I0686067

Edward P. Cardillo

Shadow of the Automaton

I Am Automaton Book 3

Acknowledgements

I would like to thank my wife Sandra, my mother-in-law Charlene Nunez, Alan Basso, Arno Kolz, Robert Rubicco, James Nunez, Jack Daly, and Phyllis Reis for their feedback and support. Thank you to Gary Lucas at Severed Press. I would also like to thank Sandra and Alexander, whose love and support were essential to my completion of this novel.

This novel is dedicated to my wife, Sandra, and son, Alexander, who are my family, my rock, my core.

Part I

O Brother Where Art Thou?

Prologue

Peter Birdsall ducked down an alleyway and ran behind houses. He passed under an arch as he heard the motorcycle tear around the corner and up the hill pursuing him.

Bullets hit the ground at his feet and flew past him as he ran in zigzags, which made him harder to hit. However, this allowed her to catch up quicker, as he was covering ground more slowly.

Just as she was practically at his back, he jumped left into a doorway and she soared right on past him. He jumped out and ran in the other direction as he heard the slowing of the motorcycle throttle and the hand brakes being applied. It was too narrow for her to turn around easily.

He bolted back down the alleyway and turned left in between two houses. As he re-entered the street he was previously on, he noticed a shadow dancing above his head in the waning moonlight. It was Kafka jumping from rooftop to rooftop, tracking Peter like a predator of the sky.

Instead of running back down the street, Peter ran across it and into another alleyway on the other side. That bastard would have to leap across the street to follow. Given his injuries that would seem unlikely, thus buying Peter another few seconds.

He ran up another steep alleyway as he heard the growl of the motorcycle somewhere behind him, searching for him. Suddenly, a great shadow leapt in front of him, and Kafka hit the ground. Kafka knelt where he landed for a moment, the exertion and the fall having taken something out of him.

Peter ducked between another couple of peach and pink colored buildings and re-emerged out onto the main street in front of a wine artisan shop. He looked up the street and saw Yvette perched on her motorcycle. Unfortunately, she noticed him, too, and began careening down the sloped main boulevard right at him.

The streets were largely empty, save for a few locals taking in some crisp early morning air. Peter ran to the side by an outdoor café. The place was vacant, locked up, and the umbrellas closed.

He reached over a wrought iron railing and snatched up an umbrella, pointing the tip at the oncoming Yvette like a joust. She saw the point coming at her, but couldn't stop her momentum. She tried to take aim at Peter with her submachine gun, but it was too late.

The point of the umbrella crunched into her chest cavity, knocking her off the motorcycle and sending Peter and the motorcycle flying into the café, crashing into the tables and chairs.

Peter opened his eyes. He was caught in the opening between the seat and backrest of a chair, his right arm radiating pain as he tried to hoist himself up. It was broken. Blood trickled down the side of his face from a gash on his hairline.

He rolled over, taking some chairs stuck together with him. He agonizingly shimmied his way loose and slowly got to his feet. He saw lights turning on and faces appearing in windows.

He stepped out of the café and saw the body of Yvette lying on the uneven stone, blood running out of the right side of her mouth, her eyes wide open with shock, the last emotion that ran through her...before the umbrella did.

Peter took her submachine gun and walked down the street, his body aching and paining from all directions. He saw a smart car parked on the side of the road in a little nook next to a staircase leading up to an apartment.

He preferred a Mack truck, but this would do. He smashed the window with the stock of the submachine gun and opened the door from inside. He slid into the seat and closed the door gently.

If he was going to beat Carl, it wouldn't be mano-a-mano. He would need help, and unfortunately, this little shitbox was the only thing on hand. He pulled the wires from under the steering column and severed them with a shard of broken glass. He stripped the ends and began to hotwire the car with his good hand.

He heard a shrill screech, like an enraged banshee in the distance behind him. Carl had found Yvette. Poor bastard. He tried so hard to meet a woman. When he finally did, Peter had to go and kill her. He felt awful. But in his defense, she was trying to kill him.

Soon, Carl would be coming for him, and if he wasn't pissed off before, he was going to go nuclear now. The poor kid had gone crazy with all that talk of perfect beings and invasion.

He peeked above the dashboard and saw Carl's lithe shadowy form and four red eyes stalk down the hill past him. Peter reached down and crossed the wires. The engine turned over and he twisted the exposed tips together.

He put the car in gear and crept out of his spot slowly. He couldn't see in the waning darkness, a reverse twilight, so he turned on the headlights totally prepared to gun it.

There was no one down the stretch of the street. Where did he—

Suddenly Kafka descended on the little car, his long limbs stretching over it like a spider overwhelming a morsel. Peter floored it and sent the car bowling down the street as fast as it would go.

Kafka was reaching into the broken window and grabbing at Peter, unfazed by his forearm being sliced by shards of broken glass. Peter was leaning inward, avoiding the swiping hand.

Peter saw around Kafka's hideous form and saw the jetty approaching fast. He sped past rows of multi-colored boats on either side of the road and onto the narrow cement jetty. Kafka looked behind him to see the sea rushing at him.

For a moment, the little car's engine gunned as it popped up on the lip, smashed through the top of the cement barrier, and flipped over the rocks on the other side. Peter and Kafka were weightless for a brief moment. The front of the car slammed into the water so hard that the jagged glass on the broken car window severed Kafka's right arm, causing it to land in Peter's lap.

Peter was slammed forward against the steering wheel, knocking the wind out of him. The windshield spider-webbed around the impact of Kafka's face. Water rushed into the little car as it sank into the water.

Peter got his bearings, grabbed the submachine gun, and drifted out of his seat and to the surface of the water. The car sank, taking Kafka with it, but the water wasn't that deep. Peter hoped that Kafka was pinned under the weight of the car.

He climbed up the rocks to the top of the jetty where the cement barrier was smashed to pieces. He lay prone, catching his breath as the sun rose over Monterosso, chasing out the monochromatic night and bathing the many colors of the town in golden light.

Peter heard splashing behind him and he turned around to see his mother climbing up the jetty one-handed. She looked up at him imploringly, the sight of her rendering Peter speechless.

She reached out for him, and he so badly wanted to take her hand. Then he reminded himself that she was gone. Peter grabbed the submachine gun and fired into his brother. Kafka was hit over and over, sliding down a little each time, but he kept coming.

Kafka grabbed Peter's right ankle tight and looked up at him. Peter wasn't able to classify the expression on his brother's face—hatred, betrayal, shame. It was horrible and made Peter's stomach turn. Kafka let go of Peter, and Peter delivered a boot to his face, sending him rolling down and into the water.

After Kafka disappeared under the surface, Peter waited for some time, but his brother never returned.

***

"Be ready," said General Ramses biting into a mini quiche. He swallowed it, savoring the sounds coming from the jazz band. "We go online in twenty-four hours. We'll need the encryptions for the data streams."

"Don't you worry," said Jon Wolff, Assistant Director of the NSA. "Everything's in place. Once congress passed the Second Patriot Act, our cryptographers went into overdrive. We have some beautiful algorithms for you, new Suite A stuff, 920-bit elliptic curve."

"I have no idea what you just said," admitted Ramses, looking around the room that was dimly lit by opulent crystal chandeliers, "but it sounds good to me. There's some concern that this data can be intercepted via satellite."

"Yes, I've heard about the extra-terrestrial concern," smirked Wolff.

"Yes, well, let's just say that the crazy ramblings of a certain rogue operative before his death made an impression on some of the brass."

"Aren't you the brass, General?"

"Just tell me that this data cannot be cracked," demanded Ramses impatiently.

"Maybe not by the Predator or ET, but perhaps by the Romulans."

"Great," huffed Ramses, "I'm talking national security and he's referencing old movies."

"Relax, General. It should be secure."

"Should be?"

"It will be. Besides, no one knows we are using this technology."

"Except for OIL," corrected Ramses.

"I understand that your man took care of that, and at great personal cost," said Wolff.

"Yes, he did. But we don't know if anyone else knows."

"Our cypher is nearly impossible to crack, even by space aliens."

"That's real reassuring, Jon. Now if you'll excuse me, I have to drop the bomb on Japan."

Jon shook his head at the crude reference to a bowel movement. Ramses excused himself and made his way across the crowded room of politicians, governmental officials, and socialites, and went toward the staircase.

He climbed the staircase to the second floor and walked down a long hallway. He passed a couple talking rather intimately in the hallway next to a painting of the French countryside. He found the men's room door on the right.

He opened the door, entered, passed an attendant rearranging his towels, perfumes, and mints, and took the closest stall. He put down the paper guard on the toilet seat, pulled his pants down, and plopped himself down on the bowl in the nick of time.

He thought he heard the attendant lock the door. "Excuse me. There's someone in here."

A head popped up over the side of the stall, black as an oil slick with four red eyes. It was the attendant. When he smiled, he revealed pearly white fangs.

"YOU!" said Ramses, aghast.

Kafka flipped over the side of the stall and landed in front of Ramses, who tried to stand but was slammed back down on the bowl.

"Please, General, don't stand up on account of me."

"You're supposed to be dead! Help! Help!"

Kafka rolled his eyes. "Oh, don't waste your breath, General. I've taken the liberty of putting a 'do not disturb' sign on the door and posting a drone in a custodian's outfit outside, so our meeting isn't...interrupted."

"How can you be here?"

"Well, I have a saying...well, it's actually more of a credo for me: what doesn't kill me makes me stronger."

"The chip. What about the chip?"

Kafka reached into his tuxedo breast pocket with a white-gloved hand and pulled out a small, thin, square chip with dried blood crusted around it. He tossed it into Ramses' naked lap. Ramses bobbled it a bit and took a look at it. "How?"

Kafka pulled back his greasy hair and turned his head to reveal a hole in his skull. "I dug it out myself with my finger. Not a very pleasant thing to do, but absolutely necessary under the circumstances."

"If you kill me, you won't make it out of here alive."

Kafka looked genuinely amused. "I don't want to kill you, General."

"Then what do you want?" snapped Ramses.

"I want you to live. I want you to launch the RGT program, and I want it to flourish."

"Oh, that's right," said Ramses contemptuously, "you and your alien overlords."

"If you weren't so concerned about it, why did I just see you chatting it up with the Assistant Director of the NSA? Let me guess...they're using KG-250 with a TCP/IP accelerator, Suite A algorithms...Am I getting warm?"

"Even if you could break the encryption," Ramses said, "what would you possibly do with data on millions of people's memories and experiences?"

Kafka shrugged. "Me? Personally, nothing. But my friends from outer space, well, they would just eat that data up."

"Why? For what purpose would they use the data?"

"That's for me to know and earth to find out, and it will soon enough," Kafka teased with a hint of menace.

"Why are you telling me all of this?"

"Because I know that you know that no one believes in this UFO theory of yours, and it's going to eat you alive to know that you have to go ahead with the RGT Program constantly wondering if I'm really crazy."

"Oh, I think we've established the answer to that question," answered Ramses.

"Maybe so, but you'll always wonder."

"So that's my punishment? To live in fear and guilt?"

"No," answered Kafka, "your punishment is coming. When it arrives, you'll wish I killed you with my bare hands in this bathroom."

"What about your brother?" Ramses asked, trying to deflect the attention off of him.

"Peter? He'll get his, too. Everyone will."

"Well if that's the case, then why don't you get out of here so I can finish my shit in peace?"

"Certainly, General. But first, a memento of our time here together." Kafka opened his mouth to reveal fangs, and he bit into Ramses before he could react, sinking his fangs into his shoulder. Ramses struggled on the bowl, attempting to pry Kafka from him.

Finally, Kafka pulled away. "One of my new tricks. Now I will always be with you, General. I will see what you see. I will haunt your dreams. We are now inexorably connected."

Ramses clutched his shoulder, "Get out! GET-OUT!"

When he looked up, Kafka was gone. He pulled up his pants and flushed the toilet. He burst out of the stall and threw the door to the outside hallway open. He peered down the hallway, but it was empty.

He went back into the bathroom and took off his jacket, throwing it on the sink platform and knocking over the attendant's tip bowl. He unbuttoned his shirt and took it off, placing it on top of his jacket.

He turned on the faucet to the hot water full blast and let it run into the sink. When the water was hot, he scooped some up in his right hand and washed the bite on his left shoulder. He grabbed some paper towels and dabbed at the two holes until the blood began to coagulate.

Then he turned off the faucet. The hot water had steamed the mirror above the sink. He was startled at the sight of a four-eyed smiling face drawn on the mirror at face level, overlapping his. The crude features smeared as the moisture on the mirror ran, creating an unnerving effect.

He threw the paper towels out and put his shirt and jacket back on hastily. He spilled out into the hallway and strode back to the staircase. He looked at the room and all of its occupants, social butterflies bouncing from clique to clique in almost random patterns.

He descended the stairs with heavy feet, holding onto the bannister, looking at Jon Wolff talking to one of the young female socialites, the one with the reality show…flirting was more like it. He couldn't blame Jon, given her reputation.

On his way down the stairs, he bumped shoulders with a passerby. He looked up to excuse himself and caught a glimpse of the man he bumped. An odd chill ran down his spine…

…he could've sworn the man bore an uncanny resemblance to him.

Chapter I

Pelham Train Station
Southern Westchester County, New York

Bill sat on the train platform in his sweat suit that he plucked from the hamper and threw on last minute. He kept his large, black duffle bag close to his slippered feet. The train was running late.

As he looked up at the television screen displaying the arrival and departure times, there was a faint buzzing coming from somewhere, a nuisance sound like a persistent insect that he just wished would stop.

As he looked up at the screen, random memories began to fill his mind, the most palpable being Helen's infidelity with another teacher from his job. Bart McKinney. Ten years younger and in much better shape. A real cougar chaser…and he caught Helen.

The train pulled up at long last, and Bill reached down and grabbed his duffle bag by the handles. As he rose from the bench, the memory of Bart quickly faded, leaving an unpleasant taste in his mouth, and he realized that the buzzing…or was it clicking… was coming from inside his head.

He boarded the train and took the nearest seat by the door, the four-seater with facing seats. As he took his seat facing in the opposite direction that the train was going, he tucked his large, black duffle bag under his feet protectively, forgetting that he suffered from motion sickness when riding backwards.

He felt so strange that he didn't even notice. Helen thought he was home sick, or at least that was what he told her. Maybe he was really sick. Maybe that buzzing in his brain was a tumor.

But it didn't matter. Once he reached Manhattan, nothing would matter anymore. Helen could go run off with Bart; they deserved each other.

It was a twenty-or-so-minute ride into Grand Central Station. He found the rundown of the Bronx brownstones flashing past the windows a little more disheartening than usual, the ruins of a better civilization.

He looked around the train car. Some were checking their cell phones and mini-coms. Others were paging through items on their tablets. Holographic ads danced around the car, white noise in the hustle and bustle of rush hour.

When the train came to a stop, he grabbed his large bag and strolled off the train and onto the platform, blending in with the crowd, mindlessly moving as one large school of fish.

The stroll to Times Square was a pleasant one. It was a bright, warm, sunny day, not a cloud in the sky. He relished the feeling of the warm sun on the back of his neck as he meandered through the crowd, dodging and sidestepping like the pro that he was. The Manhattan streets were old hat to him.

He reached West 47th and Broadway and saw the bleachers. He placed his bag down at his feet, wearily rubbed his eyes, and then massaged his temples with his two forefingers. The buzzing from all of the giant monitors and holographic advertisements inciting a hell of a migraine, tearing up Bill's poor, overtaxed brain.

As he reached the bleachers and climbed to the top, horrible memories from his youth filled his consciousness. He took a seat, placing his large black bag next to him on the bleacher, and looked out over the bustling crowd.

They all looked like ants to him, and for all intents and purposes, they *were* ants to him. It was watching an ant farm, like children do, as the ants go about their busy day, unaware of being observed by the children.

Yet, with all of the buzzing from the monitors and holographs, Bill felt like he too was being observed, and by a malevolent presence no less. The sensation was disquieting, and as Bill gazed down upon the harried pedestrians, he envied their ignorance.

However, he was no longer blissfully ignorant. He had been painfully aware that he had eyes on him for quite some time now, and he didn't like it. No, he didn't like it one bit.

It was time.

He swiveled over and unzipped his large, black duffle bag. He hesitated as one of New York's Finest passed in front of the bleachers. After the police officer passed him by, he reached inside his bag and pulled out an AR-15, purchased after the latest expiration of the assault weapons ban.

Bill stood up, took aim at the nearest monitor looming over Times Square advertising lingerie, and pulled the trigger again and again until the monitor projected disjointed fragments of its video advertisement.

There was a delayed reaction on the street and sidewalk below. At first, people were startled by the gunfire, stopping in their tracks and looking around. A few looked up in horror and pointed at Bill, but he continued to shoot at the monitors.

A police officer—the one who passed by the bleachers moments ago—was shouting something at him, but the buzzing in his brain and the gunfire drowned it all out. The officer drew his gun, but Bill got to him first. The officer went down clutching a hole in his chest.

Government employee. Government enforcer. Bill mused that he got what he deserved. The government couldn't expect to reach into their lives, snoop into their most private memories, and not expect some kind of pushback.

There were more officers coming, but the crowd was running every which way in a panic, obstructing their progress. Bill took the opportunity to fire into the crowd at the police officers, sometimes tagging an innocent bystander.

The ants were scurrying around the farm. They noticed their observer, who was now imposing his will on them, and all they could do was scurry. There was no queen to protect, only drones. They were all drones.

Overhead, an armed autonomous aerial vehicle (AAAV)—an armed domestic drone—received data on Bill's position. Its camera trained on Bill firing into the crowd below the bleachers, placing him in its cross hairs. It received a transmission to lower its altitude and engage.

As it dropped between the skyscrapers into the city and approached street level, it received authorization to neutralize the target. It screeched over cars, taxicabs, and pedestrians, zeroing in on Bill until it achieved tone.

The Gatling minigun began to spin as bolts of light flew out and pelt the bleachers at a rate of two thousand rounds per minute.

Sparks flew as bullets tore holes into the bleachers and Bill, reducing both to Swiss cheese. Bill's blood splattered everywhere as his riddled body shimmied on the bleachers. After a brief forty-second burst, the firing stopped, the drone zoomed past overhead, and Bill's mangled body dropped off the back of the bleachers.

The last thing he saw on this earth was the flashing lights of the Gatling munitions streaking towards him and silence…

…the buzzing had finally stopped.

***

Tyler-Skylar Show
Docutainment Network
Los Angeles, California

The effeminate twins sat in tall stools on the stage of their cramped studio in front of their live audience, their poofy hairdos with blond highlights lending them the appearance of two oversized poodles.

"Skylar, 11,020 hits on Skylarblog agree with me that *all* guns should be banned in this country. They're primitive, they're obsolescent, and completely unnecessary. What say you?"

There were cheers and jeers from the live studio audience. This was docutainment, what passed for news in this day and age.

"Dear brother," said Tyler with a dismissive flip of a well-manicured hand (his cuticles were flawless), "apparently you haven't heard of the Second Amendment to the United States Constitution...something about the right to keep and bear arms."

"Tyler, I don't think that right applies to you. Please, put those batwings away. At least wear a sweater or something." There was more noise from the audience and a very artificial laugh track played over the din. "But seriously, the Second Amendment. How archaic. We don't have any foreign standing armies to contend with...that is unless Canada grows a set and invades. But I find that highly unlikely."

"13,908 hits on Tylerblog agree that the Second Amendment is still valid. Guns are as American as tobacco and apple pie."

"Tyler, brother, tobacco kills people."

"Skylar, tobacco doesn't kill people. People who smoke tobacco kill themselves."

"Tyler, guns were a part of our history when we were a frontier nation. Back then, settlers had to worry about wild animals and Native Americans. In modern society, we don't have to worry about those things. 14,158 hits on Skylarblog agree with me. What say you?"

"Au contraire, brother of mine," replied Tyler. "We in modern society have to fear the most dangerous animal of all...our fellow man. Our fellow citizens have been going off the deep end lately. Mass murders from shootings are on the rise."

"Exactly my point, Tyler. The fact that guns are legal and easily accessible are the very reason for these atrocities."

"Chew on this for a moment, Skylar: Just think, what if in any of these shootings, the innocent victims were armed? The shooter in each case would've been taken down before too many lives were taken. What say you?"

"Tyler, are you suggesting that we use guns to fight guns? The last thing I think we need is more guns. 14,572 hits on Skylarblog agree with me."

"Skylar, there will always be guns out there. Even if there is a ban, the government can't just go around confiscating weapons from the citizenry. Weapons that were purchased legally and within the proper parameters. No, realistically those already in possession will be grandfathered in, leaving the rest of us defenseless against them when they decide to go postal. 15,672 hits on Tylerblog agree with me. What say you?"

There were shouts and hoots of agreement mixed with jeers of dissention as camera four panned across the audience. Audience members were shouting at each other, and a few isolated shoving matches began to break out.

Skylar nodded to the production engineer, who in turn hit a red button. *Quiet Please* signs began to flash over the audience, and after a few moments, an uneasy hush fell over them.

Skylar flipped his permed hair flippantly at his brother. "Tyler, your paranoia about your fellow man astounds me. Do you mean to tell me that you don't feel that you can walk down the street in modern society and not feel safe unless you're packing heat? This isn't the Wild West, you know."

"First of all, Skylar, I don't know how you know what I'm packing..."

"I'm your brother, we grew up together, we shared a bedroom and bathroom..." There were ooh's and hoots from the audience at the bawdy reference. "...but we're talking about guns, remember?"

"Yes, guns," said Tyler, pretending to blush to the pleasure of the live audience. "The answer is no. I don't feel safe. In fact, anyone can be a threat." He stood up and walked over to a darkened part of the stage. Tyler gestured to a stagehand who came out holding a pink AR-15. He handed it to Tyler. There were gasps and the crowd began to stir with anticipation.

Tyler gestured to the darkened part of the stage, and the lights came up revealing a mockup of a quaint suburban scene. There were two facades of houses, with flowerbeds under the windows, two front yards with artificial green grass and white picket fences. In the window of one of the houses was a cardboard cutout of a housewife holding an AK-47. In the front door of the adjacent house was an old lady holding a shotgun. In the front yard was a mailman holding an uzi.

Tyler strode up to the set. "As you see, dear brother, a typical suburban neighborhood. But wait. Holly Homemaker in the window there isn't putting a pie on the sill to cool. She's packing heat and eyeing me suspiciously. I don't much like the way she's looking at me. Time to *stand my gound*."

Tyler raised his pink assault rifle and fired into the window, blowing the cardboard cutout's head clear off. The audience was on their feet and erupted in cheers and applause.

The *Quiet Please* lights began to flash and the audience quieted down in anticipation. Tyler flashed a mischievous grin as Skylar buried his face in his hands in an exaggeration of disgust with his brother.

"Hey, it was her or me, dear brother. Uh-oh, grandma's off her meds today. She thinks she's Davy Crockett and I'm a Mexican invading her fort. She's demented and can't be reasoned with. There's only one thing to do…" Tyler put a hand to his ear as the audience egged him on, shouting "Stand your ground!" They knew what they wanted, and Tyler was going to give it to them.

He raised his rifle and fired at granny, taking off the tops of the pickets and spraying the front of the house with holes. The audience went wild.

"Well, there's one less Medicare recipient draining our tax dollars," quipped Tyler. The audience roared with hysterical laughter, drunk with bloodlust and vicarious pleasure.

The sign flashed and the audience hushed in momentary anticipation.

"What's that I see? Postal Pete is about to go…well, postal!" He looked expectantly at the audience who responded with shouts to blow the mailman away, "Stand your ground!"

"It's either him or me." He raised the rifle and tore the postman cardboard cutout apart. "Return to sender, bitch." The audience exploded in cheers and thunderous applause.

Skylar wailed in outrage. "Enough, brother. We get your point. But do you need automatic weapons for protection? 20,040 hits on Skylarblog agree that they are unnecessary for protection and are overkill."

"Skylar, brother, these guns aren't just used for protection. There are many Americans who hunt with them as well."

"Hunting?" Skylar was dramatically incredulous. "Why would one need an assault rifle to hunt? There'd be nothing left to mount on your wall."

Tyler put an index finger up as if telling his brother to wait. A dark part of the stage next to the suburban set lit up revealing a stuffed deer posed on two legs and holding a rifle. There was an American flag on the floor next to it that suddenly went ablaze. The audience gasped collectively.

"Look, Skylar. Bambi's packing heat, and he's burning an American flag." The audience responded with boo's and hissing. "There's only one patriotic thing to do. Don't tread on me!"

Tyler raised his rifle and shot at the stuffed deer, blowing bits and pieces away until there was nothing left but a heap of wasted taxidermy. Stagehands came out onto the stage with fire extinguishers and put out the flame.

The crowd went wild, standing in the aisles, yelling and gesticulating wildly.

Skylar went to stand by his brother, who struck a rather unconvincing manly pose with his pink assault rifle. "And that's all the time we have for today. Thank you for watching America's number one docutainment show. Be safe, and don't forget to spay and neuter your pets."

Tyler raised his rifle one last time and shot the deer in the crotch, blowing off its member as the camera cut to a commercial.

***

Central Security Service:
Liaison Between National Security Agency and the Service
Cryptologic Elements of the US Armed Forces

Woodlawn, Maryland
11:00 HRS

In an air-conditioned room, technicians were poring over the countless streaming transmissions of Retinal Gateway Technology (RGT), monitoring memories transmitted from cell phone screens, computers, and television sets, as monitors interfaced with brainwaves of the unsuspecting populace. The center was one of many nodes throughout the country empowered by the Second Patriot Act for surveillance to detect the operations of terrorist agents.

A young agent in his mid-twenties scratched his head as something gnawed at the back of his mind. Something in the patterns of brainwave transmissions didn't quite sit right with him, but he was unable to put his finger on it. He picked up the phone.

"Hi, Marty. What's up?"

"Fred, there's something strange about the noise in the transmissions."

"What, exactly?"

"I'm not sure, but it has to do with the signal-structure. There appears to be something within the wideband."

"I'll be right there."

Fred appeared moments later in Marty's cubicle. "So show me what you're talking about."

Marty called up the wideband signal structure on his computer. "Here is the wideband. See?" Fred nodded. "Well, if you apply a signal detection model to this particular transmission source, look what happens."

Fred watched the screen intently. "There's a pseudorandom spreading across the bandwidth."

"Exactly," said Marty. "Someone's attempting to transmit backwards through the broadband."

"How? Direct-sequence spread spectrum? Time-hopping? Chirp?"

"All of them, Fred."

"Jesus. How didn't we know about this?"

Marty rubbed his eyes with his index finger and thumb, pinching the bridge of his nose. "We've been so occupied with securing the transmissions from outside detection that we never thought to look to see if someone was hiding communications from us within the transmissions."

"We'll get on it, isolate the source."

"That's not all," Marty interrupted.

"What is it?"

Marty typed furiously on his keyboard calling up multiple broadbands. "It's not just that one transmission…it's pretty much all of them."

"Low probability of intercept," said Fred gravely. "Right under our noses. Good work, Marty. I have to notify the NSA."

"Right."

Fred stalked through the bullpen of cubicles back to his office. His secretary, Nancy, looked up at him. "Sir, General Ramses is here. He's passing through security now."

He looked at his watch. "We don't have a scheduled meeting, Nancy."

"No, sir. You don't."

"Well, tell him he has to wait. I have to attend to something urgent."

"Yes, sir."

He entered his office cursing General Ramses' timing under his breath. He closed the door behind him, plopped himself in his leather chair behind his desk, and picked up his phone. He activated the encryption grid and hit speed dial.

"Assistant Director Jon Wolff, please. This is Agent Fred Eberhardt, identification number 0489270, Codename: TEMPEST."

Fred looked up, startled by some kind of commotion in the bullpen.

"We are locating Assistant Director Wolff for you, sir."

There were thrashing sounds from outside the office. Fred stands up and walks around his desk, taking his cordless phone with him. He hears Nancy emit a high-pitched shriek.

"What in God's name…" He was in here dealing with a potential national security crisis and they were carrying on outside. He flung the door open to see red all over the walls.

In the seconds it took him to register that the red was high volume blood spatter, he saw Nancy slumped over her desk, red pooling on her desk from where her throat—or what was left of it—rested.

He dropped the phone at his side as he saw General Ramses standing before him, as if he had just noticed he was even in the room. He wasn't there before, was he? There was something…different about Ramses. His eyes were feral, and he flashed a toothy grin. His teeth were coated in red.

Ramses picked his teeth with a rather long fingernail. "Hello, Fred. Thought I'd drop by."

"Connecting with Assistant Director Wolff," a faint voice said from the phone at Fred's side.

Ramses looked at Fred expectantly. "Well, go ahead. Answer it."

Fred nodded slowly, like a child being instructed by a parent. He put the phone to his ear. "Hello?"

"Mr. Eberhardt, is General Ramses there?"

"Yes, sir. He…he is."

"Good. The two of you can discuss the spread spectrum hidden transmissions your team has stumbled upon."

How could Assistant Director Wolff possibly have known about it before they found it?

Ramses was gesturing with his left hand. "Come on, give me the phone, Fred."

Fred obediently handed Ramses the phone, who proceeded to crush it with his hand. "There, that's better."

"B-but how?"

"How what, Fred?" answered Ramses, too casually given the situation.

"How did he know about the hidden transmissions already when we just found them?"

Ramses gawked at Fred in amusement. "Fred, you mean to tell me that you step out of your office to find blood splattered all over the walls and your secretary's throat ripped out, your whole team murdered..." Fred looked over Ramses' shoulder and out onto the bullpen. There were blood and bodies everywhere. "...and the first question you think to ask me is how the boss knew about the transmissions?"

Fred again nodded like a child being questioned by a teacher. Ramses shrugged. "Well, I guess that answer is obvious."

"H-he... he knew about the tr-transmissions..." Fred stammered.

"Good, good," Ramses waved his hand as if he was extracting the answers from Fred.

"...and he must somehow... have authorized the transmissions."

"Good. Good. Almost there," mocked Ramses.

"...so the RGT transmissions must be...two-way?"

"Excellent! A gold star for you."

"But they're not supposed to be two-way. Who's transmitting backwards in the broadband?"

"Why, the aliens, of course."

And then it dawned on poor Agent Fred Eberhardt. He remembered meeting about why the NSA wanted the RGT transmissions encrypted. Some low probability event, something about extra-terrestrial interception. Fred thought the notion was a joke at the time, the Assistant Director compulsively covering all the bases.

But Fred wasn't laughing now.

"Are-are you..."

"Am I what? One of them?'

Fred nodded like a scared child who saw the boogeyman for the first time.

Ramses felt his prey's heartbeat thundering in his chest and the artery in his neck throb like a primal drum egging on his dark urges. Fred's pupils were dilated. His fear was intoxicating. "So which will it be? Fight or flight?"

He was hoping for flight. He so enjoyed it when they tried to run. To his surprise, Fred pulled his sidearm.

Fight it was.

Ramses' features began to change before Fred's eyes, as he weighed his chances against whatever Ramses was. He knew Ramses must have moved quickly to have murdered everyone in the office while he was trying to get through to Wolff.

Ramses' nose elongated into a snout and his shoulders grew so large he began to hunch over. He grew taller and longer, and his face sprouted hair like a time-lapsed video in a Chia Pet commercial. His teeth elongated into fangs and he sprouted two more eyes that opened slowly, taking Fred in.

Fred didn't want to wait for the transformation to be complete. He saw this movie before.

He fired several shots into the head and chest of the lupine Ramses, but to no avail. Ramses leapt forward, swiping the handgun out of Fred's hand. Fred ducked a flash of sharp claws and rolled over and behind Nancy's desk.

"You have a little fight in you," growled Ramses. "I like it. The thrill of the hunt."

Suddenly Fred popped up from behind Nancy's desk with a shotgun in his hands. Even Nancy was trained in security measures…a lot of good it did her.

He aimed at Ramses' chest and fired, sending him flying backward. As he recovered a little too quickly for Fred's taste, Fred fired another shot, and another. Ramses fell backwards, crashing into the water cooler.

"I don't suppose silver would work on you?" Fred chided.

Ramses stood upright and brushed himself off. "Why? You got any?"

Fred reached out and pulled the fire alarm. If he wasn't going to survive this encounter, he wanted everyone else in the building to get out.

The cacophony appeared to disorient Ramses momentarily, and Fred fired a few more shots into him.

Ramses staggered backward, steadying himself against the door to Fred's personal restroom. He tipped up his head and let out a howl.

Fred was stepping carefully around to the entry to the bullpen. "So you aliens are a bunch of werewolves?"

"We are whatever you fear most?"

"Well then I must warn you," said Fred, "I am an avid hunter."

Ramses chortled, "And I must warn you that you are out of ammunition."

Fred backed out into the bullpen of cubicles, holding out the shotgun horizontally to block the doorway. Ramses came raging after him, slashing claw marks in the wall as he advanced, and ran right into the shotgun. The ends caught the sides of the doorway, clotheslining him.

As Ramses fell backward, the wind knocked out of him, Fred dashed into the cubicles, getting on his hands and knees. The room was a labyrinth of fabric-covered cork partitions. It wouldn't hold Ramses off, but it would slow him down.

Peter scrambled down a narrow aisle and crawled into a cubicle with an agent hanging off of his wheeled chair, his face torn off. It was

Nell, wife and mother. He heard Ramses snarling toward the front of the labyrinth.

"That wasn't very nice, Fred." There were sniffing sounds and heavy breathing. "Old Spice. I bet the wife just goes gaga over it."

Shit. He could smell that? Fred had to think quickly.

He heard cubicle panels being torn down and he saw them flung across the room. "Come out, come out, wherever you are! Or I'll huff, and I'll puff, and I'll rip your lungs out!"

There were no windows in the office, part of security. There was only the exit to the hallway, and then two elevators and a door to the stairway. But there was no way he was making it to the exit without Ramses seeing him. The thrashing and snarling was getting closer.

Fred looked up and saw Nell's computer was on, and she was logged in. He opened up a search engine to the internet and queried about the exact frequency of a dog whistle. Fifty KHtz. He queued up the audio signal generator and turned the volume up to its maximum. Since the Central Security Service was in the business of signals, their equipment was state-of-the-art. Perfect.

Ramses was now only a couple of cubicles away. "Fi, fie, fo, fum, ready or not here I come!"

Fred kept his finger poised over the mouse.

Ramses snatched the wall of Nell's cubicle and broke it in half with his bare claws, tossing aside the remains like cardboard. He looked down at Fred.

"Ah-ha. There you are. Keeping the young lady company, I see."

Fred clicked the mouse and Ramses began to yelp and hold his ears. This was Fred's chance. He jumped up, yanked out the computer mouse—hurling it across the room—and pushed himself over the opposite wall of the cubicle.

As he closed the distance and made it to the door to the hallway, he looked back and saw Ramses frantically trying to turn off the computer with his large clumsy claws.

He knew it only bought him several extra seconds, so he spilled out into the hallway and passed the elevators. He nearly overshot the door to the stairwell, but he grabbed the handle and flung the door open as he heard the computer crash against the wall.

He flew down the stairs, taking two at a time, and nearly fell a couple of times. He heard the door to the stairwell fling open three floors above, but he was almost to the garage.

He heard grunting and snarling as he bypassed the lobby. Ramses wouldn't stop, even in public. Fred knew too much. There was no use endangering the rest of the building.

He threw open the door to the garage and bolted in the direction of his assigned space as he heard a grisly reverberating howl cut off by the closing of the stairwell door. Ramses was right behind him.

He sprinted across the row of cars to spot number four, which was fortunately a stone's throw away. It was good to be regional director.

The stairwell door exploded off the hinges as Fred snatched his mini-com multi-tasker from his pocket and disengaged his car's digi-locks. He threw himself into the driver's seat as Ramses sprang across the garage.

As the car engine turned over, Ramses vaulted the car and a large claw came crashing through the driver's side window. Fred grabbed the claw, using all of his strength to push it away from his chest. But Ramses was unnaturally strong.

He wanted to throw the car in reverse, but he needed both hands to keep Ramses razor sharp claws from piercing his chest. However, the beast's strength was relentless, and Fred cried out as his arms began to fatigue and the claws drew closer and closer.

He gave another cry as he saw them puncture his shirt, his skin giving way like butter to hot knives. Blood welled up around the entry wounds staining his perfectly pressed white dress shirt.

His hands released their grip on Ramses claw as he accepted his fate. Ramses leaned in, his hot breath stinking up the car and fogging the windshield.

When Fred opened his eyes, Ramses was gone. He looked down at his chest, at the source of the sharp stabbing pain that racked his body. The engine of his car was still revving. He eased his foot off the gas pedal and saw a team of first responders enter the garage.

There was also someone else…in between the cars. Someone, who looked just like him, staring at him. He was even dressed the same.

Fred mustered up whatever energy he had left, and he pressed on the car horn on the steering wheel. It blared out and quickly faded away as Fred closed his eyes and faded from consciousness.

***

Otay Mesa
California
23:02 HRS

Major Peter Birdsall stood outside a warehouse with a platoon of men armed to the teeth with automatic weapons.

"All right, men. Listen up." All eyes were on Peter. "RGT provided intel that the tunnel inside this warehouse connects with another in Tijuana. Two squads, led by Lieutenant Harper, will enter the tunnels at exactly 12:00 HRS. Captain Romagossa will take two squads across the border and take the warehouse from the other end. I will establish HQ in a hotel nearby with Lieutenant Farrow where I will coordinate the strikes.

"Intel places the Navajas cartel and OIL operatives at that warehouse right now, and they're ready to make a cocaine run, but we're not going to let that happen. Am I right?"

"HAROO!" the men hollered in response without missing a beat.

"Glad to hear it ladies. The Mexican government is not privy to our little operation here, so it's in and out. Nice and quick. Let's get moving. Time's-a-wasting."

Captain Romagossa and Lieutenant Harper saluted Peter and were off to their tasks. Peter remained behind outside the warehouse with a small security detail in the warm day in late May.

His recent promotion to Major was unconventional but meant to keep him quiet. Although most Majors rode desks, Peter was in Special Ops now, so he was in the field. He would rather be leading the men into combat, but he was thankful that the Army decommissioned the undead infantry drones.

General Ramses' sighting of Peter's younger brother, Carl (AKA Kafka), a few months ago was unsettling. Peter thought he left him for dead in Monterosso. He hit the kill switch in Carl's brain himself to make sure the deed was done. When Ramses reported that he was assaulted by Carl in the men's room at a Washington D.C. function, no one in the know rested easy.

It was the main reason why the army decommissioned the drones. Well, that and the fiascos in Xcaret and Siena. With Carl alive, kicking, and unrestrained by his kill chip, the undead drones were compromised. Carl could order them to turn on anyone at any moment.

However, since that night in Washington D.C., no one had seen hide nor hair from Carl. His alter ego, Kafka, had been referenced in several RGT transmissions involving Order for International Liberation operations, but Carl had dropped off the grid.

Every operation, Peter waited for Kafka to surface and start tearing his men apart, but he never showed. As far as the media knew, the Automaton was alive and well, especially thanks to Peter's impersonation in Siena. There was some confusion about what happened with the drones attacking the hostages, but the media seems to have cleared up the confusion.

That's all there was on the news: the Automaton vs. Kafka. Good vs. evil. What they all didn't know was that both were the same monstrosity.

Since Kafka dropped off the grid and the drones were decommissioned, neither character had to make an appearance. Peter hoped it would stay that way.

He got into a large SUV with Lieutenant Farrow and the three-man security detail. As the doors slammed shut and they began to move, Lieutenant Farrow was regarding Peter curiously.

"Something on your mind, Lieutenant?" asked Peter without looking at Farrow.

"How are you holding up, sir?"

"Fine. Thanks for the concern," Peter said with sarcasm that he immediately regretted. Farrow was a good man, which was why Peter brought him along to Special Ops. Besides, with the drones decommissioned, Farrow had to have something to do.

"I didn't mean any disrespect."

"I know," said Peter pensively. "I think about him being out there, too."

"Do you think he'll ever pop up again? Resurface?"

"If he does, we'll be ready," said Peter gravely. But would *he* be ready? He went through the emotional pain of killing Carl once…or so he thought. He was not sure what would happen the next time.

"If they encounter any homemade undead drones at the warehouse," added Farrow with substantial concern, "we won't have any amygdala kill switches."

"The Sweepers will pick up any undead presence, and we'll adjust accordingly. Right?" Peter looked at Farrow for confirmation. Farrow only nodded tentatively.

There were two significant encounters with the undead drones in combat. The first in Xcaret was a complete failure. The one in Siena was barely a victory. Farrow wasn't being pessimistic. He was being a realist.

They crossed the border without incident and the SUV pulled up to a real dive of a hotel, a dilapidated art deco four-story building jammed in between two storefronts.

Peter sized up their temporary digs. "Peach. My favorite." The color was an attempt at a tropical splash in an ocean of diarrhea. Even the sea foam green balcony railings looked dingy.

Peter and Farrow, in civilian clothing wheeling small luggage, exited the SUV and stepped into the lobby of the hotel. The lobby was a small improvement over the exterior, but still poorly maintained. But that was the point—to blend.

Peter checked in at the front desk and obtained the digital room key sequence onto a civilian mini-com. A military standard issue multi-tasker would blow their cover to anyone watching, and Tijuana had cartel eyes and ears everywhere. The three-man security detail, also in civilian dress, checked into two separate rooms to keep up appearances.

When they reached Peter's room, Peter swiped his mini-com over the digi-lock and the three-man security detail entered first, guns drawn, and cleared the area.

When the lead soldier nodded his approval, Peter and Farrow entered the room casually, closing the door on a quiet hallway.

"I'm going to set up the laptops on that little desk," announced Farrow, walking over to a rickety wooden table by the balcony.

One of the security detail, Kessler, turned on the television as another, Michaels, swept the room for bugs. The third, Nomura, stepped out onto the balcony and casually surveyed the street below. When Kessler was finished, he nodded to Peter.

"Good," said Peter. "Let's set up com-links on the double. The sooner we complete the mission, the sooner we can get out of here. The bed bugs look hungry."

Farrow had their mobile communications center up and running in no time. There were two laptops synched with two ear pieces for Peter and Farrow.

"Echo Team, do you read?" Peter spoke aloud in the room.

"Bravo Team Leader here, on schedule and in position. I have eyes on the nest. Over." Captain Romagossa was awaiting Peter's signal.

"Bravo Team, hold position."

"Copy."

"Farrow, do we have a fix on Echo Team?"

Farrow was watching a laptop screen. "Harper's almost in position."

"Echo Team Leader, you are getting close to the exit point. Maintain radio silence. Switching to text messaging." Peter produced his military-grade multi-tasker and looked down at the screen, which read *Copy* in text from Lieutenant Harper.

"Echo Team is closing the gap and almost in position," said Farrow, stroking his chin nervously. Remote coordination always made him nervous. He knew that if he made one minor miscalculation good men would die.

Peter was also uncomfortable with this game of chess, moving men around strategically, based on laptop screens. He would've preferred to be in the mix with the boots on the ground. Chess was Carl's game.

Carl...

"Echo Team is in position," reported Farrow.

"Bravo Team, move on target," Peter announced. He saw a satellite depiction on his laptop. Thirty multi-colored heat signatures moved into the warehouse in formation. The heat signatures representing Navajas and OIL began to drop off the screen, one-by-one and then in clusters. The remaining enemy bogies retreated further into the structure.

"Echo Team, move in on target," Peter ordered. Suddenly, heat signatures emerged from nowhere on the screen and flanked the retreating bogies.

"How's the street, Nomura?" Peter asked.

"All clear, sir."

Within minutes, the enemy bogies were wiped off the computer screen. "Bravo and Echo Team, mission accomplished. Proceed to extraction point. I'm sending the nav coordinates now."

Peter nodded to Farrow who transmitted the coordinates to the two team leaders and their mobile pickup meandering a few blocks away.

"Nice work, everyone. In and out, no casualties. Stack 'em, pack 'em, and rack 'em."

Farrow began to break down the equipment and pack it away. Kessler and Michaels stepped into the hallway. Kessler manned the door to the room while Michaels stepped down the hall to clear the stairwell for their exit.

Nomura was looking down at the quiet street. They chose a location away from the bars and cathouses, so that any approaching enemies would stand out rather than blend in with a crowd.

Nomura was looking at a holographic advertisement flashing something about a local beer when he saw something move swiftly down below, almost out of his field of vision. He looked down, but there was nothing there. Maybe it was a stray cat.

"Kessler, how's the hall?"

"All clear, sir."

"The stairwell is clear as well, sir," crackled Michaels into Peter's earpiece. "Hanretty, we're ready for exit," Peter said into his microphone. *"Copy that."*

Farrow was zipping up the luggage shut to some TV commercial blasting trumpet music and a clown riding around on a unicycle, when Nomura saw it again.

If he wasn't mistaken, it looked like something jumped from the second floor balcony up to the third floor balcony right beneath him.

Peter saw Nomura looking over the edge. "Everything cool, Nomura?"

Nomura was peering over the edge, his sidearm now in his right hand with the safety off. There was a shadow moving around on the balcony below, but it was too dark for him to make anything out.

"Nomura," Peter demanded impatiently.

Nomura saw something flitter to his left. When he turned his head, he saw a man clinging to the sea foam railing on the balcony. The man looked at him with cats' eyes…four of them…and hissed, flashing long fangs.

"JESUS." Nomura swung his right hand over the railing to take aim when the shadow grabbed his hand from below in a vice like grip, yellow fingernails digging into his flesh.

Farrow was with Kessler by the door, ready to leave. Peter stepped onto the balcony as he saw Nomura pulled over the side.

"Holy shit!" Peter cried out, and he drew his gun as two figures landed on the balcony from either side. They hissed and bared jagged fangs. Peter heard Nomura screaming and pleading for his life down below.

"Get Farrow out of here!" he barked at Kessler over his shoulder. Kessler didn't need to be asked twice.

"So what the hell are you supposed to be?" Peter quipped, training his Beretta M9 at the two…men. They blinked their four yellow eyes at him.

In the background, the host of some ludicrous game show was consoling a contestant who was apparently losing, prompting the obnoxious trumpet music and some buxom woman in a bikini to jump into a vat of pudding.

The two men didn't answer. They just smiled at him viciously, brandishing fangs dripping with saliva as Peter realized that Nomura had gone quiet.

Peter shot one in the head, sending him backward into the third from below, who had just climbed over the railing to join the party.

He fired another shot at the one on the left, but the man moved too quickly. Peter sidestepped as the assailant flew past him.

The one he shot in the head stood upright, fingering the bloodless head wound curiously; the one who caught him now stepped around to advance upon Peter. The one that flew past him into the room was now coming at him from behind.

"Ah, hell," Peter said, sounding like John Wayne, and he rushed the two on the balcony, catching each of them with an arm and pushing them against the balcony railing. The one from behind hit him so hard in the back that they all fell over the railing in a heap of bodies.

Peter felt the wind knocked out of him from the impact with the sidewalk and the guy behind him that landed on his back, but he was cushioned by the two assailants he positioned in front of him. They, too, were momentarily disoriented. The third one rolled off his back and on the sidewalk.

"Nice teeth, but you bastards can't fly," Peter muttered as he rolled off of the two under him. He got to his feet as the three fiends got to theirs. They recovered a little quicker than he would've liked.

He fired shots into the two near him and then the third a little further away, but it didn't even slow them down. They only mocked him with their toothy grins. Peter had seen zombie soldiers before, but nothing like this.

He darted in between two parked cars and across the empty street, the three monsters quick on his heels. As he looked around for his ride, the SUV came careening down the street and plowed right into the three pursuers, crushing one beneath its wheels and sending the other two ricocheting off the grill.

A door swung open and Farrow yelled, "Get in!"

Peter jumped in, as he heard tires screech on pavement, and the SUV pulled away with the back door still ajar. Farrow was clutching Peter's wrists as Peter pulled himself into his seat and closed the door.

"What took you guys so long?"

"What were those things?" Farrow's face was white."Something new," replied Peter. He was looking out the window at the blur of palm trees and short, multi-colored buildings, all appearing to be different shades of blue in the moonlight.

As the SUV made a sharp right turn, there was a tall lithe shadow in the middle of the road. It was holding something over its shoulder.

"Sir," said Hanretty.

"Carl," gasped Peter.

The figure fired off an RPG that whistled toward the SUV, but the driver swerved in time as it shot right past and blew up a storefront behind them.

The SUV careened into a parked car, pushing it onto the sidewalk. Hanretty had slammed his head into the steering wheel and was feeling woozy.

"Get us out of here!" Peter shouted at him as he saw Kafka reloading. Hanretty shook his head and put the SUV into reverse, but the front bumper had become attached to the parked car.

Peter saw Kafka aiming the next RPG. "Gun it, Hanretty!"

Hanretty floored it, and the SUV pulled free. He put it in drive and gunned down the sidewalk as Peter heard another whistle. This one caught the rear of the SUV, sending it flying forward, rear end up, until it landed upside down. It skidded to a stop on the sidewalk, crashing into a storefront window and tearing down the striped cloth awning.

Peter put out his hands and feet to get his bearings and unbuckled his seatbelt. He crashed headfirst onto the roof of the car.

"Farrow, you all right?"

"I-I think so." He had blood running down the side of his head. He appeared to be cut from flying glass.

"Kessler, Michaels, you all right?" Peter shouted, as he helped Farrow with his seatbelt. There was no answer.

"They're dead, sir." Farrow said, his eyes wide with terror.

Peter grabbed Farrow by the shoulders. "We need to get out of here. You can do this, Farrow. You're a soldier. Remember your training."

Farrow swallowed hard and nodded. Peter had apparently gotten his wish. He was no longer moving the chess pieces. He was on the board. In the mix, just like he wanted.

Peter slid out of the broken window, shards of glass scraping his back through his golf shirt. He felt warm, wet blood mix with sweat, making his shirt stick to his back. Farrow followed behind him.

Peter crouched and waddled to the broken rear window of the SUV, and he pulled out two AK-47's. When Farrow was out, he reached back in to grab the luggage.

"Forget it," said Peter. "We have to keep moving." He held up his right hand and showed Farrow a thermite grenade.

Farrow nodded and retracted his hand. Peter grabbed him under his left armpit and hoisted him to his feet, shoving an AK-47 into his hands. Then he pulled Farrow deeper into the store. "Follow me."

They quickly waded through canned food, opened boxes, and various other food products strewn about, and headed down one of the grocery aisles to the back of the store.

Peter pulled the pin and tossed the thermite grenade down the aisle. It slid right up to the overturned SUV whose front protruded through the broken storefront.

They ducked through a back door into a small storage room. As the door shut behind them, the store shook with a boom as the grenade went off.

"There's a back door," said Farrow, pointing to an exterior door in the back of the storage room. There was a cheap metal shelf stocked with more canned goods in front of it. "They don't seem to care about fire codes."

Peter gave Farrow a sardonic look. "Let's get out of here before the gas tank blows." Farrow nodded, and they each took a side of the shelf and pulled it down, sending the cans rolling everywhere.

"Wait," Peter said, and he disappeared into the storefront. The SUV was ablaze, blocking the breach with flames. He didn't have much time. He went behind the enclosed glass counter and turned on the gas grill, blowing out the pilot light underneath.

As he rounded the counter, he thought he saw the wraithlike silhouette of Kafka stalking up to the bodega. He wasted no time.

Farrow, who was waiting by the rear exit, saw Peter re-emerge from the front. "What did you do?"

"Something Carl told me he did in Xcaret when trapped in the resort with the drones. A little taste of his own medicine."

He pushed Farrow out the back door, and they spilled into a narrow alleyway. They ran down the alley, followed by a louder boom, and the bodega began to cave in on itself, flames shooting out of the collapsing roof.

"Do you think we got him?" asked Farrow.

"I think we bought ourselves a few extra minutes," panted Peter as they sprinted as fast as they could down the alley. He grabbed his mini-com multi-tasker. "This is Team Leader, exit compromised. We need immediate extraction at new coordinates."

"Roger that, Team Leader. We have your location. Sending coordinates for extraction."

Peter looked down at his screen as the coordinates uploaded, and a navigation map appeared with the extraction coordinates indicated in flashing green. ETA, twenty minutes.

"It's six blocks away," said Peter. We won't win a straight-up fight with Kafka, so we have to evade until our ride comes."

Farrow nodded.

They came to the end of the alleyway and turned back onto the street. They hit an intersection and turned right onto a busier boulevard. Peter and Farrow shoved past pedestrians in the dark under flashing holographic ads, onlookers recoiling from the sight of the AK-47's, and jogged until they hit another intersection.

"We've got to get out of here before the authorities catch up with us," said Farrow.

Peter knew he was right. They didn't want to be intercepted by Kafka or the local police. Either way would end in certain death.

"Three more blocks this way," Peter said, pointing down the boulevard. "We've gotta get out of public, or we'll definitely run into local law enforcement. It's an aerial extraction."

Farrow understood. "Rooftops."

Peter nodded. He kicked in the front door of a yellow apartment complex covered in graffiti, and they ran down the hall to the stairwell. They climbed the stairs, two-at-a-time, and ran down another long hallway, toppling a drunken resident standing in the middle as they passed.

Peter pointed to the stairwell at the other end of the hall. "There's the roof."

Peter shot the lock off the chained door at the top, and they burst out onto the roof. He checked his multi-tasker as Farrow bent over with his hands on his knees, trying to catch his breath.

"Eleven minutes. We need to be there." Peter pointed to a rooftop several buildings away.

He went to the edge of the roof and looked down at the street. They were on a main boulevard, and the street below was teeming with nightlife.

"Do you think he's been following us?" asked Farrow, walking over to Peter. He, too, was looking down at the street.

Peter frowned. "Let's not stick around to find out." He shouldered his AK and Farrow followed suit.

They ran to the edge of the roof and hopped the four-foot gap between the buildings onto another flat, asphalt rooftop. They ran across that rooftop, dodging waste stack vents and skylights.

The next rooftop was pitched and covered in Spanish tile. Peter and Farrow jumped simultaneously. Peter landed and began to scale the pitch on all fours. Farrow landed less gracefully, tiles sliding out from under his feet.

Peter heard the clinking of dislocated tiles and turned to look back to see Farrow sliding towards the edge. Farrow got a grip and held it right at the edge, but he was afraid to move.

Peter turned and slowly crab-walked back down the pitch. When he reached Farrow, he turned sideways and reached out a hand. "It's okay. I've got you."

Farrow reached out with a trembling hand and took Peter's. Peter's grip closed around Farrow's hand like a vice, and he pulled Farrow away from the edge. Farrow struggled to find secure footing as more tiles slid off the rooftop.

Peter was suddenly reminded of a story Nolan Kettle told him about how Carl coaxed a terrified soldier through the dreaded rope bridge of the Victory Tower exercise in Basic.

"Just follow me on all fours. Slow and careful."

"Got it," said Farrow, recovering quickly.

They crawled up to the peak and then crab walked slowly down the other side, Peter leading to stop Farrow in case he began to slide again.

They made it to the edge, and Peter heard the staccato blade of a Black Hawk cutting through the night sky. He checked his multi-tasker. "Three minutes."

They had two more roofs to cross. The next two appeared flat, as did the third where the extraction was to take place.

They jumped together, grabbing the edge of the flat roof on the other side. They pulled themselves over the lip and rolled to standing position. They crossed the rooftop, hopped across to the next one, and hopped to their final rooftop.

Peter and Farrow heard sirens from below. The police were on the scene. The sound of the Black Hawk was getting louder. Farrow looked up as it approached. "We made it."

However, Peter was looking at the rooftops they just crossed and saw two of the fanged men from the hotel leaping from roof to roof with unnatural speed. They were only two rooftops away.

Peter grabbed his AK-47 and opened up on the two men, but the men moved too quickly and easily dodged the fire.

Farrow was calling it in to the Black Hawk. "Enemy bogies approaching on rooftops."

"Copy that."

The Black Hawk, which was flying over the fanged men heading towards the extraction point, turned in the air and the guns opened fire on the leapers. Bolts of light shot across the sky as the two pursuers were lit up like Christmas trees.

After their motionless bodies slid down and off the pitch of the Spanish-tiled rooftop, the Black Hawk swung back around and hovered over Peter and Carl. A rope ladder unfurled and landed between them.

"Age before beauty!" Peter shouted at Farrow over the helicopter blades.

Farrow didn't need a second invitation. He grabbed the rope ladder and began to ascend the rungs.

Peter looked around, his AK trained on the rooftops in case they had more party-crashers. He looked up and saw that Farrow was almost up and in the helicopter.

He shouldered his AK and grabbed a rung of the rope ladder, when something in a blur snatched him away from it, sending him staggering backward and falling through a large skylight.

As he fell, he saw the helicopter quickly recede from his view and he landed on a pile of boxes. Winded, he rolled off the boxes and landed face-down onto the harder laminate flooring. The room smelled like leather.

He pushed himself up on his hands and knees as he heard gunfire on the roof and saw the Black Hawk pull away. He felt for his AK-47, but it must've been thrown off his shoulder in the fall.

Peter looked around and saw piles off boots, belts, and women's purses on tables by the boxes. A lithe form descended through the skylight and landed in front of Peter.

"That wasn't very nice, Carl."

Kafka smiled, his four eyes glinting in the low light like a twisted cat. "Oh, that? It was just a love tap, Pete." He saw Peter's expression. "You don't like it now that the tables are turned. Now, I'm smarter *and* stronger than you."

Peter hated to admit it, but Kafka was right. "You look like shit, Carl. How's that gypsy girlfriend of yours? Sorry I got to stick her before you, but the last thing that went through her before she died was...well, I'd like to say it was thoughts of you, but it was the point of that umbrella."

There was a micro-expression of barely contained fury on Kafka's face.

Peter smirked. "So you *did* sleep with her."

Kafka grinned in a horrible display of tooth and fang. "Sorry about Fiona, Pete. I heard she gets around...as in all over the place. You might say she went to pieces over me."

"How did you find us?" Peter demanded, quickly changing the subject.

Kafka cocked his head sideways, amused at the question as if the answer was obvious. "I followed your little trail of crumbs, Pete. You really need to be more careful."

Peter had no idea what Kafka was referring to. He reached at his side, concealed by the dark, and silently activated the touch screen on his multi-tasker. "So where've you been hiding all of this time?"

"Who says I was hiding?" croaked Kafka. His voice made Peter's skin crawl.

"You dropped off the grid for a while after Monterosso. I heard you paid Ramses a visit." His fingers were typing furiously on the touch screen.

Kafka stroked his black, oily chin with elongated fingers that ended in sharp wisps. "He nearly shit himself when he saw me, but he was on the john anyway, so I guess it was okay."

"Still with OIL these days?" Peter probed, trying to sound like he was engaging in small talk. He was dragging out this reunion to stall for time.

"More like OIL is still with me," Kafka corrected. "I serve a higher purpose now."

"How are your Martian friends?" chided Peter. "Coming to take you back to the mother ship?"

"On the contrary," said Kafka menacingly, "it is I who has brought them here."

"So that explains your dentally well-endowed friends."

"Those were a few, but there are many," answered Kafka cryptically. "You might say they're everywhere."

This was news to Peter. He wondered how many more were out there. "And your OIL friends are okay with your new crowd?"

Kafka chortled at the question. "They have no choice. If they are true believers, they will join us. Those who lack faith will perish with the rest of you."

"You seem very confident in your chances. Invasion won't be so easy."

Kafka laughed, a horrible flittering sound. "Not only will it be easy, but the military will help us achieve it."

More riddles. "How is that, exactly?"

"You don't think I'm going to reveal my master plan to you just like that, do you?"

"I guess not," replied Peter. "But it was worth a shot." There was an uncomfortable pause. "You know I can't beat you in a fight."

Kafka shrugged two bony shoulders. "Who says I want to fight? If I wanted you dead, you'd be dead already."

"So what *do* you want?"

"Why not join the cause? General to general—"

"Actually I'm a Major now," Peter corrected.

"Leader to leader," Kafka said with an undercurrent of growing impatience. "Like Grant and Lee at the Appomattox Court House."

"And let me guess," quipped Peter, "I'm supposed to be Lee. Bad example."

"Actually, unbeknownst to you, the example is quite fitting," replied Kafka.

"I'd have thought you'd be rather pissed at me for killing your little gypsy girlfriend in Monterosso," pushed Peter.

"Your heartbeat is accelerating," said Kafka, the impatience escalating to an edge of anger in his voice. "You are trying to push me.

Why?" Kafka cocked his head sideways, reaching out to the outside of the building with his senses. "You called for help."

Peter smiled at his brother as he heard the blades of the Black Hawk outside the building.

"They can't get to you in here," said Kafka. "Your valiant effort is wasted."

"Who says I wanted them to get to me?" taunted Peter, and he threw his mutli-tasker at Kafka.

Kafka caught it reflexively as Peter hit the ground. Suddenly, bolts of light crashed through the wall as the Black Hawk opened fire on Kafka.

Peter commando crawled across the floor as bullets flew above him. He passed another stack of boxes that were being minced by the gunship hovering just outside the building.

He made it to a doorway on the far side of the room, and he crawled through. He got to his feet and descended a flight of stairs, crossed a leather shop, and kicked open the front door.

He stepped out onto the street and all manner of drunks, junkies, and assorted low lives were cheering the lightshow the Black Hawk was putting on for them up above, pounding the second floor with a barrage of bullets. Tijuana had become so lawless that gunfire was viewed as entertainment rather than something to hide from.

Peter looked up, wondering when the gunfire would stop and the rope ladder would unfurl for him, but something out of the corner of his eye caught his attention. It was the two four-eyed, fanged men from before, minus the one crushed by the SUV. They were staring at Peter, hungry with vengeance, giving off a horrid clicking.

"Oh, shit," Peter said to himself, and he crossed the street, mingling with the crowd.

The two fanged men followed him, meandering through the crowd, brandishing fierce canines. No one noticed. Everyone was looking up at the show above.

Peter stepped onto the sidewalk and entered a building with a crowd of nighttime partiers. He walked down a narrow hallway that smelled like an armpit, pushing the people in front of him forward as he heard the thumping bass backbeat mixed in with Norteno music.

He entered the club proper: a large dance floor with three bars, one on each side of the room (excluding the entrance), two cages, and a small stage containing half-nude dancing girls.

Peter wiggled his way through the throng of dancers, making his way to the opposite end of the room. He looked back at the entrance and saw the two vampires enter the club, scanning the crowd for him. These bastards were persistent.

He hoped he could lose them in the crowd, music, and flashing lights. Peter passed by one of the cages containing a buxom young woman wearing pasties. She was gyrating slowly to the music, her teeth, eyes, and fingernails glowing in the black light.

Suddenly, one of the vamps caught sight of him and began to make a beeline for Peter, now shoving its way through the crowd. Peter looked down at his shirt and saw his blood illuminated in the black light. It was like a goddamned bull's eye.

Peter knelt down as if he was going to tie his shoelaces, and he pulled up his pant leg. He pulled a large knife out of a leather sheath. When he stood up, he felt a hand on his shoulder.

He spun around, but a quick hand with a strong grip caught the knife. It was the other vamp. Peter felt a sharp pain in his ribs, and when he looked down, he realized the vamp injected him with something.

Peter slapped the needle out of the vamp's hand, but it was too late. He struggled to twist his hand and press the knife into the vampire as he was bumped by oblivious dancers around him, but the vampire was too strong.

Suddenly, the sounds took on a frightening quality and the colors from the lights and glow sticks began to streak in slow motion all around him. Peter shook his head, but the pulsing music took on a horrible quality.

Lights and faces flashed before his eyes, smiles turned to toothy grins, glassy eyes took on a nightmarish intensity, and Peter began to see demons interspersed in the crowd.

As he recoiled in terror, trying desperately to convince himself that these were all hallucinations induced by whatever the vampire injected into him, he loosened his grip on the knife.

The vampire snatched it out of Peter's hand and slid it inside its shirt. It then backed away from Peter and disappeared into the crowd.

Peter stood there dizzy, trying to keep his balance. He didn't know why the vampire backed off, but he knew an opportunity when he saw one. He began to stumble his way through the crowd, falling into neighboring dancers.

One girl smiled at him and kissed him on the cheek as he leaned on her momentarily for support. When he looked at her face, it was grotesquely contorted and demonic. She was trying to tell him something, but he couldn't hear or understand her.

He backed into a man, who promptly shoved him so hard he nearly fell into another girl. When he turned around, he saw a monster snarling at him, snapping its teeth.

Was this real? He had vampires following him; he used to work with zombies...was this so crazy? It was like everyone in the club, upon taking notice of him, transformed into something else. When they looked at him, they dropped their human veneers and revealed something ugly and horrible underneath.

He looked across the room and saw Kafka standing tall over the crowd, his four eyes luminous, all gazing at him. Peter began to back up, but there was a wall of dancers behind him pushing back. The club suddenly felt saturated with people, and it was standing room only.

Kafka made his way through the crowd like a great wraith wading through humanity, undetected. Peter tried to push, but the crowd was dense and he hadn't the coordination to slip in between the tightly packed clubbers.

When he realized he had nowhere to go, a wave of panic washed over him, flooding his mind with terrible possibilities. He began to claw at people in desperation, trying to shout his way through the people.

However, the music drowned him out and scandalous fiends glared back at him in disapproval, flicking forked tongues at him in protest.

Peter turned around and Kafka was upon him, opening his mouth and licking venomous fangs. All Peter could do was look up at what was once his brother, a thing that now embodied hatred and evil and was fueled by vengeance.

Kafka sunk his teeth into the side of Peter's neck, and for a moment, the room had gone quiet and dark. The bite was excruciating, yet it blocked out the terror of the hallucinations—a brief moment of respite, cleansing through pain, redemption through contamination.

Peter embraced his brother, accepting his fate at Carl's hands. He had failed his little brother and was now prepared for his penance. He had been the sole survivor of too many missions, lost too many men. He had failed to protect his mother, and he lost her, too.

It was his time.

Kafka released Peter and pulled him close, whispering in his ear, "We are one, although we are many."

He released his grip on Peter, letting him fall to the floor, and he disappeared into the crowd.

Peter lay on the floor, the horrible music faded into the background, white noise. The demon faces vanished, and Peter was only aware of faceless people crowded all around him in the sweltering room...

...except for one face.

While everyone was looking everywhere else, this one face was looking right at Peter. It would appear somewhere in the mix and then vanish, only to reappear somewhere else in the crowd.

Peter was weak but forced himself to sit up, leaning on his right arm, and he strained his eyes to peer into the crowd. He saw the face again, this time closer. He rubbed his eyes frantically, struggling to make out the face.

Then there it was, right in front of him, looking down at him. It was like he was looking in the mirror, because standing before him in dirty khakis and a golf shirt stained with sweat and blood was Peter, himself.

This impossibility was more than his mind was able to handle, and he leaned back, closing his eyes, allowing himself to drift down the current of madness gently into sweet oblivion.

Chapter 2

University of Texas at Dallas
University Village Apartments
Building 58
24:00 HRS

Elicia Corti fired up what was to be her final podcast. After tonight, she was taking herself off the grid...or at least her illegitimate self.

She still had projects to do for the mobile phone companies, debugging their operating systems, but it was a major step for a nineteen-year-old L33T hacker in modern society to drop off the grid. No more blogging and no more podcasts as Tronika. After tonight, she was closing her Tor account.

In essence, she was killing off Tronika, but she saw it as ending on a high note. She had done some legendary cracking and had nothing to prove to anyone. One of her greatest trophies was posting a zombie apocalypse survival manual on the CDC website.

She, or Tronika rather, had been invited into some pretty elite groups, but she had always declined. They were too Black Hat for her, even the vigilante groups. The Nation State had already dubbed her the Seditious Blogger, and she didn't need any more agencies looking for her.

Elicia decided to use her skills for good, and more importantly for profit, portscanning and updating operating systems and firmware. The money was very good and there was no risk of going to prison. A couple of close shaves with the authorities and the hacker life had begun to lose its luster.

However, she was going to be on the grid as a regular, every day n00b. She still had to purchase her online digital textbooks and post her homework for her professors to grade online. She still had to pay her tuition, check her e-mail, and update her social networking sites.

"Good evening, listeners. This is Texas Pirate Podcasting, the underground revolution watching the Man for you, John Q Citizen."

She never referred to herself as Tronika in her broadcasts, but her followers knew who she was.

"As you know this will be my final broadcast via the internet. Things have been heating up around here, and your gracious host has to watch out for her own skin. If something were to happen to me, then who would look out for you? Who would risk life and limb in this fascist regime to bring you the truth?

"I have been noticing…neighbors being carried off in handcuffs by the FBI, who have been very active as of late. With the Second Patriot Act in place, they are scouring the highways and byways of the digital realm, looking for terrorists and likely finding them where they want to.

"Is this a legitimate use of tax payer dollars in the name of national security or a Federally-sponsored witch hunt? The jury is still out on that one, but what has recently come to my attention is not the *Why* but the *How*?

"Just how are these Federal stooges conducting their surveillance? Phone tapping? Internet honeypots in chat forums posing as hyperlinks for those with a penchant for terrorism? Video cameras?

"All of these are well-documented ways of detecting and ensnaring terrorists. So if you have nothing to hide, you have nothing to worry about…right?

"Well what if the government was using your cell phones, your mini-coms, your computer screens, and your television sets? Different story? There are advertising applications in Japan where screens can scan the retinas of passersby on the street and flash advertisements tailored to the individual.

"Now that's all private enterprise, corporations jockeying to snare your attention so that you will purchase their unique product. But what if the government was using this technology, or something similar, to read your retinas without your awareness or consent?

"Still feel this is kosher? Hey, if you have nothing to hide, then what is there to worry about? Privacy? Intellectual property? There is a fine line between clandestine surveillance and espionage, and when the government engages in this sort of behavior it becomes tyranny.

"So it is because of the dangers of tyranny that tonight's broadcast will be my final one on the grid. For those of you who have been following my podcasts for the past year or so, I thank you.

"You all must keep alert. Be aware of the technology that you are using and who might be viewing your behavior, or even worse…your thoughts. Although my podcasts are finished, I will never rest in my endeavor to seek out the truth. Somehow, someway, I will get the truth out to all who will listen in the hopes that someone in a high place will initiate policy change to protect our individual liberties.

"These are frightening times, but in our fear we must not trade in our liberties for empty gestures that do nothing to protect us but give us baseless senses of security. The terrorists try to take away our freedom, our way of life. Let's not hand over our freedoms to the government so the terrorists can't have them.

"And now I must say to all of my listeners good night. It has been a pleasure to serve you. God bless America, and God bless you all."

She turned off her microphone and shut down the podcast. She deleted her account with the podcast service, dismantled her proxy servers and proxy IP addresses to conceal her identity and location.

This was no longer a joke. When she was a freshman, she started her podcasts as a social commentary on what was going on in the country, in the world. While philosophically for individual liberties and against big government, she found that her following always spiked when she went on rants and sometimes speculated beyond facts.

Hell, it was entertainment, and if it spiked her following then she was game. That was what it felt like…a game. Night after night, she would pour out her opinions into cyberspace and watch her numbers go up and down. Soon her numbers were way up, and consistently so.

The UTD Mercury, the university newspaper, praised her anonymous rants, calling her a courageous iconoclast. The administration panned her broadcasts, calling them the ravings of a confused, naïve girl who was vastly uninformed about politics, sociology, and the real world.

Both reactions amused Elicia, but she stopped laughing when she saw fellow students being taken away, their computers, cell phones, mini-coms and such all confiscated. All right around the time when she was harping on the government spying on the citizenry using every digital interface under the sun.

Elicia didn't actually believe in any of this. At least not at first. It was more part of her entertainment portion of the show, not factual content. However, when she saw the apprehended students return, she knew the feds weren't looking for these other students.

They were looking for her.

Apparently, she had touched a nerve with this particular thread of rants. The government didn't like being accused of spying on the populace. While most would dismiss Elicia's podcasts as juvenile, paranoid crap, she did garner quite a large following.

It was time to quit while she was ahead.

Her roommate Darcy staggered into the room drunk off her ass. "Hey, Elicia, you're still up?"

Elicia smiled at Darcy. Although she wasn't into the drinking/drugging lifestyle (that was more her older sister Brittany's ball of wax), she still liked Darcy. "It would appear so."

Darcy accidentally slammed the door behind her, dropped her purse on the floor, and plopped down in her bed smelling of cheap beer and cigarettes.

"So what were you doing all of this time?" she slurred.

"Typing up a paper for sociology." Elicia noticed that Darcy's makeup was smeared on her face.

"You know," said Darcy sitting up, "you're always worrying about that shit. You should've come out. It's finals week. I won't see you over the summer."

Oh, *this* dance again. "Darcy, I would only cramp your style. I'm pretty much guy repellent."

Darcy looked deeply perturbed by this. "You shouldn't say that about yourself." She was wagging her finger. "You are a very pretty girl."

It was true. Elicia was pretty, in a natural, girl-next-door kind of way. Unlike her sister, whose main mission in life was to be glamorous 24/7 to land a husband, Elicia did not wear much, if any, makeup. She was thin and she didn't dress like a total librarian, but she played down her looks, which always boggled both Brittany and Darcy.

"Matt Brauer thinks you're pretty."

This got Elicia's attention. "He was there?"

"You're damned right he was there, and he asked me about you."

"Go to sleep, Darcy."

"No, really, he did."

"What did he say?"

"He asked where you were. He probably wonders why you never come out."

Dammit. Matt Brauer was asking where she was. This was one of the costs of being a dedicated iconoclast. She had taken a couple of classes with him now, struck up some small talk on a few occasions, but never had the guts to take it any further.

The truth was she was afraid. Her mother, Brittany, and Darcy all accused her of being too serious. What if she *was* too serious? Matt seemed like a nice guy. He wasn't a hardcore partier. He was cute as hell.

She was afraid that, if left unchecked, small talk would evolve into politics and then she would go on one of her tirades, and the dialogue would quickly become a soliloquy. She supposed that was why she liked doing her podcasts. There was no one in front of her, no feeling self-conscious.

But that was over now.

"You know what, Darcy? Next time you go out, I'm coming with you."

Darcy looked incredulous, which was all the more comical in her inebriated state. "You mean it? You'll really come out?"

"It's only Thursday. I'll go out with you tomorrow night. Maybe even have a couple of drinks. Promise."

"That's great, Elicia." Darcy lay her head back down on her pillow and began to snore.

Elicia got up from her computer desk and walked over to Darcy. She took her sheet and covered her gently. Then she turned off the light and walked back over to her computer desk. She shut down her computer and lay in her bed, wondering if Darcy would remember the promise she made tonight.

It didn't matter because she planned on keeping her vow. She had dedicated so much time to making Tronika a rock star that she had neglected her analog life.

***

Fort Bliss Medical Facility
13:07 HRS

Peter came to in a white room with a one-way mirror, hearing the familiar blips and beeps of all kinds of monitors. Given all of his recent adventures, this was not an unusual way for him to wake up.

He tried to sit up, but he was unable to move. He was still unsteady from…that's right, what that fanged bastard injected him with. The memories began to flood his consciousness.

He wanted to reach up with his fingers and feel his neck, but he was unable to lift his arm. He tugged and began to feel a restraint secured with Velcro around his right wrist. He tried to move all of his limbs but found them to be tied down as well.

He began to remember the Black Hawk and Farrow…Christ, was Farrow all right? Did he make it out? As his mind raced with ideas and hypotheses, the door to his room opened with a swish. He was in a negative pressure room, which meant only one thing…

Quarantine.

General Ramses stepped into the room, and he wasn't wearing any protective gear. Peter found this curious given all of the precautions that were taken.

"General," said Peter craning his neck to look at Ramses.

"Major," replied Ramses coolly.

"What happened, sir?"

"We found you in a dance club. You were incoherent."

"Farrow?"

"He's fine."

"Thank God."

"Which is more than I can say for you," said Ramses imperiously.

"Sir?"

"When we extracted you *seconds* before the local authorities arrived, we brought you straight here for evaluation. You had narcotics in your system."

Ramses' tone was accusatory. Peter had to explain what had happened without sounding defensive or crazy. Shit, if Ramses oversaw a platoon of zombie soldiers, he wouldn't think a trio of vampire terrorists to be too far-fetched.

In theory.

"Sir, Kafka was there. I was injected with narcotics to disable me." He thought about the bite. Surely the physician saw it during his evaluation, so there was no point in hiding it. "He...bit me, sir."

Ramses gazed upon Peter stone faced. "So, you botch yet another mission, lose more men, draw the attention of the Mexican authorities to our operations, we find narcotics in your system, and you try to explain it all away with fantastical explanations?"

"But, sir, he did bite me."

"Yeah, and your dog ate your homework. Not to mention, you let your brother get away yet again. Do you think I'm stupid, Major Birdsall?"

"Sir?"

"It does not escape my attention that every step of the way, when we get close to taking out your brother, there you are getting in the way."

Peter was speechless...almost. "Sir, with all due respect, if the army hadn't tried to kill him we wouldn't be in—"

"Oh, that's rich. It was *your* responsibility to keep your brother out of trouble."

"Sir, we didn't even understand what was happening to him. We still don't."

"And thanks to you, Major Birdsall, we will never get the chance. I've tolerated your incompetence for too long, lost too many men. You are to face court martial upon your convalescence, be it ever so speedy."

This was all happening too fast for Peter to process. Court marshaled. After everything he had been through? After everything the army put him through?

The Boy Scout act no longer applied. He was pissed...had been pissed for quite some time. If he was going to be court marshaled, he was going for broke.

"That's it! I bled for this army hunting down dangerous cartels and terrorists. I herded zombies like a twisted Bo Peep for the cause because one of you bastards thought it was a good idea, only to have them turn on me because the army couldn't control the traitors in its own ranks.

"I almost lose my brother to those MONSTERS only to bring him back safely so you guys can murder him. But you assholes can't even do that right, and now Carl is tearing the ass out of the army and this country, embarrassing YOU in the process.

"Because that's what you are, General, an EMBARRASSMENT. You've been rubbing elbows with the politicians too long, you've forgotten you're a soldier. You actually think you're one of them.

"It's just one dinner or benefit after another for you now. You don't even know what's going on under your very nose. My only regret was that I wasn't there in D.C. when my brother, the good man you tried to kill, made you shit your pants in terror."

By the end of his rant, Peter's fists were clenched, he was panting, and he had gone hoarse. Both men were silent in the negative pressure room, Peter's words hanging out there in the filtered air.

A cruel grin spread across Ramses' face. "Thank you, Major. That will be all."

He stepped out of the room.

Peter lay back sweating. He had always wanted to let the brass have it, and boy did they have it coming. To Peter's surprise, it actually felt good. Cathartic, even. He was tired of being the good boy.

These jerks created Kafka, let them clean up the mess. He was tired of it all, and as far as he was concerned, it was no longer his problem to try and fix. Even if the end result meant wasting the rest of his natural born life in a cell, it was a well-deserved respite from bailing an increasingly incompetent government out of the messes they made.

Ramses shut the door behind him and found Colonel Betancourt looking at Peter through the one-way mirror.

"Don't you think that was a bit harsh, sir?"

Ramses stood next to Betancourt, but Betancourt didn't make eye contact. He kept watching Peter through the glass. Ramses spoke anyway.

"The man's incompetent. He's botched too many missions."

"That man's been through a lot, too much," corrected Betancourt. "And, for the record, he's always tried to do the right thing *despite* how we've managed to screw things up."

"So you're defending him, Colonel?"

"I don't think he deserves a court martial."

"I'll take your opinion under advisement," said Ramses a little too dismissively for Betancourt's taste.

"Particularly after you promoted him to Major and insisted that he remained in the field."

Ramses practically snarled at Betancourt. "As I recall, Colonel, you backed my decision to keep him in the field."

"I believed that he was more effective in the field than behind a desk like some half-assed bureaucrat...sir."

"And I suppose you agree with him about his brother."

"Permission to speak freely, sir."

"Why not? You're on quite a roll, Colonel."

"I do believe that mistakes were made. That man is not responsible for what happened to his brother."

"And we are?"

"That is my opinion, sir."

"Well then, by court marshaling Major Birdsall, I guess I'm going to make one more mistake."

Betancourt turned around to face Ramses, looking into his eyes. "He's been bitten, sir."

"Surely you don't believe any of that hogwash."

"If you don't, then why the quarantine, sir?"

"What are you trying to say, Colonel?"

"There are people disappearing, important people. There was the animal attack that you witnessed in Maryland, sir. You don't really believe it to be an animal attack, do you?"

Ramses didn't respond one way or the other.

"I mean, if it was an animal attack, then why did the supposed animal tear out all of the security cameras. The footage is missing. Major Birdsall is right. There *is* something happening under our very noses. I don't know if it is OIL or something else, but this country is in danger."

If Betancourt wasn't mistaken, Ramses was growling under his breath, low so that it was almost undetectable. And his eyes...there was something different about his eyes.

Finally, Ramses spoke. "Major Birdsall is a liability. Once he's out of the way, we can deal with this theory of yours, as paranoid as it may seem."

"He shouldn't do any time."

Ramses grinned, bearing too many pearly whites. "Time? I wouldn't dream of it, Colonel." And he stepped out of the room leaving Betancourt to ponder their conversation.

Betancourt turned back toward the one-way mirror and watched Peter thoughtfully. The last thing that man deserved was to be court marshaled. However, there was something different about Ramses, something he couldn't quite put his finger on.

He left the observation room and walked down the hall to the serology lab. When he entered, he saw technicians disassembling equipment. Lieutenant Mary Keegan saluted him.

"At ease, Lieutenant. I've come to inspect your progress with the serum."

"Yes, sir." She seemed taken off guard, flustered even. But who wouldn't be. The army created undead drones using THV before even coming up with a cure, which was irresponsible in her opinion.

To add insult to injury, the army poured ninety-nine percent of the funding into the development of the drones, largely neglecting the development of a cure. However, it was not her place to point out such problems. She had to follow orders.

"Well, sir, the project has been discontinued."

This surprised Betancourt. "What? By whose authority?"

"General Ramses gave the order, sir. With the drone program discontinued, he saw no need to waste funding on developing a cure. All funding has been rerouted to…"

"Retinal Gateway Technology," he said.

"Yes, sir. That is correct. General Ramses wants the lab dismantled and samples destroyed by 17:00."

This whole thing was, in Betancourt's opinion, premature and short-sighted. THV was still out there, and possibly in OIL's possession. Discontinuing development of a cure was foolish. He couldn't question the general in front of Keegan, although he suspected from her demeanor that she was right there with him.

"How far did you get?"

"Well, the animal trials were unsuccessful in killing the virus. The best we were able to achieve was slowing it down, significantly even."

"But no cure."

"That's correct, sir."

"Can I see the samples?"

Keegan hesitated, obviously dubious about the request, given Ramses' orders. He mistook her hesitation for confirmation that they had already been destroyed.

"They haven't yet been—"

"No, sir. We still have them."

"Well, by all means, I'd like to see them then…and all documentation of their effects," he added so it didn't look like he only wanted to see the vials, which would've been an odd request.

"Yes, of course, sir."

She led him to the back of the lab to a Plexiglas enclosed area containing refrigeration units. "They're right in there, sir."

"I see. And the records?"

"They're back in the other room, sir."

"Well, by all means, go get them."

She nodded tentatively and left to go get the records.

Damn, she was making this more difficult than it needed to be. He guessed that she felt the same way he did about all of this, but dammit, she was going to follow orders. Good soldier.

The area containing the vials of serum required security clearance, specifically Keegan's fingerprints and retinas. He knew the only way he was going to get a vial was to ask her for one. There was no way around it.

She returned with the files on a memory stick that she slipped into a slot in the computer, which immediately called up the contents of the stick. "Everything you need is right here, sir."

Then she walked over to the containment area, submitted to finger and retinal scans, and opened the door. "Forgive me, sir, but I must oversee the breakdown of the lab, or the General will have my head. Can you watch these while I find a tech to dispose of them?"

Betancourt suppressed a shit-eating grin. "Yes, of course, Lieutenant. Don't let me prevent you from carrying out your orders."

She smiled, holding her gaze for a significant extra second or two, and left Betancourt alone with the vials. Good soldier. She apparently picked up on his ambivalence and decided to help him. They both knew the vials were to be destroyed anyway, so who would miss one or two?

He wondered if he should take more. He only needed one, but what if they needed more? They needed to be refrigerated, and the extra vials wouldn't likely survive unrefrigerated transport. One it was.

He slipped into the containment area, pilfered a syringe, and opened a small refrigeration unit. He swiped one of the vials, removed the rubber stopper at the top, removed the cap off the syringe, and slid the syringe inside. He slowly drew serum into the syringe, emptying the vial, and replaced the empty vial.

He closed the refrigerator door, replaced the syringe cap, and slipped the whole thing gingerly into his pant pocket. He slipped back out of the containment area as Keegan returned with a young technician.

"They're all yours," said Betancourt, gesturing to the containment area and the remaining vials within. Keegan looked down at the slight bulge in Betancourt's pants and then quickly averted her gaze elsewhere so as not to tip off the technician.

"Let's just say I'm happy to see you," quipped Betancourt clapping Keegan appreciatively on her back and leaving the lab like his pants were on fire.

He was quickly outside Peter's quarantine suite, but this time there was a guard. "Sir."

"As you were," Betancourt replied and made to enter the suite.

"Sir, General Ramses made it clear that no one was to enter the quarantine suite."

Damn. Something was definitely up with Ramses. Why the sudden paranoia? It was like he was covering his tracks, but why? He thought of Ramses' remark about Peter doing time. *He wouldn't dream of it.*

Suddenly, he feared for Peter's safety, but then he regained his senses. There was no way Ramses was going to harm Peter. Why would he do such a thing? Even if he were, it would be too suspicious. Wouldn't it?

"I have a few questions for Major Birdsall that would help shed some light on any possible contamination threats."

"I have my orders, sir. I am to let no one into this suite. Even you, sir." He said that last part rather tentatively.

"Lieutenant Keegan has just informed me that there is a definite contamination threat that may not be contained by a negative pressure room."

"Sir?"

"The contaminant isn't airborne. It's radiation."

The guard looked at him quizzically.

"Do I need to spell it out for you, Private? We have all been exposed. General Ramses isn't even privy to this yet. I need to get in there on the double and find out what I need to know."

"Yes, sir."

"And you need to get your ass checked out right away for radiation exposure. Report to Lieutenant Keegan immediately, and then the physician."

"Yes, sir." The guard saluted and stalked down the hallway to Lieutenant Keegan.

Shit. He only had a few minutes before the guard would realize that his story didn't check out. Ramses was going to hear about this, but he couldn't act on it. The slippery bastard looked suspicious as hell already.

He wouldn't want to draw any more attention to whatever he was trying to hide.

But one thing was for certain…Ramses would now know that he wasn't to be trusted. He'd worry about that later.

Betancourt slipped into Peter's room.

"What are *you* doing here?"

Betancourt walked right up to Peter's bed, keeping his back to the one-way mirror. He slipped the syringe out of his pocket and popped off the cap.

"Wait a minute. What in the hell are you doing?"

"Major, I'm on your side." He tapped Peter's forearm and a vein readily revealed itself in relief against his skin. He threaded the vein and sent the serum into Peter's bloodstream.

Before Peter could protest, Betancourt spoke in hushed tones. "This is a serum to counteract the bite. It won't kill the THV, but it will slow it down."

"I-I-I don't understand."

"By doing this, I've placed myself in danger, so you have to trust me. I'll be pulling for you at the court martial. Once you're discharged, I'll be in contact."

"Assuming I'll be discharged," whispered Peter.

"I don't think Ramses wants you imprisoned, but I'm not sure why."

"Sounds like a lot of guessing to me, sir."

"There's something going on. I agree with you. The army's going rotten from the inside, and I plan to find out why."

"Why risk all of this?"

"Not all of us are bureaucrats and wannabe politicians, son. I'm a patriot like you."

Before Peter could say anything else, Betancourt winked at him and whisked out of the room like a tornado. He felt a burning sensation in his veins that made him arch his back and clench his fists in his restraints.

Then just like that, it stopped. He suddenly became very calm, medicated calm. He fought the drowsiness, trying to process what had just transpired. He played and replayed Carl's last words to him in his head, struggling to make sense of them, because there was a reason Peter was still alive. *We are one, although we are many.*

In the end, his mind succumbed to numbness and he drifted off to the drumming of his own pulse inside his head. All the while, he swore someone was watching him behind the glass…

For some reason it was like one of those dreams where he was looking down on himself.

***

"I am telling you, he's unstable," said Al Razi, his voice trembling.

Kojic was frowning. "He has been very different, ever since Italy."

"Different? He's barely even human at this point. And he's changed the entire direction of the organization. All of this talking of true believers. In what?"

"He still believes in the cause," answered Kojic quickly, his eyes shifting around the room nervously as if he was afraid they would be overheard.

"And which cause is this, now? Liberation? Anarchy? He speaks of these *Outworlders* like he's some kind of half-assed Scientologist."

"It is not as if they don't exist. Just look at him. He appears to be in their image."

"Then we are all doomed. What if these Outworlders come? What happens to us? Slavery...death?"

Kojic truly did not know the answer to this question that had crossed his mind more than a few times since Italy. Belmont was dead, murdered at the hands of this Kafka. Yvette was dead, murdered by his brother. "So what are you saying?"

"I am saying that we should not stray from Belmont's mission. He is the original founder of the Order. It is his vision we must follow, not this monster's."

Kojic started at that last word and became even more uneasy. "You must keep your calm," he urged through clenched teeth. "You know he can hear from far away."

"I am frightened, Kojic." He was. He did not think twice about strapping a bomb to his chest, stepping out into a public square, and pressing the detonator...for the cause. But Kafka represented worse horrors and unspeakable possibilities.

Just then, Farooq entered the room, making both men jump out of their skins. He looked at them, perplexed by their reaction. "What is it?"

"Nothing," answered Kojic with an artificial coolness that barely, if at all, passed for casual.

"He wants to see us," announced Farooq.

"Kafka?" asked Al Razi.

"No, Santa Claus," said Farooq reproachfully.

Kafka relished the thought of converting his big brother. All this time, Peter somehow escaped death, so many times that he now wished for it to come. However, Kafka granted him the irony of an immortal existence, an eternity to suffer with his survivor's guilt.

In time, Peter would shed his humanity and embrace the existence of the Outworlders, for theirs was an existence of conquest and infinity, not frailty and limits.

His mini-com sounded off. "Yes."

"We have a problem."

"What is it, General?"

"It's Colonel Betancourt. He is suspicious. This business about court marshaling your brother. He's not buying it."

"He doesn't need to. My plans for Pete have nothing to do with him."

"Well, he went and made it his business by injecting your brother with the antidote serum R&D was working on."

Kafka became irritated. "I thought you disposed of the serum."

"I did, or was about to. He somehow got his hands on it and injected it into your brother."

"No matter. It's not a cure. It will only prolong the inevitable."

"What about Betancourt?"

"Oh, I'll take care of him personally. Just stick to the plan."

"Yes, Kafka."

"Fail me again and I'll be taking care of you."

He terminated the call to spare himself Ramses' pathetic response.

There was a knock at the door. He could sense their elevated heartbeats; taste their anxiety, rolling it around on the back of his tongue like a fine wine.

"Come in."

Three of his best OIL operatives entered the room at his bidding.

"You called, Kafka," said Kojic reverently.

"Yes, I suppose I did. Please, sit down." Kafka gestured to three chairs. Kojic, Al Razi, and Farooq all sat down. "You served Belmont well."

They each nodded in loyal confirmation.

"Such a pity we lost him," said Kafka without any pity, "but he died for the Cause."

"He was a good man," said Kojic.

"Which brings me to a very important question: what are each of you willing to do for the Cause?"

They looked at each other in confusion.

"I'm not sure what you mean," replied Farooq.

"You've been in OIL for years, each of you, and you've climbed the ranks. You three represent OIL's best men."

The three men smiled uneasily, wondering just what point Kafka was trying to make.

"The point I'm trying to make," said Kafka practically reading their thoughts, which clearly was uncomfortable for them, "is that I am asking whether or not you are willing to make the ultimate sacrifice."

"Clearly, we are each willing to die for the Cause," said Kojic.

"I'm not talking about death," growled Kafka. He noticed their pulses flutter, for he knew they heard the rumors of Kafka's conversions.

"W-we are prepared to do what is required," said Kojic, swallowing hard.

"Does Kojic speak for the rest of you?"

Al Razi and Farooq nodded in unison, wide-eyed.

"Good. Kojic, come here."

Kojic looked at the other two and then stood looking like he didn't quite know what to do with his hands. He tentatively stepped around Kafka's desk and stood in front of him.

"Kojic, Serbian national, world renowned computer hacker, way to step up to the plate."

Kafka rose very suddenly, practically causing poor Kojic to jump out of his shoes. He reached out and caressed the back of Kojic's neck with long fingers.

Then, moving with great speed, he lunged and sank his teeth into Kojic's neck so that it appeared as if he barely moved. Kojic began to convulse in Kafka's arms.

Farooq cowered in a corner of the small room, and Al Razi turned heel and bolted out of there as fast as his legs would carry him.

Kafka released Kojic from his bite and glared at Farooq in the corner, his face demonic. "Go fetch Al Razi or you'll pray for death by the time I finish with you. Time to join the family like Kojic here. The pay sucks but the fringe benefits are to die for."

Chapter 3

Two Weeks Later
Birdsall Homestead
20:12 HRS

Peter had recovered remarkably quickly, in time for an expedient court martial. As promised, Colonel Betancourt vouched for him, but in the end, Peter was handed a dismissal with a forfeiture of all pay and allowances.

He had moved back in with his father who, despite the circumstances of Peter's stay, was happy to have one son home.

"You're better off," Barry insisted in between draws from his beer. "You can come to work at the hardware store. At least no one will shoot at you there."

Peter ran his fingers through his hair in exasperation. A big part of him was relieved, yet it was beginning to dawn on him that he was now a civilian. He abruptly went from being a Major in the U.S. Army Special Forces, commanding multi-million dollar equipment and highly trained soldiers, to a boomerang kid living with his father.

Christ, now he knew how Carl must've felt.

"What do you think he's doing now?" Barry asked, reading Peter's mind.

"Damned if I know, but he got what he wanted: me out of the picture."

"It could've been worse, Pete. You could be dead."

His father was right. He could've been dead, but truth be told, he felt better than he ever had before. However, strange things were happening to him…changes.

For one, he felt his father's heartbeat across the table. He also became faster, not just physically, but mentally. "I suppose you're right, Dad."

"Working at the hardware store will be good for you. Hell, with everything that's been going on, it's the only thing keeping me going." He smiled warmly at his son. "And now I have you."

"I don't think we've heard the last of Carl though," said Peter, feeling his father's heartbeat accelerate from the comment. "I'm scared, too, Dad."

Barry looked puzzled. How did he know?

Peter didn't want to tell his father about the changes. It wasn't a matter of top secret classification. Not anymore. He just didn't want to frighten him by telling him that he was going through the same changes that Carl was going through, because they both knew what Carl became.

"Do you think we're in danger, Pete?"

Peter knew Barry was in danger, but probably not from Carl. He had to come clean, for his father's safety.

"Dad, I've been going through these changes."

Barry smiled in a fatherly way. "Your whole life has been uprooted and twisted around. You'll bounce back."

Peter sat forward, his palms flat on the kitchen table. "No, I mean *changes*. Like what Carl went through."

Barry looked like his skin went suddenly cold. "Oh. I see. Changes."

"Yes, Dad."

"You, too? But how?"

"During a mission in Tijuana I ran into Carl...and he bit me."

Barry almost dropped the beer right out of his hand. "Wh-what do you mean, he *bit* you?"

"I mean he sprouted fangs and bit me. On my neck."

Barry didn't know what to say. He knew what Carl looked like, what he had become, but this was too much.

"There were other men," Peter continued, "his men, and they also had fangs." He felt comfortable speaking freely. After what had happened, his father had thrown away his television, and their mini-coms were powered down."Jesus," gasped Barry. "What do you think this means? That Carl is some kind of monster? Like Dracula?"

"There was what the press called an animal attack in Maryland. The building where it occurred happened to be NSA."

"So you don't think it was an attack," Barry said.

"Exactamundo," replied Peter.

"But Carl wasn't bitten, was he?"

"That's exactly what bothers me. He wasn't. Not in Xcaret. Not during training."

"And what about you?" Barry gestured to Peter with both hands. "You mean to tell me that you were bitten, and the army just let you go?"

"Especially after what happened to Carl," Peter added. "That doesn't sit well with me either."

"Maybe they're using you as bait...for Carl," Barry offered. "Thinking he'll come back for you."

"Maybe," said Peter thoughtfully. "The thought did cross my mind. That may be the reason for the public disgrace. If Carl believes that I'm out—truly out—he'd come back for me."

"What do *you* think, Pete?"

"I don't think Carl is that stupid. He bit me before any of this happened. This is their reaction after the fact. He could've killed me, easily. I think that he bit me for a reason, and it's for that reason that he won't be coming back."

"I hope you're right," Barry said with a shiver, the thought of his prodigal son returning giving him the willies. However, it wasn't just that. He knew that if he did return the army would kill him. Although he didn't have—or for that matter want—his son home, he took some consolation in the fact that Carl was still alive.

"Carl's reason for biting me can't be good," said Peter gravely. "I just wish I knew what it was."

Barry stood up, clearly tired of the direction the conversation was heading in. "Well, it's late and I'm heading up for bed. I suggest you do the same. You can bring all of your magic powers with you to the store tomorrow. I could use the help."

Peter sat back in his chair nursing what was left of his beer. "Good night, Dad."

"Good night, Pete." Barry lingered for a moment; drinking in the sight of his son like it was going to be the last time he was ever going to see him that way again. It made Peter uncomfortable.

Barry left the kitchen, and Peter heard his father's footsteps up the stairs. He heard the water turn on and the pipes become noisy. It was June and already hotter than the hell itself. His Dad was taking a shower before bed.

Peter finished his beer, got up, shuffled his way to the fridge, and got himself another. Before he knew it, another turned into three more and he was working on a good buzz.

He felt his father's pulse slow down and become regular, the throes of slumber. Peter was tired, but a weary kind of tired, not the sleepy kind. He wanted to go to bed, but he was in the grip of a nasty insomnia that all the beer in Texas wouldn't fix.

He looked out the deck door off the kitchen and almost did a double take. He thought he saw someone looking in at him. He slammed his beer bottle down on the kitchen table and rubbed his eyes, but the shadow was still right outside the deck door.

"Who is it?" Peter cried out to the darkness just outside. He reached out with his senses, like Carl said he used to—it was remarkably easy, like reaching out for a beer—but he felt nothing.

The presence was oddly familiar and disconcerting at the same time. He knew it was this goddamned doppelgänger that was following him around for the past two weeks. It was like it was secretly keeping tabs on him in the most private of moments, but every time he went to confront it, it vanished.

"Leave me alone," Peter demanded, his speech slurring slightly.

He stood up with heavy feet and left the kitchen. He trudged up the stairs slowly, one-by-one, until he reached the top. He didn't know why, because he knew sure as shit he wasn't going to sleep.

Then the idea occurred to him out of thin air, plucked from the night: he wondered what it would look like if he finger-painted with his father's blood all over the walls of Barry's bedroom.

The idea came so quickly, like second nature, that he was overcome with nausea and repulsion at the very notion. Where the hell did that come from? He chastised himself silently in the dark hallway.

Yet there it was again. The idea of murdering his father, ceasing that heartbeat of his and tasting his blood. Peter wretched in the hallway. Composing himself, he stomped down the stairs, went back into the kitchen, unlocked and flung the deck door open, and ran out into the night.

He wanted to see him, the sick bastard who planted these evil thoughts into his head. He searched the shadows by the moonlight for him and by-God, if he found him he was going to wring his neck, this thing that wanted him to become like Carl.

Peter laughed horribly in the moonlight, like a demented miscreant with sin on his soul. He felt the anti-dote serum pumping through his veins, fighting the THV that Carl gave him, the diabolical gift that kept on giving.

He had to leave his father's house or he couldn't be held responsible for what was going to happen. He was dangerous. A weapon, planted by his brother.

His life had become a ticking time bomb. It was only a matter of time before he lost control, before he turned into a monster like Carl.

He looked up and saw a man standing there in front of him waiting. He didn't even hear the guy approach. "Can I help you?"

When he looked up, he saw his own face. He was looking at him looking at himself. What? His weary brain raced to process the sight before him—

"Are you all right, Son?"

Peter was startled by his father's voice behind him, but he suppressed the reflex to turn around. He was still getting used to his heightened senses and, distracted, had not detected his father's presence.

He didn't want his father to see him in his current condition. He couldn't see himself, but he knew he had at that very moment changed...transfigured.

"I'm fine, Dad," he called over his shoulder as he stared straight ahead at the perfect image of himself. It was leering at him. Did his father see it?

His father was silent for a moment, and Peter could sense his concern behind him as he wrestled down his homicidal impulse to eviscerate the man where he stood. After a brief moment, Barry turned and went back inside.

Peter, who didn't realize he was holding his breath, gasped for air as he relaxed, the primal urges subsiding for the moment. He realized his twin was gone.

It was then that he realized that it was unsafe for him to stay with his father. He would have to come up with some reason to leave, and his father likely wouldn't understand, but it had to be done.

He walked over to the patio set and dropped wearily into one of the chairs. He decided he would spend the night outside, away from his father. Then he thought twice about it, stood up, stepped through the sliding door and into the kitchen, and locked the sliding door behind him.

He reached into his pocket, fished out his now civilian issue mini-com multi-tasker, and placed it on the kitchen counter. He left the kitchen, exited the house through the front door—locking it behind him—and walked back around to the backyard patio set.

He took his place in the patio chair and took some consolation in the fact that the only way he would be able to get into the house would be to break his way in. He felt confident that he would be able to suppress the urge to do so, but he didn't want to tempt fate by leaving himself easy access to the house.

He thought...hoped that for the night his father was safe. He allowed the rhythm of his father's heartbeat to lull him into drowsiness and then an uneasy sleep, keeping the primal urges that Carl planted at bay at the fringes of his volition.

*****

Elicia sat with her feet up on the desk at the front of the computer lab, lazily paging through a novel as her laptop was searching for kernel mode rootkits in the Planar Mobile operating system. She was about to abandon the novel due to what she deemed poor writing. It was one of those zombie novels where corpses wandered the post epidemic landscape in search of romance and validation with other zombies. And, of course, they were all teens re-enacting adolescent dating rituals and tweeny politics.

The last straw for her was a love triangle between two zombie boys and a teenage human survivor. Disgusting. She put her digi-reader down on the desk in front of her and considered the empty lab that lay before her under her watch. She enjoyed the job. The campus was a ghost town during the summer sessions, particularly summer session one, and it gave her time to kick back without the intrusion of human interaction.

Her mind wandered to her blog and all of the FBI activity on campus. Since she abandoned the blog, federal activity had not slowed down. In fact, it had appeared that their presence had doubled. With the internet, there were all kinds of way to track people.

The FBI was fond of using hyperlinks associated with websites of interest as honeypots to glean IP addresses. So all one had to do was click on a link to her seditious blog, and boom...IP address logged, search warrant obtained, and the Feds were knocking on your door the next day. They were following breadcrumbs.

Short-wave radio would have been much more difficult to detect and out of the reach of the FBI. Elicia supposed the NSA would have the means to pursue it, but she laughed at the thought and chastised herself for being so paranoid. Besides, she was protected under the First Amendment.

She had seen in the news that authorities believed that OIL was regaining strength and stepping up their activities. She recalled some incident in Tijuana regarding a possible scuffle with Special Forces, but the government denied everything.

As she looked out across the rows of vacant computers, she became aware of an electrical hum that made her uneasy. All computers hummed. It was a combination of heat synchs and fans working to keep the dormant computers cool, but this was different. It was more palpable than the usual ambient hum. It was a buzzing...

...and it felt like she wasn't alone in the lab.

Just then, someone crossed her view in the lab, and her skin went cold as she registered who it was. Her illustrious Matt Brauer had entered the lab, about twenty minutes before closing, and took a seat in the first row, the third computer in, placing him front and center before her.

He didn't look up. He only grabbed the mouse with his right hand and began clicking, staring at the screen intensely.

She sat up, pulling her feet off the desk in front of her and nearly sending her toppling off of her chair. Her cheeks burned from her apparent clumsiness, and she straightened herself and looked up to see if he had seen her near accident.

Thankfully, his eyes were on the screen in front of him, the screen which mostly blocked her view of his face. This meant that his view, too, was mostly blocked.

She heard Darcy's insistent voice in her head. *Go for it, Elicia. You have him all to yourself. There's no one else around. You'll never get a better opportunity.*

But truth be told, Elicia wasn't sure what "going for it" entailed. She thought about it and quickly came to the obvious conclusion that whatever it entailed it had to begin with a conversation.

To begin a conversation, she had to get up and walk over to him. The only problem was that she appeared to have lost all control of her legs. As she pondered their frozen state, excuses of why she shouldn't go over to him began to pop conveniently into her head.

It was late, and she had to close up soon anyway. So why begin a conversation now? He was obviously busy and didn't come into the computer lab to talk to her. Leave him alone.

When he came in, he didn't even look at her or acknowledge her presence. He obviously had no interest in speaking with her.

After closing the lab at 9pm, she had to compose patches for the Planar operating system in her dorm room. She had a deadline to keep, and she had already used up her good graces with her supervisor at Planar.

However, as these very appealing excuses popped into her head, she chased them out and steeled her resolve. She wasn't going to chicken out this time. Darcy's voice was drowning out the excuses with success, and Elicia began to will her legs to move.

She stood up, stepped from around her desk, and rounded the end of the first row of computers, exposing Matt's profile. He was dressed in a faded blue tee shirt exposing athletic arms and a pair of broken-in blue jeans and white sneakers. Then there was his chin, her favorite feature. He had a strong, masculine chin. A jolt of excitement shot through her at the sight, propelling her toward him with such force that she almost didn't stop.

She applied the brakes and stopped just a couple of inches short of colliding with him. He looked up at her startled by her quick approach, smiling awkwardly. "Hi."

This was it! She was fully committed. No turning back now. "Hi."

He waited, looking up at her expectantly. It took her a moment, but she realized that he was waiting for her to speak. She did, after all, approach him.

"I just wanted to let you know that I have to close the lab at 9." Shit. She finally summoned the courage to speak to him and the first thing she did was throw a rule at him.

"Okay. I won't be long."

Elicia was about to walk away with her tail between her legs, and she began to turn but she stopped. "You're Matt, right?"

He looked up from his screen and back at her. "Yeah. Art Appreciation, right? You were in my class with Dr. Hanson."

"That's right," she said encouraged by his recognition. "I'm—"

"Elicia. I know."

This was getting even better. She was even beginning to smile now. "So, I didn't know you were taking summer classes," she probed, emboldened.

"Yeah, I'm taking Anatomy and Physiology. It's a tough class, lots of memorization. I figured I'd get it over with."

"Smart. That's what I'd do."

"So what about you?"

"Oh, I'm taking Literature during summer session one. Figured I'd just get it over with. I'm just watching the labs during summer session one."

"Smart," he replied.

"So, are you working on a project for your class? Because if you are, I can close the lab a little later if you want."

"No, nothing like that. I'm just checking my email. The FBI came into my room and confiscated my laptop."

"What? Why?"

"I'm not sure. They wouldn't say, but I think it had something to do with this podcast I was following. Some girl on campus has been railing against the government and all of the surveillance they're using on the population."

Shit. Shit. Double shit.

"Oh, I've heard something about that," she answered, trying to sound as casual as possible but probably overdoing it. "Tronika, right? So what do you think?"

"You mean about what she says?"

Elicia nodded.

"I think she's right. In this digital age there's a million different ways the government can track what any John Q citizen is doing on or offline. It's not just the internet. They can track cell phone or mini-com usage, credit cards, digi-lock access to tell where you go and when you are or aren't home. They have surveillance drones patrolling the skies, *armed* no less."

Elicia frowned. "Yeah, I heard about that thing in New York City. So there's something to this podcast? What about the girl who does it? The University is stopping short of calling her a terrorist. I think 'seditious' is the term they are using."

Matt was now turned toward her, and he looked fired up. "I think she's brilliant. She seems like one of the few girls on campus who has any kind of original thought going through her head. And, let me tell you, she's got balls. Big ones…"

She was in love. As she listened to him go on about her, her grin widened to Cheshire Cat proportions.

"…the FBI has been combing the campus, but she's announced that she's dropped off the grid, which sucks. People need to hear what she has to say."

This was it. This was her chance. "Well," she looked up at the clock, "I have to close up the lab in a minute, but I was wondering if you would like to grab a cup of coffee at the café. I think they're still open."

His expression suddenly changed, the enthusiasm from discussing the podcast draining from his face, replacing it with an awkward smile. "Oh. Well, I have to get going. I have lots of studying to do."

"Well, maybe another time then. You tell me."

He stood up. "I-I'm going to be very busy this session. It's a heavy class. Won't have much free time." He was now backing away from her, making his way towards the door. "See you later." He turned and left.

Elicia was still standing there by Matt's computer, the reality of his blowing her off still registering. The room suddenly felt like it was one hundred degrees and she felt strange being so embarrassed in an empty room.

She listened for Darcy's voice in her brain for some words of support or encouragement, but apparently, it too had been rendered speechless. Great. Just great.

When she heard Matt rave on and on about Tronika, she forgot that he had no idea she was Tronika. The fact was Matt was interested in Tronika, and it was clear he had no interest in her.

She immediately became jealous of her now defunct avatar, and she was glad Tronika was dead (so to speak). She wondered what image of her guys like Matt conjured up in their immature little minds. She imagined raven black hair, leather, and whips and such.

She shook her head, clearing the image out, and turned off the power strips at the end of each row of computers, the incremental noise reduction making the peculiar hum that was detectable before only more apparent. However, strange buzzing was the last thing from her mind. She just wanted to lock up the lab and get back to her room.

She walked through the quadrangle alone and across campus back to her apartment. She absent-mindedly slammed the door behind her, dropped her bag on her bed, and sat down in front of her computer.

She was in no mood for writing code. Her interaction with Matt seemed to be a vacuum, sapping her enthusiasm as well. Rejection never felt good, which is why she tried to avoid social interactions with the opposite sex like the plague.

She switched on her computer, paused, and then switched it back off. Planar would be disappointed, but they would have to wait. She walked back over to her bed, placed her bag on the floor next to it, and lay down with an awful heaviness of body and soul.

What was the point of all of this anyway? Maybe her sister was right. Maybe she hid behind all of this shit—the podcasts, the blogs, her side jobs—to avoid her discomfort with people, particularly boys. It was a crutch that she was beginning to grow tired of using.

She needed to learn how to socialize with the opposite sex. She had to realize that small talk was not stupid or useless. It was a way people connected. Social media and technology were great for sharing ideas but was incompatible with chemistry and vibes and all of that horseshit Darcy droned on about.

But that was just it! Maybe it wasn't all horseshit. She had to start realizing that. Really realizing it, not just recognizing it on an intellectual level. Dammit, it was time to stop thinking and start doing it. For God's sake, Darcy was no rocket scientist but she knew exactly what to do and how to do it.

Elicia realized that she had made it more complicated than it actually was, putting it up on some kind of pedestal, and therefore placing it out of her reach. She had psyched herself out.

She lay there angry at herself. It was time to stop blaming all of the guys on campus for being superficial and stupid. She was the one being stupid. Resigned to her failure with Matt Brauer and resolved to do something different, her last thought was that she was going out to the local bar tomorrow night and she was going to force herself to flirt with guys.

***

Luka Kojic tossed and turned in the night with the sensation that his blood was literally burning in his veins. He wanted to tear his skin off for relief, and he thought of his parents and sister as they were years ago before they were slaughtered in retaliation by Serbs in Bosnia.

He wondered if the young girls ripped from their beds went through as much agony in the rape houses as he felt now, for he too felt violated. Kafka had invaded his body and changed it somehow, and Kojic knew that it was never going to be the same again.

He fingered the bandage on his neck as he wondered if Farooq and Al Razi felt the same way. Kojic's wife, Marina, stirred next to him, shaking the bed. In her sleep she reached out for him, lightly stroking his forearm with her fingertips. He became aroused and hunger for her welled up inside him.

He reached out for her and placed his right hand on her arm. She stirred again and as he applied pressure, her eyes opened and met his in the dark. She reached out and touched the side of his face, slick with sweat, with her hand.

As he rolled over on top of her, she rolled on her back and received him, the two of them moving in one fluid motion like only a married couple who knew each other could.

As he entered Marina, they began to squirm together in unison, the rhythm slowly building momentum and picking up speed. His fever began to worsen and his hunger exploded into frenzy, feeling like it would never be satiated.

He began to bite her neck gently, the soft skin between his teeth feeling right, and she scratched her nails gently down his back. Pain melded with pleasure as they wrestled in the sheets.

He slid his hand over her face and clamped down over her mouth and nose. She was initially startled by the gesture, as it was new in their repertoire, but she began to feel the effect of the air depravation. She felt her lust rise up in waves and the rush of an impending orgasm when she needed air.

She placed her hand on his wrist, a sign to let go so she could breathe, but her eyes widened in terror when she realized his grip was not relenting. She began to squirm under his grasp, shaking her head from side to side, but his grip on her face only tightened as sweat rained down from his face onto hers.

Her panic only fueled a lustful rage that he had never felt before. He had felt the two sensations separately, but never in synergy like this. As his gaze met her eyes, wild with the instinct for survival, it felt like a new level of intimacy they had not yet experienced. However, this moment was interrupted when she bit down into his hand hard enough to cause him to release her.

Outraged by her act, he slapped her across her face so hard it made his own ears ring. She cried out in horror, "Luka!"

He struck her two more times on the face. Then he jumped off of her and backed into the corner, panting as if he would never catch his breath.

She sat up clutching her eye and only stared at him in incredulous terror. She rolled off the opposite side of the bed, ran into the bathroom, and slammed the door behind her.

As he heard her lock the door, he slid on his back down to a crouching position and tore at his receding hair with his hands, digging his fingernails into his scalp.

He all at once became ill, physically ill, as guilt became shame. This was not the first time he had ever struck Marina. He had many times before, as was his right as a man. His father had done so with his own mother right in front of him on many an occasion.

But that was right. It was not undeserved. He did not indulge his wife like American men did. They pampered and forgave, and the end result of their mercy was spoiled wives who weren't fit to live in a man's home.

This time Luka knew he crossed a line. Violence had no place in the bedroom as part of pleasure, but in the moment that had just transpired, he felt pleasure and punishment to be one in the same. Depravation and climax, two sides of the same coin. His infliction became foreplay to a greater need...murder. The idea felt foreign and degenerate to him, yet it was planted in his mind and took root.

"Marina," he called out. He could hear her trying to suppress sobs on the other side of the door. He so badly wanted to apologize. It was normally bad form for a man to apologize to a woman, but in this case warranted. That bastard Kafka had planted this in him. He infected him with this poison.

Luka got up and walked barefoot over to the closed bathroom door, leaning on it. "Marina, I am sorry." He did not know what else to say.

But his apology must have had some kind of impact, because he heard her sobbing slow and eventually downgrade to wet sniffling.

"Marina, I am sorry. I don't know what came over me. I think I am sick."

There was silence on the other side of the door. She was listening. That was something.

"There is no place in our bed for such things. I don't know what I was thinking."

The door slowly opened, and he stood up so that he wouldn't fall in. She stood before him with a puffy face and a swollen left eye. Normally the sight of this did not move him, but tonight it made him sick with remorse.

"My Marina. I am so sorry." He reached out and gently placed his hands on either side of her face. She let him, but her body tensed with anxiety. She knew better not to resist.

"Why?" she whispered, her mouth trembling as she was on the verge of tears. "Why, Luka?"

"I do not know, my Dear."

"Do I not please you anymore?"

"No," he blurted out. "Never."

"I thought you were trying to murder me."

That word stabbed him in the heart like an icy blade. "Murder? My Marina. Never." He pulled her close and embraced her. He felt her trembling against his body.

On the floor, from his side of the bed, he heard his cell phone ring in his pants. He knew who it was, and it filled him with bitterness.

He released his wife, gently lifting her face to meet his eyes with his finger. She looked at him and nodded. What else could she do?

He rounded the bed and picked up his pants, pulling out his cell phone. "Yes."

"Wake up Farooq. We need to meet."

"Yes." Kafka terminated the call before Luka could reply, but there was no need to reply. Only to respond.

He pulled on his pants and checked his watch. Just before midnight. He looked at his wife apologetically.

"Go," she replied. "For the Cause."

He nodded solemnly and touched her swollen cheek gently. He kissed her injured eye and left the bedroom.

Marina heard his footsteps on the linoleum through the kitchen and she heard the front door close. She was angry with her husband as she stood there in the dark bedroom with the bathroom light blaring behind her. The light stung her eyes and hot tears streamed down her face.

She reminded herself that her husband was a good man. She was not exactly sure what kind of work he did, but she knew it was for the Cause. It was greater than jihad. He was to teach the Western pigs the price of their indulgences.

There were times where she almost liked living in America. The food was plentiful, such exotic treats in great abundance. She liked clothes shopping. She even liked television.

But when she looked around her and saw the fat, lazy American women out stuffing their faces and spending their husbands' money on ridiculous luxuries while people in other countries suffered, she hated America. They profited while they pushed around and bullied the people who were true believers. All Americans believed in was money and things.

Suddenly, her anger towards her husband began to wane and, although she didn't like the way he treated her sometimes, she knew he did it for her own good. She knew in her heart that she was better off than her undisciplined American counterparts were. She was thankful that she had a husband who cared enough to see that she didn't stray from her path in this land of inequity.

They were here for a cause, and she wished Luka success. He rarely spoke about his work to her, and it wasn't her place to ask. However, once he spoke of this Kafka with such fear and reverence that she figured him to be a great man. She had never seen her husband regard another man with such caution. He was blessed to follow such a man.

She lay back down in bed, her residual resentment evaporating and her resolve stronger. She turned on her right side and felt her tears on her left side begin to dry, pulling her skin tighter. She closed her eyes with visions of salvation swirling in her head and drifted off into a dreamless sleep.

Chapter 4

Birdsall Homestead
06:27 HRS

Peter woke when he heard the sliding door open and his father step out onto the deck. He rubbed his eyes and slowly straightened up in his chair, his back complaining from the position he slept in.

"Pete, have you been out here all night?"

"Yeah," said Peter, as he yawned and stretched.

"Why would you go and do something like that? It must've been freezing out here."

"Dad, a Texan's version of freezing is not a valid one. I've been in all kinds of uncomfortable terrain before, spending nights out in the open."

"What, you don't like beds anymore?"

"I like the night air. I find it soothing."

Barry just looked at him as if the explanation didn't satisfy him. Then he shook his head, dismissing the topic. "Suit yourself. Just remember that you're not in the army anymore."

"Old habits die hard, I guess," said Peter.

"Come inside. I'm brewing a fresh cup of joe. Unless you want to eat tree bark instead or something."

"No, Dad. Coffee sounds good." He stood up, rubbing the soreness in his neck, and followed his father into the kitchen. He was quickly greeted with the aroma of fresh made coffee, a welcome scent.

"You're up early," Peter said.

"I usually get up around now," Barry explained. "It's part of getting old." He pointed to Peter's multi-tasker on the kitchen countertop. "Your phone is flashing."

As his father went to the cabinet to take out two coffee mugs, Peter checked his multi-tasker. It was flashing. He touched the screen and it indicated that he had a message titled, "O Brother Where Art Thou?"

He looked up at his father, who was pouring coffee into the two mugs. He quickly shoved the multi-tasker into his pocket.

His father noticed the motion. "Everything all right?"

"Yeah, fine, Dad." He took the Las Vegas mug his father handed him. Barry had an oversized Lake Tahoe mug himself. They both sat down at the kitchen table. Barry began to chuckle.

"What's so funny?" Peter asked in an almost accusatory tone.

"You never sit at the table. You usually lean against the counter." Peter smiled in recognition and shrugged his shoulders. "Your brother is the one who sits at the table."

Peter stopped mid-sip as a chill went down his spine. He suddenly wanted to end this conversation and head to the bathroom where he could view his message from Carl.

Barry saw Peter's expression and took it to be in synch with his. "Yeah, your brother. I guess things are different now."

Peter was sipping his coffee quickly. "Yeah, I guess so."

"Well, I could sure use you at the store. I had to lay off three employees. Good ones, too. I hated to do it, but I didn't have any alternative. I had to."

"Well, at least it's not because you're replacing them with computers or technology. Unemployment is skyrocketing because most storefronts have gone digital. Now the internet takes orders. No more clerks."

"Well, the hardware store is no exception, Pete. I have automated orders, but the plumbers and contractors who come in still need a human to consult with. They run into problems on the job and need someone to help them work around it."

"Well, there you have it," said Peter with resignation. "The only jobs that are progress-proof are doctors, shrinks, dentists…the services."

"Cops, firefighters, teachers, mailmen," added Barry. "All government jobs. Meanwhile, the private sector, whose taxes pay for government workers, is shrinking. Who is going to support all of this? And welfare and food stamps are through the roof."

"So all we have left are business owners with no employees, just technology."

"That's right, Pete. And not everybody can be a business owner. There have to be some Indians, not just Chiefs."

"Well, I know one government job they are trying to replace with technology."

"Oh, yeah?" Barry took a long sip of his coffee. "And what's that?"

"Soldiers. Dead heads instead of jug heads. Autonomous aerial drones instead of pilots."

"Well, you better than anyone else knows that didn't work out, Pete."

"Yeah…I suppose I do. The armed autonomous aerial drones seem to be working out fine."

"Not if you heard about what happened in New York City," said Barry frowning.

There was an uncomfortable silence.

Peter suddenly stood up. "Well, I'm going to take a shower. What time do you open?"

"Eight o'clock, but I get there at 7:30 to get ready."

"Seven-thirty. Gotcha."

"It'll be good having an extra pair of hands around. I'm all alone, and moving boxes of heavy hardware is getting a bit tough on an old man like me."

"No problem, Dad. It'll be like old times. Working at the hardware store was my first job, and now it looks like it'll be my last."

"Don't talk like that, son. One day at a time."

Peter nodded. "One day at a time."

He took one last sip of his coffee and could barely contain his anticipation as he left the kitchen. He climbed the stairs, taking two at a time, and grabbed a large towel out of the hallway linen closet.

He rushed into the bathroom, locking the door behind him, and began to run the shower full blast. He hoped the sound would be enough to mask, or at least distort, the audio of the message in case his father was in the hallway.

Then he remembered his new abilities. He closed his eyes and reached out with his senses, and he found his father's heartbeat downstairs in the kitchen. He was apparently helping himself to a second cup of coffee.

Satisfied that he was indeed alone, he pulled his multi-tasker out of his pants and touched the screen to view his message. It was Kafka, obsidian face and four eyes blinking in unison.

"Hello, Pete. Little brother, here. I heard about your dishonorable discharge from the army. Believe me, you are better off. Look what happened to me. The army made me the man I am today.

"By now you should be experiencing some changes. It's different for everyone. You may have some new abilities you didn't have before. You have also, by now, encountered…well…yourself.

"I know this must all be very confusing right now, and I'd like to make it up to you. Pete, the only reason you are alive is that I know you had nothing to do with the army's treachery and my betrayal.

"Listen, Pete. The army screwed us both over, so I drafted you to the winning team. In the near future you will thank me. You deserve an

explanation of what is happening to you. We also need to discuss how we are going to keep Dad safe. If he remains the way he is, he is in danger.

"Meet me tonight at Frisky's. I'll be sitting in a booth by myself. I will be alone and unarmed. This I promise. Together we can get through this. If you worry about my intentions, just remember that if I wanted you dead, you'd have been dead a long time ago.

"If you see yourself in the meantime, don't run from it. It will be better if you welcome it. Trust me. I know. I hope to see you tonight, Pete."

He blinked twice and the message terminated.

Jesus Christ. Was he serious?

Peter placed his multi-tasker back into his pocket and carefully slid off his pants. He placed them on the sink and stepped over to the toilet. The seat was already up. He took a leak and stepped into the shower, adjusting the hot water down a little.

As he stood there in the shower, he replayed Kafka's message over and over again in his head. *The only reason you are alive is that I know you had nothing to do with the army's treachery and my betrayal.* Of course he didn't. He tried to save him.

Just remember that if I wanted you dead you'd have been dead a long time ago. Peter remembered the dance club in Tijuana. He remembered feeling weak and powerless. He remembered Kafka's grip on him and his bite.

Peter shook his head in the shower to scatter his thoughts to the wind. Enough of that. He had to focus on the little details, the ones that would tell him something. *It's different for everyone.* Apparently, Kafka turned others before Peter. That explained the fanged assailants jumping rooftops in Tijuana like hopscotch.

By now you should be experiencing some changes…You have also, by now, encountered…yourself. His doppelgänger. He knew that this was significant. Did Kafka still see his? What was its purpose?

You deserve an explanation of what is happening to you. He was trying to butter Peter up. For what? The bastard was up to something. *We also need to discuss how we are going to keep Dad safe.* He wanted to bite Barry. Infect him. Worse, he wanted Peter's blessing.

Peter finished rinsing and turned the shower off. He stood there for a moment dripping, pondering Kafka's intentions. He was back in the country. Was it to go get Dad? Or was it for something bigger?

He stepped out onto the towel on the floor and grabbed the large one he brought from the linen closet. He wrapped himself in it, drying himself off. He stepped in front of the fogged up vanity and opened it.

He grabbed a brand new toothbrush in its wrapping and the toothpaste. He unwrapped it, tossing the packaging in the small pink garbage pail between the sink and the toilet—no doubt, his mother's purchase—and rinsed the brush. He lavishly applied some toothpaste and brushed.

He thought about his poor mother. He prayed her death was quick, but he knew it wasn't likely painless. He cursed God for having smote her from his family's life. No warning.

There was an emptiness in the house now. Even though his father lived there, it was her home. It had her touches, her décor, and now it was a shell of what it formerly represented to him. It no longer carried the sentiment of home sweet home. Now, more than ever, it felt like he was in a house unfamiliar to him except in a few shallow ways.

He reached out with his senses and felt his father downstairs in the kitchen. He was listening to the radio. Ever since their discovery of RGT in the TV and what happened to Carl, Barry threw out his television. He smashed it under his boot repeatedly and threw it out.

The television.

Suddenly it hit Peter. In Tijuana, in the leather shop, he asked Kafka how he found them in the cheap hotel. Kafka said he followed the trail of breadcrumbs. The television in the hotel room, blaring one of those annoying shows with the loud music. He remembered now.

One of the security detail must've been watching it, even glancing at it. They all must have. Kafka was looking right back at them with his own stolen RGT apparatus. That was how he knew where to find them. He accessed their recent memories and gleaned their location.

He looked at his pants crumpled up on the floor. That also meant that Kafka knew that Peter saw his message. Shit, it also meant he read Peter's recent memories. Peter panicked for a moment, reviewing recent events. Kafka must've seen Peter running into his doppelgänger and sleeping outside on the deck to protect his father.

He also must've seen his quarantine and court martial. His disgrace. His being drummed out of the army unceremoniously. Somewhere his brother laughed at him, taking pleasure in his big brother's fall from glory.

Peter decided from that moment that he was not going to use his multi-tasker again. Not unless he wanted Kafka to know something. His little brother was watching.

That's when Peter felt a strange sensation. It wasn't his new ability. It was something more visceral, instinctive even. He looked at his reflection behind the fog in the mirror. It was blurred but he could see that the outline didn't measure up with his. He was holding a toothbrush up to his mouth with his right hand, but the outline of the reflection appeared to have its arms down at its sides.

He rinsed his toothbrush and laid it down on the sink. He then wiped the mirror with his hand, revealing the face of his reflection in a single swipe, and he was startled by what was revealed.

It was sneering at him, grinning wickedly with a feral, toothy grin. It looked more animal than man, and it looked right at him.

Peter didn't want to alert his father downstairs. So he spoke to it. "What do you want?"

It only grinned maliciously at him.

"I said what do you want, you son-of-a-bitch?" he spat through gritted teeth to control his volume. He saw movement in the reflection, but it was concealed by the fog. Peter wiped the rest of the mirror and saw the reflection pointing a long, sharp fingernail at him.

"You can't have me," Peter taunted.

The reflection began to claw at the surface of the mirror, its claws squeaking against its side of the glass. It looked hungry for him. Peter was emboldened by his position on his side of the mirror.

"That's right, you piece of shit. Claw all you want. I want some goddamned answers. What do you want?"

It cocked its head sideways in amusement, but Peter thought he saw frustration building in its horrible eyes, two pools of blackness that threatened to swallow him whole.

It thrust its sharp finger at the glass again, pointing at Peter.

"Why don't you come and get me then."

Peter felt his father stir downstairs. He was probably growing impatient and wanted to get to the hardware store. When Peter looked back at the mirror, the reflection was no longer staring back at him.

It was behind him.

He swung around wildly, knocking over his father's stack of medicine containers on top of a small storage cabinet.

"Pete, are you okay?" Barry called from downstairs.

Peter looked around and saw he was alone. "Fine, Dad. I'll be right down."

When Peter descended the stairs and walked into the kitchen, he found his father standing at the counter in front of an empty mug.

"Sorry, Dad. I'm not used to getting up this early."

Barry knew this was a lie. He was certain the army didn't let their soldiers sleep in. "I heard a commotion up there."

"Oh, I'm just a little clumsy. I knocked over some of your pill bottles by accident."

Barry knew that, too, was a lie. Peter was many things, but clumsy wasn't one of them. An athlete and soldier, yes, but not clumsy. He knew Peter was going through something. Maybe it was the adjustment to civilian life. He decided to let it go…for now.

"Well, we have to get going. The store isn't going to open itself."

Peter nodded. "Right. Let's go."

Barry turned off the radio.

"Anything interesting in the news?"

Barry opened a draw and pulled out a set of old-fashioned keys he made with an old machine he found in the basement of the hardware store. A relic from the days before people used their phones to unlock doors. It appeared Barry had gone completely analog. Peter smiled at his father's accidental wisdom.

"The authorities seem to be close to finding that seditious blogger they've been after. Or so they would have us believe. Oh, and they were going on about the Automaton and Kafka. They don't even know the two are one in the same. They mentioned your scuffle in Tijuana as a sign that OIL was alive and well, and that they are masterminding something. The FBI and CIA are supposed to be on the case."

He left the kitchen. Peter followed.

"I think they're right."

"About what?" Barry asked absent-mindedly as he stepped out the front door and locked it with an old-fashioned metal key from his new set. Peter noticed the old-fashioned mechanical lock his father must've retrofitted recently.

"OIL is up to something." He wanted to tell his father about Kafka's message, but now wasn't the time. He had to figure out what he was going to do about it.

"Well, I hope you're wrong," said Barry as they walked side-by-side down the path to his car. For this, he had to use his phone to unlock it. "But I wouldn't be surprised. These terrorists never really go away."

They got into the car. Barry started the ignition. "We pound them, they quiet down for a while, but they always regroup."

Peter sighed heavily. "So you're saying that they are an inevitability?"

Barry thought about this for a moment. "I am saying that it is difficult to slay a hydra. You kill one terrorist here and there and several more pop up to take his place."

Peter remembered learning about mythology in grade school. He always hated the subject, but his father's reference wasn't lost on him.

Carl loved it. He loved the creatures and their powers. It was ironic really. Carl had simultaneously become two figures of myth. The mighty

Automaton and the nefarious Kafka. Hero and villain. The savior of freedom, the defender of democracy, and the most dangerous man alive.

Peter chuckled bitterly to himself as he pondered the paradox. Barry took note of his son's odd disposition but decided to ignore it for the time being. He put the car in gear and pulled out of the driveway.

***

Fort Bliss
Texas
09:00 HRS

Colonel Betancourt was striding down the hallway to General Ramses' office. There was an update about the search for Tronika, the seditious blogger and notorious computer hacker. They had been collaborating with the FBI and Assistant Director Wolff of the NSA. Wolff and Ramses had made it a top priority, asserting the girl had terrorist connections.

Betancourt had concluded it to be a waste of time, but after the Kafka sighting in Tijuana, Ramses and Wolff appeared emboldened in their crusade.

The retinal scan on Ramses' door registered Betancourt and opened. He stepped into the office where Ramses was standing behind his desk looking engrossed.

Betancourt stepped forward, removed his headgear and saluted. Ramses saluted back. "Have a seat, Colonel."

Betancourt sat and took in Ramses' desk. It was aflutter with papers and digital files. He had never seen the General's desk in such a state of disarray.

"Sir, I assume you have some new information on the seditious blogger."

Ramses gawked at him perplexed for a moment, and then he sat waving a dismissive hand. "Oh, yes, her. She's a college student at the University of Texas at Dallas. Elicia Corti. We're going to pick her up tonight."

"I assume we are using the local authorities on this one, sir. She's just a kid."

"And Adolf Hitler was just another Austrian artist," said Ramses sarcastically. "*We* aren't doing anything. I have something much more important for you, Colonel."

"Oh?"

"It would appear that Kafka is back across the border and he has made contact with his big brother, the ex-Major Peter Birdsall."

"That's unbelievable. He just contacted him out of the blue on an open frequency?"

General Ramses regarded him with what Betancourt could only surmise to be suspicion.

"As unbelievable as it may appear to you, Colonel, the NSA picked up the message via RGT. It would appear that the program is working as designed."

"What was the content of that message, sir?"

"He wants to meet—get this—at Frisky's, some shithole dive bar in their hometown."

"That seems rather bold."

"Or rather clever," added Ramses. "Hiding in plain sight."

"But he had to have known we would've picked it up."

"I don't think so," said Ramses. "He knew about RGT, but I don't think he fully grasped the extensiveness of the program. Besides, the communication was hidden in a reverse transmission picked up by our brethren in the NSA. I don't think he expected us to find it. To our obvious advantage it would seem."

Reverse transmission? This was the first time Betancourt had heard anything about reverse transmissions through the RGT network. Ramses slipped up. "Yes, so it would seem. So what are we going to do?"

"I want you to put together a team. If he is in Texas, we are going to grab him and bring him to justice."

"Sir, this man is clever. I don't think it is going to be that easy. In fact, this whole thing reeks of a set-up."

"What are you saying, Colonel?"

"I am saying that this man has set us up time after time. He set us up at Guantanamo Bay, and he set us up in Siena, Italy. Every time he has been one step ahead of us and every time, it has ended in the death of innocent people and good soldiers."

"You think this is a trap?"

"I know it is, sir. He is picking a public place. I'm sure he's going to have the bar stocked with OIL operatives. As soon as we move in, he's going to start killing innocents. It is going to be yet another fiasco."

"Besides, why contact his brother? Why now?"

Ramses was quick to answer. "Kafka could've killed him in Tijuana and he didn't. Why do you suppose that is, Colonel? In his message, he talked about keeping Peter Birdsall and their father safe and explaining what was happening to him. He wants to help his brother. Recruit him, even. And we are going to exploit his sentimentality and box him in."

"Why do I get the sense that Major Birdsall's dishonorable discharge was all part of a plan to use him as bait for his little brother?"

"You know darn well, Colonel, that in operations we sometimes have to sacrifice smaller fish to catch the big ones."

"But never with our own men, sir."

"He was a liability. Too many failures surrounding that man. We have a chance to catch this Kafka. Why not take it?"

"At what cost, sir? Kafka may be sentimental, but he's not stupid?"

"What do you propose?"

"We go to the bar first. We install a metal detector at the door. We replace the management and staff with ours. If anybody asks, we'll say there have been some fights at the bar recently and the detector was installed recently for security. I want facial recognition of everyone that walks through that front door. We'll cross reference the faces with known terrorists in the FBI and Interpol databases. If an OIL operative sets foot in that bar, I want him unarmed and I want to know about it.

"I want a security perimeter in place around the area as soon as we confirm he's in the bar. I want roadblocks in place manned by local authorities. I want the whole thing buttoned up good and tight."

Ramses was smiling. "Good. This is all good, Colonel. This is why I want you in charge of this operation. Elicia Corti is small potatoes. I need you to handle this personally."

Betancourt found it interesting that he brought up the girl again. "Yes, sir. I have to get started right away."

Ramses stood up, and Betancourt followed suit.

"Get to work, Colonel. Dismissed."

They both saluted each other, and Betancourt left the office. Ramses sat back down behind his desk and dialed his phone.

"Assistant Director Wolff...yes, it's Ramses. Tell the Alpha that the sheep are coming to his den."

He hung up the phone and grinned to himself. That nosey do-gooding bastard Betancourt was a problem. Ramses was well aware of his slipping Peter Birdsall the antidote serum, which meant that Betancourt was well aware that he couldn't trust Ramses.

Betancourt suspected him, which made Betancourt dangerous, and now Ramses had to put him away. After tonight, he would no longer be a concern.

Chapter 5

10:37 HRS

Marina watched her husband from the living room as he tinkered away furiously in the kitchen. He stumbled through the door at around 8 am after having been out all night, and now he refused to sleep.

She wiped the sweat off her brow, the simple motion making the room spin. Luka occasionally looked up from his work on his strange apparatus to ask her if she needed anything. He had already brought her tea and Tylenol to bring down the fever that raged inside her skull and made sure she was comfortable.

This work of his, the machine he was tinkering with, was no doubt an assignment from this great man, Kafka. And it was no doubt an important assignment, as Luka has been working on it like some kind of deadline was approaching.

She pondered what this Kafka must've looked like. He was important, so she figured he must be tall...and strong. Yes, if Luka feared him so, he must possess the strength of several men. The more she thought about Kafka, the more she felt she knew him.

She wasn't sure if it was the fever, but she found her hand and her fingers straying towards her lap and creeping towards her nether regions, when Luka looked up at her. She slid her hand back onto her knee.

Luka wiped his brow, but his sweat was from his labor, his fever having already passed. He glanced up from his work, his eyes magnified by his work glasses giving him the appearance of a large insect.

He felt awful about Marina. It wasn't just his aggression towards her last night. He couldn't help but feel that he made her sick with whatever he had. He brought home Kafka's gift, and now she too felt his bite.

It was bad enough that he had been violated, but now he had introduced something terrible to his wife. This after he took great pains to keep what he did with the Order a secret from her.

To be honest, he didn't do it to protect her. He did it to protect himself. If the authorities were to apprehend her and interrogate her to get to him, using deportation as leverage, she would have nothing to tell them.

Except for the name of Kafka. For some unknown reason he had allowed that name to escape his lips. It was the only thing she knew about what Luka did outside the house. That and the portable RGT headset that he had been working on. She wouldn't be able to make heads or tails out of that. To her it was some kind of equipment. That was all.

After what Kafka did to him, and now what he spread to his wife, he didn't much care about the authorities tracking him down. Although he labored under Kafka's direction for the Order, for the Cause, he resented Kafka.

He dared not show it, for Kafka would kill him on the spot. Luka harbored no illusions about who would win in a fight. He knew that Kafka was more than his match, with his Outworlder powers.

There were a few who initially challenged Kafka's leadership. One, a brutish man named Hamidi, who mocked Kafka's talk about Outworlders to his face. One night, during a heated discussion about the new direction of the Order, Hamidi jumped across the table and lunged at Kafka trying to sink a rather large knife into his heart.

Kafka moved like he already knew Hamidi was coming, dodging the knife by mere millimeters and smashing Hamidi through the table. Everyone seated stood up suddenly and backed away.

Hamidi stood up, dusting himself off, as Kafka laughed at him. This only enraged the mountainous Hamidi, who rushed Kafka only to find the knife that he held only seconds before plunged into his gut.

Kafka clicked at him like a large cicada in apparent delight, all four eyes gazing into Hamidi's two, and he flung Hamidi across the room. The back of Hamidi's skull smashed against the cinderblock wall, and as his body slid down there was a large red mark left behind with bits of skull and grey matter clinging to it.

That was the first, but not the last attempt on Kafka's life. The would-be assassins recognized Kafka's speed and apparent precognition in hand-to-hand fights, so the attacks became sneakier.

One man, Hassan, a bomb-maker, planted one of his creations in a room full of Kafka and his supporters. He made sure he left enough time on the timer so that he was out of the building and in his car before it detonated.

Hassan reached his car, opened it, and got in. He turned on the ignition and waited, but to his profound disappointment, Kafka stepped out the front door and waved to Hassan. Kafka waved and then turned his long hand over, raising a protracted middle finger.

Hassan did not have a chance to register the gesture when his bomb detonated in the back seat sending him to hell in many little pieces.

The third and final attack came from a man named Malik, who was a chemist for the Order. Malik took the liberty of slipping a potent poison into the water supply. He didn't want to take the chance of getting caught slipping the poison into Kafka's cup, so he poisoned the supply from a distance.

When he stormed into Kafka's quarters, he found Kafka and his guard all lying dead on the floor. Malik, being a thorough man, took out his gun and fired eight shots into Kafka, two of which were a double tap into his skull. He then dragged Kafka's body outside into the dirt, doused him with gasoline, and lit his body on fire.

Satisfied that the deed was done, he went home, made love to his woman, and slept like the dead. Malik was later woken in the middle of the night to find a charred Kafka standing over his bed clutching his woman by the hair. It was her screaming that woke him.

He tried to turn and reach for his gun on his side table, but his wrists and ankles were bound to the bed frame. Kafka flung the woman across the room and demanded that she watch. She crouched in the corner, whimpering in horror.

Kafka took a funnel and pried Malik's mouth open. Malik kept pushing the funnel out with his tongue and tried to turn his head, so Kafka punched him in the mouth, knocking out his front teeth.

Kafka then jammed the funnel through the space and grabbed a large gas can on the floor next to him. He poured gasoline down Malik's throat as the man writhed on the bed in pain from the gasoline burning his esophagus.

As the gasoline began to poison Malik's body, Kafka shoved a long rag down his throat. He then produced a lighter and lit the rag. He backed away and stood next to Malik's trembling woman as Malik's body burst into flame from the inside.

Kafka began to walk out, and then—as if just remembering—he took out his pistol and shot Malik's blazing corpse eight times. He took the woman and made her recount everything she saw about the way Malik died to the members of the Order.

From that point on, Kafka's leadership was not questioned. Each assailant was murdered with their own methods, and Kafka's Outworldly powers were no longer questioned.

It was at that point that Kafka began to talk about Order members "getting some skin in the game." Luka didn't quite know what the expression meant, but Kafka announced that there were going to be some sacrifices made and lieutenants chosen. All for the Cause.

That was what Luka wrestled with. He did not agree with using Outworlders to further the Cause. It was not their cause to push, but after being bitten—he had heard about Ramses' bite and what he now was—

was Luka now an Outworlder? Was he to become an Outworlder, or have a part of him become such?

He turned the portable companion unit, slid the RAM home into its slots, and adjusted the heat synch. The processors would generate a good amount of heat. If Kafka wasn't careful he would set himself on fire.

Maybe not such a bad outcome.

No, he would take care that such an outcome wouldn't happen. He remembered what Kafka had said about Belmont and what he said right before he died at the hands of an army soldier in Italy.

As Kafka cradled Belmont in his arms, Belmont passed the torch— the Order and all of its operations—to Kafka with very specific instructions. Belmont himself entrusted Kafka with their mission, and it was Belmont who wanted to enlist the help of the Outworlders.

Or so Kafka said.

Belmont knew about the UFO crash site in the Congo, the origin of the RGT, and the undead that surrounded the craft.

I know the war you are fighting against the oppression of the world's great superpowers, said Kafka. *But you cannot win this war with sporadic attacks of terror. You cannot topple society with bombings and shootings. The Outworlders have provided us with soldiers for the Cause. I am their general, selected by the Outworlders, and I in-turn have chosen you to be my lieutenants.*

Kafka went on about how special they now were, and how after the destruction of the world they would inherit the earth. Kojic thought about Marina...

Maybe by infecting her with Kafka's poison he spared her life. If Kafka's plan worked and society indeed fell, Luka wondered how Marina would fit into the picture. Would she have been spared because of his sacrifice?

Either way, the question was now moot. She was now in on it, like it or not. He guessed that she now had "skin in the game." He had saved her life from what was to come, and she would share a special place with him in the new world order.

"Are you all right, my sweet?" he called to her from the kitchen.

"Yes, Luka."

"Do you need anything?"

"No."

"Why don't you take a bath? It will help with the fever." He stood up and walked into the living room. He gently took her by the hand and lifted her up to standing. He gently guided her through the kitchen and into the bedroom.

He opened the bathroom door, turned on the light, and began to run her a tepid bath. She slid off her robe and stepped gingerly into the bathtub, wincing from the aches and pains stabbing her body like daggers.

Luka helped her lower herself into the tub, as she was dizzy and light-headed, and she rested her head on the back of the tub.

Luka knelt down and felt her forehead. Then he leaned over and kissed it. "Everything is going to be okay," he whispered to her.

He stepped out of the bathroom and returned after a couple of minutes with a glass. He ran the cold water at the sink for a moment and then filled the glass with cool water. He turned off the faucet and placed the full glass on the floor next to the bathtub within Marina's reach.

"You have to drink, to stay hydrated."

She nodded appreciatively. "Thank you."

He stood there for a moment, taking in her bruised face from last night. He blew her a kiss and returned to the kitchen.

He sat down in front of the RGT apparatus and began to put the final touches on the assembly. Kafka told him that it needed to be completed by the afternoon and ready for a field test. It looked like Luka was going to be on time.

However, there was the menace of expectation in Kafka's command. There were unspoken consequences implied if the apparatus was finished and it didn't work. He needed to test it first.

He finished his work twenty minutes later and powered it up. It worked, but he needed to know that it was functional.

He got up, grabbing the headset in one hand and the portable tower in the other hand, and brought it all into the bathroom.

Marina looked up at him. "What are you doing?"

"Sweetheart, I need your help."

"For what?"

"I need to test this equipment out."

She looked at him uncertainly.

"A quick test. It will only take a minute." He reached out to take her hand. She gave him her hand and hoisted herself with his help out of the bathtub.

Luka reached out, grabbed a towel, and wrapped it around her naked body. She was shivering. It was the fever. He put down the toilet lid and guided her to sit on the toilet. He dried her hair tenderly with another towel and then reached down and picked up the headset.

Marina put her hands up. "What is it?"

He gently lowered her hands with his, placing them in her lap. "It won't hurt, I promise."

"Luka, I want to know what it is before you place it on my head."

"I will, my Dear. After I see if it works."

She hesitated but then nodded. He placed the headset on her head and then plugged it into the tower. He switched it on and took out his cell phone. He turned a knob while looking at his cell phone and then stopped.

Marina, in her half-delirious state, did not understand any of this, but she trusted her husband.

"Okay, sit still." He pressed a button on the tower. Images began to flicker on his cell phone screen. Marina putting groceries in the refrigerator, Marina walking home from the supermarket, Marina shopping in the supermarket—it was her memories in reverse transmitted to his cell phone in perfect clarity. The apparatus worked.

He reached up to remove the headset when images of Marina lying in a bed with a naked man on top of her played on his cell phone screen. He didn't want to see himself bite her. He was ashamed. But the scene passed.

Then it showed her waking up in the morning.

Wait a minute. The sex occurred after she woke up. Luka was out of the house all night. He didn't return until morning, and Marina was already up.

He took the headset off her head as his thoughts raced to make sense of what he just saw. Marina smiled up at him, looking for his approval.

"Good? It worked?" she asked.

Luka placed the headset down gently on the floor and switched the tower off. He couldn't look at her. He wasn't sure what he felt exactly at that moment. Sad, angry, confused.

"Who is he?" Luka's voice trembled as he barely contained his rage.

Marina looked confused. To her the question came out of left field, apropos of nothing. "Who? What do you mean?"

"The man...you were having sex with," he practically choked on the words.

Marina didn't know what was happening, but when the significance of his question dawned on her, her eyes went wide. "I don't know what you are talking about."

"DON'T LIE TO ME, MARINA."

She was startled by his outburst and in her dizziness nearly fell off the toilet. Luka did not reach out to steady her. In fact, the gentle, tender man that was looking after her but a moment ago appeared to have left the apartment.

"I would never lie to you." The pitch of her voice was higher.

"Then tell me who he is."

"What was that machine you put on me?"

"Just tell me who he is."

She hesitated, looking down at her feet. "Our neighbor, from downstairs."

"Yuri?"

"Yes."

"Why, Marina?"

"Luka, you are always out of the house doing your work. I got lonely."

He suddenly seized her by the shoulders, the impact sending the room spinning around her. "Why, Marina? Why?"

"You are never here!"

"My work that I do, it is for us! It is for you!"

She lost her timidity and lashed out at him. "You and your work! You drag me to this evil country and hold me captive in this little apartment while you do your work."

"It is for the Cause. We were chosen."

"Chosen by who, Luka? This Kafka?"

"You have desecrated our bed, our marriage!"

"I bet Kafka knows how to please his woman." She regretted it the moment she said it, but she didn't have time to regret it for long.

Luka lifted her off the toilet seat and threw her into the bathtub, her head hitting the side nearly causing her to black out. Her ears rang as she gripped the side of the tub to hold her aching head out of the water.

Luka descended upon her, grabbing her throat with both hands, and he shoved her head under the water. She clawed at his wrists and forearms wildly as her legs thrashed about in the water.

A vein popped out of Luka's forehead as he held his wife's head under the water. With his people, there was no question. Adultery committed by a woman under any circumstance was punishable by death. It was law. Their Law.

After a moment, the thrashing slowed down and Marina's hands slid off his wrists. Her body shuddered and her eyes went wide one last time as he saw the life slip out of her. When she was still, he let go of her throat and sat back on the floor in the water that splashed out of the tub.

He sat there with his hands tearing at his hair at the horror of what he was compelled to do, of her betrayal of their marriage. Then he remembered the RGT apparatus and spun around. It was not sitting in water, thank goodness.

He stood, snatched it up, and stalked into the kitchen, putting it carefully on the table. He paced back and forth, his eyes still seeing red as he remembered Yuri downstairs.

He ran through the living room, threw open the front door, and spilled out into the hallway, slamming the door behind him. He dashed to the stairwell and descended the stairs, taking two at a time, until he reached the next floor down.

He shoved past a man that…looked just like him, but he didn't take the time to stop and look. He was moving too quickly, like a runaway train about to go off the rail.

He ran to Yuri's door and was about to pound on it, but then thought better of it. He took a deep breath and then rang the bell. He waited, listening for sounds of life on the other side of the door. To his surprise, he heard Yuri…no, he felt it, his heart beating on the other side.

He was struggling with his impatience and about to ring again when he heard heavy footsteps approach the door. The digi-lock disengaged and the door cracked open, the chain preventing it from opening any further.

Luka was thankful that this shitty ghetto building still had chains instead of the door magnets. He could break the chain.

Yuri's eyes went wide when he saw Luka, and in a guilty reaction, he attempted to push the door shut. However, Luka's boot already hit it, sending the edge of the door into Yuri's forehead with a crunch.

Yuri stumbled backwards clutching his forehead, and Luka gave the door another swift front kick, snapping the chain. He shoved his way into the apartment as Yuri ran for the kitchen, blood running between his fingers from the wound beneath.

Luka was right on his heels. He felt Yuri's pulse race, and it excited him. He was the lion, and Yuri was the gazelle. The chase was on.

Yuri opened a drawer and pulled out a large knife, but Luka was on his back. He reached around and held Yuri's knife hand, controlling it. It was a part of his training. When in a knife fight, control the knife hand.

Yuri had no training. He only had an intense instinct for survival. He shoved the counter, pushing himself and Luka backwards, but Luka pushed back while controlling Yuri's knife hand.

Yuri kicked hard against the counter, sending the two of them flying backward and onto the shoddy wooden kitchen table. It collapsed under their combined weight, sending both men crashing to the ground.

Yuri lost his grip on the knife, and it flew from his hand across the kitchen floor. He tried to sit up and make for it, but Luka reached his arm around Yuri's throat and tightened his grip.

Yuri clawed at Luka's already torn arm and tried to pull it away. He lurched his head forward and then slammed it back, catching Luka on the bridge of his nose.

Luka knew his nose was broken, and in that moment, he loosened his grip on Yuri...and that was all Yuri needed. He flung Luka's arm off of him and threw himself forward on all fours, his fingers reaching out for the knife.

He wrapped his fingers around the handle and turned around on his knees, but Luka had a leg of the table in his hands. He swung it like a bat, connecting with Yuri's temple, and Yuri dropped the knife.

Luka swung again and missed, his eyes running from the broken nose obstructing his vision. Yuri had enough time to stagger to his feet, but Luka swung and hit him on the side of his neck.

Yuri collapsed against the refrigerator, pulling down several papers that were held up with little magnets. Luka stood over him with the table leg in his right hand trying to catch his breath.

He licked the corners of his mouth as he panted, and his tongue found his canine, first the right one, then the left. They were...big. He raised his hand to touch them, but Yuri groaned on the floor. Luka gave him a swift kick in the ribs.

He wanted to kill the lecherous bastard, but in that brief moment he was struck with an uncanny clarity, as if seeing the plain truth of things for the first time. He had Marina's body lying in a tub upstairs. If he wasn't careful he was going to have a body down here as well.

Too many bodies.

Luka looked down at Yuri, who was lying on the linoleum moaning. The son-of-a-bitch learned his lesson. No more killing. He dropped the table leg and grabbed a dishtowel off the countertop and pressed it to his nose, which was leaking blood and mucous.

He left the apartment and began to climb the steps back to his floor. If necessary, he could explain to the police why he had attacked Yuri, but he wouldn't be able to explain Marina's body in the bathtub.

As he climbed the steps, he quickly worked out a plan in his head. First, he would wrap up her body and quickly clean the bathroom up. It wouldn't be hard. There was no blood. Only water all over the floor. Then he would hide her body at the Order safe house until he would be able to dispose of it. Then he could say she left the country to return to Serbia to be with her mother.

He opened the door to his apartment and closed it carefully behind him. He looked around the living room and then shoved the coffee table over to the side. He reached down, pulled the rug from underneath, and dragged it behind him through the kitchen.

He was careful not to bump the kitchen table with the portable RGT apparatus on it. Shit. He forgot all about it. He stopped in the middle of the little kitchen and checked his watch. He had some time, but not much.

He proceeded into the bedroom and then the bathroom, where he stopped dead in his tracks, perplexed by what he saw. The bathtub was empty.

For the first time in all of this Luka began to panic. Where was she? He couldn't believe she wasn't dead. He saw her die, he felt himself smother the life right out of her.

He heard a wheezy growl behind him, and he turned around in time to see her rounding the tall dresser in the bedroom. Her eyes were practically white and glazed over, and she snarled as she reached out for him.

He dropped the rug, and she lunged at him. They both stumbled backwards into the tub, once again splashing water everywhere. As he tried to push her off of him, she snapped her jaws at him like a wild animal.

He heard screaming and it took him a moment before he realized it was he who was screaming. He pushed her up and managed to pull his knee in and place his foot on her chest.

She lunged forward again, but he held her at bay as she swiped at him with her hands and growled like a bobcat. He kicked hard, shoving her back into the sink, knocking it off the tile where it was bolted down.

As she got her bearings and prepared for another lunge, he pulled himself out of the tub. She ran forward but tripped right over his back falling forward into the tub face-first.

He got to his feet and backed away, staring at Marina in terror. "Marina! What happened to you?"

She pushed herself up and out of the water. She spun around, her maniacal features dripping with water, her teeth bared. She pushed herself up to a standing position, snarling and snapping.

Right before she came at him again, he backed into the bedroom and shouted, "STOP!"

To his surprise, she listened.

He looked at his wife, taking her in for what she was now. He didn't understand what had happened to her. He knew she was sick. Was this what he was to become?

Then he remembered General Ramses. He didn't turn into...this. Luka hypothesized that when he killed her, the infection in her body had not yet been complete, but it was there.

So it stood to reason that, given the limited progression of the infection, this was all she could become. No speech, no intelligent thought, just an animalistic killer. She would be one of the drones after all, not a lieutenant.

He stepped forward, approaching her carefully. "My poor Marina. I am so sorry."

She growled at him, a low, guttural sound, but she made no move to attack him. He moved in a bit closer, reaching out a hand to caress her face. She let him do it.

"My poor, dear Marina. I will take care of you. I am so sorry. I will take care of you. Everything will be all right."

As he uttered the words, he knew they were a lie, but he didn't know what else to tell her. Maybe Kafka would know what to do. He was in touch with all of this Outworlder bullshit. He rigged the portable RGT; Kafka had to do something to help him.

Maybe there was a way to bring her back, restore her. Or at least to give her the faculties of speech and thought. She snapped at his hand like a puppy playing but didn't actually bite him.

Just then, he heard the door to the apartment open. Heavy footsteps stomped through the kitchen. Yuri was coming, but all Luka could think of, was his poor Marina.

Yuri caught sight of him standing in the bedroom and came at him. He was holding the knife in his right hand. Luka did not care. He didn't know how to think or feel anymore, so when Yuri rushed into the bedroom, he stood there as Yuri plunged the knife in between his ribs on his left side, burying it to the handle.

The force of the blow sent Luka falling on his right side. Yuri stood over him, blood dripping down his face, panting and looking vindicated. He heard a growl come from the bathroom.

When Yuri turned he expected to see some kind of dog, but instead he saw Marina lunge at him with her arms reaching out for him. She grabbed his head with both hands and bit his nose and lips right off his face.

He pulled free and fell backwards onto the bed, clutching his face and screeching hysterically. Marina stood there for a moment chewing. Yuri rolled off the bed and onto the cheap carpeting spurting blood from his face.

He tried to commando crawl out of the bedroom, but he was unable to move. He looked back over his shoulder with a mangled face and saw Luka clutching his ankle and smiling.

"Please, Luka, let me go," he tried to say, but without his lips it came out as, "Leez, Luka, let ree go."

Luka did not.

Marina got down on all fours and sunk her teeth into Yuri's thigh. He yelled out in horror and pain. Blood poured out of the wound and began to spatter the shoddy beige carpeting. Yuri's pant leg became drenched in a dark liquid.

Luka laughed wickedly. "She wants your body, Yuri." He crawled over to Marina. "That's it, my Dear. Feed. You are a soldier now and you need to keep up your strength."

He stroked her hair lovingly as he watched her slowly eat the neighbor from downstairs alive on their bedroom floor.

Part II

Something About The Road to Hell and Good Intentions

Chapter 6

"Well, I don't know about you, brother, but I agree with the notion of requiring a license to become a parent," said Skylar with obvious contempt in his voice. "It would certainly decrease the amount of people dependent on our tax dollars." There were cheers and boos from the live studio audience.

Tyler rolled his eyes. "But don't you think it's a little too Big Government? Don't you think it infringes on our civil liberties? 50,112 hits on Tylerblog agree. What say you?"

"It's not like the welfare state wants these kids anyway," replied Skylar. "Most of them are accidents. Besides, it would cut down on the amount of abortions, which you and your Religious Right detest anyway. 59,008 hits on Skylarblog agree. What say you?"

"Skylar, dear brother, I just don't think it's up to the government to decide. I think that the decision to have a child is a deeply personal one, and the decision to abort is forbidden by the Church."

"But, Tyler, your camp is always complaining about the amount of lazy people dependent on public assistance. They reproduce like rabbits, their numbers increasing exponentially. Public assistance dollars delivered to each household increases with each child born into it, and the tax code favors them as well. If you want to reverse this welfare/food stamp culture, you have to hit them where it hurts. For every unlicensed child born into a household, that household is hit with a tax. Or decrease the amount of public assistance. Either way, it is a financial penalty for having unlicensed children. 71,231 hits on Skylarblog agree. What say you?"

"You know what I say, Skylar? I say that your plan reeks of Social Darwinism. Such a policy, already being applied by several states, affects certain socio-economic groups. This is government-designed natural selection weeding out certain groups of *undesirables* in favor of a dominant class. 75,009 hits on Tylerblog agree. What say you?"

"*Dominant class*? Really, Tyler. Tell me, if there is a shrinking group of tax paying producers pulling a large cart of growing dependents, how are they a dominant class? They are being taxed into oblivion to support an ever growing number of nonworking, nontax-paying leeches. The non-producers have been exponentially outpacing the producers in reproduction rates. The producers are being punished for hard work and success. This system of government dependency cannot sustain itself. 78,095 hits on Skylarblog agree. What say you?"

"I say, where is your humanity, brother? Not all of those receiving public assistance are lazy. What about the ever-growing number of those unemployed or underemployed, victims of the Great Rollercoaster Recession? Are you saying that they want to be dependent on the government for a pittance that barely puts food on their table? 82,529 hits on Tylerblog agree. What say you?"

"Oh, please, Tyler. They get a heck of a lot more than a pittance. They collect food stamps that studies show are being used at restaurants and movie theater concession stands rather than for groceries. They get free, top of the line mini-coms and cable television with all of the premium channels. What motivation do they have to go out and work when all of their basic needs are already taken care of for them?"

"Skylar, I think that those individuals that you are referring to are a minority. There is always waste in public programs. That is unavoidable, but we don't want to throw away the baby with the bathwater. I think it's only fair that those who are fortunate enough need to pay in a little more, a small price to pay for the success that is elusive to so many. 84,291 hits on Tylerblog agree. What say you?"

"Tyler, I do not wish to punish the unfortunate victims of the Great Rollercoaster Recession. I am fully aware that there are many talented, skilled individuals who wish to work and be productive. I just don't want these unsuccessful people to have children. It would just mean more mouths to feed on the public dime. To be honest, if you are not a tax-paying producer, it would be irresponsible of you to reproduce. In fact, unless you are a tax-payer and even a property owner, you shouldn't even be able to vote! 87,083 hits on Skylarblog agree. What say you?"

"Skylar, brother dear, are you suggesting that the government employ voter suppression tactics on the lower socio-economic groups?" More boo's and hisses than cheers. It all blended after a while into indistinguishable, collective outrage directed against both sides of the argument.

"Tyler, I am saying that if you don't have any skin in the game, you shouldn't be given the opportunity to direct policy that affects the greater whole. The significant portion of the population dependent on public assistance will never vote to end it. Why work when the government will support you for free? I think that the current politicians know this, and they use entitlements as currency to garner votes. 92,199 hits on Skylarblog agree. What say you?"

"Skylar, I don't think there is an easy solution to this problem. It wasn't enough that a great fence patrolled by drones on the Mexican border reduced the amount of illegals flooding our ranks to practically nil. Now you want the government to decide who should and who shouldn't have children."

"Tyler, we largely fixed the immigration problem, but those who were already here have already reproduced, growing exponentially in just a few generations. Add that to the already dependent welfare culture fostered in this country and we have a real problem of solvency. The Baby Boomer generation already decimated Social Security and nearly destroyed Medicare."

"Well, Skylar, that concludes another evening of docutainment. We'd like to remind everyone that tomorrow is monthly Take You Parents to Work Day. Do you have a pain in the ass boss that you just don't have the nerve to stand up to? Have you wanted to demand that raise or promotion that you deserve, but the right opportunity never arose? Well, why not ask Mommy or Daddy to do it?"

"That's right, Tyler. Your parents have raised you since birth, feeding you, putting a roof over your head and clothes on your back. They've kept you safe and looked out for you all of these years. Why stop now? They love to do it anyway."

Tyler waved and threw his arm around his brother, kicking up his heel. "Thank you, and good night."

***

10:35 HRS

"It is finished," announced Kojic, rubbing his eyes.

Kafka studied the man with all four eyes, cocking his head slightly to the right as if pondering something. "You look like shit, Kojic. Rough night?"

"You might say that."

"How's the wife?"

Kojic didn't believe Kafka's audacity to ask such a thing. The fact that he even asked out of the blue indicated that he knew damned well how his wife was.

"Not so good," was all he could muster.

Kafka let the words hang out there displaying Kojic's anguish for all in the room to see. Then at last, he answered. "Let's see what you've brought me. Then I might be able to help you."

It was all Kojic could do to keep himself from breaking down. He was sleep deprived and exhausted from the arduous night prior. He resented and was grateful to Kafka all at once. The bastard gave him what now plagued his wife…if she was even still his wife, but maybe it wasn't as bleak as it appeared. Maybe Kafka would offer some bit of comfort about Marina's condition.

"First the apparatus."

Kafka displayed a toothy mockery of a smile and all eyes blinked simultaneously. Kojic thought he noticed two sets of eyelids.

"That's what I like about you, Kojic. Straight to business. I can see why you were Belmont's right hand."

Farooq stirred uncomfortably in the corner, which made Kafka grin wider. His statement was for Farooq's benefit. He liked to keep things competitive amongst his lackeys. If they were preoccupied fighting each other for his favor they didn't have time for mutiny.

"Let's see now," said Kafka, eyes wide, as he walked over to the table on which the portable RGT apparatus sat. "Farooq, get me a few of our men. Any three, I don't care."

Farooq stood up, nodded, and briskly left the room.

"I like what you've done here, Kojic."

"Thank you, Kafka."

"And it is completely portable?"

"Yes, but the tower must accompany the headpiece. I made it small with a handle for easy transport. The case is as small as I could make it without interfering with cable management. I installed a state of the art heat synch."

"Excellent." Kafka truly looked pleased. There was a strange, guttural clicking that seemed to come from him. "The parts Assistant Director Wolff was so kind to provide were adequate?"

"We can pick up cell communications from all of the major providers, DBS and DTH signals between 12.2 and 12.7 GHz, the Cell Broadcast Channel, tapping into Galaxy-18 and 19, AMC-4, Satmex, and all of the Atlas satellites, the internet, television broadcasts—"

"I get it. Well done, Kojic. What's the radius?"

"Within 3.63 miles, adjustable downward."

"Private military feeds?"

"Yes."

Farooq returned with three men as Kafka requested and awaited further instruction.

"Leave us," commanded Kafka looking at Kojic and the Farooq. The two men glanced tentatively at each other and then excused themselves from the room.

Kafka was alone with the three men he requested. He looked up from the RGT apparatus and smiled menacingly at them.

"Himmel," he addressed the one furthest to the right, "do you know why I have summoned you here?"

The young man thought about it for a moment, uncertain of how to answer and, more to the point, terrified of answering incorrectly. "No, sir."

"Of course you don't," whispered Kafka. "The three of you all have something in common. Do you know what that is, Tsang?"

Tsang took a good look at the other two men. "We are all young, sir?"

"Yes, that is true, but it wasn't what I was thinking of." Kafka was like a cat toying with its prey right before it brutally ended its life. It was unbearable. "How about you, Mikos?"

Mikos swallowed hard. "I don't know, sir. I am Greek, Tsang is Chinese, and Himmel is German. I can't think of anything we have in common."

"There is one thing...one significant thing you all have in common," said Kafka, the clicking rising softly.

All three men looked at him expectantly.

"None of you have been infected," Kafka stated, as if the answer should've been obvious to them.

All three men stirred uneasily. Although none of them were infected, they had heard stories about some of the higher ranking operatives. Men like Kojic and Farooq.

Kafka picked up the headset to the RGT apparatus and gently placed it on his head, the electrodes making contact with his jet black, oily skin. The visor slid over all four eyes but only appeared to line up with the inner two.

He reached out, powered up the tower, and began turning a dial. "Bear with me. This will only take a minute."

The three men glanced at each other uneasily, unsure of what to anticipate. Kafka finished turning the knob and pressed another button. All at once, the three men's cell phones went off. They looked down at their pockets quizzically.

"Well, go ahead. Answer it."

Each man reached into his pocket and produced his cell phone. The screens were flickering...

Kojic and Farooq waited outside in the hallway.

"What do you think he's doing in there?" asked Farooq.

"I don't know."

"You should know," demanded Farooq. "You were working on it all night."

"He asked for a portable RGT unit. He didn't tell me anything about what he planned to do with it."

"Do you think he will tell us?"

"I don't know, Farooq. I'm sure he will. Whatever it is, it's something important to him."

Suddenly the door opened, and both men made way as Kafka stepped into the hallway, closing the door to the room behind him.

"Farooq, ready one of the vans with tinted windows. Slap on a decal for a florist or something and commercial plates."

Farooq nodded and stalked down the hallway, a man on a mission. Kojic was looking at the door to the room beyond and nearly jumped out of his skin when Kafka slapped a bony hand on his shoulder.

"You've done well, Kojic. So now I will tell you about your wife."

As Kojic wondered how he knew about Marina, Kafka began to lead him down the hallway away from the room with the closed door. Kojic made a cursory glance over his shoulder at the room that was quiet as a tomb.

"You killed your wife before the infection was complete, my friend."

"But how? How do you know?"

"Because I can feel her, Kojic. She is one of my children now. She has a condition known as Kluver-Bucy Syndrome. I learned about it when I was in the military. It will make her hyper oral, hyper aggressive, and hyper sexual."

This explanation conjured several unpleasant images in Kojic's mind's eye.

"You are a lieutenant," Kafka continued, "but she is a soldier. It doesn't make her any less important."

"Is there a way to help her?"

"I am afraid there is nothing you can do. She will not regain her ability to speak, and she has lost the capability for higher order cognition." Kafka saw the look of horror and barely contained outrage on Kojic's face. "My friend, I never told you to try to murder Marina. That was your doing."

Kojic looked down at his feet, his face hot with rage. Kafka was right. He had never ordered him to murder Marina. He couldn't have known about her and the neighbor downstairs. That piece of shit, Yuri.

"I-I have a body that needs to be disposed of."

"Ah," said Kafka grinning sympathetically, "the paramour who violated your marriage."

Kojic nodded.

"You were right to kill him."

"Actually," Kojic corrected, "Marina killed him."

"But you let it happen?"

"Yes."

"How did it feel, to let your undead wife eat the man who destroyed the sanctity of your marriage—who questioned your manhood—alive?"

"I-I don't know…"

"Oh, come on, Kojic. How did it feel? I mean how did it *really* feel."

"It…it felt right."

"Of course it did," said Kafka triumphantly. "It *was* right."

"But Marina…" said Kojic trailing off.

"She probably had it coming," said Kafka, adding insult to injury. The words were daggers in Kojic's stony heart. He knew it was true. "She will be much easier to control now. All you have to do is focus."

"Control her how?" Kojic was suppressing hot tears, but they streamed down his dirty face. "What am I to do with her?"

"When the time is right I will call on her. Until then take comfort in knowing that she will be spared a horrible fate."

However, Kojic couldn't imagine anything that was worse than her current fate

"Go home, be with her. You have done well. Rest up, for tonight we will bring my brother into our fold and tie up a dangerous loose end. It will be a night for family to be together again before we go to war."

Kojic only nodded, choking back sobs. He was like a small child being consoled by a parent. He didn't quite believe what Kafka was saying, but he had no choice but to accept it.

"Soon you will be part of a new dominant race that will end oppression in the world. We will end pain and suffering and become part of something bigger."

Kojic heard talk like this before. When he spent time in Albania, he heard communists talk like this. That everyone would be the same and cared for by the few chiefs in the communist party, but the end result was the chiefs feathering their own nests at the Indians' expense.

"Remember," added Kafka, as if reading Kojic's mind, "you are a chief. You are my chief. Do not forget that. And anyone who is not one of us will convert or perish. It is our way."

Kojic nodded, drying his eyes with his sleeve. This part sounded familiar. He was about to wage a jihad, a much bigger one than he had anticipated, and he was a member of what was surely to be the winning side.

"In the next few hours, you will begin to see an exact replica of yourself. Do not be afraid."

Kojic looked at him confused.

"You will see. When it happens, do not run from it. Embrace it. It will make you powerful."

Kojic nodded obediently, not having the faintest idea what Kafka was talking about. He remembered the man in his apartment building that he shoved past, failing to get a good look at him in his haste. Kojic had an idea this was a part of his own transformation, a progression of the infection. Kafka's gift.

"Good. Bring me your body if there is anything left. I will take care of everything. Not to worry, my friend."

Kafka slapped him on the back and continued down the hall leaving an anguished Kojic to his thoughts.

***

Birdsall Hardware
11:47 HRS

Peter found working at the hardware store blissfully distracting. He was helping his father repair a holographic advertisement in the aisle containing plumbing equipment. Other than a couple of contractors roaming the store, they were alone.

"Jesus, Dad. You weren't kidding when you said you were all by yourself."

"I appreciate your help," said Barry. "Hand me the video card."

Peter reached into the advertisement kit that came in a box of plumbing joints and nipples and pulled out a video card wrapped in plastic. He handed it to Barry.

"How do you know how to assemble these things?"

"Your brother isn't the only one in the family who's good with electronics," said Barry, who then became lost in thoughts of Carl. "I wish he were with me now, helping me out, too."

Peter sensed the two contractors roaming around the aisle with T-squares and dry wall saws. He thought about Carl's invitation. He wanted to tell his father about it, but the meeting wasn't going to be a social call. He had to kill Carl tonight, or die trying.

He quickly changed the subject. "I'm impressed. Really."

"Well," said Barry snapping the card into its slot, "you just learn as you go. The manufacturer makes the directions pretty simple. They want their wares properly advertised. They want to be first to catch the customer's eye. It increases sales."

"What about competing brands? Who gets what placement on the shelves?"

"They actually pay for shelf placement. It's part of my revenue. The money's good. Pass me the screwdriver."

Peter grabbed it off the floor and slapped it in his father's palm like a nurse handing a scalpel to a surgeon. Barry replaced the outer cover of the holo-projector and screwed it in place.

"Okay, let's get it on the shelf and turn it on."

Peter nodded and watched as Barry placed it on the designated shelf and flicked a switch. The holographic ad began to flicker in mid-air.

"Oh, shit," complained Barry. "Gotta open it up again."

As he unscrewed and removed the outer casing, he began to fiddle with the components inside. Peter just stood there, mesmerized by the flickering holograph. It was the pattern of the flickering. It registered on his retina and seemed to render him immobile.

As he saw the ad flicker, the store and its shelves disappeared. At first, all he saw was the light patterns. Then, memories that weren't his began to flood his mind.

His back and neck became rigid as sights and scenes rushed before him. Somewhere in the distance he heard his father rambling on about something, which was strange because last he saw, he was standing next to him.

Suddenly, he was in a setting vaguely familiar to him...

He was inside the dance club in Tijuana where Kafka infected him with a bite on the neck. It was dark except for strobe and neon green laser light effects flickering in tune with the glitchy holographic advertisement. Even the stenches of sweat and sex were present. Was this a dream or some kind of illusion?

Across the expansive dance floor, where hundreds of young hormones bumped and grinded up against each other to a rapid beat of techno music in tune with the lights, Peter saw Kafka standing on the main stage. There were scantily clad women around him writhing to the beat.

Peter began to push his way through the crowd. Oddly, the interior of the club felt larger than he remembered. He snaked his way through the crowd, his progress slow, but never taking his eyes of Kafka, who stood amongst his entourage like an emperor.

His progress was slowed as girls reached out for him, placing their hands all over his body, beckoning with sultry eyes containing the promise of all kinds of depravity. He called out to his brother.

"Carl! Carl!"

The music was too loud. With his newfound abilities, Peter reached out and felt the crowd around him. Or they reached out and found him. He wasn't sure which exactly.

What at first felt like the scattered beats of individuals quickly coalesced into a thundering tribal beat of a human forest that pounded in time with the music, as if the DJ were directing all of their vitals.

The feeling was overwhelming, and Peter was caught up in the waves of rising and falling human beats, a tide of life exploding all around him.

After some time, he reached the stage. When he looked up at Kafka, he saw a large pyramid looming behind him, as if the back wall of the club had opened up on some other dimension revealing an ancient scene. Two other pyramids flanked the middle one, but set back a little further in the distance.

Kafka looked down and saw Peter, calling his name without actually using his voice. *Pete.* It was more of an idea that entered Peter's mind without tone or timber. He reached out a lithe hand and snatched Peter up out of the crowd, pulling him onto the stage.

Peter had always been taller than his brother, but now Carl towered over him with inhuman features. For the first time Peter was intimidated by his younger brother.

Pete, welcome.

Suddenly the tone of the music shifted, the tide of the vibe emanating from the crowd shifting with it. It became more explosive and darker in tone. The effect was disconcerting.

"Carl, where are we?"

We are at the dawning of a new era. The Endgame is about to begin.

"I don't know what you mean. What is the Endgame?"

You will reap the rewards of having joined a superior race. The Outworlders have come.

"What Outworlders? What are you talking about, Carl?"

There is no Carl, only Kafka. I, the Harbinger of Doom, the Deadly Lieutenant, the Opener of Floodgates, am to usher their arrival on this planet. And you will be by my side. I have seen to it.

"What are you talking about? Invasion?"

For centuries, the Outworlders have made contact with our kind, planting the seeds for their arrival, but fear and superstition have chased them out before their plans could come to fruition.

Now, in the modern age, with the rise of secularism and timeless superstitions forgotten, our seeds are now ripe and the great Reaping will begin.

"What are you saying? That these Outworlders planted technology on this planet to make way for their arrival?"

Throughout time, they have bestowed the gifts of knowledge and mastery of technology in the hopes that one day, the gate for their arrival would be opened.

"The RGT."

Kafka nodded emphatically.

The pyramids, the printing press, the internet, all gifts bestowed by them unto us. RGT is the most modern example. The Outworlders knew that our kind's propensity for paranoia and domination would one day assist them in the development of the tool needed to open the Floodgates between our worlds.

"If these Outworlders are so powerful and advanced, why don't they just come on their own?"

Kafka pointed a long, bony finger at the crowd. Peter was horrified by what he saw.

The crowd of young dancers was now a crowd of writhing undead. Milky, glazed over eyes glared at him from down below as they wheezed and swayed to the dark music.

Kafka shoved Peter so hard he fell backward into the sea of undead like a crowd surfer at a concert. Hands reached up and groped for him as he was engulfed in a collective moaning.

Terrified for his life, he screamed and struggled out of their grasps and fell between them to the floor. He felt their terrible vibrations, an antithesis of the vitals he felt before, thunder through his mind like a horrible cacophony. All he could do was crawl up into a ball.

They will not harm you, for you are one of us.

After a moment, when he realized that he wasn't being eaten alive, Peter began to uncurl. He rolled over on his stomach and slowly pushed himself up on his palms. The sea of undead parted around him as he stood up.

"What about Dad? What's going to happen to him?"

Look.

Peter saw Barry standing right in front of him in the clearing. He was wearing his hardware store uniform.

He must join us.

"I-I don't understand."

Suddenly, Peter felt an alien hunger seize his body, surging through his veins like liquid fire. He felt his features change, and his father shrunk back in reaction.

"Pete, are you all right? What's wrong?"

Peter's mind raged with a sadistic appetite, ebbing and flowing with Barry's pulse that was quickening in front of him.

Barry reached out for him. "Son, what's wrong?"

Peter snapped his jaws at him, bearing sharp fangs, like a rabid animal. Barry was so startled he fell backwards.

"No! I won't do it!" shouted Peter as he turned away from his father. Barry's pulse beckoned him like a dinner bell.

You must, brother. If you don't, his fate will be much worse.

Peter hunched over with hunger pangs, his heart beating in his throat. Kafka was implanting these impulses in his mind. He was sure of it. He had to clear his mind.

He began to think of his mother.

What are you doing, Pete? Stop that.

Peter closed his eyes and just thought of his mother. He thought of her smile, the way she made a fuss cooking for him and his brother. The way she always made them feel cared for. Warmth began to spread over his body, a feeling that he could only describe as home.

Stop that. Save Dad. You must do it. He will suffer, Pete.

Peter opened his eyes and stood up straight, pointing a finger at Kafka. "Why don't *you* do it?"

Kafka only shook his head disappointedly.

This was your opportunity to save Dad. Now his fate will be on you.

All at once, the whole scene vanished. The nightclub, the music, the pyramids, the sea of undead. All gone.

Peter found himself in the aisle of the hardware store with his father and the two contractors staring at him in disbelief.

"Are you okay, pal?" one of them asked.

Peter looked at his father, who just stood there trembling.

"Dad, are you all right?"

Barry backed away from Peter.

"Did you see any of that?"

Barry was incredulous. "Any of what, Pete?"

Peter looked around. Apparently, he never left the hardware store. What he saw must have been some kind of private event. That was why Kafka couldn't infect their Dad. He was never here.

"What's wrong with your face?" asked the other contractor.

Peter reflexively reached up with his hands and felt his face. Sharp ridges were beginning to recede as his features began to smooth out and return to their original configuration.

What the hell had just happened to him? Had he changed in front of his father and these two contractors? It wasn't entirely a private event. Carl wanted him to infect their father. He was attempting to command it remotely.

Damn, he was powerful. They now shared some kind of connection, but it wasn't foolproof. He was able to chase it all away with the thoughts of his mother. Peter wasn't sure if it was the warm feelings that dispelled Carl's commands or if there was still a human side of Carl that was vulnerable to thoughts of their mother.

Carl did refer to the human race as *our* kind, meaning that despite his transformation he still identified himself as human. Either way, it was a weakness. One that he could exploit.

Then there were all of the titles Carl had for himself. He was a human that was selected for a very special role in what was to be an alien invasion.

He stepped out of his own head for a moment and saw his father and the two men gawking at him.

"I'm going to call 911," said one contractor. "This boy needs help."

Peter held out a hand. "No, I'm all right. Don't do that."

The man held his mini-com out in front of him, frozen, not sure if to take Peter's objection as a threat.

"Dad, I'm leaving. I have to go."

"But, Pete," Barry began to protest.

"I-I have to go. I'll explain later."

Peter ran out of the hardware store before anyone could say anything else.

***

Kafka sat back in his chair behind his desk contemplating his interaction with Peter when there was a knock at the door. He checked his watch.

"Illumination at ten percent." The lights in the office dimmed until it was shrouded in shadow. Then he switched on a copy of the therapeutic ambience program that Ramses pilfered for him from the late Captain Fiona London's office.

The office transformed. The exposed brick and cracked plaster now looked covered and new. There were a couple of digital paintings on the wall and a holographic representation of a cybernetic digital desktop on his desk.

Kafka, himself, was transformed into a raven-haired, handsome man with a thin mustache in a pin-striped suit. He looked like Clark Gable.

"Come in."

There was a tone and the door opened. Two Chinese spies, with whom Kafka had recently been in contact with, entered, followed by Kojic.

"Please, gentleman, have a seat," said Kafka cordially, never leaving his seat. His voice retained its tinny reverberation, lending it an inhuman quality.

The two Chinese glared at his obvious gesture of disrespect and then took seats in the chairs in front of Kafka's desk. Kojic sat in a third chair to their right.

One of them started to speak, but it was in Chinese. Kafka put up his long finger to tell him to wait.

"Translation mode, Chinese, scan for dialect."

The digital décor in the room glitched as the program waited for a sample of speech to analyze.

"Go ahead," said Kafka, gesturing with an open palm for the man to continue.

After about a sentence of more Chinese, the man's words were translated and re-spoken by the ambience program.

"...seen the facilities, as shown by your man, Kojic, but we want to know exactly what we are investing in."

"Mr. Joeng, your government has been hacking into the American's networks for decades. However, the access I am offering is unprecedented."

"What kind of access are we talking about?" asked the other man.

"Mr. Kao, as you have probably heard, the United States government has been employing the use of Retinal Gateway Technology."

"Yes, what is it, exactly?" asked Joeng.

"It is an intelligence gathering technique that reads retinas and extracts memories. Under the Second Patriot Act, the government has been monitoring the populace through their television sets, cell phones, mini-coms, computers...anything with a monitor. It's pervasive."

"And you are proposing that we can gain access into this network," said Joeng.

"Exactly."

"How?"

"My man, Kojic here, has been developing an apparatus that allows a user to remotely gain access to this RGT network, but we have run out of funding."

"How close are you?" asked Kao.

"We can gain access, but within a proscribed radius. Unfortunately, the radius is too small; hence the access isn't as remote as we would like it to be."

"I see," said Joeng. "How much?"

"I will need twenty million."

Kao chortled and shifted in his seat. Joeng just glared at Kafka. "That's a bit, as you would say, steep."

Kafka sat forward in his chair, flashing his digit million dollar smile. "C'mon, boys. I'm talking about unprecedented, pervasive, undetectable access into the thoughts and memories of billions of Americans. This includes military, law enforcement..."

"How is it undetectable?" asked Joeng.

"The NSA has not developed a means to track the usage of RGT other than their own because they think they are the only ones that have it."

"If you possess this kind of technology, why share it with us?" asked Kao, barely trying to conceal his suspicion.

"Because I need the funding, remember?"

"What about OIL?"

"They don't have that kind of money. You guys, however, have one of the strongest economies in the world. You can afford it."

"Do you have OIL's blessing?" asked Kao.

"OIL, sure! They hate this country as much as you do. If you could help bring it down, they'd be happy to help."

"Mr. Kafka, we are *not* terrorists. We do not hate America," corrected Joeng.

"I understand. I really do. You guys are the other big kid on the block. You're rivals. I get it."

"Good," said Kao. "As long as you understand our position. We do not normally consort with the likes of anarchists such as yourself."

"I know, I know," reassured Kafka, "you guys are communists. I understand. But we have a common enemy, so why not...help each other out?

"Of course, if you want to sit here in my office and insult me, I can always go to the North Koreans. They'd kill to have access to this kind of technology."

Although both men kept poker faces, Kafka felt their heartbeats flitter for a moment.

"The North Korean government hardly has twenty million to offer you," said Joeng with an edge of irritation in his voice.

Kafka sat back and put up his hands in a gesture of resignation. "Hey, I'm an anarchist, right? What do I care about money? Maybe I just *give* it to them just to see what happens."

Joeng looked at Kao, who nodded his approval. Kafka found this interesting, as he was never sure from their communications which man was in charge.

"Great!" shouted Kafka, making Kojic jump. "So we have an accord!"

Both men nodded.

"Excellent. Once the money is wired over we'll be in touch."

"You can expect it within the hour," said Kao.

Kafka stood up. Kao, Joeng, and Kojic all followed suit. Kafka extended his hand. Koa took it, but when he felt Kafka's long fingers, he looked down in shock and disgust. All he saw was a digitally perfect representation of a human hand.

"We'll get cracking on the remote access device for you right away," said Kafka with a little too much enthusiasm. "Kojic, kindly show these fine gentlemen the way out."

Kao took his hand back and held it away from his body awkwardly as if he touched something filthy or germy. Kojic gestured to the door, and both men exited the office.

Kojic paused before leaving.

"Looks like we're in business," said Kafka.

Kojic nodded and stepped out into the hall with Joeng and Kao, closing the door behind him.

Kafka sat back in his chair behind his desk. "Terminate ambience program."

The office resumed its dilapidated appearance, and Kafka regained his terrible countenance. He thought about the factory floor below and the equipment that was being refurbished at that very moment, and he clicked in anticipation as he sat in the shadows.

***

Frisky's Bar
12:21HRS

"So let me get this straight," said George Newman, owner of Frisky's Bar, "you are taking over my bar. Under whose authority?"

"The United States Government," replied Colonel Betancourt coolly.

George spat contemptuously on the ground at Betancourt's feet. "I'll be damned if I'm going to let Big Brother waltz on in here with some damned executive order seizing my bar. This is a private establishment."

"I understand, sir. This is a matter of national security."

"What matter?"

"It's classified, sir. Just know that you are doing a great service to your country."

"Now you wait just a goddamned minute. I haven't agreed to anything yet."

"Please escort this nice gentleman off the premises and into protective custody." Two soldiers dressed in plain clothes grabbed George under each arm and escorted him out the back.

George shouted over his shoulder, "I didn't even vote for Rubio!" A parting shot.

Betancourt shrugged casually. "Lieutenant Farrow, install that metal detector and make sure the facial recognition equipment is operational. You need to be in and out so no one suspects anything. I am sure Kafka has this place under surveillance."

"Yes, sir. In and out." Farrow was dressed like an electrician. His white electrician's van was parked out front.

Betancourt turned to Lieutenant Villanueva. "We are going to staff this place tonight. Bar tender, bouncers, busboys. Everyone know their jobs?"

"Yes, sir. I've prepped the men myself."

"Excellent. If any OIL are flagged at the door, the bouncers snatch them up and take them in the back as quickly and quietly as possible."

"Yes, sir."

"The only people in here that should be armed are our own. Am I clear?"

"Yes, sir. The local roadblocks will fall into place as soon as Kafka enters the bar. Our men will form a wide perimeter. All air traffic above the bar has been diverted."

"Good. No way out. We'll only have one chance at this."

"Yes, sir."

"Excellent, work," said CIA Agent Kickuchi imperiously. She, too, was dressed in plain clothes, but she was acting like she was running the show. Technically, she was, but Betancourt was managing the details. The devil was always in the details. "Kafka will never know what hit him."

Betancourt pressed his finger pensively to his lips as if reviewing a list in his head. This was all too easy. Kafka was too clever to be caught this way. Betancourt smelled a rat. He was sure this was a trap...but set by whom?

Either way, Betancourt was anticipating a problem and he wasn't about to take any chances. He wasn't a betting man—his ex-wife forbade gambling—but he would bet solid money that by the end of tonight he would receive confirmation on what he already suspected about Ramses.

Once he had proof, he was going to nail that slimy bastard to the wall.

"There is some activity at the bar," said Farooq into his cell. "Some kind of technicians."

"I see," said Kafka on the other end. *"Do they look like government?"*

"I am not sure. Maybe something broke. It says Garrett Electricians on the side of the van."

There was a pause on the other end as Kafka researched the company name. *"It looks legitimate. Any cell communication in or out of the bar?"*

Farooq looked down at the portable tower of the RGT unit. "None yet."

"Well that's odd, don't you think? These electricians didn't call anything in to the office the whole time?"

"No."

"It's like they're avoiding using their cells."

"You might say that."

"It's the government. Ramses said they'd be trying something. Some added security or something. No matter. We will proceed as planned."

"Yes, Kafka."

***

Peter was rummaging in the closet of his old room in his father's house. He found his duffle bag and unzipped it. He produced a digi-locked box and keyed in the security code. He opened the box and removed his Desert Eagle handgun.

He looked it over and loaded the clip. He made sure the safety was on and shoved it under his waistband in the back. He took two extra clips in his right hand and shoved the box closed with his left. The digi-lock automatically engaged.

If Kafka really was going to show up at Frisky's tonight, Peter was going to blow his brains out all over the bar. If there was any truth to what Kafka said in Peter's vision today, he had to be taken out.

He thought he sensed something and turned around on his heel, training his gun, but there was no one in the room with him.

He turned his eyes to the window and saw it.

His doppelgänger was outside the window grinning at him and scratching the glass. Peter stood up and rounded the bed, but by the time he reached the window, it was gone.

He looked down into the backyard, but it was empty. He heard movement downstairs. He quickly and silently slipped out of his room and stood at the bannister at the top of the stairs.

He trained his gun down below as he heard some shuffling. Someone was definitely moving around downstairs. He reached out with his senses and felt that the other presence was in the kitchen.

He slowly crept down the carpeted stairs, careful to avoid the fourth one up that creaked, stepping over it. He rounded the bannister, training his gun on the kitchen.

He jumped into the room as his father stepped in his way, the two of them yelling as they collided.

"Jesus, Pete. It's just me."

"Dammit, Dad, I almost killed you." He backed away from his father, engaging the safety and shoving the gun in his waistband again.

"I left the store to see how you were doing. Something's not right, Pete."

"I know that, Dad. Something definitely isn't right."

"It's your brother. He's contacted you."

"I can't discuss it now, Dad."

"But where will you go?"

"Away from here. Trust me; it's for your own safety."

"*What's* for my own safety? Will you please explain to me what the hell is going on here?"

"It'd be better for you if you didn't know."

Suddenly Barry slapped his son. Peter stopped in his tracks, the side of his face stinging.

"Dammit, I'm your father and you *will* tell me what the hell is going on!"

Peter regarded his father clinically, the way he was trained to regard civilians in confidential matters. All business. "Sorry, sir. I have to go."

Peter pushed passed him and then out the front door.

Barry stood in the kitchen helpless to do anything to help either of his sons. He regretted slapping Peter the moment he did it, but he didn't know what else to do. One thing was for certain, he could no longer treat either of his sons like children anymore.

They were both grown men, and both made their own decisions. There was nothing Barry could do about it except stand by and watch, hoping both men did the right thing.

Chapter 7

University of Texas at Dallas
13:04 HRS

"Can anyone tell me what the message or moral of *Frankenstein* is?" asked Dr. Grotsky clutching a digital copy and pushing her reading spectacles back up the bridge of her nose.

"It is about good versus evil," offered a student in the second row. "The monster is pure evil."

"Not quite," said Grotsky tapping her lips thoughtfully with her right index finger. "While it's true the monster is pure evil, a true abomination, one can hardly say that Dr. Frankenstein was good. In the book, he dabbles with dark science, creating life from death, something considered very profane in Mary Shelly's time."

"It's a story about betrayal, the killing of the primal father," offered another student scrunching up her nose in thought. "Frankenstein is the father, and his 'son' wants to murder him. It's a playing out of Freud's Oedipal Complex."

"I can see that," said Grotsky, "but it's not the main message. Anyone else?"

"It's an indictment of modern technology, namely medicine, as unnatural and something to be feared," offered Elicia.

Grotsky stood up straight from leaning on her podium. "Exactly! Frankenstein used what in the story is considered modern technology to create life from death, and the exercise backfires terribly on him. *Frankenstein* is a cautionary tale."

"Kind of like the undead drones our military was using?" asked a student in the back.

Grotsky removed her spectacles and chewed on one of the arms thoughtfully. "Well, yes, actually. That's the perfect example. Our government used what many might consider an unnatural technology to combat terrorism, and ultimately it did backfire on us."

"What about the Automaton?" another student asked. "He's done this country some good, and *he* hasn't backfired on us."

"The Automaton is a perversity of government technology," said Elicia cynically, "and how do we know he hasn't backfired on us? We don't even know where he came from or why he has his powers."

"This Kafka character is a real villain," added Robert, a jock sitting next to her. He was on the lacrosse team, as evidenced by his stick lying next to his right foot.

Grotsky was encouraged by the discussion. It was validation that the students were truly listening and thinking about the material. "Yes, Robert, but we didn't create Kafka."

"Yeah, we don't know where he came from either," added Elicia. "For all we know, he and the Automaton may be the same person."

Robert chortled. "That's ridiculous. Kafka's a terrorist. A mass murderer. The Automaton is a hero."

"That's not what Afghanistan would say. Did you forget Tora Bora?"

"Yeah, but that was a military operation. He killed terrorists."

"I'm sure, to OIL, Kafka's actions are military operations for their Cause."

"Okay, well let's relate this all back to the story, shall we?" doddered Grotsky, afraid the conversation that was becoming a debate was derailing the lecture.

"So, what are you for, OIL?" asked the student sitting in front of her turning around.

Elicia rolled her eyes. "All I'm saying, in line with our discussion of *Frankenstein...*" Grotsky nodded her gratitude, "is that the Automaton represents a technology that is lethal and likely unnatural."

"Thank you, Elicia, for bringing us back to Mary Shelly's work."

Elicia nodded in reply, and Grotsky began to drone on about the novel. She resumed her presentation on the Smartboard, and as she did so, Elicia stared at the screen and became lost in thought.

She thought about the Automaton, who had been discussed frequently but had also remained relatively unseen. She thought about the government monitoring its populace in the name of national security under the Second Patriot Act. She also thought about her podcasts and how she missed them. She wondered if Mary Shelly would've understood her message.

Then, curiously, her mind drifted to Matt Brauer. She recalled her exchange with him in the computer lab and her humiliation. She thought about her roommate Darcy and how she blew off going out that Friday night at the end of the semester when she promised she'd go out with her.

Then in a stream of consciousness, she thought about her sister Brittany, who never had any problems meeting boys. She remembered when Brittany had found her a date for the senior prom in high school, a friend of hers named Bret.

Her face again became hot with embarrassment as she recalled a night of being neglected by him as she sat by herself sipping stale punch, only to find him making out with Britanny's friend, Lara, by the lockers. When she ran out of the auditorium upset, Brittany had caught up with her and, trying to make Elicia feel better, told her that she was pissed at Bret because she paid him to take her to the prom.

She remembered in eighth grade, after winning first place in the middle school science fair, running over to her crush, Joe Soretto, to show him her ribbon only to find him fawning all over her sister.

She remembered sixth grade when she was the first sixth grader to win the middle school spelling bee in the history of the middle school, only to have her books thrown on the floor and stomped on by the cheerleading squad. When she went home to tell her mother, her mother dried her tears and told her that it wouldn't hurt to play up her looks like her sister. Maybe then, the other girls would treat her better.

Elicia thought of all these things as a loud humming rang in her head louder and louder until it was almost unbearable. Resurfacing from her private reverie, the classroom came back into focus and Grotsky's voice became distinguishable words again.

However, the daydreaming curiously left Elicia with a headache. She found herself staring at the Smartboard, from which the now faint electronic hum was emanating. She stretched and looked around the room to find all of the other students staring straight ahead, mesmerized.

If she wasn't mistaken, they were all looking at the Smartboard in unison. Grotsky, oblivious to the sudden groupthink (or lack thereof) was content to drone on and be entertained by the sound of her own voice.

Elicia, unable to bear any more, abruptly stood up almost knocking her desk over. Dr. Grotsky ceased her dissertation and all of the other students gawked at Elicia.

"Excuse me," she said sheepishly and left the room.

She closed the classroom door behind her and strolled down the hall to the restroom, her footsteps echoing down the hallway. She stepped into the restroom and walked over to the sink. She ran the cold water and began to splash her face, looking at herself in the mirror.

Jesus. It was summer session and all, and a warm one at that, but she had never lost her concentration to that extent before. Her 4.0 GPA was a testament to that.

Yet, she wondered why her mind had wandered to such unpleasant places and she felt hung over. Why had her mind leapt from Frankenstein and Kafka to her failed social exploits and embarrassing moments?

To Elicia, it didn't feel like her mind was wandering. It was hard to explain, but it was as if the memories were being pulled from the edges of her consciousness into the light. She shook her head, dismissing the notion as ridiculous.

She took a paper towel and blew her nose like a trumpet. She tossed the paper towel in the trash receptacle, took a deep breath, and decided to return to class.

When she entered the classroom, she drew a few looks, but Grotsky was droning on about the book they had read prior, drawing a comparison.

"Remember *The Picture of Dorian Gray* by Oscar Wilde, another cautionary tale about the dangers of curiosity, self-exploration, and wanton hedonism. The relentless pursuit of pleasure without conscience."

"Sounds like Friday nights," quipped Robert, earning a few stifled chuckles. Grotsky rolled her eyes.

Elicia had already read that book in high school. She thought about the portrait that bore Dorian Gray's sins, a perfect record of all his dalliances and transgressions for all to see.

"On the contrary," Elicia interjected, "the tale was totally about the burden of conscience. He possessed the very record of all he'd done and had to hide it away."

To her surprise, rather than being delighted by the participation, Dr. Grotsky looked annoyed at being corrected. Yeah, she was one of those professors.

Grotsky cleared her throat. "Yes, well, it was Dorian's social experimentation, his thirst for carnal knowledge, which led to his record in spite of conscience."

Oh, it was on. Elicia loved professors like this. Or she loved challenging their pedantic interpretations. When they had huge, fragile egos, it only made it more fun.

Elicia smelled blood in the water. She leaned forward in her seat. "But still, it was the knowledge that the portrait, i.e. his conscience, was sitting right upstairs from him under the constant danger of being discovered that eventually led to his demise."

Grotsky pursed her lips, her eyes darting around behind her glasses. "Yes, well, we were comparing *The Picture of Dorian Gray* to *Frankenstein*—"

Elicia didn't miss a beat. "If *The Picture of Dorian Gray* were to be written today, it would be both a cautionary tale about conscience and technology."

"How could it possibly be about technology?" Robert chortled. "It's about a painting."

"The Victorian version used a painting as a metaphor for conscience…"

"Miss Corti," Grotsky interrupted, "I think I established that it was about the unscrupulous pursuit of pleasure."

Elicia ignored her and continued. "…but a modern version would use Dorian's hard drive. You see, there is a record on our hard drives—and on servers for that matter—of everything we look at on the internet. Every site, every keystroke. A modern-day Dorian, in his relentless quest for pleasure…" Grotsky nodded in recognition of her own idea "…would be agonizing over the guilt of what was indelibly recorded on his hard drive. He'd become paranoid about hackers and the FBI and it would drive him mad until he destroyed it."

"You sound like that Seditious Blogger, Tronika," chided Robert. Grotsky regarded her with an expression that Elicia could only call imperious contempt.

"Yes, well your analogy has one serious flaw, Ms. Corti," said Grotsky with no small measure of self-satisfaction. "Destroying the hard drive would not cause his demise."

Elicia sat back pondering this point. Grotsky was right about that. Still, she thought her analogy to hold water regardless.

"But a valiant effort," Dr. Grotsky added as a backhanded compliment.

Elicia's head began to hurt again, and she counted the minutes until class was over.

***

Kojic's Apartment
14:24 HRS

Luka Kojic walked through the door to his apartment and looked around the living room. It was empty and the furniture all askew as he had left it. He stepped into the kitchen, flicking on the light switch. He heard something coming from the bedroom.

It was a strange wheezing…and slapping sounds.

Thinking of his poor, dear Marina, he ran into the bedroom to find Yuri, half-eaten, plugging his wife on the bed.

"Marina, no!" Luka yelled, but the couple did not stop their disgusting relations.

Even in death, she couldn't remain faithful. In a futile gesture, Luka rounded the bed and tried to pull Yuri off of his wife. A significant part of Yuri's midsection was eaten away and his ribcage exposed, and he was slick with bodily fluids. Getting a secure grip on the man was impossible.

Luka stood there running his hands through his hair as he listened to the rasping exertion of the two zombies in his marriage bed. He was in agony as he saw Yuri attack his Marina, literally, with all he had left.

Luka ran into the kitchen and selected a large knife out of a drawer. He ran back into the bedroom, leaned over the side of the bed, and plunged his knife into the back of Yuri's head.

Yuri reached frantically with both hands to the back of his head, pulled out the knife, dropped it behind him, and continued to stab way at Marina underneath him.

Luka cried out in torment at the futility of his intervention. He rounded the bed once more, opened the closet, and pulled out his shotgun. He cracked it open, loaded two shells, and snapped the double barrels back.

He reached out and poked Yuri in the side of his cheek with the tip of the barrels. Yuri turned his head and opened his mouth, but Luka shoved the tip of the barrels in his mouth.

Yuri reached clumsily for the barrel, but Luka didn't give him the chance. He pulled the trigger, emptying both barrels and effectively taking off the top of Yuri's head.

Yuri dropped on top of Marina, motionless, as she continued to take her pleasure from him. Luka pulled the now entirely lifeless body of Yuri off of his wife and threw it to the ground beside the bed.

Marina sat up growling at her husband as he sat on the bed beside her. He caressed her hair matted with blood and bile as she snapped at him.

"Now, now, my Marina. You had no idea what you were doing. It wasn't your fault. I deserved it, anyway."

She snarled and spat blood at him, but he patiently wiped it from his face. He was not angry. This was his penance for neglecting and murdering her.

But he still loved her. She was his under the Law, even now in her current state, and he never walked away from what was his. Never.

"Tonight I have to do something very important," he explained to her, as if she was comprehending him, in denial of the harsh truth. "It's what I've been working on all of this time. After tonight you will no longer be alone."

He nearly choked on that last part. He now felt the guilt of months of long hours and late nights pour into him, making his soul heavy. As he sat there on the bed gazing into her milky white eyes, he suddenly was able to understand how alone Marina must have felt.

She sat there wheezing loudly, shaking the mattress as he ran his hand down her face. Her skin no longer retained the softness that he had grown accustomed to. It was dry and stretched tight over her high cheekbones.

He stood up, backed away from his bride, and stared at her…Kafka's creation. Kafka's soldier. His mind began to engage in mental gymnastics, rationalizing the tragedy before him.

Marina always stood on the sidelines, watching her husband come and go and work silently in the kitchen. She never knew the exact nature of his work, only that it was going to bring down the infidels, the Western oppressors. Now she was a part of his work…an integral part of it as a matter of fact.

His twisted reverie was interrupted by Luka's sudden awareness of the pungent smell of blood and bile. His expression soured. He never viewed his wife as an equal. He had felt that contempt that men from his culture had for women, but now he felt revulsion at the sight of her beyond misogyny. It was more basic. More primal.

"I must leave you now, Marina. Please stay in the apartment. I will come back for you."

She grunted randomly, but he took it as a response and smiled warmly, seeing the woman he married. He leaned over and kissed her head and she grimaced. Then he left the bedroom.

She sat there alone on their marriage bed staring into oblivion as she heard the front door close and the digi-lock engage.

She was alone again.

***

20:03 HRS

Elicia nearly jumped out of her skin when there was a knock at her dorm room door. She had been staring at her blank computer monitor for God knows how long. For some reason, she had been afraid to turn it on. Ever since her Lit class, she felt uneasy.

She stood up and cracked her back. "Who is it?" she called through the door.

"It's your roommate, stupid," said a voice on the other side of the door.

Elicia's face lit up. She strode over to the door and opened it. "Darcy, what are you doing here?"

"Good to see you too, bitch." Darcy stood in the hallway wearing a wry smile, her trademark smile that stopped traffic and made all the boys (and even a few girls) come running.

"I mean I thought you were home for the summer."

Darcy shrugged. "I got bored."

Elicia turned around and walked back toward her powered off computer. "I didn't think you were ever capable of being bored."

When she turned back around, she was puzzled to see that Darcy was still standing in the doorway looking pale in the fluorescent lighting of the hallway. "What are you doing standing in the hallway? Come in already."

Darcy smiled mischievously, "Don't mind if I do." She stepped into the dorm room as if she were crossing some invisible barrier.

"So really, what are you doing here?"

"I came to take you up on my offer to go out."

Elicia rolled her eyes and tipped her head back in an exaggerated gesture of exasperation. "Oh, that."

"Now you promised me at the end of the spring semester, and then you chickened out. You have no excuses this time. It's summer, and you only have one class to worry about, and it's a total bullshit class, so I don't want to hear it."

"Do I have to?" Elicia groaned.

"Yes, you do. You have no choice in the matter whatsoever," Darcy declared.

"And if I refuse?"

"Well then, we'll just have to kidnap you."

"We? Who's we?"

"Oh, I almost forgot," teased Darcy with her trademark smile. "I have a surprise for you," she sang.

"What surprise?"

Matt Brauer stepped into the doorway, the lighting giving him a pale appearance too. Elicia felt her skin go cold. "What's he doing here?"

Darcy stood next to Elicia, placing her arm around her. Her grip was strong, and there was a weird clicking sound. It was coming from...

"Now, Elicia, there's no reason to be rude to the guy you've been crushing on all year."

Elicia felt her face flush. "Darcy! Jesus Christ!"

"Hi, Elicia," said Matt from the doorway.

"Come in, Matt. We're all friends here. I mean, Elicia invited *me* in."

"Groovy," said Matt, and then he too stepped into the room.

Elicia felt ambushed. After their interaction in the computer lab, Elicia had written him off. Or at least she had convinced herself she had. Her thoughts began to race. Maybe it hadn't gone as badly as she remembered. Maybe she had misinterpreted his reaction. Maybe he was playing hard to get. She was always terrible at reading people.

"Relax, I'm here, aren't I?" he said as if reading her mind.

This startled her even more, and she looked into Darcy's eyes for guidance. Darcy's eyes put her at ease, and the weird clicking sound began to fade away. Darcy would never hurt her. She knew that. This had to be right.

Yet somewhere a voice screaming in the back of her mind told her that it wasn't right. That nothing was right about this scenario. However, as she looked into Darcy's big, blue eyes that voice, too, faded away until it was forgotten.

"But the computer lab…I-I—"

"I was taken by surprise," said Matt, shrugging his shoulders sheepishly. Damn he was cute. "I didn't know how to react. You see, I *have* been secretly crushing on you all this time. I had no idea you felt the same."

Darcy licked her lips as she saw Matt drown Elicia in the depths of his black eyes, his fangs protruding from underneath his lip.

Elicia gazed languorously at her crush and shook her head in disbelief. This was like a dream. It was all too good to be true…and happening so quickly.

"See," whispered Darcy in her left ear, "you don't give yourself enough credit. You're way prettier than your sister."

She was careful not to let the tips of her fangs brush Elicia's ear, but in Elicia's state, it probably wouldn't have been noticed. The darkness in Darcy's eyes swirled like whirlpools of oil.

Elicia looked at Darcy, who still looked pale, and noticed two bite marks on her neck. Darcy read her mind. "Oh, these damn mosquitos. I hate bugs."

That voice in the back of her mind was screaming again, refusing to be drowned out. It was a primal scream…a scream for self-preservation.

"Why don't you say we all go out and have some fun, just the three of us," said Darcy, squeezing Elicia harder. "It'll be a blast. You and Matt can get to know each other."

Matt smiled, and Elicia was immediately lost in his dimples. "I'd really like that, Elicia."

He held his hand out to her. She hesitated. The voice in her head began to fade as she took notice of that strange clicking sound, like cicadas…in her dorm room.

But it was too early for cicadas…

She took Matt's hand and he and Darcy whisked her out of the room on the fuzzy wings of a summer night's dream.

***

21:10 HRS

Peter stood outside of Frisky's on a line snaking out the front door like a serpent. There were bouncers at the front entrance and what looked like a metal detector.

Shit. He had to ditch the gun he had strapped to his ankle under his jeans, and inconspicuously. What was Frisky's doing with a metal detector? This was Texas for Chrissake!

He waited until the line took him by some parked cars in the gravel parking lot. "Gotta take a leak," he said casually to the guy behind him, who didn't seem to give a rat's ass one way or the other.

He stepped off the line for a moment, stepped in between two cars, and unzipped his fly. He glanced over his shoulder to find a couple of guys behind him on line glancing at him and then quickly losing interest.

Fortunately, there was some urine in his bladder to void and he did so, his stream splashing lightly on the gravel. Then he zipped up, stepped away, knelt as if he was tying his shoelaces, he reached up his pant leg, and pulled out the handgun. He quickly threw it and the extra clips into the bushes and then made a mental note of where it all landed.

When he returned to his place in line, the man behind him backed up to make room. He nodded at the man, who in turn nodded back and quickly became disinterested again.

Great. Now if Carl actually were to show up, he wouldn't be able to blow his brains out. Peter remembered the last time they were in Frisky's together. That was when he met Yvette. Peter hoped Carl wasn't still sore about that.

He remembered Carl's way with the women in the bar, and afterwards his way with the cowboy antagonists and the bouncers. Peter was suddenly reminded of how strong and fast Carl was now, and the notion was sobering.

Peter didn't know what to expect. After all, Carl was still his little brother. There still appeared to be a part of Carl that cared about Peter and their father. Then again, ever since he started calling himself Kafka and looking less and less human, he became ruthless...diabolical even.

Finally, he reached the door and was asked to step through the metal detector by two really well muscled bouncers. They looked like mercenaries or paramilitary.

As he stepped into the scanner, he wondered how Carl planned on getting into the bar undetected. One thing was for sure. He wasn't coming in armed. However, since the bouncers were only looking for weapons, there was the possibility that Carl's other...attributes might go unnoticed.

The one bouncer nodded to Peter, and he stepped into the bar. Despite the amplified security, Frisky's was the same old shit dive bar it had always been—dark, smoky, lousy music and even lousier women.

It was crowded, particularly for a Thursday night. He saddled up to the bar and took in his surroundings. The clientele looked the same, but the staff looked different. However, Peter wasn't a regular these days, so he had no basis for such a claim.

But that wasn't it. Nope, something else was different about the staff. They looked like the bouncers at the front door. Now that he thought of it, all of them did from the bar maids down to the bus boys. And there were more of them than usual.

He saw Carl sitting alone in a booth on the far side of the dance floor. He knew it was Carl before he saw him. It was something he felt, and Carl must've felt it too because he nodded to Peter as their gazes met.

Peter crossed the dance floor, navigating past men with no rhythm and girls flailing their arms about, cigarette in hand. The glowing coal of the cigarette tips seemed to blur before his eyes in streaks of light as he felt each individual's heart beat like a drum.

As he approached the booth, he recognized Carl's lithe form and black as night face and wondered how the bouncers got past his appearance. Then he saw Carl wasn't alone. On the inside of the booth next to Carl sat Barry, their father.

"I see you had no trouble getting in," said Peter standing in front of the booth. Barry looked up, startled.

"Why don't you join us, Pete? Have a seat," said Kafka.

"Don't mind if I do," answered Peter wryly. He slid into the booth opposite Carl and his father. "If you don't mind me asking, Carl, how did you get into this place looking like a reject from Halloween? Your disguise is pretty piss poor, if you don't mind me saying so."

Kafka smiled, his four eyes blinking in unison. "C'mon, Pete. There's only one answer that makes sense. They knew I was coming."

So that was why there was a metal detector and staff that all looked like military. "Yet, you still came."

"Not only did they know," said Kafka slyly, "but I'm the one who tipped them off."

Peter took the bait. "Now why would you go ahead and do that?"

The barmaid walked over and was standing in front of the booth. "What can I get you?"

"A Jameson's and a Heineken chaser."

The barmaid nodded and was off back across the dance floor.

"Still drinking the same thing, I see. A real creature of habit," Kafka smirked.

"If I were you, I wouldn't be calling other people creatures. Anyway, I thought to myself 'why would you do something like that?'" Peter persisted.

"Now, boys," Barry interjected. "There's no need to start fighting. Pete, your brother came in peace."

"Did he now?" Peter never took his eyes off his brother. "You shouldn't have come, Dad. This is between me and Carl."

"There's no need to snap at Dad, Pete. I actually invited him. He's my insurance that you'll behave."

Barry smiled and nodded at this, interpreting it as a statement about his role as peacekeeper between the two boys. Peter saw it for the threat that it was. Barry was Kafka's hostage.

"I do come in peace. Take me to your leader," he said in a mock alien voice. Then his expression became serious. "If I wanted you dead, Pete, you'd be splattered across the wall already and you wouldn't have known what hit you."

"You never answered my question, Carl."

"I wanted them to know I was coming because there was no point in hiding it. I am not here for them."

"So then, what are you here for, Carl?"

"Why for you, of course." As Peter pondered the meaning of this affirmation, Kafka continued. "Have you seen your doppelgänger yet?"

"We've met."

The barmaid was back with Peter's whisky and beer. She placed them on the table. "Settle now or run a tab?"

"Run a tab," Peter answered, never taking his eyes off Carl.

Her heart beat quickened a bit as she shot a glance at Kafka. Peter felt it, and he was sure Carl did too. Something was up. She walked away.

"Well, Pete, what shall we toast to?"

"To family reunions," Peter responded sarcastically.

Kafka picked up his glass, Barry did the same, and all three men clinked their glasses together. Peter downed his whiskey and took a large gulp of his beer. Kafka downed his entire pint of what looked like a dark ale in a few hungry gulps and then took Barry's beer. He down Barry's beer in quick order as Barry sat there stunned.

Kafka took his last swallow and smacked his lips together in satisfaction.

"You've become quite the heavy weight," said Peter.

"One of the many benefits of being an evolved being," said Kafka. "You haven't let him in. Why?"

"I don't know what you're talking about," said Peter taking another gulp of his cold beer.

"Your doppelgänger. You obviously haven't let him in. If you did, you'd be...different."

Barry just sat there quietly watching the exchange between his two sons, struggling to understand what the hell they were talking about.

"Different how? Like you?"

"Carl's really not a villain," Barry jumped in. "There's just been a big misunderstanding."

"Dad," said Peter tersely, "stay out of this."

"Why, when he's very much a part of this?" taunted Kafka.

"Yeah, he's a real saint," said Peter bitterly through gritted teeth. "The Automaton, national hero. Or am I talking to the mighty Kafka, notorious terrorist, now? I get real confused sometimes."

"Saint or sinner," said Kafka. "Why choose? Why can't we be both from time to time?"

"Too bad the public doesn't know you are one in the same."

"Well, you saw to that yourself, Pete, when you played the Automaton in Italy. When you turned the undead on all of those helpless people."

"That was some trick, little brother."

"Oh, you ain't seen nothing yet, big brother."

"Why do I believe you?"

"Because you know what you're up against."

"Do I?"

"Why fight me, Pete? You know you can't win. Join me. You and Dad. There's going to be a changing of the guard around here, and believe me, you don't want to get caught on the wrong side."

"You've pretty much drafted me."

"Pete, the army threw you out. You thought you were being a good soldier, serving your country like a true blue-blooded patriot, but as soon as they thought you might be dangerous, they tossed you out on your ass."

"Maybe I am dangerous, Carl."

"Oh, no doubt, you're a killer, and pretty soon you'll be in good company. But I didn't want you or Dad to become like the drones, mindless undead with no soul. I wanted better for the two of you."

"You sold your soul to E.T., Carl. Look at you. You look like a frickin' insect. You've got four eyes. This is better?"

"Flattery will get you nowhere, Pete."

"Carl, whatever is coming, we can fight it together. We've done it before. We can do it again." Barry looked at Kafka with hope at Peter's words. He just wanted everyone to get along. They were the only family he had left.

"There's no fighting this, Pete. When they arrive in numbers, there will be no defense. It will be a war of attrition. Whoever will survive the first wave will eventually be turned. They won't stop until the human race is eradicated or converted."

"And what about OIL?" asked Peter. "They're okay with all of this?"

"They are used to the notion of global jihad. The scale just got bigger."

"Now they have to submit to a violent power, who believes in their own superiority, or face death," said Peter. "Ironic."

"You might say the whole situation possesses a certain poetic justice," said Kafka waving his clawed hand in the air loftily as he spoke.

Peter leaned forward in the booth. "You of all people should understand the importance of not submitting. Our mother was taken from us by people like this. It's why you enlisted to begin with."

"And those very people will be consumed or converted by the next dominant race," answered Kafka. "They will pay for their actions."

"So that's your big plan for revenge. Sell out the entire planet? What about those sworn to bring terrorists to justice?"

"Oh, you mean like the ones who put a kill chip in my head and then tried to use it on the remote possibility that I'd be dangerous? The terrorists, the generals, the politicians, they all have one thing in common."

"What's that?"

"They're all human."

Peter sat back in exasperation. "So that's that then? You've written off the entire human race?"

"Look at us, Pete. Half the planet is at war, poverty is widespread. We were supposed to be the greatest superpower in the world. The

United States of America. Almost a third of our population is unemployed, the rest underemployed, we have a government that no longer functions, the air is becoming toxic—not from pollution but from unchecked levels of pollen. We are in a decline. We have been for quite some time. We are the dinosaurs, and the meteor is about to strike the earth."

"You keep saying 'us,' Carl. You haven't fully committed to the aliens."

Kafka's heartbeat quickened almost imperceptibly. "Pipe dreams, Pete. You are desperate to find humanity in me yet. You're barking up the wrong tree."

"What happens if your aliens succeed in their invasion? What happens to you after you've served your purpose?"

"I will hold a prominent position in a new world order. For shit's sake, Pete, I dropped out of college because Dad could no longer afford it. The army threw me out.

"These 'aliens' have been trying to take route in our culture for ages, planting technology to aid their cause. Hell, they *are* us. Humanity has been too stupid and superstitious to develop the gifts. Thanks to me, they will finally gain a foothold on our civilization. It'll be nice to be something important."

"I had no idea the mighty Kafka had such a fragile ego. These aliens must be a real high maintenance bunch."

"They're not so bad. How do you think the damn pyramids were built? When there was a figure like me selected to lead, he was buried alive as part of superstition. They hold the key to untold technology. They are so much more advanced. RGT is only the beginning. We've only but scratched the surface."

"And the price of admission is conversion."

"It's worth the cost, believe me."

"Believe you...how can I? Look at you. You said so yourself that everyone's going to become mindless zombies. How is that worth the price? What, because you have an elevated position it makes it all okay?"

Karl sucked his teeth. "You make me sound like some communist who starves his people so he can live well. This is evolution."

"Somehow I don't think Darwin would agree. It feels more like colonization."

"Pete, you can't resist your doppelgänger forever."

"I've done a good job of it so far. Don't jinx me."

"You will join us, Pete. You'll see it's the only way. The alternative is...unpalatable."

"Maybe you should listen to him, Pete," pleaded Barry. "The world is a scary place. I don't know if I want to see nature take its course. Maybe it's better this way."

"Well, I'm not ready to give up on this planet just yet," said Peter defiantly. "It's a screwed up world, but it's *our* world. It's our responsibility to fix it, not hand it over to a hostile power. Jesus, I remember when our biggest problems were radical Muslims and anarchists. We never handed the world over to them."

"This is better," insisted Kafka.

"Really? Because it sounds like the same rhetoric to me. Jihad is jihad."

Kafka sat back in his seat and put his palms flat on the table. "Did it ever occur to you that this is nature taking its course?"

"Part of evolution."

"Look at me, Pete. I'm stronger, faster, and smarter."

"You were always smarter."

"You've got to be feeling it, too. You have to be."

Peter was feeling it, and it felt good. However, thanks to the antidote serum that Betancourt administered to him, he knew he was never going to be as strong or as fast as Carl was. Besides, Carl's offer of power was more frightening than enticing.

"Remember the drones in Xcaret, Carl? Remember how they ate everyone alive? Is that what you want to align yourself with?"

Kafka smiled in resignation. "You can't make an omelet without breaking some eggs."

Peter suddenly looked around the room. He felt a change in the ambient rhythms, an overall quickening.

"Speaking of which, you notice how the barmaid never came back over?"

Chapter 8

"They are about to make their move," stated Kafka coolly.

"Who is?" asked Peter.

"Your old army buddies."

"Shouldn't you run?" asked Barry panicked.

"No need. They will hand me my means of escape."

Peter and Barry didn't have time to ponder Kafka's cryptic statement. The staff of Frisky's began to swing into action.

They came from every corner of the bar with assault rifles trained on Kafka. The patrons who were indeed patrons were escorted off to the other side of the bar.

Betancourt came out of a room behind the bar with Lt. Farrow holding some kind of machine. "I want the civilians escorted out of the bar immediately."

"Yes, sir," said one of the soldiers and made it happen.

Betancourt strode up to the booth. Peter and Barry had their hands up. He addressed Kafka. "How did you plan on getting out of here?"

"Nice to see you, too, Colonel Betancourt."

"What is your exit strategy?"

"Pardon?"

"Don't play games with me, Kafka. We all know you just wouldn't waltz into a public place and leave yourself exposed."

"Maybe I'm hiding in plain sight," Kafka taunted.

"Exit strategy," Betancourt insisted. "What is it?"

Kafka snickered. "I'm going to walk out of here on my own two legs, and you're going to help me."

"No more games, Kafka. If you won't tell us, then we'll extract it out of you."

"I'm counting on it."

Peter didn't like any of this. It was all too easy, and he saw Betancourt was struggling with that fact, too.

"Colonel…"

"Stay out of this, sir," Betancourt replied, addressing Peter as a civilian. "We'll have you out of this soon."

Sir? This son of a bitch just waltzed into a trap, and when Peter was trying to alert him to the fact, he's treated like a civilian?

Peter realized that this wasn't just about a family reunion. Kafka had the army thinking they were using Peter as bait, but in reality, Kafka had used Peter as bait.

"What are you doing?" Peter asked Kafka.

"Cleaning house," replied Kafka.

Betancourt gestured for Lt. Farrow to bring over the apparatus he was holding. Farrow held what looked like a tiara in one hand and some kind of a computer tower in the other.

"So, I see now the army has a portable RGT apparatus," Kafka said to Betancourt. Then to Peter, "They are going to extract my memories to ascertain what my strategy is."

"If you move a muscle, I'll blow your brains all over the wall," threatened Betancourt.

"Kill him," insisted Peter. "Do it now."

Kafka grinned defiantly. "He can't, Pete. He has orders to bring me in alive."

"Let your brother and father go," ordered Betancourt.

Kafka put out his hands, palms facing upward. "I was never holding them, Colonel."

Betancourt nodded and Peter slid out of the booth. Kafka slid out and stood up in one swift motion allowing Barry to slide out. The soldiers inched in, targeting Kafka's head with their assault rifles.

"Easy," said Betancourt to Kafka. "Nice and easy."

Kafka shrugged sheepishly as Peter and Barry backed away across the dance floor.

"Go ahead," said Betancourt to Farrow, who stepped forward.

"Put this on," said Farrow nervously handing Kafka the tiara.

"But of course, Lieutenant," said Kafka, blinking all four eyes sincerely, as he placed the tiara on his oily head.

Betancourt nodded and Farrow began to turn dials and switches on the tower.

"Come with me," Kafka beckoned across the bar to Peter. "This may be your last chance. Dad's blood will be on your hands."

"Shit," whispered Peter to Barry. "He's up to something, but I don't know what."

"Why don't they just give him a chance to explain everything?" whispered Barry desperately, eyes wide watching his youngest son across the bar.

Peter shook his head. His father was lost. Something was about to happen, but for the life of him Peter didn't know what.

Lights turned on and the tower began to hum as Kafka's expression went blank. The televisions over the bar began to flicker in some kind of strange pattern of static. Cell phones chimed outside the bar in tune with the multi-taskers on each of the soldiers. After a brief moment, Peter felt the heart beats of the bar patrons outside disappear.

That was when the screaming began.

One soldier in the back looked at the flickering televisions over the bar and froze, mesmerized at the screen.

"Hold your positions," Betancourt commanded.

Farrow looked down at his chiming multi-tasker hanging from his belt.

"What is it?" asked a soldier in the back standing next to the one who was in a trance.

The mesmerized soldier looked up with milky eyes and snarled at the other soldier, as his eyes went wide.

"Jesus!"

Betancourt whirled around in time to see the newly undead soldier tearing flesh out of the other soldier's neck with his teeth and the undead patrons from outside flooding into the bar.

Peter grabbed his father by the arm and tried to pull him further into the bar, but Barry didn't move. He stood there, mesmerized by the televisions.

"Dad, we have to go...Dad?"

Peter let go as his father turned and lunged for him, snapping his jaws like a turtle. Peter shoved him away, but Barry came at him again. Peter restrained him by the wrists, holding him away at arm's length as Barry savagely snapped at him.

"Jesus, Dad," was all he could manage. He sidestepped his father, letting him fall forward under his own momentum. Barry hit the dance floor face first, and Peter stepped away, horrified.

"Don't look at the televisions," shouted Betancourt, but he was too late. He had already lost his men to the televisions or the sudden zombie ambush.

Farrow looked like he almost glanced at the televisions, but he turned his head away. Peter looked. At first he saw a pattern of lines and static, but after a moment he saw eyes looking out at him...into him.

Memories that didn't belong to him began to flood his consciousness again. The peculiar thing was it didn't feel like the memories were intrusions. They felt like they were already a part of him and were being unearthed.

"Farrow," said Betancourt pointing to Kafka, "cover him. The rest of you fire at will!"

Farrow drew his sidearm and trained it on Kafka, his hand trembling.

Another patron rounded the group and came at Peter, but Peter front kicked him, sending him flying backward into two undead girls.

Kafka's zombies were making quick work of the unturned soldiers. This was not the Infantry Drone Program. None of these soldiers had any experience with the undead and didn't even know what they were dealing with. To them, these were civilians who for some reason became aggressive.

Their lack of experience and ignorance caused them to be easily overrun, firing wildly into the crowd and only landing the occasional head shot by accident.

Peter kicked a zombie in the face and snatched up an assault rifle from a fallen man. "Aim for their heads! Head shots only!" He began popping the melons of the nearest undead patrons.

But it was too late. Most of Betancourt's unit was dead, and those that weren't were being ravenously eaten alive on the floor of the bar.

Peter ran over to Betancourt, who trained his gun on him.

"We have to get out of here!" Peter shouted at Betancourt over the screams.

Betancourt whirled around to look at Kafka only to find Farrow on the floor. Kafka was choking another soldier.

"Forget about Kafka!" shouted Peter. "We have to go!"

Farrow got up and stumbled toward the back entrance. Peter laid down some cover fire across the bar as Betancourt ran, but Kafka caught him by the arm in a fierce grip.

He pulled him close. "And where do you think you're going, Colonel?"

Peter turned and fired into Kafka's chest and neck, sending him flying backwards into the booth. Kafka held onto Betancourt, taking him with him.

Betancourt reached down for the knife in his boot. Peter saw this and continued to lay down cover fire taking down the now reanimating soldiers.

Betancourt stabbed Kafka in his right wrist, the knife burying itself in the wooden table. Kafka hissed at him as he turned the knife, causing him to release his grip.

Betancourt stood, pulled his side arm, and shot Kafka repeatedly in the face. Farrow was holding the rear entrance door open. "Come on! Come on!"

Peter grabbed Betancourt by the arm and pulled him towards the back door. All three men spilled out of the bar into the summer night air.

"Do you have a car?" Peter asked Betancourt.

"Right there," said Betancourt pointing at a sedan.

They ran toward the car when Peter felt a quickening in the distance followed by gunfire whizzing past them. Lt. Farrow went down.

Peter saw the flashes of a muzzle in the dark. There was a man by a white van firing at them. Peter grabbed Farrow as Betancourt laid down cover fire. He dragged Farrow and they all took cover next to the dumpster out back as the mystery man began to make Swiss cheese out of their ride.

"Farrow's bleeding badly," said Peter frantically.

"A copter is coming for extraction," said Betancourt. "Any minute now. We never planned on taking Kafka out by car."

A few zombies stumbled out the back door and into the gunfire. One took a headshot and dropped to the ground. The other two followed the sounds of the nearest guns around the dumpster.

They reached out for Peter and Farrow, snarling. A young girl in her early twenties, dressed in a short skirt and tight halter-top with wild eyes, almost bit Peter on the arm, but he whirled around and shot it in the face point blank. It dropped to the ground in front of Farrow.

The second one, an older male in his early thirties, stumbled over the now inert body of the girl, landing on top of Farrow. It grabbed Peter's leg and tried to sink teeth in. Peter's weapon jammed, so he rammed the barrel down into its mouth and it bit down.

"I don't think that air support is coming," he said to Betancourt.

"It should have been here," said Betancourt between bursts of gunfire.

Suddenly, they heard the Black Hawk approaching. It saw the gunman by the van and began to lay down cover fire, hurling bolts of light through the darkness.

"The cavalry's here," shouted Betancourt.

The helicopter slowly approached the rear of the building, tracking Betancourt's mini-com multi-tasker. Right behind it there was a small, fast-moving shadow streaking across the night sky and closing in fast.

"What's that?" asked Peter.

The small craft fired off a hellfire missile that collided with the Black Hawk, blowing it right out of the sky in a bright ball of orange fire.

"I-I don't understand," gasped Betancourt, flabbergasted.

Peter grabbed his shoulder. "We can't stay here. If the zombies don't get us, Kafka will."

"I don't think Kafka's going anywhere. I shot him point blank in the face several times."

"Hurt, but not dead," said Peter. "I can feel him. We need to get the hell out of Dodge."

"We're pinned. What do you have in mind?"

"Cover me and keep the zombies off of Farrow," shouted Peter. "I'll take that gunman out. Try not to hit the van. We're going to take it."

Betancourt nodded and shot at and around the gunman in the distance, trying not to damage the white van.

Farooq cursed himself for only lighting up one of the soldiers trying to escape. He hoped it was the Betancourt that was Kafka's target tonight. He had the other two pinned behind a dumpster.

He saw zombies spill out the back of the bar. He hoped that if he could keep them pinned long enough, the zombies or Kafka would finish them off.

He saw one of the soldiers move from behind the dumpster. Maybe it wasn't a soldier, but he moved fast. He zigzagged back and forth in a blur, gradually making his way up the hill towards Farooq's position while the other soldier was laying down cover fire.

Farooq shot at the fast, zigzagging man, trying to lead the target, but he was too fast. He heard bullets fly over his head from the soldier behind the dumpster. Where was Kafka?

Betancourt ran out of ammo and slammed in a backup clip as another zombie came around the dumpster. Farrow was on the ground writhing and convulsing. Fortunately, the mystery gunman was preoccupied with Peter.

Betancourt aimed just as the zombie opened her mouth over the barrel. Standing over Farrow, he blew her brains out the back of her head and then focused back on the gunman.

He didn't believe what he saw.

Peter was just walking right up the hill towards the gunman, slowly, like he was out for a stroll. The gunman was firing wildly to the right and left, but no one was there. Betancourt thought Peter was crazy just waltzing up the middle, but the gunman didn't even seem to notice him.

Farooq was now panicking as the zigzagging blur made its way up the hill. He looked to his left and saw his doppelgänger. It showed its sharp, crooked fangs as it gestured with gnarled claws. *He's coming to get you, and he's getting closer. He's coming up the middle.*

Farooq looked but saw nothing. It was impossible. The man was all over the place, first left, then right. *It's a trick. He's right in front of you.*

But poor Farooq didn't have time to react. Peter raised his rifle and, aiming high so as not to seriously damage the van, popped his head right off his shoulders. As Farooq dropped, he left a stain on the side of the white van.

Peter waived Betancourt over. He opened the driver side door and slid in. He turned on the lights and was relieved to see the gunman's cell phone on the passenger seat. He toggled to the car app and activated the ignition. The van's engine turned over.

Betancourt saw Peter walk right up to the man and shoot him in the head, but he didn't have time to make sense of what he just saw. More zombies were barreling out the back door of the bar and Farrow was lying at his feet completely still.

Poor bastard.

Betancourt ran up the hill as the undead bar patrons followed closely behind. He felt fingers scratching at his back as he jogged up the hill, thankful that he kept up his daily cardiovascular regimen.

"Come on!" shouted Peter out the driver side window of the van.

Betancourt rounded the front as the pursing patrons came at Peter, who raised his window just in time. As they smeared blood and bile on Peter's window, Betancourt jumped in the passenger side. "Punch it."

Peter hit the gas as a zombie shattered the driver side window and the van lurched forward, pulling a couple of clinging zombies with them. Peter picked up speed and swerved sharply, shaking off the hangers on.

He saw them get up in the rear view mirror and run after the van, but they disappeared in the darkness as Peter put distance between them.

"Farrow?"

"He didn't make it."

"The zombies?"

"No, his wounds."

Peter pounded the steering wheel in frustration. He liked Farrow. "He was a good man."

"Yes, he was."

There was a brief moment of silence as the two men listened to the sound of the van's engine.

"We are going to come up upon one of the roadblocks," said Betancourt. "When we do, let me handle it. You are in civilian clothing. They won't know who you are. I have ID."

"Okay."

"How did you pull off that trick back there on the hill?"

"What trick?" But Peter knew what Betancourt was referring to.

"You just walked up the hill, right down the middle of the firing corridor, and shot him in the head."

"I lead him to believe I was elsewhere."

"Yeah, I saw him firing on either side of him. You have to teach me that trick some time."

"I'm not even sure how I did it."

"How's the serum working?" asked Betancourt, changing the subject.

"I've gone through some changes that I don't fully understand, but so far I'm not turning into my brother."

Betancourt smiled pensively. "Good. Hopefully you never do." He felt the tension between them. "You know, I never meant for things to happen this way to your brother and you."

Peter looked ahead at the road, but his expression was bitter. "Well, you know what they say about the road to hell being paved with good intentions."

"I didn't agree with General Ramses' handling of either of you."

"Speaking of which," said Peter now changing the subject, "who gave you the portable RGT apparatus?"

"Ramses."

"And who put this operation together?"

"Ramses. He set this whole thing up. He's been waiting to take me out ever since I slipped you the serum."

"You had to know that wasn't going to go over well," needled Peter.

"It was a test. I wanted to know where he stood."

"Well, now you know. What I want to know is how he ordered an aerial drone to fire on the Black Hawk," said Peter.

"He couldn't have. There's safety protocols."

"Could he override them?"

"I don't think so," said Betancourt.

"Where are we going?"

"To pay General Ramses a visit. I have a few questions for him."

Kafka stepped out the back of the bar into the night air holding his mangled face. He looked around at the dead bodies of the bar patrons and then up at the top of the hill. He slowly climbed the hill and came upon Farooq's body.

"I should have turned you sooner. You might have survived this," he said to no one in particular, but he knew it differed by the individual. Although there were general principles, no two infections went the same. Farooq was not one of his stronger agents.

He walked back down the hill and stepped back into the bar. He looked at all of the dead bodies lying on the dance floor. There were a few undead patrons and resurrected soldiers milling around with bloody mouths.

Kafka stepped into the men's room and leaned on both palms on the sink in front of the dirty mirror. As he took in his damaged face, he smiled as he was struck by the memory of meeting Yvette in this very bathroom. That woman had altered the course of his life forever on that fateful night.

Reluctantly pulling himself out of that reverie, he braced himself for what he must do. He hadn't much time before the authorities would storm the bar. He saw his outer right eye was ruined, and he traced the wounds on his face with a lithe finger.

He traced the edge of a wound and began to dig his long nail into it. When he slipped his nail underneath, wincing, he began to pull. He slowly peeled the skin off the wound, and then off his face.

He hissed in pain as he peeled large pieces of his face off, throwing the bloodied black shards into the sink. He was like a horror movie actor pulling latex prostheses off after the wrapping of a scene.

When he was finished, he turned on the faucet and splashed his face with warm water. When he looked at himself again in the filthy mirror, he face looked brand new.

Peter slowed down as the roadblock came into view. Betancourt produced his mini-com multi-tasker. "This is Colonel Betancourt, coming up on the roadblock in a white van. Acknowledge."

"We see you, Colonel."

"Police?" asked Peter.

"And National Guard."

"Approach slowly, sir."

The officers and national guardsmen came into view. They had their weapons trained on the van.

"Stop here," instructed Betancourt.

Peter stopped the van and put it in park. The sheriff walked cautiously up to the van, his hand resting on his gun. His face was tense, and when he saw Peter behind the wheel, he drew his gun.

Peter lowered the window as he approached and put his hands on the steering wheel.

"Who in the hell are you?" demanded the sheriff, addressing Peter.

"He's with me," said Betancourt, leaning over Peter.

The sheriff relaxed and holstered his weapon. "Sorry, sir. We can't be too careful."

"Understood, Sheriff," said Betancourt casually. "There was a mess at the bar. My unit was killed."

"Sir."

"I want a tight perimeter formed around the bar. But no one enters until I send over a special unit. Is that clear?"

"Sir?"

"Call in Hazmat. There's been potential exposure to a chemical weapon. No one goes in until I send reinforcements. The bar is now quarantined. Anyone comes out and you shoot to kill."

The sheriff looked hesitant.

"Shoot to kill," insisted Betancourt, texting furiously on his multitasker. "I'll take full responsibility. Do you understand?"

"Y-yes, sir."

"Good. Now get moving and let us through. We have to report back to Fort Bliss."

"Yes, sir."

The sheriff ordered the other officers to back their cars off the road, and Betancourt nodded to Peter. Peter activated the car and slowly drove through the roadblock. When they were through and down the road, Betancourt broke the silence.

"I hope they follow my orders and wait for backup. They're not prepared for what's inside that bar."

"What if what's inside that bar comes out to them?"

"As long as they follow my orders they should be okay."

"And what about Kafka?"

"He's long gone by now."

"How would he get through the roadblocks?"

"I don't know, but I know he's slipped through our fingers before. He's too prepared. He's been one step ahead of us the whole way."

His multi-tasker flashed a message. Betancourt frowned as he read it.

"What is it?" Peter asked fearing he already knew the answer.

"The roadblock on Eagle Ford Road is no longer responding to dispatch."

"Kafka."

"He probably used his portable RGT to turn them. They have television monitors in the black-and-whites."

"I don't get it," said Peter. "You have to be bitten by the undead to be turned. None of those bar patrons were bitten. They just changed."

"I think it had something to do with their phones ringing and the televisions flickering," answered Betancourt. "Or at least that's what I saw with our men in the bar."

"You didn't look at the television?"

"Obviously not," replied Betancourt. "I had my eyes peeled on Kafka. Then I heard you shout not to look at the television."

"But how? It doesn't make any sense." Peter thought about those eyes he felt watching him through the television.

"Ramses let something slip about two-way communications embedded in the RGT. Apparently, he can transmit…something from that portable headset. That was why Ramses gave it to me. He said it was to extract Kafka's game plan from his memory so we could extract him safely."

"He never had any intention of you getting out of there alive," said Peter, finishing Betancourt's thought.

"It would appear not."

"So what's the plan? We can't just waltz into Fort Bliss guns blazing, coming for Ramses. By now, he's had to have heard you were coming."

"Generals are largely detached from missions. He usually waits to be briefed by me."

"But think about it, Colonel. If this was a set-up, he's going to want confirmation that you are dead. If Kafka is still out on the loose, he has probably found some way to get word back to Ramses. My guess is that Ramses will be expecting you."

"But not you," said Betancourt.

"So what's the plan?"

"Ramses is going to play it business as usual. He's not going to acknowledge that he set me up. Tonight is going to go down in the books as a mission that went wrong. He'll want to be briefed."

"What about me?"

"Remember that trick you pulled in back of the bar?"

"Yes."

"Do you think you can do it again?"

Chapter 9

Fort Bliss
Hangar 4
00:29 HRS

General Ramses entered the hangar looking at his watch.

"Where the hell were you?" asked Wolff testily as he scratched behind his ear. Darcy and Matt were giggling like demented school children.

"There's been a wrinkle. It appears Betancourt has escaped. In fact, he's on his way and should be here soon."

"What are you going to do?"

"He knows nothing of what we are doing here. I'll bring him to the hangar, and you and these two will be waiting for him."

"Goodie, goodie. A tasty treat," sang Darcy.

"First things first," reminded Wolff. "We have to find out what our little Seditious Blogger knows."

"Where is she?" asked Ramses.

"In the center of the Labyrinth strapped to a chair," said Wolff.

"Is the RGT in place and ready?" asked Ramses.

"Yes. I wanted you to be here for this."

"Well, I'm here, so let's get to it."

Darcy and Matt looked at the large, mazelike training structure in the center of the hangar in awe. A simulation of a structure with walls but no ceiling, the Labyrinth looked like a movie set with all of the lights and cameras mounted above it.

Ramses, Wolff, and crew entered the Labyrinth, Wolff leading the way. They entered a room where Elicia waited, blindfolded and strapped to a metal chair with a large RGT device sitting in front of her.

"I had to requisition a truck to bring it here," said Wolff regarding the RGT. "It took a couple of hours to set up."

"We could've, like, water boarded her or something," said Matt gleefully.

"Shut up," spat Ramses, failing to conceal his contempt for the younglings, if he was even trying. Matt and Darcy grinned defiantly at each other, licking their fangs.

"Who's there?" asked Elicia, her voice trembling.

"My name is General Ramses of the United States Army, and this is Assistant Director Wolff of the NSA. I believe you already know your two escorts."

"No names, General," said Wolff irritated.

"It doesn't matter now," snapped Ramses.

"Why am I here?" asked Elicia.

"You've been very active on your blog and podcast, Elicia. And very hard to find, may I add. I commend you on your elusiveness."

"Thanks," she said tentatively.

"What I want to know is why you've been telling people to drop off the grid. You've been talking about government surveillance technology, and frankly, I want to know what you know about it."

"I don't know anything, sir," answered Elicia quickly. "I'm just a college student. I did it...for fun. Everybody blogs about something these days," she said sheepishly.

Wolff smiled. "Oh, but you are so much more than a college student. Really, I expected Tronika to be a little less humble. So many of you 'hacktivists' crave recognition."

Elicia's mouth went dry as a bone. She found it difficult to swallow. She had been afraid this day would come.

"And for somebody who did it for fun, you garnered an awful lot of followers," said Wolff.

"She was very popular on campus," added Darcy. "Her blog and podcast, I mean."

Wolff glared at Darcy and she shut up.

"It was just for fun. Shits and giggles. You know," insisted Elicia.

"Then why did you suddenly stop?" asked Ramses.

"There were FBI agents combing the campus," answered Elicia truthfully. "I didn't want to get in trouble."

"You didn't want to get in trouble," repeated Wolff thoughtfully. "Why? If it was...just for fun, then you had nothing to worry about. Besides, you've garnered access to major agency systems: the CDC, FBI, CIA. You're telling me that, in all of your hacker exploits, you never came across any sensitive information. Recently, you started preaching about Retinal Gateway Technology. No one outside the NSA or military knows about it. Not even everyone on the inside is privy to it. No, you must be hiding something."

She had never used that term—Retinal Gateway Technology—per se.

"Please don't hurt me," she pleaded on the verge of tears. "I don't know anything. I swear."

"Oh, we're not going to hurt you...yet," said Ramses menacingly. "You see, being the cautious type, I'm not going to take your word for it. We're just going to extract your memories and see what in fact you do know. Then we'll hurt you."

Elicia shuddered and forced back a sob. "A-a-and how are you going to 'extract my memories'?"

"I assure you," said Wolff amused by her concern, "that will be the least painful part of tonight."

He grabbed the headset off of a small wooden table next to the large apparatus and placed it on Elicia's head, startling her. Tears streamed down her face and her nose ran.

"Don't worry, Dear," said Wolff softly, "you are being recruited into an elite group. I thought that's what you hackers lived for. It's a compliment, really." He pulled off her blindfold and made sure the headset lined up with her eyes.

"And what group is that?" stuttered Elicia.

"Shhh. Your questions will be answered soon enough."

Wolff walked over to the RGT console and began to flip switches and turn dials. Suddenly, images from Elicia's memory popped up on the monitor. Ramses stepped forward to get a closer look.

"Cool," gasped Darcy.

It took a while, but they sorted through all of the memories of Elicia's classes, her interactions with Darcy, the phone calls with her sister...the awkward exchange with Matt. Matt and Darcy tittered when that memory came on screen. Wolff shot them a dirty look.

They saw Elicia composing her blog and recording her podcasts. They saw her research on the internet regarding government surveillance technology, but no appearance of RGT.

Ramses stood there pinching the bridge of his nose deep in thought. After a while, he rubbed his eyes. "Enough."

"Are you sure?" asked Wolff.

"She doesn't know anything. She's just a paranoid college student who likes to hear the sound of her own voice."

Wolff turned the RGT device off. He walked over to Elicia and gently lifted the headset off her head and placed it back on the wooden table.

Elicia's vision was blurry from the RGT. As her eyesight cleared, she began to see her antagonists and the RGT apparatus take shape. She also noticed that she was in a room with no ceiling with bright lights shining down on her.

"I told you I didn't know anything," she whimpered.

"Well, that's been confirmed," said General Ramses.

"So what now?" asked Darcy.

"We turn her," said Ramses as if the answer was obvious. Darcy clapped her hands excitedly.

"Turn me into what?"

"You get to become just like me," announced Darcy triumphantly.

"What do you mean?" she asked Darcy. "What do you have to do with any of this?"

"Hey, Elicia, I'm just doin' my part, serving my country."

"You knew all along that I was Tronika?"

"Hell no," said Darcy. "These guys clued me in, but I'm real impressed, Elicia. I didn't think you had it in you. Who knew that my geeky little roommate was a secret badass?"

General Ramses' multi-tasker chimed. He took the call. "Yes...yes...I see...thank you. I'll be right there."

"Betancourt?" asked Wolff, already knowing the answer.

"Yes. You'd better come with me. He'll behave if he sees the both of us. We'll get him to come out here and we'll finish him off." Then Ramses addressed Darcy and Matt. "Now you two wait here with your friend and keep an eye on her. We'll be back shortly."

Darcy and Matt nodded like two obedient children.

"Don't touch anything. Nothing happens until we get back," Ramses ordered. "Do you understand?"

"Yes, sir," said Darcy insolently.

He glared at the two of them menacingly, as if to drive his point home, and then left the hangar with Wolff.

As soon as they were out of sight, Darcy turned excitedly to Matt. "Let's have some fun. This place is cool."

"You heard what the General said."

"It can't hurt to look around," she insisted. "Look at this setup. There's even a control tower overlooking the maze. Let's check it out."

Matt looked nervously at Elicia.

Darcy shoved him hard. "Oh, come on. She's not going anywhere."

"Why don't you guys let me go?" pleaded Elicia. "Darcy, I thought we were friends."

"No can do," said Darcy. "I wanna check this place out."

"Same old Darcy," said Elicia pensively. "Never a dull moment."

"Not if I can help it, bitch," replied Darcy smiling. "Your life is about to get more exciting, Elicia, when you turn."

"So I'm going to be like you?"

"It's glorious," sang Darcy. "I feel so sexy."

"Well, you always wanted me to be just like you. Now it looks like it's actually going to happen."

Darcy playfully flipped Elicia the bird and pulled Matt out of the room. Elicia was alone.

She immediately began to pull at her bindings, but she was secured with plastic ties like the police use. She looked around the room frantically for something she could use.

Peter waited outside the gated perimeter of Fort Bliss as he saw Betancourt pass the security checkpoint and drive the van into the base. Slinging the assault rifle on his shoulder, he ran along the perimeter fence towards the middle of the base. He crouched by the fence shrouded in the darkness and reached out into the fort like Carl told him he used to do.

He found it surprisingly easy. He could sense all of the mobile sentries roaming the grounds on patrol. He vaguely sensed Betancourt as he parked the van and entered the building where Ramses' office was.

Then he sensed two figures leaving Hangar Four. *The* Hangar Four. The Hangar Four that was supposed to be shut down along with the Infantry Drone Program. He recognized General Ramses but not the second figure. They were crossing the base to meet Betancourt.

This was interesting. What were they up to in Hangar Four? Peter had a choice. He could've either tracked the meeting with Betancourt and wait for his cue or he could've investigated what was in Hangar Four.

He figured that Betancourt would be safe for the moment in the Officers' Office Building. Ramses wouldn't dare attack him there. So Peter turned his attention to Hangar Four.

He continued along the perimeter fence until he was in line with Hangar Four. It looked quiet from the outside, but when he reached out, he sensed activity inside.

Interesting.

Betancourt was waiting in Ramses' office when he entered with Wolff.

"Colonel, I didn't expect to see you back so soon. Where's your team?" He saw Betancourt looking uncertainly at Wolff. "Oh, yes, Colonel, you know Assistant Director Wolff of the NSA."

Wolff extended his hand, and Betancourt shook it.

"There's a problem," said Betancourt. "The mission was unsuccessful." He was reluctant so say anything further, wondering what the Assistant Director of the NSA was doing at Fort Bliss with General Ramses.

"You can speak freely in front of Assistant Director Wolff. He's tracking Kafka with us. How do you think we intercepted his message?"

"My team has been wiped out. Kafka has escaped."

"But I gave you the portable RGT that Assistant Director Wolff provided us. Didn't you ascertain Kafka's escape plan?"

"We didn't get the chance, sir. When we used the device, something happened."

"What happened, Colonel?" asked Wolff.

"It triggered some kind of communication through media that somehow turned the bar patrons and one of my soldiers into the undead."

"That's ridiculous," said Wolff. "What would be the mechanism for such a thing?"

"It appeared that Kafka communicated back through the RGT, like he was transmitting."

"Two-way communication?" asked Wolff. "That's impossible. We've no detection of two-way communication across the broadband."

Ramses looked at Wolff nervously and quickly changed the subject. "So what happened to the team, Colonel?"

Betancourt raised an eyebrow. "Assistant Director Wolff, General Ramses had informed me that you picked up two-way communication through the broadband. In fact, that's exactly how you detected Kafka's message to his brother. Hidden in plain sight. Remember, General?"

Wolff looked a little flummoxed at his error, but quickly recovered. "Well, yes. That was how we found Kafka's message, but I wouldn't think he could transmit a signal turning people into the undead."

"Yes," said Ramses smiling uncomfortably, "we'll have to launch a full investigation into it. But first, Colonel, we want you to come with us. Here's something of vital importance that we have to show you."

Betancourt tilted his head quizzically. "Sir, don't you want to be debriefed about the mission? Don't you want to know the details of what happened?"

"Why, yes, of course. You can fill me in on the way."

"With all due respect, sir, the details are of a sensitive nature and should be discussed in a secure location."

"Where we're going, it's secure."

"Sir, I feel you need to hear the details right away because Kafka is at large with his new trick and time is of the essence."

"Assistant Director Wolff, would you please excuse us. We'll meet you at Hangar Four."

"Hangar Four?" asked Betancourt. "Wasn't it shut down with the Infantry Drone Program?"

"One thing at a time, Colonel Betancourt," said Ramses with a reprimanding tone. "First, you fill me in on the details. The other thing can wait." He nodded to Wolff, who then excused himself from the office.

"Please begin with your report, Colonel."

"Whoa! Look at this equipment," said Darcy like a kid in a candy store. "I wonder what all of these buttons do."

She pressed one, turning on the cameras. The whole Labyrinth popped up on a bunch of monitors. One monitor displayed it in its entirety while, others zoomed in on specific rooms. The fourth monitor showed Elicia hopping in her chair, moving it toward the RGT console.

"Look there's a microphone," Matt pointed out.

Darcy grabbed it and pressed the switch next to it. "Now, now, Elicia. You stay put like a good little soldier." Her voice bellowed out over the maze.

Elicia froze and looked up around her at the sound. She apparently saw the control tower, and Darcy and Matt chuckled as she looked right into one of the cameras.

"Now let's see what some of these buttons do," said Darcy looking over the control panel. Her eyes settled on three buttons labeled "Cages" and grew wide with anticipation. "Oh, how 'bout these."

She pressed all three buttons and a red light flashed across the maze. The doors opened on three cages, and two undead shambled out of two of them.

"Darcy, I think Ramses was saving them for the Colonel. They were a gift from Kafka."

"Oh, they'll still be here when he gets back. But Elicia won't!" Darcy jumped up and down, giddy as she watched the two zombies make their way into the maze.

"I don't know if this is what he had in mind," said Matt.

"Who cares?" replied Darcy picking her fangs with a red fingernail. "Besides, I don't want her to be *exactly* like me. A mindless zombie is much better for her."

"You bitches are so catty," said Matt smiling.

Peter hopped the fence rather deftly and landed comfortably on his feet on the other side. He sensed two roaming sentries nearby. He clung to the shadows and sprinted from building to building under the cover of darkness.

When he reached the last building, there was a long stretch to Hangar Four with no cover. The patrolling soldiers were walking towards the hangar. There was no way he could cross undetected.

He closed his eyes and focused. He felt his facial features contort out of their natural anatomical alignment. When he opened his eyes, he stepped forward out of the shadow of the last building.

"Look," said one of the patrolling soldiers pointing off to their right.

"There," said the other one pointing to their left.

"Split up," said the first one.

They each took a direction and approached the rapidly moving figures they saw darting around in the moonlight. "Halt! Identify yourself!"

Peter walked quickly up the middle, right between them, unnoticed. He heard a voice booming over some kind of loudspeaker coming from Hangar Four. He knew someone was in the control tower of the Labyrinth.

Chills shot down his spine as he recalled his first experience in the Labyrinth, and he quickened his pace. As he reached the side door of the hangar, he reached inside with his senses and detected two strange presences in the control tower. They didn't feel normal to him. Then he felt two more abnormal presences in the maze moving together, and one normal presence in the middle of the maze whose heart was beating out of its chest.

He pushed the unlocked door open and slipped in.

Elicia was looking over the RGT apparatus when Darcy's voice boomed over the loudspeaker. "They're coming to get you, Elicia," she said in a creepy voice. Elicia heard Darcy and Matt laughing.

That's when she first heard it. It sounded like growling and then footsteps, but the feet were dragging. The odd sounds were drawing closer as Elicia heard more giggling over the speakers and then that annoying clicking like cicadas.

"So what you're telling me is that Kafka turned bystanders into zombies using the portable RGT device, televisions, and cell phones to escape, and then he did the same to one of the roadblocks," said Ramses.

"Who knows where he's going next," said Betancourt, "and how many others he'll do this to. He can cause several outbreaks of the THV virus that would quickly spiral out of control. We're talking epidemic, here. We need to call in HAZMAT."

"Okay, we'll do that, but you're not privy to new developments. There's something I have to show you in Hangar Four. Something regarding Kafka. If we move now we might be able to catch him."

"But I thought Hangar Four was shut down."

"It was, but there was something we missed. Something crucial to bringing Kafka down. We have to hurry."

"We should bring some engineers from R&D," said Betancourt reaching for his mini-com multi-tasker.

"There's no time for that now," insisted Ramses, growing impatient. He knew Betancourt was stalling and wanted to bring others into it for his protection. Betancourt knew it was a trap.

Betancourt stood up resigned to Ramses' urgency. "Okay. Lead the way, sir."

Peter looked up and saw two young people in the control tower laughing and pressing buttons. Lights began to flash. As he screwed his eyes and got a better look, he saw they weren't kids at all. They looked more like those vampires that chased him and Farrow on the rooftops in Tijuana.

He noticed they were watching and talking to someone in the maze, and that someone had two zombies a few rooms away from her and closing in fast.

Peter capitalized on the two vampires' distraction and bolted across the room and into the maze. Amazingly, his enhanced senses and ability to reach out allowed him to navigate the maze rather easily.

Within a couple of minutes, he found Elicia.

"Who's that?" asked Matt.

Darcy saw someone moving quickly through the maze. He moved too fast for her to get a good look at him on camera.

She grabbed the microphone and pressed the button. "Hey, who are you? What are you doing?"

She and Matt saw the man stop for a moment and quickly look up. He was dressed in regular clothes, not like a soldier.

"Maybe he's the third zombie," offered Matt.

"I didn't see him come out of the third cage," replied Darcy. "Go down there and check it out."

Matt cracked his knuckles as the fangs in his mouth extended like a horrible erection. "With pleasure."

Elicia screamed, startled, as Peter burst into her room.

"It's okay. I'm here to help."

Just then, two zombies, both men dressed in black, spilled into the room. They looked like paramilitary. One rushed Peter while the other went for Elicia. Peter spun as he was grabbed; sending his zombie falling forward and landing face down.

He wanted to unsling his assault rifle but Elicia screamed in terror as the other zombie snarled and reached out for her. Peter reached out and grabbed the zombie from behind by its shoulders right before it closed its jaws on her neck.

It snapped at her as Peter backed away, pulling it with him. It spun around and grappled with him, trying to bite any part of him it could get its hands on.

"Look out behind you!" yelled Elicia.

As Peter turned his head, he saw that the other one was on its feet and reaching out for him. Before he could react, it sank its teeth into his collarbone. He heard, more so than felt it snap under the pressure. The other zombie got a hold of his forearm and sank its teeth into his flesh. Blood soaked his shirt by the collar and sleeve.

"Oh, the hell with this," Peter groaned, and he reached around with his right hand and wrapped his arm around the head of the zombie biting his neck. He grabbed the hair on the back of its head and held tight. He felt it pressing his rifle into his back.

Peter dropped suddenly, snapping the zombie's neck over his shoulder. It released its bite and rolled off of him onto the floor, its head dangling at an unnatural angle.

It still reached for him.

The zombie biting his forearm did not release its bite and was still standing. He slid under it in between its legs and gave it a good kick. His flesh ripped off in its mouth as it staggered backwards and into Elicia, who cried out in horror. The force of the impact toppled her chair on its side and she went crashing to the hard floor.

Peter sat up, the zombie with the snapped neck just missing him, and unslung his assault rifle. When the zombie on top of Elicia got to its feet, Peter blew its brains out the back of its head. He then swung the rifle up and sent the stock crashing down on the zombie behind him, crushing its skull.

"Who the hell are you?" cried Elicia.

Peter got to his feet just as Matt entered their room in the maze.

"Well, well, a visitor," said Matt licking his chops, clicking like a cicada. His four eyes were black as night and his fingernails were claws.

"Who's this?" Peter asked Elicia.

"Shoot him!" she yelled.

As Assistant Director Wolff crossed the grounds, he heard gunfire coming from Hangar Four. He quickened his pace into a run when he came upon two patrolling soldiers. He flagged them down.

"Sir, that's coming from Hangar Four," one of them reported.

"Alert security and find General Ramses," said Wolff.

"Yes, sir. You need to come with us."

Wolff hesitated, looking at the hangar. "Yeah, okay. Lead the way."

They began to sprint back towards the front of the base when they realized he wasn't with them.

"Where'd he go?"

They heard a strange clicking sound. When they turned around, there was a roar and a flash of teeth and claws, and they screamed.

Ramses and Betancourt saw the flashes of gunfire in the distance as some kind of wild animal tore two soldiers apart.

"What the hell is that?" gasped Betancourt.

"We have to hurry," said Ramses.

Betancourt pulled his sidearm and put it to Ramses' temple. "Not so fast, General."

"What in the hell do you think you're doing, Colonel?"

"I know you are a traitor, General. Now walk ahead, slowly. Make any sudden moves and I'll put a bullet right into your brain."

"Okay. Okay," said Ramses, putting his hands up. "Have it your way."

"Move," said Betancourt, pressing the barrel of his handgun into Ramses' head. There were alarms sounding and soldiers started dashing to and fro in the commotion.

Peter emptied his rifle into Matt, the impact throwing Matt back up against the wall, but he kept coming. Peter tossed the rifle and grappled with Matt, but he was weakened from his bites from the zombies. His flesh burned on his shoulder and forearm, but at the moment, it was the least of his worries.

Elicia was squiggling around frantically on the ground, cursing at Matt. Peter and Matt took turns throwing each other up against the wall, each never letting go of the other.

They stumbled through the open doorway and were rolling around on the floor in the next room. Matt lashed out and snapped at Peter, biting him in several places as Peter yelped and grunted in the struggle.

Elicia looked up at the control tower and saw that Darcy was gone. Great, now she'd be here any minute. This was going from bad to worse.

They all heard a door slam and a low, animalistic growl. Then they heard Darcy's voice.

"Something happened. I'm sorry, I—"

There was a wet ripping sound and then a gurgling.

Matt, currently on top of Peter, looked up. "Darcy?"

He punched Peter in the face and stood up. He stepped over him as Peter rolled around on the floor clutching his face, and he stood in the doorway to the next room.

Peter scrambled in a commando crawl into the next room. He crawled over to Elicia on the floor. "We have to get out of here." However, there was no way to cut the plastic ties binding her to the chair.

"What were you two doing?" they heard in the next room in a low, growling inhuman voice.

"Mr. Wolff, we were just having some fun."

Peter looked at Elicia sardonically. "Don't tell me Mr. Wolff is an actual wolf."

She shrugged her shoulders and smiled sheepishly.

"Great," said Peter.

They heard more wet ripping sounds and Matt's head came rolling into their room through the open doorway.

"Screw it." Peter got to his feet, grabbed the back part of Elicia's chair by her head like a handle, and he began to pull her into the next room as Wolff stepped into theirs. The legs of the chair scraped loudly against the hard floor as Peter made his way through the other part of the maze.

Wolff put his nose in the air and sniffed loudly. "Ah, someone's on the rag." Then he took off in the direction of Elicia's scent.

With his newfound strength and speed, Peter found pulling Elicia behind him in a chair rather easy, like a kid dragging a stuffed animal around. They heard Wolff tracking them through the maze, and he was right on their heels.

"Hurry! He's coming!" shouted Elicia behind him.

Ramses, with a gun to his head, entered the hangar first with Betancourt following behind him. "You know, Colonel, this hangar will be swarming with soldiers within minutes. You've taken a four-star general hostage. I see no way out of this for you."

Betancourt saw the dismembered body of a young girl on the floor and heard the commotion in the maze. "So this is what you've been up to? Stay here."

Betancourt backed away from Ramses and climbed the metal staircase to the control tower. When he burst into the control room, he saw that all of the monitors were on. There was a hulking, four-eyed beast tracking Peter and some girl tied to a chair through the maze.

"Elicia Corti," he said out loud. "So that's what they were doing back here."

Peter felt Betancourt enter the hangar. He looked up over his shoulder and saw him in the control tower.

"I have an idea," he said to Elicia.

"You'd better hurry. He's coming!"

Peter made it to the back of the maze by the cages. He straddled an exterior wall of the Labyrinth and smashed a window with his fist. He picked Elicia up, chair and all, and tossed her though the opening.

Just then, Wolff barreled into their room, his broad furry chest heaving.

"Who the fuck are you?" he snarled.

Peter bolted into the next room, and he heard Wolff follow behind him. He made his way to the middle where the open cages were. He turned and stood, placing himself behind the cage door with his back to the wall.

In a hot second, Wolff came bounding into the room and hurtled towards Peter. There was a flash of pain as Wolff smashed into the bars of the cage door, crushing Peter up against the wall.

Wolff reached through the bars and tore at his chest, slashing his already ruined shirt. Peter saw colors as he shoved the gate, only to have Wolff push it and him right back against the wall.

Screaming, Peter shoved the gate again, pushed his feet against the wall behind him, and pushed off with all of his might.

Wolff lost his footing and stumbled backwards, but because he held onto the bars of the cage door, he swung right into the cage.

Peter put his aching shoulder into it and shoved the cage door shut. Betancourt must have read his mind, because Peter heard the digi-lock engage. He backed away as Wolff lunged at him, his claws just missing him.

Peter looked up at the control tower and gave Betancourt a thumbs up. Betancourt waved back at him.

Wolff was pacing back and forth in the cage, seething with rage. He flashed all four hungry eyes and growled at Peter.

Peter looked the cage up and down and smirked. "That's a good look for you."

Wolff roared at him.

Peter walked back to the room where he smashed the window and found Elicia sitting there.

"Is he dead?" she asked through the opening.

Peter stepped through and grabbed a jagged shard of glass. "Not quite, but he's contained for the moment."

He tore off one of his sleeves and wrapped it around the base of the shard. Gripping it carefully, he began to saw away at Elicia's bindings.

He freed her right hand and then her left. As he worked on unbinding her ankles, she rubbed her wrists. When she was completely free of the chair, he pulled her towards the front of the Labyrinth.

They saw Betancourt standing there with a gun to Ramses' head. Peter marched up to Ramses, brandishing the glass shard.

"Go ahead, you chicken shit bastard. Why don't you change into whatever you are?"

"He won't do that," said Betancourt. "If he's transformed when reinforcements bust down the door any minute, he'll have a hard time explaining it."

"Looks like I live to fight another day," Ramses gloated.

"Not if I kill you first," hissed Peter through gritted teeth.

"No, Major," said Betancourt relieving Ramses of his sidearm and handing it to Peter. "He's our ticket out of here."

Suddenly, as if on cue, MP's stormed the hangar. Peter and Betancourt stood close to either side of Ramses with their guns to his head.

"Keep between us," Peter instructed Elicia, "and stay close."

She nodded and stood flush behind Ramses between Peter and Betancourt.

"Stand down," shouted an MP, the one in charge, to the others. "They have the General hostage. Colonel Betancourt?"

"We just want to walk out of here without any trouble," announced Betancourt. "But if you force our hand, we will kill the General."

"I'll kill him," vowed Peter. "Believe me, there's nothing I'd like more."

The MP's were startled by Wolff roaring somewhere at the back of the Labyrinth.

"What was that?" asked the MP in charge.

"Something that will explain all of these dead bodies," said Betancourt. "Check the surveillance footage."

"Colonel Betancourt, surrender your weapon."

"As soon as we're outside the perimeter, we'll give you the General back unharmed. We need transport."

"There's a few Humvees parked outside. Take one, but the General gets released within the perimeter."

"What guarantee do I have that you won't open fire on us once I do so?"

"This is obviously some kind of misunderstanding, sir. We don't wish anyone to get hurt."

"Good, son. Then you'll let us go. The only thing you have seen is our holding the General at gunpoint. If we wanted him dead, he'd be dead."

"And what about the bodies, sir?"

"Look at them, Corporal. They're torn to pieces. Look at us. Does it look like we could do that kind of damage, son?"

"These men are murderers!" accused Ramses.

"Look at the footage," implored Betancourt. "You'll see that's not the case."

"I ask that you leave these two civilians behind, sir. You can go on your way."

"Negative, Corporal," said Betancourt. "I don't expect you to understand this right now, but they are safer with me."

"Don't listen to them, Corporal," admonished Ramses. "Don't let them leave this base."

"Do the right thing, Corporal," said Peter. "You don't want the death of a four-star general on your hands."

The corporal nodded and gestured for the other MP's to stand down and clear a path. Now fugitives, the four walked through and out the hangar slowly (Peter was limping) as the Corporal radioed to the MP's outside to stand down.

They made their way over to one of the Humvees parked out front. "Open the door," Peter said to Elicia, who opened the front door. "Slide in to the passenger side." She did.

Peter then reached out with his free hand and opened the back driver side door. "Get in, General."

"You're not going to get away with this," said Ramses, and then he got in.

"You drive," Peter told Betancourt, who slid into the driver seat and closed the door. Peter got in the back with Ramses and closed the door.

Betancourt turned the engine over and began to pull away. There were soldiers flanking them on either side.

"You won't get far," said Ramses.

"Oh, I think the MP's will have their hands full reviewing the security footage," said Peter. "They'll see Assistant Director Wolff ripping those two vampire kids to shreds. Then he'll point the finger at you."

"He'll be quite human-looking when they find him in that cage. By the time they view the footage, he'll be long gone," said Ramses.

"He's right," said Betancourt. "Our objective now is only to escape with our lives. We'll worry about the rest later."

They were pulling up to the front gate. The gate operator received a call, and the gate slowly opened. The soldiers surrounding the Humvee had their guns trained on them.

"Who's that?" Elicia asked, pointing at a dark figure standing at the opening of the front gate.

"Call off your man and we'll let the General go," ordered Betancourt into his mini-com multi-tasker.

"He's not ours, Colonel."

Betancourt strained to look at the dark figure.

"Shit, it's Kafka," said Peter.

"What's he doing here?" asked Betancourt.

"Your ass is grass now," taunted Ramses.

Kafka walked up to the Humvee. Betancourt lowered his window, clutching his handgun in his right hand and pointing it at the inside of the car door. The soldiers weren't sure if this new character was a part of all of this. Police cars were racing in the distance, closing in on the fort.

"Good evening, Colonel," said Kafka coolly. "Leave the General. I'll take it from here." He was wearing his high tech tiara and carrying his portable RGT console.

"You're going to let us go?" asked Betancourt suspiciously.

"At this point you're better to me alive than dead, Colonel."

"Don't use that on these soldiers," Betancourt implored. "These are good men."

"That will be entirely up to them, Colonel. You'd better get going. The local law enforcement is almost here."

"He's going to kill everyone," said Peter from the back.

"I just want the General," assured Kafka, "but if you want to stick around, I can turn everyone into flesh eating zombies and be on my merry way. Or I can call in a drone strike on this base, with a single idea in my brain, killing all of these good soldiers."

"So that was you back at the bar," said Betancourt.

Kafka nodded.

"No, we don't want that."

"Then hand over the General. They'll think I'm with you and let me go with my prominent hostage."

Betancourt turned around and nodded to Peter.

"Out," Peter ordered Ramses. "Another time."

"Somehow I don't think you'll get the chance," Kafka said.

Ramses chortled and opened the back door. He stepped out and Peter closed the door behind him. Betancourt hesitated for a moment.

"You'd better get moving, Colonel," said Kafka. "Time is of the essence."

"We could kill him now," said Peter to Betancourt. "Then we can explain ourselves to the MP's."

"Pete, you couldn't kill me before. What makes you think killing me will be so easy?"

"He's right," said Betancourt. "Now's not the time. We're in a tight spot."

"I say we do him now," said Peter urgently.

"You're welcome to try," replied Kafka. "Everyone around me will be undead with a single thought."

"He's going to do it anyway," said Peter. "I say we take him now."

"The MP's will cut us down, so unless you think you can kill him in one swift move, we don't stand a chance," explained Betancourt.

Peter was silent. He knew Betancourt was right, and it pissed him off. Their only option was to leave.

Betancourt put the Humvee in gear and drove forward and out of the fort, leaving Kafka standing there with General Ramses.

Kafka put his RGT console down on the ground and stood behind Ramses, pointing his assault rifle straight ahead. The police cars were closing in.

"Lay your weapon down on the ground and step away from the General," ordered a soldier over a bullhorn.

"So what's the plan?" whispered Ramses to Kafka.

"You failed to serve your purpose assigned to you, so now you'll serve another." Kafka laid his rifle down on the ground.

"What are you doing?" asked Ramses confused. "Turn them all into zombies. Do it now."

"Then there won't be any witnesses," explained Kafka. "I need witnesses."

"For what?"

There was the squeak of a bullhorn turning on. "Sir, back away from the General and lay face down on the ground."

Kafka flashed his teeth in a gruesome smile.

"For this."

Kafka reached behind him and produced a smoke grenade. He pulled the pin and dropped in on the ground at his feet. He and Ramses were immediately consumed in a thick cloud of smoke. He reached behind him and pulled two machetes out of sheaths strapped to his back.

The approaching police cars came to a sudden halt, skidding on the asphalt, the monitors in the dashboards flickering and the lights flashing behind the smoke.

When the smoke began to clear in the night breeze, one of the police cars sped away and Ramses lay in pieces on the ground. Four zombie police officers staggered out of the smoke and towards the base.

"Hold your fire!" shouted the MP on the bullhorn. "There are police officers in the line of fire!"

The zombies, encouraged by the call to dinner, picked up their pace as they shambled towards the front gate.

Kafka was gone.

***

"Jesus, does somebody want to tell me what the hell just happened?" asked Elicia, her eyes wide as platters and her heart beating out of her chest.

"You were abducted," answered Betancourt with his usual matter of fact tone, as if it was no big deal.

"Abducted? Abducted by who?"

"The US Army," said Peter gravely.

Betancourt kept his eyes on the road as he drove. "The question is why?"

"It's my blog...and my podcasts."

"Yes, we know you are the Seditious Blogger," said Betancourt impatiently. "We just don't know why you were abducted and taken to an abandoned hangar on an army base to be murdered."

"Wait a minute. *You're* Tronika?" asked Peter dubiously.

Elicia, irritated by his disbelief, narrowed her eyes and ignored Peter.

"How the hell am I supposed to know what they wanted?" she asked Betancourt.

"What did they ask you about?" interjected Peter, turning on the charm. He flashed his best million-dollar smile. He had done it in Frisky's countless times.

"You don't look so good," she said, unconvinced.

Peter nodded for her to continue.

"They were asking me why I was urging people to take a walk off the grid. They asked me about RET—"

"RGT," Peter corrected.

"Yeah, I guess. RGT. Whatever. They asked me if I knew anything about using cell phones and televisions to read people's minds."

"Their memories," Peter again corrected.

"Well, did you?" Betancourt asked.

"I talked about that kind of stuff on my podcasts, and I always figured the government was developing some new spy technology. But those didn't look like government back there."

"It's because they weren't," stated Betancourt.

"They looked like monsters. What were those things following me in that maze?"

"Those were zombies," stated Peter, "developed by the government."

Elicia was incredulous. "What the hell is the government doing developing zombies? What about my friend, Darcy? She wasn't a zombie. And who the hell are you guys?"

"I told you those weren't government," said Betancourt. "They once were, but now they're not."

Elicia ran her hands through her long brown hair in exasperation. "Why can't I get a straight answer out of you people?"

"We might as well tell her everything, seeing as her life now depends on it," Peter said to Betancourt.

"This information is classified," insisted Betancourt, being a total hard ass as usual.

"We need to know why they took her," added Peter. "They perceive her as a threat, and we need to know why."

"He-llo. I'm right here," said Elicia, obviously annoyed by the fact that they were talking about her as if she wasn't there.

Peter decided to tell her, despite the protest from Betancourt. "The army developed zombie drones to flush terrorists out of caves. At the same time they were developing Retinal Gateway Technology, or RGT, a technology that can be used to read people's memories through neuropathways by tapping the retina in the eye."

He smiled as he mused that he sounded like Carl. Carl... "Both technologies are linked in their origin, and my brother developed a brain tumor that allowed him to communicate with the zombie drones. As it ends up, he began to change himself, and now it appears that he is about to lead an invasion on this planet. Oh, and he infected me too, but the Colonel here gave me a serum to stop my transformation."

Elicia looked at Peter as he sat there triumphantly, thinking he explained everything.

"You guys are crazy. You're escaped mental patients, is that it? I was rescued from monsters by a couple of escaped mental patients. Why does this kind of shit always have to happen to me? Why can't I just be normal?"

"I know this is a lot to digest," implored Peter, "but you saw what you saw at the hangar."

Elicia was thoughtful for a moment. "How do I know *you* guys aren't a couple of monsters?"

"I'm perfectly human," stated Betancourt.

Elicia turned to Peter.

"Hey," he said putting up his hands defensively. "We just rescued you, didn't we?"

"So you're one of...them?"

"I was bitten by them, but the serum the Colonel gave me is preventing it from turning me fully into one of them."

"Fully?"

"Well, I can sense people's heart rates and pulses and I'm stronger and faster than I was. I can also do this cool trick..."

"Major, you digress," said Betancourt testily.

"It's all information," said Peter defensively. "She has a right to ask questions."

"*You're* a Major?" said Elicia with equal parts question and sarcasm, mocking his disbelief that she was Tronika.

"Yes. I mean, I was."

"Aren't you a little young to be a Major?" said Elicia suspiciously.

"Well, it's a long story."

"Major," Betancourt reminded.

"Elicia," said Peter, taking his assault rifle off his lap and leaning forward in the back seat, "you said you knew one of the...monsters."

"I knew two of them, but I only called one a friend."

"How were they involved?"

"They came to my dorm room and convinced me to go out with them."

Peter turned to Betancourt. "They used her friends to get to her."

"Only one of them was a friend," Elicia reiterated. "The other was just a creep." She blushed a little.

"The RGT," said Betancourt. "They used the RGT to find out who was close to her." Then he said to Elicia, "Your podcast was about getting people to fall off the grid. Like how? What were you recommending?"

"I had a feeling the government was tracking our every move. Cell phone calls, web sites surfed, credit card purchases...and all under this Second Patriot Act, and all in the name of national security." She put those last two words in air quotes. "People aren't even aware of half the shit the government is doing."

"This podcast and your blog…did you have a lot of followers?"

"Millions."

"Jesus," said Peter to Betancourt. "They were afraid she was onto them and getting the word out."

"Onto who, exactly?"

"You saw what Kafka did with the portable RGT," said Betancourt. "He's turning people into zombies through their cell phones, computers, and televisions no less."

Elicia thought about the humming of the computers in the lab she babysat at school, and how she felt she wasn't alone. She remembered the other students mesmerized by the Smartboard in her medieval lit class.

"Okay, you guys are losing me again. Kafka? As in the international terrorist, Kafka?"

"The very one," said Peter gravely. "He's behind all of this. If you were on to RGT and tipping people off, it would put a damper on his plans."

"He must plan on doing this on a large scale," said Betancourt. "That's why he wanted Ms. Corti, here. He wanted to silence her."

"Well, maybe we can explain to these monsters that I didn't know anything about this RGT and certainly had no intention of foiling their plan to turn people into zombies with their freakin' electronics. Jesus, this whole thing sounds nuts. This doesn't sound nuts to you guys?"

But in a way it didn't feel nuts. She had felt strange in recent days, as if the computers in the lab she was babysitting were somehow watching her. Then there were those terrible memories that came up in her lit class.

Peter regarded her with a very sincere expression. "Honey, you wouldn't believe all the shit that I've seen."

"Major Birdsall, here, was in the Infantry Drone Program. He helped develop it," added Betancourt.

"Well great," said Elicia. "Remind me to thank you personally."

"Well, I did save your life back there," Peter pointed out, deflating her sarcasm. "Oh, so I'm a Major now," he said to Betancourt. "I thought you threw me out on my ass. Dishonorable discharge."

"That was General Ramses, not me," reminded Betancourt. "I helped you, remember? You're reinstated to active duty, given the special circumstances."

"Do I have a choice?"

"No."

"Remind me to thank *you* personally, sir."

"I have an idea," interjected Elicia. "This Kafka is a terrorist. Why don't we just call up the President and have him put the Automaton on him?"

"That would be a good idea, if only for one small thing," said Peter with a pained expression.

"What's that?"

"He *is* the Automaton."

Elicia threw her hands up in exasperation. "Oh, this just gets better all the time."

Just then, Elicia's cell phone began to ring. A creature of habit, she reached down for it.

"No, don't!" shouted Peter. He snatched it out of her hand, lowered the back window, and threw it out of the car.

"What are you doing?" asked Elicia outraged.

"There's a terrorist turning people into zombies with their cell phones, remember?" said Peter.

"Oh, right."

"That's twice I saved your ass."

She blushed and he sensed her heartbeat flutter.

"That was probably Kafka trying to silence you through your cell," said Betancourt. "That means he's close."

"That could've been my sister trying to call me."

"At this time of night," said Betancourt. "Unlikely."

"We need to get off this road and to a desolate place," said Peter. "You know, off the grid." He said that last part for Elicia's benefit. He figured she needed to start feeling like a part of the solution or she'd start becoming a part of the problem.

"Wait," she said. "First, we have to pick up my sister."

"We don't have time for that," said Betancourt stoically.

"The hell we don't," snapped Elicia. "If they want to get to me they'll use her."

"She's right," said Peter. "We have to get there before they do." He knew that picking up her sister was a good tactical call, but it wasn't just strategy. He lost yet another family member today and knew how it felt to lose family to these monsters.

"Where does she live?" asked Peter.

"Close by. A few minutes away. My parents are in Italy through the month of July, so she's all alone."

"I'm sorry, Ms. Corti, but your sister isn't a priority," insisted the Colonel.

Elicia stabbed a finger into Betancourt's right arm. "Listen, asshole. She's a priority to me."

"Colonel, Elicia's with us. They can use her sister to get to her, which would mean they'd be getting to us. We'd be compromised," said Peter.

Elicia's sister wasn't a priority, but Peter was tactically correct from a certain point of view.

"Besides, if Kafka wanted us dead he would've killed us back at the base. He could've done it in the blink of an eye."

"Yes, that was curious," said Betancourt, "letting us live and all. He said he just wanted the general."

"Carl let us live because we somehow serve his purpose better alive."

"Yes," reflected Betancourt. "He wanted me out of the picture. Although he would've preferred me dead, I'm on the run from the army, which must be just as good. We're all fugitives now."

"He wants us out of the way," said Peter, "and we need to find out why."

"But first we get my sister," insisted Elicia.

"This is going to be close," said Betancourt.

"In and out," assured Peter.

Betancourt hesitated. "Okay, but if she puts up a fight, we leave her behind."

"She'll come quietly," said Elicia, lying through her teeth. She turned around and mouthed *thank you* to Peter, who nodded his *you're welcome*. He wasn't sure if she was thanking him for saving her life or convincing Betancourt to pick up her sister. Either way, it worked for him.

Betancourt sped down the street taking direction from Elicia on how to get to her parents' house. Peter lay down in the back seat weakened from his injuries, but he already felt his body mending.

He just needed time.

Chapter 10

Corti Residence
02:09 HRS

Betancourt pulled up to a fancy mechanical gate that hung open at the mouth of a long driveway.

"Nice digs," said Peter taking in the size of the property. "Your parents must be loaded."

"Why is the security gate hanging open?" asked Betancourt.

"It's Brittany," said Elicia rolling her eyes. "She comes home from a night of clubbing and always forgets to lock the gate."

Betancourt looked at Peter, cut the headlights, and then proceeded to slowly coast into the driveway. "Keep your eyes peeled."

They pulled up to the house. Every light was on.

"She must be home," Betancourt said.

"Yeah, she tends to leave all the lights on, too," said Elicia.

"Your parents' electric bill must be astronomical," remarked the Colonel.

"You must be a father," said Elicia.

"Why do you say that?" asked Betancourt, surprised.

"Because that's such a dad thing to say. I'll go in and get her."

"Wait," said Peter putting a hand on her shoulder. "We'll all go."

"You stay here," ordered Betancourt. "You're in no condition to be walking around. I'll go with her."

"Oh, who cares? Let's go already." Elicia jumped out of the Humvee.

Betancourt turned to look at Peter in the backseat. "Now don't get all caught up in trying to impress this girl. I need your mind on the mission, not getting laid."

Peter mock saluted. "Yes, Dad."

Betancourt shook his head and left the Humvee. He quickly caught up to Elicia as she let herself in the front door. They stepped into a rather large foyer, and Betancourt followed her into the living room.

The furniture was all black leather and the décor very modern. There was a 100-inch LED television mounted above a large, stone fireplace.

"Nice place," Betancourt said in genuine admiration.

"Brit!" Elicia called out. "Brittany!" She ran up the stairs to the second floor. Betancourt was right behind her.

They walked down a long hallway to the second to last bedroom. Elicia knocked, and she heard someone moving around. Betancourt drew his handgun, but Elicia pushed the barrel with her fingers so it was pointed down at the floor. She shot him a dirty look. He shrugged.

"Brittany!"

"Elicia? Is that you?" asked a slurred voice from within.

Betancourt raised his gun again. "She might be one of those monsters."

"Chill out, GI Joe. She's fine."

Elicia pushed the bedroom door open. Brittany was staggering around in a red mini dress, makeup smeared over a pale face. She was making her way to Elicia. Betancourt trained his gun on her and was about to pull the trigger when Elicia stood in front of him.

"Don't! She's drunk, not a zombie," said Elicia reproachfully.

"Elicia? What are you doing here?" Brittany wrapped her arms around her little sister's neck. "Aren't you supposed to be at school?"

She pushed off of Elicia and straightened herself up. She took a long look at the middle-aged, very stern looking black man standing behind Elicia. Her eyes were sultry.

"Whoa! Elicia, you little slut," she slurred. "Mom and Dad are going to be pissed." She sounded impressed. Brittany stumbled backwards, lost her balance, and fell on her pink bed.

"We don't have time for this," said Betancourt testily. He looked a little embarrassed at Brittany's implication.

"Relax, Colonel. She'll be easier to deal with this way."

Brittany sat up but was wobbly. "Who's your boyfriend, Elicia?"

"He's a friend, Brit. He wants to bring me to a party with lots of cute guys. I figured I'd drop by to see if you wanted to come."

Brittany eyed the two of them suspiciously. "Elicia, I thought you didn't like parties."

Elicia shrugged her shoulders and looked sheepish. "College changes people, I guess."

Brittany frowned at them for a moment, and then her expression changed to a smile. "Good for you, sis. I knew you had it in you."

"Brit, listen to me. We have a guy in the car. He's coming with us, and he's just your type. Tall, strong, very cute, and military."

Brittany perked up at the last word. "Military? What, like army?"

"He's a Major, and a young one, too."

"I bet he's a major cutie," slurred Brittany, nearly falling off the bed.

"For crying out loud," Betancourt murmured.

Elicia held out a palm to silence him and shot him a quick look that told him he wasn't helping. "Brit, you can come, but we have to leave now."

Brittany belched loudly as she pondered the situation. "Okay," she said smiling, and she hiccupped.

"Help her up," ordered Elicia.

Betancourt glared at her.

"You're bigger than me and can get her out of here quicker than I can."

Betancourt let out a long sigh, and then walked over to the bed. He slipped his hands under Brittany's armpits and began to lift her off the bed.

"Okay, sweetheart. Upsie daisy."

Brittany smiled at him and practically threw herself into his arms. "You're sexy." The alcohol content of her breath nearly rendered him unconscious.

"Okay. Right this way," he said as he guided her away from the bed. "Get the front door open," he told Elicia.

Brittany began to retch.

"No. No," pleaded Betancourt, "God no."

But it was too late.

Brittany emptied the contents of her stomach all over the front of Betancourt's uniform. It came flying out of her in a projectile stream. When she was finished, she started to cry.

"I'm sorry," she whimpered, as Betancourt held her away from him with outstretched arms.

He looked down at all of the puke. "Damn, girl. How much did you eat?"

Peter crouched low in the back seat of the hummer reflecting on everything that happened. What was Carl up to? However, his thoughts quickly turned to Elicia. She was not what he expected.

He expected the Seditious Blogger to be some overweight paranoid schizophrenic with an overactive imagination, not a college student. She definitely was not overweight. In fact...

He saw it peering into the window, looking at him. His doppelgänger. He sat up a little too quickly, causing pain to radiate down his body.

"You son-of-a-bitch! What do you want?"

It pointed an eerie claw at him. It looked a little less human every time he saw it, but he supposed he was a little less human since they last met.

The image of his twin faded as Peter saw flashing lights in the distance. It was the police, and they were at the front gate.

"Shit," said Peter.

He wanted to use his mini-com, but he knew the danger of doing so. He would probably be fine, but he didn't want Betancourt and Elicia shambling out of the house as zombies.

He reached forward and honked the horn twice. He heard the police officers' voices, responding to his honking the horn. The police had a skeleton key app in their mini-coms that opened most digi-locks. First, they would try to use the intercom at the gate. Then they were coming in. Peter figured they had mere minutes before they were through the front gate.

Betancourt picked Brittany up in his arms and was carrying her down the steps like Clark Gable when he heard the car horn.

"It's Peter. Look out the front door."

Elicia ran to the front door and saw the lights at the front gate. "It's the police."

Suddenly the intercom by the front door began to talk. *"This is the police. Is anyone home?"*

Elicia froze and looked to Betancourt for guidance.

He was at the bottom of the stairs and crossing the living room. "Talk to them. Buy us some time."

Elicia cleared her throat. "Yes, officer."

"Who am I speaking to?"

"Brittany. Brittany Corti."

The cop forgot to take his finger off the speak button, because she heard him say, *"It's the sister."*

"Is there a problem, officer?"

Betancourt was out the front door with Brittany.

"We need to speak with you, ma'am. It's about your younger sister, Elicia."

"Oh. I see. You have to hold on. Let me get dressed and I'll let you in."

"Please hurry, ma'am." He still had his finger on the speak button. There was laughing. *"Yeah, she's the hot one."*

Elicia rolled her eyes and ran out the front door to join the others. When she reached the Humvee, Brittany was already in the back seat and all over Peter.

Elicia rolled her eyes again.

"Come on, we have to go," said Betancourt impatiently.

Elicia climbed into the front seat, and Betancourt was off before she could even close her door.

"What's behind your back yard?" asked Betancourt urgently.

"Our neighbor's back yard."

"Is there a fence?"

"No, just short hedges."

"Good."

He gunned the engine and sped around the side of the large house. He came up quickly on the short hedges, but the Humvee plowed right through them. Peter and Brittany bounced around in the back seat, and Elicia held on tight in front.

"This neighbor has a gate, too," said Elicia.

"Great," said Betancourt.

He pulled around an in-ground swimming pool and around the side of another big house, and then he was barreling down the driveway towards the gate.

"That's a sturdy gate," remarked Peter from the backseat.

"We're in an army-grade Humvee," stated Betancourt, as if that explained everything away.

"Ramming speed!" shouted Brittany raising a fist and giggling up a storm in Peter's arms.

Elicia held on to her seat and turned her head away as they came up on the gate. Betancourt floored the gas pedal.

They crashed through the gate and spilled out onto the street. As the rods of the gate clanged on the pavement behind them, Betancourt jerked the steering wheel to the right like in one of those old black-and-white movies, and the Humvee narrowly avoided the front gate of the house across the street.

After running over some garbage cans, Betancourt straightened out and tore off down the street.

"Now what?" asked Peter, fending off Brittany's drunken advances.

"I know a place we can go where the authorities won't know to look for us," said Betancourt.

Brittany finally passed out in Peter's lap. "Oh, thank God," he said. "I thought the zombies were bad."

"Major, meet Brittany," said Elicia.

"The pleasure's all hers, I'm sure," quipped Peter.

Elicia turned around facing the road and smiled. She smiled because Brittany was, for the moment, safe. It was also the first time her gorgeous sister ever made a bad first impression with a guy. She felt a little guilty, but the notion positively tickled her.

The Humvee disappeared into the night barreling towards Betancourt's secret destination.

"Hey," asked Peter, "why does it smell like puke?"

***

Kafka barged into headquarters alone.

"What happened?" asked Kojic. "Where's Farooq?"

Kafka grabbed an operative, Qasim, by the throat and lifted him off the ground. The man clawed at Kafka's fingers, his face turning red and then a shade of purple.

"Kafka, please, stop," begged Kojic, frightened.

Kafka tossed the man across the room like a ragdoll. Marina, chained to the wall by her wrists, reached out for the man and almost got him. Another operative grabbed Qasim by the ankles and pulled him away in time.

"Leave us!" demanded Kafka.

Everyone dashed out of the room except Kojic. Kafka stood in the empty room blinking his fours eyes. The only sounds were Marina's wheezing, grunts, and the clinking of her chains.

"Incompetent idiots," hissed Kafka bitterly.

"What happened?"

"Farooq is dead."

This news didn't really trouble Kojic anyway. The man was an animal as far as he was concerned. "And the Colonel?"

"Betancourt escaped, but no matter. My brother, the Colonel, and the Seditious Blogger are all wanted for the murder of a four star general."

Kojic's eyes went wide at the recognition of who Kafka was referring to. "They got Ramses?"

"No. But that idiot failed me for the last time. I gave him a simple task and the tools to do it. Let's just say he was useful one last time. The authorities will be pursuing those three to the ends of the earth, which will keep them out of my hair."

Kojic unconsciously looked up at Kafka's bald, black head.

"It's a goddamned expression, Kojic. You foreigners are so freakin' literal."

"Sorry, sir…your brother…"

"Yes. What about him?"

"Perhaps you shouldn't have let him live."

Kafka stepped forward menacingly. "You are not my brother's keeper, Luka. You'd be wise to remember that."

"I-I-I just figured he'd be dangerous left alive."

Kafka stopped baring his fangs in anger and smiled wickedly. "Why Kojic, he's my brother, my own flesh and blood, the last of my family. Besides, he wouldn't be so easy to kill. He's infected, but he's somehow controlling it. He won't let it advance past a certain point."

"Really?" Kojic regretted how he sounded the moment he said it.

Kafka stepped even closer, looming over him. "Why Luka, you sound almost...hopeful. You're not having second thoughts about this gift I've given you, are you?"

"No, sir." But Kojic knew it was a lie. In fact, he was pretty sure Kafka knew it was a lie.

"And what do we have here?" asked Kafka, looking over at Marina. Marina was staring into space with those milky eyes. These two might as well have been furniture to her.

"You aren't thinking about keeping her here like a pet."

"No, sir," replied Kojic. "To be honest, I don't know what I'm going to do with her."

Kafka cocked his head sideways. "Look at poor Marina, chained to the wall like a dog. Is that any way to treat your wife?"

Kojic just looked a Kafka horrified. He had no words.

"She needs to be free with her own kind, Luka. Not chained to a wall." He walked over and clutched one of the chains in his hands, examining the links carefully.

"This gift I've given her was not intended to place her into bondage. She is to be set free." He yanked hard, pulling the chain and its anchor right out of the wall. Marina stirred, grunting pathetically.

Kafka walked over to the other chain and pulled it out of the wall. "These are my children. Even Marina. To chain her to the wall is to place me in chains."

Marina, directed by Kafka, shambled toward Kojic menacingly.

"Th-that's n-not what I meant. I meant no offense, Kafka."

Marina stopped before him and clicked her jaws at Kojic like a demented marionette, and Kafka was pulling the strings.

"Go," commanded Kafka, "be with the others."

Marina regarded him momentarily with blank eyes. Kafka opened the door, and she shuffled out of the room.

"Kojic, I need you to focus. The time has come for us to spread my gift to the masses. I need you now more than ever."

Kojic was trembling. "Yes, Kafka."

"And pull yourself together, man. You're infected. She would have done you no permanent harm...Speaking of which, I want you to assemble a small team. Then I want you to submit to torture and punishment. Trust me. It won't kill you, but it'll make you stronger. I need you stronger, Luka."

"Yes, Kafka."

"Excellent."

Kafka stepped out of the room.

Kojic stood there alone for a moment, trying to quiet down his soul. If he were to be a part of the winning team, he had to commit himself fully to the Cause.

The Cause...which Cause was this now? It wasn't Belmont's Cause. Nor was it jihad. At least not an earthly jihad. Now Kafka was killing their own as he saw fit. General Ramses. He nearly killed Qasim without provocation.

Who was to say that Kafka wouldn't kill *him* when he had the urge? And yet he spoke of mistreatment of his mindless drones, as if they were an extension of him. Perhaps they were.

Kojic finally came to his senses and left the room. He walked to the back of the building. He was going to round up a team and submit to Kafka's punishment, but first he had to see.

He came to one of the back windows and looked out across the fenced in yard. There were a couple of dozen undead milling about, mostly OIL operatives that were turned using the RGT transmission. There were only a few human operatives left after several others deserted in fear for their lives.

He searched the crowd until he saw her. Marina was milling around with a few others. When Kojic saw her and how she was at home with the other drones, he raised his fist to his mouth and bit it, choking back sobs of terrible grief.

He had always kept his Marina sequestered in their home, wherever that was, according to the Law. He protected her from the outside world of thieves and adulterers, and if that meant subjecting her to his own brand of abuse, then so be it.

But now, she had escaped his grasp, his protection, and she was no longer subject to his cruelty. Now she wandered this lot with her own kind, out of his reach. She no longer belonged to him. His pride mortally wounded, a great shame welled up inside him.

The loss of his wife had become, at this point, unbearable for Kojic. He pounded the windowsill and cried out in anguish. Where was Belmont when he needed him? The Cause had been corrupted by another, who twisted it to wage his own kind of jihad.

Kojic ran down the hall and down the steps until he found the few remaining human operatives. He barged into the room and closed the door abruptly behind him.

"Who here is afraid?"

They all looked at him dumbfounded.

"Luka, please," pleaded Adnon. "You'll get us all killed."

"What is better? Becoming one of those out in back, milling around like a simple animal? Or worse, being the only intelligent life left with a world full of those things."

"Luka, better that than dead," said Mehtab.

"You are all cowards," Kojic hissed at them. "This is not our jihad. He has you fighting for allies that have yet gone unseen, and when they arrive, they will seem more like overlords than allies. Is that what you want?"

"What are we to do?" asked Adnon. "It is too late."

"He will murder us," said Ehsan.

"Like he did General Ramses," said Kojic. "Belmont would have never murdered his own. He protected us until it was our time to pay the ultimate sacrifice. This Kafka spills our blood wastefully, without sacrifice. There is no honor in it."

"What do you propose we do?" asked Mehtab.

"We run," said Kojic. "We find other OIL cells. Not all of them are aware of what is going on. We need to inform them. We need to fight. They follow the ways of Belmont, not Kafka."

"They cannot win against Kafka," said Mehtab. "What you are asking is suicide."

"Then you will not go?" asked Kojic.

Mehtab straightened up and puffed his chest out defiantly. "No, I will not."

"Well then, you are a coward. Anyone else? Will anyone else go with me?"

After a pause, Adnon stepped forward. "I will go."

Ehsan sighed loudly. "I will go, too."

"This is mutiny," cried Mehtab, stabbing his index finger emphatically into the air. "I will have no part of this."

"Then you must die," said Kojic gravely.

Mehtab made for the door, but Kojic stood in front of it. Mehtab reached out to grab him, but Adnon and Ehsan grabbed him and pulled him off Kojic. They forced him down to his knees as Kojic produced his knife.

"No! Kojic, you will pay for your treachery!"

Kojic rammed the knife deep into his throat. It slipped in like a hot knife through butter. Mehtab gagged and struggled briefly with his holders until his eyes went wide and then vacant as his life left his body.

Kojic pulled out his knife and wiped the blade on his jeans. Adnon and Ehsan dropped Mehtab's lifeless body to the ground.

"He is infected. We must dismember him."

Adnon swallowed hard, but nodded. Ehsan nodded too. They began to pull Mehtab's body apart, piece by piece until there was nothing left but a heap of parts.

All three men stood there panting, covered in blood.

"We must go now," said Kojic in a harsh whisper, "before Kafka finds out what has happened."

Kafka sat in his office tinkering with the portable RGT. He reached out with his senses and felt the three men run out of the building.

"Cowards," he said aloud. "Kojic, you are already infected. When the world turns, you will have no choice but to turn, as will your fellow conspirators."

He no longer needed them. He would make his army as he went, and as he recruited to his ranks, the opposition would in turn shrink and eventually succumb. It was a zero sum game. There was no stopping it now.

Kafka looked over at the corner of the room, where a zombie stood gurgling and wheezing.

"Looks like it's just you and me, Dad...

...Just you and me."

Part III

Reach Out and Infect Someone

Chapter 11

The set lit up and the audience clapped as the twins came into view on stage. Tyler looked like his usual ridiculous self, but Skylar sat slouched in his chair looking a bit under the weather.

"Good evening and welcome to another edition of America's favorite docutainment show. I'm Tyler…"

He waited for his brother to jump in and introduce himself, but Skylar just sat there silent looking extremely pale under the hot stage lights. He had very dark shadows under his eyes.

"…and this is my brother, Skylar, who is looking a bit under the weather today. How are you feeling, Skylar?"

Skylar just looked at his brother and nodded as he sat there wheezing in his high chair.

"Well, it looks as if somebody rode you hard and put you up wet. Nice hickey by the way." The camera zoomed in on what appeared to be a rather large love bite on Skylar's neck. "Hot date last night?"

Skylar made a sound that sounded almost like a growl. Tyler was a bit startled, but it was showbiz and he recovered quickly.

"Well, we have a lot to discuss tonight: OIL, Kafka, the apparent absence of the Automaton." Tyler shot a nervous look at the producer off camera who only shrugged his shoulders.

"I guess we'll begin with OIL. There have been recent reports of OIL activity in Texas where the military intercepted an OIL meeting in a local watering hole in Blueberry Hill. Authorities say that the notorious terrorist, known only as Kafka, may have been in attendance, but according to reports, he has once again eluded capture."

Skylar was rocking back and forth in his chair, moaning softly. Tyler looked nervously at the producer who signaled that they were going to take a commercial break.

"More on that after we return from this brief commercial break."

The lights dimmed as they went to commercial and there was a stirring of confusion in the audience.

The producer came running onto the stage. "What the hell is wrong with him?"

"I don't know," replied Tyler annoyed at the producer's tone. "Maybe he's sick." He stood in front of his brother. "Skylar? Are you okay?" No response. "What's wrong, buddy?"

Skylar looked up at Tyler with cloudy eyes and snarled at his brother like a rabid dog.

"Jesus Christ," gasped Tyler, as Skylar reached out and snatched him. He pulled him close, opening his mouth, but Tyler wriggled away.

Skylar lunged forward and grabbed the producer, who dropped his clipboard. He pulled him close and sunk his teeth right into his neck. The producer screamed and blood came spurting out of the hole in his neck. Skylar chewed the torn off flesh noisily.

"Holy shit! Skylar, what have you done?"

The audience watched in shock and terror as the reality of what was unfolding before them began to sink in. One woman screamed, and then the people in the first few rows began to climb back over the seats behind them to put some distance between them and the stage.

A stagehand pulled the producer out of Skylar's grasp, but Skylar grabbed her arm and sunk his teeth into her forearm. She yelled as he chowed down on her flesh, and the stage became chaos as staff ran to and fro in a panic.

Tyler watched in horror as his brother pulled the stagehand closer and bit off her nose and lips. He then ran backstage and disappeared.

The lights went on as Skylar dropped the girl to the stage floor, his mouth dripping blood and her body convulsing at his feet.

"Go to commercial! Go to commercial!" yelled a tinny voice over a loudspeaker. The lights dimmed again as a message flashed on the monitors stating *We Are Experiencing Technical Difficulties. Please Stand By.* Then another commercial came on.

Skylar staggered off the stage, and to the horror of the now frantic and confused audience members, began to shamble towards them with hands outstretched and jaws snapping.

Tyler burst out onto the stage holding his pink AR-15. He raised it and pulled the trigger. The muzzle flashed in the dim lighting as Tyler lit his brother up, tearing holes into his chest and arms. One of the bullets burst his skull like a melon. Skylar's headless body dropped to its knees, hands still reaching out, and fell forward onto the floor where it became inert.

The producer was clutching his neck, and his screams melted into a wild growling as he lunged for Tyler. Tyler shot him in the head at point blank range, and the producer dropped like a stone.

The female stagehand was clutching her face as blood and other fluids squirt out between her fingers.

"Oh hell," said Tyler, resigned to the reality unfolding before him, and he shot her in the face through her left hand. She, too, fell to the floor and was still.

"I guess I was right about guns," mumbled Tyler to himself, as he was pleased with himself for taking out the murderers and minimizing the casualties of what could've been a worse tragedy.

"Damage control," he declared to himself, as security burst onto the set with the police.

They saw him standing there with his pink assault rifle and three bodies around him. "Put down the gun!"

He instinctively turned towards them, still holding the AR-15. "No, wait."

There were claps of thunder, and Tyler looked down at the holes in his chest to see blood welling out, soaking his designer shirt.

"Dammit."

He released his grip on the rifle and dropped to his knees, but the life slipped out of his body before he fell face down on the floor.

***

03:42 HRS

Elicia glanced at Peter and Brittany dozing off in the back seat. "Where are we going?" she asked rubbing her eyes. It had been a long night.

"To see a friend," replied Betancourt. "She is an epidemiologist who works for the CDC. I think she might be able to shed some light as to what is going on and what Kafka might be up to."

"So we're just going to wake her up in the wee hours of the morning and tell her about terrorists, monsters, and aliens?"

"Not *we*," corrected Betancourt. "I. She has a family. I can't just bring an infected soldier and the Seditious Blogger into her home. Besides, Major Birdsall isn't in any condition to be walking around right now."

Elicia nodded, stifling a yawn. "How about you? Don't you have anyone we need to warn? Kafka and Ramses may try to come after your loved ones."

"My wife died of ovarian cancer four years ago. I remarried, but it was a huge mistake. We divorced after six months. She's like a stranger to me."

"Any kids?"

"Two. Both grown. I have a daughter living in England working as a psychologist and a son stationed in Germany."

"He's army, too?"

Betancourt nodded. "Both are out of harm's way at the moment."

"It must be difficult having them so far away."

"Not as difficult as you would think. The army keeps me busy. When you go career like I have, it becomes your whole life."

"Do you still think about her?"

"My first wife?"

"Yes."

"Every day. She was the one. There's no one else that can fill her shoes."

"What was her name?"

"Penelope."

"She must've been pretty."

Betancourt allowed a small smile to grace his stern face for a fraction of a second. It was the first that Elicia ever saw on his face, and she wished Peter was awake to see it. "She was beautiful."

"I'm sorry," said Elicia, not sure of what else to say. It was awkward talking like this with the Colonel.

"You remind me of my daughter when she was in college," remarked Betancourt. "She was sharp like you, but she stayed out of trouble. None of this hacking or blogging stuff about such controversial topics."

Elicia flushed a little with embarrassment. "Yeah, well, if I had a time machine...I don't suppose the army has one of those sitting around..."

"Not that I know of," said Betancourt. "Why did you do it?"

"The blog and the podcasts?"

Betancourt nodded.

Elicia sighed. "It's the whole invasion of privacy thing. I get it. I'm sure the government foiled lots of terrorist plots with all of their surveillance under the first Patriot Act. And yes, if you have nothing to hide why care? All in the name of national security."

"But..."

"But, what if the government started using it against the people? Look what's happening in Washington. There's all of this polarization and in-fighting between the Left and Right. People are out of work, suffering, and pissed off. What if the government no longer is serving the people and the people want a change?"

"What, like a revolution?" asked Betancourt skeptically.

"It doesn't even have to be that extreme," said Elicia. "But what if the people wanted a change? The government would do everything in its power to keep the status quo. They don't want things to change. They don't want to give up their power."

"That's a generalization, but I see your point," conceded Betancourt.

"So what if the government started using its agencies to spy on the populace to thwart any kind of dissention?"

Betancourt hated to admit it, but the girl was right. Such power in the hands of a governmental ruling class could be dangerous.

"And what about all of these shootings and mass murders," continued Elicia.

"What about them?"

"My psychology professor said that when individuals lash out against complete strangers, it's usually a sign of paranoia."

"So what does any of that have to do with government surveillance?"

"Everything. There's no privacy anymore. You can't make a call, send an email, or buy anything without it being recorded and analyzed by various government agencies. Maybe people are on to it."

Betancourt sniffled. "Civilians aren't privy to half of what's going on. How could they know?"

"Maybe it's just a feeling. They might not be able to put their finger on it, but they can feel it. Maybe it's a general sense of feeling ill at ease."

"And you think that government surveillance is causing this."

"Look what's happening now with this RGT," said Elicia. "Has the government conducted studies to look at the long term effects of secretly extracting memories through people's retinas?"

"But this isn't government," reminded Betancourt. "These are...terrorists."

"From another planet," said Elicia.

"Yeah," said Betancourt, "but they're not here yet."

"It's like everything we do leaves a digital imprint somewhere."

"But that's accountability," pointed out Betancourt. "Crime is down because you can't commit a crime without leaving something behind that leads right back to you."

"What about Kafka? He's not only been able to elude capture, but from what's been happening lately, it looks like he's using the technology to his advantage."

"There will always be those with the know-how to exploit the technology. Is that what you are saying?"

"Exactly," said Elicia.

Betancourt thought she made a good, if not grim, point. What good was all of this technology if it could be used against them? That was exactly what Kafka was doing.

They rode on in silence for a while, listening to the sound of the tires on the road over the hum of the engine.

"You know, Major Birdsall might agree with your view of government. He lost two squads to Mexican cartels and OIL, he lost his mother in a terrorist attack, and he just lost his father tonight. He only has his brother left, who happens to be the most dangerous man in the world right now."

"What does that have to do with government?" asked Elicia.

"Let's just say that some less than ethical parts of government had a hand in all of that."

"Jesus," remarked Elicia, "that's unbelievable."

"Is it, after everything you're telling me? The kid's a true hero. No matter what's thrown at him, he just keeps coming back. He has a tremendous sense of duty."

"Maybe you should tell him that when he's awake," suggested Elicia.

"He's not my biggest fan right now."

"Why's that?"

"I wasn't responsible for it, but I was involved in what his brother became, as well as Peter's discharge from the army."

"What was his brother like? Before he became Kafka."

"He was kind of like the Major. Not as big or strong, and kind of a nerd, but he had a strong sense of duty. He enlisted after his mother was killed in a terrorist attack. The one on the mall last year."

"I remember."

"He was recruited into the Infantry Drone Program under the Major's command, but something happened to him over time. He developed a brain tumor that allowed him to communicate with the undead drones. We had never seen anything like it before. Over time, Carl began to change. He became faster, stronger."

"So what happened?"

"General Ramses ordered a kill chip to be placed into his head, in case he got out of hand. He was captured by OIL, and Ramses gave the order to trigger the kill chip."

Elicia put her hand over her mouth in disbelief.

"Well, needless to say, the chip didn't kill him. Carl knew we tried to terminate him, and it pushed him over the edge…"

"…and onto the opposing side," said Elicia.

"That's right."

"Was he dangerous?"

"I don't think he was, and I tried to convince Ramses of that, but he wouldn't listen. But he got his. Carl apparently paid him a visit and infected him. I guess he wanted an inside man."

Betancourt pulled down a quiet street and slowed down. "We're here." He pulled in front of a large, modern house with a good-sized front lawn.

"Nice," said Elicia.

Betancourt put the Humvee in park and killed the engine. "You wait here with the Major and your sister."

"You said she had a family," said Elicia concerned. "You're not just going to ring the doorbell at four in the morning."

"Ms. Corti, I am a highly trained commando. Her family won't even know I'm there." He saw the dubious look on her face. "Trust me."

"I don't trust government, remember?"

"I'll be back, but it's going to be a while. Sit tight and keep an eye on the Major and your sister. Honk the horn if there's trouble."

"Will do, Colonel."

Betancourt rounded the house to the back door. He produced his mini-com multi-tasker and utilized the Skeleton Key app that the army had standard, in case the need to breach a premises arose.

The digi-lock disengaged with a chime and he slipped inside, gently closing the door behind him. He was inside a very spacious kitchen. He circumvented the island and made his way into the living room. He passed through and found the staircase situated in the center of the house.

He crept silently up the stairs, past the two young children's bedrooms, and was standing outside the master bedroom. The door was cracked open. He peeked inside.

Dr. Marcy Cummings was sound asleep on the opposite side of the bed next to her husband, who was snoring like a chainsaw.

He crept silently into the room and around the bed to the other side. She was lying on her side facing away from him. He tapped her gently on the shoulder, mimicking one of the children. She stirred a bit but didn't wake. He tapped again, gently, but more insistently.

She mumbled and rolled over to face him, her eyes slowly opening. Before she could get a word out, he reached out and clamped his hand over her mouth. Her eyes went wide, and she tried to sit up, but his hand over her mouth kept her down.

"Shhhh," he whispered. "It's Darius. I need to talk to you."

The chainsaw faltered, as Mr. Cummings rolled over on his side facing away from them, and resumed again. She nodded her head in recognition, and he took his hand off her mouth. She carefully slid out of bed and he followed her out of the bedroom.

They slipped past the children's bedrooms and descended the stairs in silence. When they reached the living room, Betancourt made as if he was going to say something, but Marcy put her index finger to her lips and he waited.

She descended the stairs off the kitchen into a large finished basement with a full kitchenette, a regulation size pool table, and an expensive looking foosball table.

She turned on him, "Darius, what the hell are you doing breaking into my home?"

"I'm sorry, Marcy, but I needed to speak with you in an official capacity. It's an urgent matter of national security."

"How's the new wife?"

"Jesus, Marcy. It's been that long? She left me, but enough about that. There's something I have to discuss with you."

Marcy was a physician, but she was also an agent of government, so she understood. She gestured for him to sit at the counter in the kitchenette, and they both took a seat in high stools with nice beige cushions.

"I'm just an epidemiologist. What's going on that you need to talk to me?"

***

Elicia sat patiently in the Humvee watching her sister and Peter sleep. Brittany was quiet and still, but Peter shifted around, moaning in the back seat. Elicia turned on the light inside and glanced at Peter's wounds. They looked severe, and she wondered how he was even still alive.

She scanned the road for police, but the block was quiet. The authorities had no way of knowing Betancourt would come here...or at least that was what Elicia hoped.

Peter was groping around in the dark. It was pitch black all around him, and there was something wrong with his face. He felt it with his fingers and knew his features were distorted.

A voice called out to him in the darkness. *Pete.* But it wasn't really a voice at all. It was more like a suggestion or an idea. *Pete, why did you let Dad die?*

"I didn't let him die. You killed him, Carl. You did it."

I warned you, Pete. You wouldn't listen. I just wanted what was best for you and Dad.

"You want us to be monsters, like you."

I made you better, Pete. Faster. Stronger. All I wanted was for you to do the same for Dad. I tried to will you to do it, but you resisted, and now he's dead.

Peter was suddenly plagued with an unbearable guilt. "I couldn't. I couldn't do it," Peter cried out into the void.

And because you couldn't, Dad is dead. Why resist, Pete? Why resist improving, becoming a better being?

"No, you're not better. You're not better."

You put your faith in an army that was corrupt, in people who would murder your brother for their own perverse ends. People who allowed Mom to be murdered, who created the very murderers that erased her out of our lives. You have this obligation, this sense of duty to them, but what about your family, Pete? Where was your duty to your family?

Peter clawed desperately at the blackness all around him, hot tears streaming down his demoniac features. "I tried to protect them. Dammit, Carl, I tried to protect you!"

And you failed, Pete, but now I'm in a position to protect you. You know what it feels like to have lost family and friends because of your weakness. So why deny me my duty to protect you? Do you want me to suffer in guilt and remorse as you have all this time?

"You don't know what I've been through."

Oh, I know very well. Mom is dead. Dad is dead. I lost comrades in Xcaret, too. I know the loneliness of survival, to be the only one safe, but I don't have to be alone. You can be safe with me.

"I don't want to be safe with you as the world dies. I've outlived too many good people already. If it's the end, I want peace."

There was illumination from above, revealing a tall mirror in front of Peter. His reflection flashed an evil grin back at him.

It is too late for that, Pete. I'm already a part of you. You will be spared from the terrible fate that waits the world. That is my gift to you, but you cannot stop death.

"You are not a part of me. I reject your gift," Peter said bitterly. He reached out and smashed the mirror with his right fist. The glass shattered and Peter reached out, grabbing his doppelgänger by the neck and squeezing.

You know, you should really see a therapist, said his double. *Way to reach out and touch yourself. You're going to go blind if you keep that up.*

"Screw you. You're not real."

So, I'm a hallucination, which means you're crazy. Oh, that's right. I forgot. I blew up your therapist, so I guess you're screwed. She wasn't very good, anyway.

"Tell me about this invasion that my brother is planning! Tell me everything!"

The double reached up and tried to claw at Peter, but it was unable to make contact. It was as if some invisible barrier was preventing it from seizing Peter.

Why can't I get to you?

"You give me some answers and then I'll give you yours," demanded Peter, tightening his grip on its throat. What the hell? If it knew about the serum, it wouldn't change anything...or so Peter hoped.

Oh, I see. Quid pro quo. Okay, I'll bite.

Peter tightened his grip around its neck.

It's an expression, asshole. I'll tell you what you want to know, but then it's my turn.

"That's more like it." Peter loosened his grip so it could talk easier. That's right. It wasn't actually talking.

The invasion has already begun. There is nothing you can do to stop that now.

"Begun? What do you mean it has begun?"

I am not the only one of my kind. I am one of many, walking unseen amongst your ranks except by individuals. If your people ever catch on, it will be too late.

"What do you mean you walk among us? You aren't real."

Yet you hold me by my throat and are having a conversation with me.

"You're a figment of my imagination! A hallucination!"

Then why question a hallucination? What truth do you hope to uncover?

"I'm not the only one who can see you. General Ramses or Assistant Director Wolff were both bitten by Carl. Those are the others you are talking about."

And your brother.

Betancourt laid everything out for Marcy from soup to nuts. He told her about the Infantry Drone Program, THV, the crash site in the Congo, RGT, Peter, Carl, Carl's tumor, his ability to communicate with the drones, the kill chip, and the birth of Kafka.

She sat there in her den listening intently, unquestioningly. She had known Darius for years, and she knew that there had to be truth to this outlandish tale he was relating, or he wouldn't be telling it.

When Betancourt had finished, she was silent for a moment, absorbing everything. "So there was nothing found inside the ship at the crash site?"

"No. The ship was empty."

"Yet there were infected found around the crash site? These…zombies?"

It was odd hearing an official at the CDC refer to them as zombies. Then again, in the new millennium the CDC actually posted information on their website about a zombie pandemic. After facing harsh criticism, they took it down.

"Exactly."

"Perhaps those that piloted the ship succumbed to this virus— THV—and then it spread to anyone who found it."

"But if that were the case, there should've been at least one undead extraterrestrial left to be found."

"True. It wouldn't have been able to eat itself," Marcy conceded. "Maybe it escaped the craft after the crash, before anyone found the craft."

"Possible, but there weren't any sightings of an undead alien." Betancourt thought for a moment. "A Captain who monitored the psychological impact of the program on the men, including Carl Birdsall, had a theory about all of this. She said that THV existed for a purpose. Something about clearing a path for something."

"Well, if viewed as a pandemic, the living would eventually lose ground to the dead through attrition—"

"Undead," Betancourt corrected.

"Yes, undead. Taken to its ultimate conclusion, the pandemic would wipe out the dominant species on the planet. If you say that the virus is transmitted through bites, it becomes a zero sum game. The virus' gain would be humanity's loss."

"That's what I said. There's been talk by Kafka about ushering in an invasion of this planet."

"Wiping out the dominant species would make the invasion rather easy," said Marcy.

"What if I told you that Kafka found a way to facilitate the attrition even further?"

"How?"

"He's sending a signal through RGT to electronic devices that are somehow turning civilians into the undead."

"Through a non-biological means of transmission?" asked Marcy. "That's impossible."

Peter was engaged in an internal dialogue with his doppelgänger.

"So you're telling me that Carl has one of you inside him, too? But he was never bitten," said Peter.

There is more than one way for a virus to spread.

"How? And what about using the RGT to turn people? How is that even possible?"

You humans are electrical beings, your nervous system running on impulses. All ones and zeroes.

"I don't understand."

Viruses can be spread through non-biological means.

"What, like computer viruses?"

The abomination smiled at Peter's recognition.

"What about THV? How can it jump from a biological virus to a non-biological virus?"

Marcy stood up, gesticulating wildly. "All pandemics start with a virus that affects a nonhuman species, like birds."

"Yeah, I remember reading about the Avian Flu," said Betancourt.

"Right. Then there's some kind of gateway animal—in the case of the Avian Flu it was swine—that becomes infected and then can infect humans. The virus, mutating in the gateway animal, makes a jump to the human species."

"So you're saying that was how Carl Birdsall contacted THV without being bitten?"

"Exactly."

"But there was no gateway..." Betancourt froze as a chill went down his spine, causing a global breakout of goose bumps.

"Darius, what is it?"

"There were pigs."

"Pigs?"

"We used pigs in the training exercises with the undead drones. We used them as bait to lure them."

"But the virus began in humans," Marcy pointed out. "Why would it go from human, to pig, and back to human?"

"You said it a moment ago," said Betancourt, "to mutate. Now Kafka can create other types of infected, like Ramses and Wolff."

"But the digital transmission still doesn't make any sense. There has to be a separate mechanism."

We frequently select a subspecies to use as a gateway for transmission to the dominant species. Your swine did nicely.

"When you talk about transmission, it's as if *you* are the virus," observed Peter.

That would be an accurate statement. A virus is a life form. On this planet, they are primitive, devoid of any intelligence. You have seen nothing like our kind before, but other civilizations in this universe have fallen to us.

"What about the RGT?"

Most beings in this universe share an electrical essence. Our civilization has unlocked the secrets of a biological-digital interface that has not yet even been imagined by your people. The distinction between the biological and the digital has been breached, what your kind calls the soul.

"So using the RGT, which you planted on this planet, you are downloading yourselves into…us?"

We possess bio-digital copies of our genome that have been transmitted into your own bio-digital genomes and corporal vessels, but that transmission occurred at the inception of your species. Therefore, I would use the word "activated" rather than "downloaded."

"What do you mean by activated? You mean we've been walking around with you already inside of us?"

You're not so stupid after all, human. We share a common ancestry, so the source code of our genome is already implanted into what you would call your collective unconscious. It is why, although we communicate differently, we understand each other. The activation key is what is actually downloaded.

"Not all of you are the same, though. Why are some of you like vampires, others like werewolves, and others like zombies?"

I do not fully understand your references, but I can tell you that passage through the gateway organism and subsequent mutations can result in variations in our manifestations.

That was what all of these horror figures had in common. Vampirism, lycanthropy, the disease creating zombies—they were all spread through infection. Even demonic possession was exactly that—possession by a foreign entity (i.e. infection of the soul). It was all starting to make sense.

Peter had another question, but he was almost embarrassed to ask it.

"So how is it that you can speak English?"

I am not speaking to you right now, remember? You are perceiving me as ideas. As to your comprehension, it's all ones and zeroes. What you call binary is a universal modality.

"So why come here to this planet? Why us?"

"The ultimate fate of a virus," said Marcy, "is to wipe itself out once it runs out of hosts or perishes before it can spread itself. As long as it is alive, it is always searching for new hosts to prevent its own demise."

"So the extraterrestrials who designed the virus want it to eventually die out so they can swoop in," speculated Betancourt.

"It seems to fit the paradigm you're laying out."

It is our mandate. We travel the universe searching for life, and then it is conversion through infection or death, which in-turn leads to conversion.

"What about my brother?"

Enough questions. I have given you plenty of answers because your knowledge of the truth will not impact the course of things. Now it is my turn.

"Fine. You want to know why you cannot download yourself into me."

Exactly.

"Well, I might as well tell you because it won't change a damned thing anyway. I was given a serum that is acting as a blocker to your ass. Think of it as biological virus protection to your digital disease. You won't ever be able to have me."

And this information pleases you. Why? It will stop nothing.

"So what are you going to do, Darius?"

Betancourt was momentarily lost in his own thoughts. "If everything we've speculated is true, then I think I know what Kafka's next move is." He suddenly stood up. "I have to go. Thank you, Marcy."

"Wait a minute, Darius. You can't wake me up in the middle of the night, drop this doomsday scenario in my lap, and then cut and run."

Betancourt held her hands in his appreciatively. "You've been most helpful, Marcy. Thank you."

"Wait a minute. I can tell—"

"Marcy, there's no one in our government that you could tell that would believe you, and if it's really infiltrated by enemies, you'd be putting yourself in danger. Sit on this for a while. When I need you and the time is right, you can help me. In the meantime, I have an infected ex-soldier and a young girl wanted for sedition parked in your driveway. I've imposed enough."

They heard the honking of a horn outside.

"Speak of the devil," said Betancourt. He kissed Marcy on the cheek and started to walk away.

"Wait," she insisted.

"What now?"

"Follow me upstairs."

"I have to go."

"It will only take a minute," she insisted. "Please, Darius."

They ascended the steps into the kitchen. Marcy took her civilian mini-com and called up a digi-lock key sequence. "Where's your multi-tasker?"

He took it out and showed her. She sent the key sequence to his multi-tasker.

"What's this, Marcy?"

"It's the key to my father's house. The address is in the message. No one will know to look for you there. We haven't sold it yet. We've been so busy with the funeral arrangements and keeping things together."

"I'm sorry, Marcy."

"He had stage-four pancreatic cancer, Darius."

"I'm sorry about dragging you into all this."

"If you're correct, then we're all going to be dragged into this."

There were footfalls down the stairs. Marcy's husband, Red, walked into the kitchen. "Marcy, what's going on?"

"I'm sorry," said Betancourt, bowing out, "but I have to go."

He heard the front door close behind him as Red began to question Marcy. "Honey, who was that at this time of morning?"

Betancourt didn't envy Marcy. She had to come up with a story and fast, or at least a truncated version of the truth, omitting some key parts. Hopefully, Red understood.

Peter was wearing a shit-eating grin. "It pleases me because it means that you are dependent on our bodies. It also means that you have your limitations, and limitations can be exploited."

Before his double could respond, he was shaken awake by a commotion in the Humvee. Betancourt was getting in the car. Brittany was awake and crouched into a corner of the backseat, away from Peter.

"Where are we?" asked Peter groggily.

"Why did you honk the horn?" Betancourt asked Elicia.

"I got bored, so I turned on the radio. It appears we're all wanted for the murder of General Ramses."

"What? Ramses is dead?"

"The news said that as we escaped, Kafka came and dismembered him in front of everyone and took off in a police car. They think we're with Kafka."

"Jesus Christ. Now we're fugitives wanted for the murder of a four-star general. We'll have every agent of government gunning for us."

"How did it go in there?" asked Elicia.

"If my friend is right, then THV is being used to clear the way for an invasion."

"No," said Peter sitting up. "THV *is* the invasion. The aliens are the disease; or rather the disease is the aliens."

"What? How do you know that?"

"I've been seeing this double of myself ever since I've been infected. I'm pretty sure Carl did, too, in the beginning. The serum you gave me is preventing it from possessing me fully, but let's just say we...had a frank discussion."

Betancourt switched on the ignition of the car. "So you're saying this thing copped to everything? Why?"

"Because it thinks that the invasion is inevitable, and it is already counting me on its side. These things are already inside of us. They download digital activation codes into us."

"So you're saying these aliens are like herpes?" asked Elicia. Everyone gawked at her. "What? It's just an analogy."

"That's why Kafka is using RGT to turn people into zombies," said Peter. "It's a bio-digital infection that can be spread through man and machine. They download something that activates their possession of us."

"Bites and megabytes," Elicia quipped.

"Exactly," said Peter. "Apparently that's what our souls are made up of, and they have the technology to steal it."

"They're hacking our souls," gasped Elicia.

Betancourt put the Humvee into gear. "Ramses let something slip about Kafka being able to communicate backwards through the RGT broadband. That must be how he's using the RGT to turn people into zombies. If you're right about this, then I definitely know Kafka's next move."

"And what's that?" asked Elicia.

"He's going to attempt to transmit through the master RGT console. It's where all of the RGT in the entire country is filtered through."

"Where's that?" Peter asked, still feeling woozy.

"Area 51."

"Are you shitting me?" Peter exclaimed. *"The* Area 51? That's where these viral aliens are going to transmit from?"

"Yes, Major, and the irony isn't lost on me either."

"Well, we have to stop them," said Peter.

"You're not up to any more action tonight," said Betancourt. "I've found us a place to stay while you heal and we formulate a plan. Kafka is also on the run tonight with the authorities hot on his tail. That should buy us some time."

"Where are we going?" asked Brittany, who appeared sobered up and terrified.

"A safe house where no one will know to look."

"You trust this person?" asked Elicia.

"Marcy's a friend. She and I have known each other for years. It's our best option right now," said Betancourt entering the address of the house into the navigation. He gunned it out of Dr. Marcy Cummings' driveway and tore down the street following the navigation.

Chapter 12

04:36 HRS
Beeville Summer Carnival
Beeville, Texas

Kojic, Ehsan, and Adnon wandered in between carny tents amongst the din of games and rides, doing their best to blend in. Kojic told Adnon to buy a cotton candy, and Adnon did it grudgingly, holding it out in front of him as if it were a bomb.

Ehsan found the whole thing mildly amusing, but Kojic was focused. He waited until they reached the center of the carnival, and he pulled out his mini-com. He sent out a ping, a tone containing a unique sequence, and waited.

After a brief moment, he received a ping back.

"I've got it," said Kojic casually to Ehsan. "Follow me."

They walked around the carnival until the ping became strongest. They stopped to look around right in front of the tent advertising a freak show.

Anon looked up at the hand-painted banners advertising the Bearded Lady, the Human Fetus, and Bat Boy. "Americans are disgusting."

Kojic shot him a reproachful look, but before he could say anything, the dingy-looking carny with a waxed mustache and slicked down black hair standing in front of the tent gestured to the three men. "This way, gentleman, and you will all become true believers."

It was the code.

The carny gestured to the entrance of the small tent and Kojic lead the way. Ehsan followed and Adnon discarded his untouched pink cotton candy into a waste receptacle before going in.

They were guided to a small, dark seating area that consisted of long, backless wooden benches on dry dirt. At the front was a crude stage with a closed curtain behind it, the resting place of Bat Boy and such.

The carny joined them momentarily and stood theatrically in front of them. He was holding what looked like black rags in his right hand.

"Gentlemen, if you'd place your hands behind your backs."

Ehsan shot Kojic a weary look, but Kojic nodded his approval.

"Wait a minute," Adnon protested.

"Do as he says, Adnon," said Kojic. "This is for the safety of everyone."

"Yes, it's for safety," said the carny. "If not, I'll have to ask you to leave."

However, Kojic knew that if they didn't follow protocol, they would not be leaving this tent alive. "Do as he says, Adnon."

Adnon put his hands behind his back, as did Kojic and Ehsan. The carny pulled out plastic ties from his ragged pants and began to bind their wrists. When he was finished, he stood in front of them, the master of ceremony.

"I'd like to draw your attention to the stage, please."

All three men looked at the stage as the carny stepped out of the way, gesturing grandly.

But nothing happened. The curtains to backstage remained closed and no one came out.

Kojic heard the soles of shoes crunching on the dry dirt behind him, but before he could turn around, someone had thrown a heavy sack over his head. The same must've happened to Ehsan and Adnon because he heard them startle and grunt. Adnon cried out.

The weight and thickness of the sack material was oppressive on Kojic's breathing, which caused him to hyperventilate for a moment, but then he pictured his Marina in his mind's eye and quickly replaced his panic with icy hatred.

He felt hands slide under his armpits and he was lifted off the bench and dragged. His escort turned in a semi-circle, which led Kojic to believe that he was being dragged around and behind the stage.

Then he felt a breeze on his bare arms and the din of the carnival reappeared for a moment. He was lifted into the back of what must've been a van. He felt another body next to him, and then a third was shoved in after him. Then he heard the back doors slam shut.

The driver and passenger side doors opened and shut, and there was a brief conversation in Arabic that Kojic didn't understand.

"What is happening?" It was Adnon's panic muffled by the thick sack cloth. Poor, meek, Adnon.

"It's okay, Adnon," Kojic reassured. "We are in our brethren's hands now."

"Quiet back there!" shouted one of the men up front.

The three men were silent for the rest of the ride. They were intercepted by another cell and were en route to the OIL safe house, and Kojic was mentally planning out his precarious appeal.

***

Order for International Liberation Safe House
Undisclosed Location
05:02 HRS

"Why have you called us here, Kojic? Cells are not supposed to be in direct contact. It compromises us all." said Bushaj. "Where is Belmont?"

"I would not have sent out the signal if it wasn't urgent. What I have to tell you is too important to be delivered by courier. Belmont was killed," said Kojic. This response elicited mumbling and whispers from the group. "...and I believe that his killer has taken over one of our major cells. My cell. His name is Kafka." This brought more whispers and furtive glances.

"We have heard of this Kafka," said a man named Murati. "He is a high ranking agent."

"He is something else," corrected Kojic. "He is not a true believer, and he is deviating from Belmont's vision."

"If he is not a true believer, then how did he achieve such a high rank in the Order?" asked Bushaj.

"He killed Belmont and told everyone that he was carrying on his work. He has been...corrupting agents with THV."

There where chortles and scoffs from around the table. "This is impossible," said Murati. "Why would he use THV on agents?"

"Because he can control the agents once they are corrupted," said Kojic.

There were laughs around the table. "How is this possible?" asked Bushaj. "Only the Automaton has been known to control the undead."

"He *is* the Automaton," replied Kojic. "Belmont recruited him by revealing his government's treachery, and when they tried to kill him, it sealed his fate with our Order. However, somewhere along the way, he began to change, and he is no longer human anymore."

"No longer human," chided Murati. "Then what is he?"

"He no longer talks about jihad. He now talks about an invasion of Outworlders."

"Outworlders?" asked Murati, incredulous. "Gentleman," he addressed the others in Kojic's party, Ehsan and Adnon, "I think this man is crazy and is wasting our time."

"He speaks the truth," asserted Adnon. "Kafka infected agents and corrupted Kojic's wife."

Kojic looked down at his folded hands and swallowed back his pain at Adnon's mention of Marina. He cleared his throat. "If he is not dealt with, Kafka will corrupt other cells and eventually the world with THV."

"Maybe that was Belmont's plan all along and Kafka is just carrying it out," said Bushaj.

"Once again, he is infecting our own ranks. I do not believe that to be part of Belmont's vision," insisted Kojic, "unless you all want to become undead monsters."

There was more murmuring around the table.

"We are all prepared to sacrifice ourselves for jihad," said Murati. "We don't fear death."

"I am not talking about death," said Kojic. "I am talking about something worse than death, an abomination. These Outworlders are outsiders, gaijin, and are not a part of our jihad. From what Kafka says, they have a jihad of their own."

"What proof do you have of these *Outworlders*?" asked Bushaj. "Have you seen one?"

"This Kafka must resemble one of them. He is very tall with long legs and arms, black skin, and four eyes."

"Four eyes," said Bushaj disbelievingly.

"Yes, you heard me correctly," said Kojic. "He can sense the presence of others and can sometimes appear to read thoughts."

"Then how is it you three were able to escape?" asked a man named Sylaj.

"He doesn't think it necessary to pursue us," said Kojic. "He has his mission, and we no longer serve a purpose in it."

"And what is this mission?" asked Bushaj.

"He is going to go to Area 51, where the master console of RGT is located, and he is going to transmit a signal turning everyone into the undead."

There was more uneasy laughter around the table.

"And you expect us to believe this...fantasy?" chortled Murati.

"I know this sounds ridiculous," admitted Kojic, "but our mission, our vision is in danger of being corrupted by a gaijin. We are for the liberation of our people, not their enslavement by alien overlords."

"Alien overlords," chuckled Murati. "Listen to this man. You, Ehsan."

"Yes."

"Have you born witness to what this agent is telling us or has he gone completely mad."

"He speaks the truth," replied Ehsan gravely. "I wish it were not so, but it is. Kafka is very dangerous."

"What do you propose we do?" asked Murati.

"We have to stop him before he reaches the master RGT console at Area 51. We must kill Kafka," insisted Kojic.

"We cannot penetrate Area 51 with all of our forces. It is fortified to the hilt," said Bushaj. "What makes you think he will be successful?"

"He will use his portable RGT unit to turn any of the defending soldiers into the undead. He will then be able to control them," said Kojic.

"We will need proof of this," said Sylaj. "We will need to meet with this Kafka ourselves."

"That would be suicide," said Adnon.

"How do we know that you three aren't traitors to the Cause and Kafka isn't pursuing you to bring you to justice?" asked Bushaj. It was a fair question that Kojic would ask if he were in their shoes.

"I understand your position," said Kojic, "and if I were you, I wouldn't trust us either, especially with the tale I bring to you. Send a small team to make contact with Kafka, but change the location of your headquarters without informing the team. This way they cannot lead him back to us. If they return unharmed, you will tell them the new location."

"You do not expect them to return?" asked Murati.

"No, I do not, but if they do with a report of our treachery against the Cause, then you may dispense with us as you see fit." That last part made Adnon and Ehsan shift nervously in their seats.

Sylaj took notice. "Does this arrangement make you uncomfortable?"

"No," replied Ehsan.

Sylaj then looked at Adnon, who shook his head.

"If what you say is true, then you have nothing to fear," said Murati.

"If I am right, then you have everything to fear. We must begin to consider how to kill this gaijin," said Kojic.

"One matter at a time," said Bushaj. "First we make contact with Kafka. In the meantime, you are free to stay with us, but under guard."

"I understand completely," said Kojic.

"Your companions do not appear to share your conviction," said Sylaj.

"I fear for your team, that they may lead Kafka back to us," corrected Adnon.

"I fear that Kafka will succeed in his mission," added Ehsan.

"For right now, you just fear us if you are not telling the truth," said Bushaj. "We don't like traitors to the Cause."

"I knew Belmont well," said Kojic. "I knew his vision, and this is not it."

"If you are correct, then this will be a major schism in the Order, for I'm sure Kafka has contact with other cells. I'm sure he has other followers in the Order." said Sylaj. "This will cause many problems."

The meeting dispersed and Kojic, Adnon, and Ehsan were all escorted to new quarters. An armed guard was placed outside of their room.

"Why didn't you tell them that we were infected?" whispered Adnon as Kojic laid down the bedding provided to him by Bushaj.

"They would've never believed it," whispered Ehsan.

"And if they did, we'd be dead by now," said Kojic. He felt the guard outside of the room. He felt his heartbeat. He wasn't sure if the other two did, and he didn't want to tip them off to his emerging abilities. If they became suspicious of him, he had to worry about them as well.

Kojic lowered himself wearily to the floor, placing his back against the wall. He thought of Marina—his Marina—wandering in that back lot with the other dead, Kafka's personal menagerie of lost souls.

"I am hungry," declared Adnon. "Why did they not offer us food?"

"We are lucky to be alive," answered Kojic.

"But we are the same as them," insisted Adnon. "We follow the Law and we fight for the Cause, yet they treat us like enemies."

Ehsan stepped in front of Adnon, ignoring his outburst. "Kojic, what if Kafka tells them lies about us? What if he tells them we betrayed the Cause?"

"If this cell sends out a party to make contact, I don't expect them to return."

"But we don't know that for certain," said Ehsan. "Kafka is clever. Why kill them, when he can use them to get back to us and convince this cell to follow him?"

Kojic in his heart knew that this was a possibility. "Ehsan, what other choice do we have?"

"We can run," interjected Adnon, now stepping in front of Ehsan. "We can leave the Order."

Ehsan hissed in disgust at the suggestion and crossed to the other side of the room, turning his back on Adnon.

Kojic looked Adnon in the eye. "Do you betray the Cause so easily, brother?"

"It would appear that our Cause has betrayed us, Kojic."

"There are people and there is the Law from which the Cause springs. People come and go, are strong and weak, but they are all subject to the Law and they all fight for the Cause."

Ehsan turned on his heel quickly, facing Adnon. "We are foreigners in an unfamiliar land, Adnon. Without the Network, we'd never survive."

"They will take one look at Kafka and they'll see he's not one of us. He looks like a reptile or insect. There is no hiding that fact," reassured Kojic.

"He would not let any other cell questioning his authority survive," said Ehsan, finishing the thought.

"That's right," said Kojic. "I am fairly certain that anyone Bushaj or Murati send out will not return."

"And then?" asked Adnon impatiently.

"And then we will be vindicated. It is not the first time an individual has been corrupted and had to be dealt with by the Order."

Kojic looked up suddenly, as if startled.

"What is it?" asked Ehsan.

"They've made a decision," said Kojic.

Within seconds, the door opened and Murati stepped into the room. He looked at Adnon, then Ehsan, and finally his eyes rested on Kojic, who he ascertained to be their leader.

"We send out a team tonight. Gather yourselves. In a half an hour, we move to another safehouse. You will be bound and blindfolded as a precaution."

"Of course," said Kojic, answering for the triad, but he knew that Murati and Bushaj didn't want them knowing the location of one of the cell's safe houses…in case their story didn't check out.

"I will need the location of Kafka," demanded Murati.

"Of course," said Kojic.

Murati gave the nervous Adnon a final look and left the room, closing the door behind him.

"So we put my theory to the test," said Kojic gravely.

"How did you know?" asked Ehsan.

Kojic avoided his gaze, which he was sure aroused greater suspicion from Ehsan. "Know what?"

"That they were coming with a decision?"

Because I could feel them, you idiot. "I just had a feeling."

"Well, I hope your feeling about Kafka is correct, Kojic."

Kojic slowly rose to his feet. "We do not need to worry about if I am right. We need to worry about what to do about it once Bushaj realizes I am right."

***

06:12 HRS
Marcy's Father's House

Elicia sat on an old, plush armchair in the corner of the bedroom watching Peter toss and turn in a fitful sleep in the bed. The darkness was waning outside the large window and the horizon began to glow a burnt orange.

She watched the man who saved her life from monsters twist under his bed sheet in agony. The Colonel told her that his infection with THV allowed his body to heal from trauma, making him stronger. He told her about Peter's brother Carl and how the healing changed his morphology.

However, the Colonel thought that the serum he injected Peter with would prevent any such metamorphosis...or at least he hoped that was the case. Peter's body was covered with scars, which made Elicia wonder if this was the worse trauma he's ever experienced.

Given what the Colonel said in the car, she doubted it.

She was outright exhausted from the night before, and she envied her sister in the other bedroom who was sleeping soundly. But Elicia, as tired and weary as she was, could not bring herself to give up her vigil.

The Colonel kept watch for a couple of hours and came in to check on her and ask about Peter. Once he saw she wasn't going to sleep, he smiled and told her he was going to catch some shut eye downstairs and to holler if there was trouble.

The softness of the armchair beckoned her to rest her tired eyes. She was sure there were brief moments when she did shut her eyes, despite her best intentions to keep them open, but she never allowed herself to drift off for more than a minute or two. Peter's moans and cries would wake her, and the rising sun was bathing the room in light to support her cause.

She was grateful to Peter, not just for saving her neck, but for convincing the Colonel to save Brittany. The least she could do was stay up with him as he writhed in the bed soaked with sweat, his body mending itself while struggling to retain its humanity, even if he had no awareness that she was there with him.

She thought he was good-looking—tall, athletic, strong...the type of guy that Brittany led around by the nose. The type of guy that wouldn't give Elicia a second look.

She had become resigned to this fact years ago and had avoided the jock in favor of the tall, thin, brooding iconoclast, that deep guy who waxed philosophical over a coffee and would write songs about how he secretly pined away for her. In theory, those specifications sounded intriguing, but in reality, those guys tended to be huge douche bags.

Yet here was a guy who went against everything she looked for in a man, and she found him attractive. Even more, she found herself attracted to him.

But that was just it. He was a man. Most of the guys she ran into were frat boys and college *boys*. Peter was older than her—she wasn't sure by how much exactly—but he was no boy.

He had seen too much, had taken on tremendous responsibility. She had always admired those who served in the military. She believed they had a certain courage and conviction that wasn't for her, but she respected the hell out of it.

Peter felt suspended in darkness, but not midair. It was as if he was in some gelatinous kind of matrix that oppressed his body and breathing, as if it was smothering his lungs. Yet, as it oozed into his pores and orifices, he felt his wounds mend, the fibers of his body becoming taught and stronger.

But the ooze wanted more. It wanted him to become something more...something else.

His body fought the ooze with every cell, struggling to retain its anatomical integrity. The process was excruciating. Then there was that voice that presented itself as cognition...

Peter, I wish that I could save you this pain, but the serum in your bloodstream will not allow the full transformation. Such a shame because you would become something powerful...something beautiful.

"Screw you. This hurts like a bastard, but it beats becoming whatever you are."

If you knew what it felt like to become what I am, you would feel very differently, I think.

"I can feel the fibers of my muscle and the cells of my skin weaving themselves back together."

Yes, one of the benefits of being a 'monster.' Actually, in your case, a half-monster. But really, doesn't being half-a-monster make you a monster? Period.

"You're just pissed that you'll never take my humanity."

It is not I who has robbed you of your humanity. Your own species has already done that. Your own government has disowned you because you are only half-different, and now they hunt you down like a monster. So doesn't that, in effect, make you a monster?

"A person isn't defined by how they are treated by others. Each person decides who they are."

Really, Peter? Are you that naïve? Do you really believe that any individual has that kind of volition over their own lives? There are many forces that operate on an individual that are outside of their choosing that direct who they become.

"Oh, I get it. I'm the victim of my circumstances, right?"

We cannot help our circumstances.

"We each have free will, the ability to defy the odds and determine our own path."

Oh, yes, because you know that kind of thing happens all of the time.

"I don't appreciate your sarcasm."

Well, your argument is, once again, naïve. I have statistics on my side, but go ahead. Hold out hope. Maybe you'll be that one who bucks the system. The unruly primitive who defies an empire. The whore with a heart of gold.

"Is that how you see us? As urchins living in a bad corner of the universe?"

Something like that.

"So what is all of this? Your white man's burden? Your attempt at missionary work to enlighten us as a species?"

You don't perceive us as enlightened? We are higher order beings. No question about it.

"You are a virus."

Once again, Peter, you are viewing us as a species from your very limited understanding of a virus. A virus, according to the understanding of humans, is a contradiction. It is life, yet it is not. It can carry on many of the activities of life, yet it is lacking in some important areas. Most importantly, it lacks the machinery to reproduce. The only way a virus can proliferate is to infect a host.

This is why your species cannot wrap its brain around the state which you call 'undead.' Your zombies and vampires, for example. They are not alive, yet they are not dead. They carry on certain activities of life, namely feeding, yet they cannot reproduce without infecting another host.

"Yes. Yes. I get it. What we call zombies, vampires...you guys...you *are* the virus and the virus is you."

Finally, some progress. Perhaps you aren't as dense as I originally thought.

"But how can you be higher order beings if you are limited in things like reproduction? We humans have no problem reproducing."

So I've noticed. And you wonder why we consider you the cockroaches of the universe. I forgot you Texans don't believe in evolution, let alone comprehend it. Your understanding of what you call evolution is incorrect as well. In fact, your Charles Darwin never referred to it as "evolution." He called it descent with modification. He never referred to species as higher or lower ordered. Some species were just better adapted to their environments. It had nothing to do with intelligence or culture.

Look at reptiles—cold-blooded, relatively less intelligent fauna on this planet. Yet, in the climates in which they live, they are perfectly adapted because they do not waste energy generating their own body heat—they absorb it from their surroundings, they have more energy for more important activities. They have volition over their own heart rate, and can slow it down at will, allowing themselves to be submerged underwater for long periods of time to evade predators. Can you do that?

"What does that have to do with us?"

Remember we share a common ancestry going back eons. Don't you think we made the same mistakes as you humans? Using up the resources around us until there were none left. Succumbing to degradation of our bodies—famine, disease.

"Oh, great. A tree-hugging race of warlord aliens. What, is your mother ship a hybrid? Like a Prius mother ship? Now I suppose you're going to tell me that it's not too late to reduce our carbon footprint or some bullshit like that. Did Al Gore send you? My father always thought he was an alien life form."

You can make jokes all you want, Peter, but I'm not going to preach to you about conservation. In fact, we are all about consuming everything around us. We are viruses, remember? But we have devised a way to survive the exhaustion of resources.

"Your digital representations."

Ah, very good. That's right. Who needs a body when your digital "soul" or "software" can live on? It only needs to be transported to a new world with new resources to be consumed.

"So as long as you can send copies of yourselves to new worlds, you are pretty much immortal."

Not so much immortal as having a long life span. Immortal implies that we can't be killed.

"You can be killed, if you cannot get your digital copies to new hosts on a new world."

Silence.

"Oh, what, is the topic of your mortality making you uncomfortable?"

We do not die. We simply become dormant. Unactivated code sitting on a shelf somewhere in the universe. You would call it Purgatory, but that is not a worry. Your world has plenty to offer in the way of hosts and resources, and we have just begun to consume.

"For now, anyway. If you're not immortal, does your species believe in a God or gods?"

We do not have any use for religion. We travel and we consume.

"Don't you wonder where you came from? Who wrote the original code for your digital souls?"

Does a virus contemplate where it came from? It lives to infect. When the host dies, if there is no other host available it dies. There is no virus heaven or hell.

"As far as you know, anyway."

You Texans, clinging to your bibles and your guns. You always need a purpose and you fight to protect it.

"Don't you feel empty without a purpose?"

Our purpose, much like yours, is to reproduce. Since you reproduce via sexual intercourse, evolution has given you a sex drive. Since we reproduce through infection, we are given a lust to infect. To infect and murder is like an orgasm to us.

"That's why when Carl planted thoughts of murdering my father in my head it was arousing. I never felt anything like it before."

It was what your brother felt when he fantasized about murdering Captain London...and even you.

"But he didn't murder me, and that bothers you."

We wanted him to, and he almost did after what you did to his girlfriend in Italy...

"Hey, in my defense, she was trying to KILL me, but hey, why let the truth get in the way of a good story?"

...but his sentimentality towards you, because you tried to protect him from your government, changed his mind, and now I'm trapped as a voice in your mind, never able to fully realize my destiny.

"You can always kill yourself. End your suffering now, because it isn't going to get any better than this. I'm a lousy roommate; I don't play well with others..."

Believe me, at this point if I could, I would, because there is no point in remaining in this state indefinitely.

"But you can't kill yourself."

I can only die if you die and there is no other host to infect, but that is no longer an option because the serum prevents you from infecting others.

"So you're trapped."

In a matter of speaking.

"Good. So there is a hell for viruses."

Your mortality has been altered as well. Other than being dismembered, your body and mind will age slowly and your natural lifespan will lengthen.

"How long?"

Generations.

"My brother, too?"

Yes, even more so. To the other humans you will appear to be immortal.

"Like vampires."

That is what your species has perceived us to be. Over the ages, through countless contacts and attempts at invasion, humans have constructed this mythology about us. It was a way to make sense of what they couldn't possibly understand.

"So why are you telling me all of this? Why not keep me in the dark?"

What's the point? You are going to live through your own hell, in time. If we win, you'll get to witness the mass conversion of humanity. You'll be a half-human living in a monster's world and then you'll wish Colonel Betancourt never gave you the serum.

"And if you guys lose..."

Then you'll be a half-monster in a human world, a pariah among men. All who you care about will die as you live on. You'll witness loss after loss until you decide to end your live or live out the rest of your long lifespan in self-seclusion.

"So either way, I'm screwed."

We've been defeated before, but we always pop back up, and perhaps you'll be so lonely that you'll not only welcome our reintroduction into this world...you'll facilitate it. So you see, all we have to do is wait.

"But it won't benefit you. You'll still be trapped in my body unable to jump to another host."

The others will find a way. Corrupted data can sometimes be salvaged, transferred to new hardware.

"So you do pray for something. How human of you. My species calls it hope."

There's no need to get insulting.

"So, now you have to find a way to pass the time inside me while you wait for your unlikely salvation. We've got a long time to get to know each other."

I have some form of entertainment while I wait.

"Oh yeah, and what's that?"

Suddenly Peter felt a rush through his body, and it shuddered in the matrix with bloodlust.

You might say I can press your buttons.

"Wh-what are you doing?"

More specifically, I can press the buttons on your amygdala.

"Oh shit, no!"

Elicia wasn't sure if she drifted off, but she suddenly saw Peter sitting straight up in bed. But there was something wrong with his face…with his features.

He suddenly leapt out of bed and lunged for Elicia, hands reaching for her throat. She screamed, but she didn't have time to fend him off. He had her hands around her throat and they both toppled over with the chair.

Betancourt came running up the stairs and into the room. He grabbed Peter around his neck in a kind of headlock and pulled him off of Elicia.

"Stand down, son! Stand down!"

Peter looked up at Betancourt with wild eyes, but he went limp in his arms. In a matter of moments, his features went back to normal and Betancourt released him.

Peter sat on the rug in the middle of the floor panting, as Elicia was backed into a corner trembling, her eyes wide in horror.

"What the fuck is wrong with you?" She was rubbing her tender throat.

"Elicia, I'm…sorry."

Betancourt was sitting on the bed panting from his exertion as Elicia ran out of the room. Peter heard her sister talking to her, asking her what happened.

"I see you're stronger," said Betancourt.

"Yeah, it would appear so."

"You need to control whatever that is that's got a hold on you."

Peter looked down at his socked feet in shame. "I know."

"You know, she stayed up all night with you."

If Peter didn't already feel like shit, this guaranteed it. "Christ. I didn't mean to…"

"I know," said Betancourt. He lost the commanding officer tone in his voice and replaced it with something that sounded like compassion. "She'll be all right."

"I feel awful."

"She's a tough girl. She'll get over it."

However, that wasn't what Peter wanted to hear. He didn't just want her to get over it. It pained him that he hurt her. He didn't want forgiveness. He wanted more. Did he want her to like him?

"Well, there's no time to feel awful. We have work to do." There was the old Betancourt that he knew and resented.

Peter stood up deftly. "First, I want to brief you on my…dream."

"I'm not Sigmund Freud, Major. We have more important…"

"It communicated with me, sir. In fact, we had a whole conversation. It has weaknesses."

Betancourt appraised him for a moment. Peter knew he was calculating whether or not he should devote serious time to Peter's dream encounter. "Okay. But bullet points. Time is of the essence."

"Yes, sir." Peter looked at the wall and felt Elicia's rapid heartbeat as she sought comfort with Brittany in the other room.

"There'll be time for that later, Major."

"Yes, sir."

"Let's leave them alone for a bit. We'll go downstairs and you can tell me about your dream."

"Yes, sir."

Chapter 13

Kojic opened his eyes and he was in the middle of a street at night. The buildings around him, stark, looming, metallic structures, were on fire and there was screaming all around him.

He stood up, brushing himself off, and he saw that Ehsan and Adnon were standing there with him, along with three wraithlike, four-eyed, silent figures. He looked up and saw three moons in the night sky.

"Where are we?" asked Adnon, frightened.

"I do not know," answered Kojic. He turned to the one wraith standing next to him. "Where are we?"

It didn't answer. It only pointed a finger.

Kojic, Ehsan, and Adnon, all looked in the direction that it was pointing and saw a throng of diminutive figures running towards him. They weren't human, but they looked like…children.

He saw Marina, in her current zombie state, pick one up. She turned it over in her hands as it struggled to break free. There were larger figures bounding down the street in her direction…the parents.

You must protect her. It was the figure standing next to him. It didn't speak, yet Kojic heard its voice in his head.

Kojic didn't hesitate. Desperate to protect his bride, he rushed forward and lunged at the larger figures as they descended upon Marina. In an unnatural fury, he reached out and slashed at their throats with elongated claws on the tips of his wispy fingers.

The parental creatures grabbed at their torn throats as others wrestled with them. Kojic pleaded for the others to join him. "Help me, Ehsan! Adnon!"

They looked at each other and then their own four-eyed monsters, which nodded in answer to their unspoken question.

They rushed forward, bodies twisted, fangs bared, and bit and slashed away at Kojic's antagonists. Marina opened her mouth wide and chomped down into the flesh of the youngling she held as it squirmed and screeched in terror.

When they silenced all of the figures around them, Kojic stood tall amongst all of the blood and bodies, feeling powerful and aggressive, like a predator at the top of a food chain. He looked around as legions of zombie creatures, like the ones he just killed, flooded the streets killing and destroying everything in sight.

Kojic looked around for his four-eyed shadow, but it was nowhere to be found. As if wondering the same thing, Ehsan and Adnon looked around for their shadows as well.

Marina grinned horribly, her mouth slick with the youngling's juices, and pointed at a reflective metallic surface next to Kojic. He looked and was startled by the reflection looking back at him.

It was wraithlike, had four eyes, and fangs protruded from its mouth. It reached up, as he did, with long, razor-sharp claws, and felt the accentuated ridges on its face that lent it a demoniac quality.

Ehsan and Adnon stood next to him, gazing at their reflections, which were in kind with Kojic's.

"What have we become?" asked Adnon.

Although we are many, we are one.

***

08:56 HRS
Outside Kafka's Headquarters

Four OIL operatives from Bushaj and Murati's cell waited in an unmarked van across the street from a large, abandoned building with a fenced in back area.

A man named Bejko produced his mini-com, sent out a unique pulse, and waited for a response. There was a unique tone transmitted back within seconds.

"I've got tone. We go in," said Bejko. "Petrela, I need you in a sniper position on the rooftop next door. Be careful not to be seen."

Petrela nodded.

Vllasi checked the explosives under his long coat. The air conditioner in the van was not working properly and he was sweating from the heat and the fact that he might have to meet his virgins if the meeting went awry.

They were briefed about this Kafka, but largely based on Kojic's account, which they had difficulty believing in its entirety. They had all heard of Kafka, but none had ever met him or seen him in person before. He was a legend in the Order, and legends had a way of falling victim to hyperbole, often in their favor.

Bejko was certain that all they were going to find was a very regular man who was cunning and resourceful. Whether he was a friend or enemy to the Cause was another matter entirely, but Bejko had been given authorization to use lethal force if necessary.

They exited the van, save Petrela. They crossed the street casually and strolled up to the old building. Petrela pulled away and around the corner, where he was going to park and enter the building next door from the other side. He had a tracker to follow the signal of Bejko's mini-com.

Bejko and Vllasi stopped in front of a rusted, windowless front door. Bejko sent out a second tone and the digi-lock disengaged. The two men looked at each other and Bejko opened the door. They both stepped inside.

They waited in the dark for a brief moment when an unearthly voice croaked over a PA system.

Greetings. Please stay where you are. I will send someone to get you."

Vllasi looked nervously at Bejko, fingering the detonation switch he ran up his right coat sleeve to his hand.

"Calm down," snapped Bejko, "or you're going to kill us both over nothing."

Vllasi nodded and released his grip on the detonator switch, but he wiped a hefty amount of sweat from his brow. Although he was a true believer, walking around with thirty pounds of C4 strapped to one's chest was hell on anyone's nerves.

They heard the echo of shuffling coming down the hall at some distance. Before long, a dark shape appeared whose gait matched the shuffling. As it passed by windows and was briefly illuminated, Bejko hoped that what he saw for only a moment was only a trick of the shadows.

He looked over at Vllasi, and the look on Vllasi's face confirmed what Bejko thought he saw and prayed wasn't real. At last, the shape stopped in front of them, its face concealed by the shadows. It gestured for them to follow it.

They trailed behind it, squinting their eyes at the sickly sweet odor of death, which reminded Bejko of a killing field in Albania where they shot captives in cold blood and left the bodies to rot. The communists called them dissidents. Bejko called them poor bastards who never stood a chance.

He put out a hand and touched Vllasi's arm to still his fidgeting, which had only gotten worse as they followed this shadowy figure into the bowels of the decrepit building. Vllasi's uneasiness was making Bejko nervous, but the more he thought about it, the more he realized that it really wasn't Vllasi making him nervous. He was picking up on something unexplainable that made his palms sweat and his skin go cold. Vllasi was picking up on it, too.

They reached the end of a long corridor and stopped in front of an elevator. The figured gestured for them to wait, and then it made its way down another dark corridor until it vanished from sight.

"Are we supposed to push the button?" asked Vllasi.

Bejko reached out with his right index finger to press the button when the doors creaked open, startling them both. They looked at each other and Bejko stepped inside first. Vllasi, terrified that the figure might return, jumped in right behind him.

They waited for a moment, but the doors remained open.

"Press the button," said Vllasi nervously, wiping his chin with the palm of his trembling hand.

"Which one?" snapped Bejko.

Then they heard the shuffling coming from the dark corridor that the shadowy figure retreated down. It was coming back in their direction. Before long, the figure reappeared cloaked in the shadows, its horrible countenance revealed for a second at a time as it passed windows.

Bejko looked up and saw a camera mounted inside the elevator car. "Which floor?" he called out to whoever was on the other end watching them.

There was no answer.

The shuffling grew louder and the shape larger as it was almost at the elevator. Bejko and Vllasi heard wheezing and what appeared to be a low growl.

Bejko began to push buttons—second floor, third floor, fourth—he didn't care at this point. Nothing happened.

"Bejko, do something!" cried Vllasi.

Bejko put his hand on Vllasi's arm, his signal to him not to have an itchy trigger finger with the C4, and he pulled out an AK-47 without the stock. "Get back!" he commanded the figure.

However, it pressed on unimpressed by his display of firepower.

"Stay back! I warn you!" He shoved the barrel of the gun outside of the elevator. Vllasi grabbed his arm in terror, like a younger brother looking for protection in the dark from the bogeyman. It looked as if the figure was going to walk right into it.

There was the grating of metal on metal and the elevator doors began to creak closed. Bejko pulled the barrel of his AK inside the elevator car as the doors closed. A hand reached out for them but didn't make it in time. There was a loud ding and the elevator slowly began to rise.

"Jesus!" shouted Bejko, unnerved. He looked up at the camera. "What the hell was that about?"

There was no answer.

"Maybe Kojic was right about this Kafka," said Vllasi.

"Shut up, Vllasi."

"There's something wrong with this Kafka. This isn't normal."

"Shut up, Vllasi! This elevator is probably bugged! He's probably listening to every word!"

Vllasi clutched his hand over his mouth at the realization that Bejko was probably right. If Kafka was watching, why wouldn't he be listening?

"Mere theatrics!" bellowed Bejko in a poor attempt at bravado, the tremor in his voice betraying him. "It's all part of the illusion."

The elevator came to a stop on the third floor, but the doors didn't open. Bejko pressed the Open Doors button, but nothing happened. The PA system crackled.

Place your weapon on the floor and leave it behind.

"It was a test," said Bejko annoyed. "He was testing to see how we would react. Now he knows I'm armed."

He placed the AK-47 on the floor of the elevator car and there was another loud ding. The doors scraped open and both men stepped out. The doors closed behind them and they heard the elevator descend...with the AK-47.

Bejko was now unarmed.

Please, down the hall, last door on your right.

"At least he's not sending another one of those things," said Vllasi.

Bejko shot him a disapproving look, and Vllasi shrank. Bejko began to walk down the hallway lined with doors, offices over a factory it seemed. Vllasi followed at a distance behind him, happy to let Bejko lead.

As they passed windows looking out over the fenced in area in the back, they saw dozens of people milling around. The way they were walking was odd, like their shadowy escort downstairs, and they were bumping into each other. It was like a yard full of very drunk people.

Bejko stopped to look out one of the windows. "Look, Vllasi. Look at those people down there. What's wrong with them?"

There was no answer.

"Vllasi." He tore his gaze away from the window in annoyance at his cowardly...

Vllasi was no longer with him.

He was gone, vanished, and Bejko thought he saw one of the office door digi-locks re-engaging.

"Vllasi! Where are you?"

He walked over to the door and turned the doorknob, but it was locked. He then knocked on the door and waited. No response. He put his ear up to the door and listened.

Silence.

The last door on the right. Please.

The voice made him jump out of his skin. The out dated public address system gave the voice an unnerving, tinny quality, but there was something else…something shrill about the voice itself. Something that had his subconscious screaming for him to turn and run.

He was unarmed and lost his compatriot armed with enough C4 to blow them all to kingdom come, but he had to see it through. He had his combat training. Plus, Petrela was on the rooftop next door. If he had to run, he had coverage.

At last, he reached the final door on the right. He reached out to open the door, but the digi-lock disengaged and the door slowly swung open.

Bejko looked in and saw a tall, lanky man…with four eyes…standing behind a desk. "Please, come in. Have a seat."

Bejko swallowed hard and entered the room. Kafka gestured for him to sit in one of the chairs in front of the desk. As he sat in the chair to his left, he heard the door to the office close and the digi-lock engage behind him.

"You must be Kafka."

Kafka sat in his chair and smiled. Bejko though he looked like a cross between a lizard and a praying mantis…with four eyes. Kojic said he'd have four eyes. The man actually had four eyes.

"Guilty as charged."

"It is good to meet you. I've heard stories—"

"All good, I hope," quipped Kafka, but his humor was lost on the petrified Bejko.

"You are something of a legend."

"Thank you…what shall I call you?"

"Bejko."

"Ah, yes, Bejko. So you're from one of the other cells?"

"Yes."

"And how, Bejko, did you find me?"

Me, not us. Bejko saw this as possible confirmation that Kafka was the only one left in this cell, as Kojic had explained. Alone…except for those things milling around out back.

"We were told to make contact by a courier from Ishmael Irani."

Kafka heard this name before. Belmont had mentioned him—he was some kind of bigwig, but Kafka sensed Bejko's pulse quicken.

He was lying.

"Oh, Ishmael Irani. Well, why didn't you say so?"

Bejko looked around the office, trying to look casual but failing miserably. "So this is your base of operations. Very nice."

"Yes, it serves its purpose," said Kafka. Bejko realized that it wasn't the PA system. This man's voice was really that creepy in person. "The Rollercoaster Recession has left a veritable wasteland where the manufacturing sector once was. These factories are great. They are sturdy, have limited access points, and are easy to defend. And spacious! Let me tell you about spacious!"

Kafka's expression, if it could be said that his face had expressions, quickly changed. "But I take it you're not here for a tour." There was a hint of menace in his tone, an unvoiced threat that sent a chill down Bejko's spine.

"No, I'm not."

"So what brings you by, Bejko?"

"Ishmael Irani heard of Belmont's death and he wanted a report on who was taking his place." Quickened pulse. Another lie.

"I see," said Kafka. "As you may have heard, Belmont, in his last hours, entrusted his mission to me."

"Where do you come from? No one has heard of a Kafka coming up in the ranks until recently."

"Belmont recruited me," said Kafka without missing a beat. "You know how he likes to collect people."

Bejko managed a smile. "He had a reputation. And what of Yvette? She was his right hand."

Kafka's expression soured. "She was murdered by an American. An army soldier. She was…indispensable."

Bejko found Kafka's reaction intriguing. It appeared this monstrosity was exhibiting some kind of emotion…sentimentality.

"I am sorry to hear that," replied Bejko. "She was a true believer. One of the best among us. So what have you been working on?"

"These are an awful lot of questions coming from another cell. The whole point of decentralized cells is that if one is compromised, the activity of another is not."

"This is for Ishmael Irani," Bejko reassured.

"Ah, yes. I forgot. The only thing I find strange about…well, you— not to put too fine a point on it—is that usually couriers from the higher ups are not members of other cells. They're usually independent. This way if they are compromised, they can't give up any of the cells."

Bejko's pulse quickened again, faster than before. "My cell has moved on without me. I don't know its location, nor do they know mine." This was the truth. "I am working with Ishmael Irani now." This was a lie.

Bejko quickly tried to change the subject. "So what are all of those people wandering around out back? What is wrong with them?"

Kafka smiled like a vampiric used car salesman. He liked to toy with his prey before eating it. "They're drones."

"Drones?"

"Yes, infantry drones. More specifically, United States Army Infantry Drones."

"I thought that program was discontinued after the incident in Siena, Italy."

"It was, but through American military mismanagement, I was able to obtain some from Mexico and Italy."

"Why aren't they wearing drone uniforms?"

Kafka grew serious, his eyes glaring.

"Why, Bejko, it sounds like you're accusing me of something. I don't know if I like the tone of your questioning."

"No, Kafka. Please. I did not mean any disrespect. It was merely an...observation." Kafka found Bejko's racing pulse intoxicating at the moment, and his fangs began to extend from under his top lip like a horrific erection.

Bejko wasn't sure if he was seeing correctly. Kafka laughed, as Bejko did a classic double take. "Wh-what is that?"

Kafka pointed to his protracted fangs with an abnormally long finger. "What, these? I'm just happy to see you."

Bejko knew the ruse was up. He stood up, flung his chair over the desk, hitting Kafka clear in the face, and he made a run for the door. Only Kafka was faster than Bejko and caught the chair before it hit him...

...and the office door was still locked.

"Shit!" cried Bejko as he pulled on the doorknob, snapping it off in his hand.

Kafka stood at an impressive six-foot seven or eight and loomed over Bejko. "What kind of guest treats his host like this?"

Bejko was pounding his fists on the door. "Vllasi! Vllasi, where are you?"

There was a large explosion a few rooms away that shook the entire office. Bejko held onto the wall and a dusty plastic office tree in a pot to steady himself. His ears rang as Kafka was upon him.

He struggled in hand-to-hand combat, blocking, striking, and twisting out of Kafka's grip, but Kafka was too fast and too strong. Kafka pulled him close in a horrible embrace, too close for Bejko to strike back or slip out of it, and he sank his teeth into Bejko's neck, his four eyes rolling back into his skull in ecstasy.

Petrela heard the explosion from inside the abandoned factory. He trained his sniper rifle on the windows where his tracker said Bejko's mini-com was located, but it was inside an interior room, so he couldn't get a visual

Petrela's mind raced to make sense of what was happening. Vllasi triggered his suicide bomb, which must have meant that the meeting went wrong. Yet, he was still receiving a clear signal from Bejko's mini-com. Had Bejko survived the blast?

He waited, watching the windowed corridor through his scope. There was no movement from within. He scanned

the perimeter of the building, even the fenced in back area with those strange people shambling around.

Nothing.

He checked his watch anxiously and did one more sweep of the exterior of the building with his scope. Nothing. Finally, he decided to pack it up.

He exited the building and ran for his van parked at the curb. He threw his rifle inside and hopped into the driver's seat. He looked around nervously to see if he had garnered the attention of any by-standers, and then he sped off.

***

"So you're saying that this thing is always with you, like a voice in your head?"

Peter sighed. "It's kind of like a voice, but it's more like an intrusion of ideas into my mind."

"Well, we now know of another weakness," said Betancourt. "If they run out of hosts and can't transport themselves they become…inert."

"That's right, sir."

"Well, if Kafka is going to do what I think he's going to do, he's going to be spreading digital copies of these aliens to everyone." The Colonel took a deep breath and held it for a moment. "What I am about to tell you is highly classified. It could very well end my career."

"No offense, sir, but you aided and abetted a fugitive—me—and you are wanted for the murder of a four-star general. Anything that happens to your career, at this point, would be an improvement."

"I see your point, Major…"

Peter waited expectantly as Betancourt became momentarily lost in his own thoughts, as if he had never realized his situation until Peter pointed it out. "…Area 51 houses the master console for Retinal Gateway Technology through which all transmissions in the country are filtered and analyzed."

"How can all of the RGT transmissions in the country be filtered through one location?"

"It's the ship," said Betancourt. "The entire craft serves as a magnet or beacon for the transmissions."

"That makes total sense," said Peter. "These aliens are nothing if not efficient. They travelled to this planet in the craft that would become their apparatus for pandemic infection. Waste not, want not."

"Kafka's likely move would be to access that apparatus and interface with it…"

"And convert everyone into alien zombies with his new trick," said Peter finishing the thought.

"He'd communicate backwards through the broadband, and Assistant Director Wolff will let it happen undetected," added Betancourt.

"So what do we do, sir? I take it we can't just waltz into Area 51 and tell them that the notorious terrorist, Kafka, is coming to use their space ship to turn everyone into zombies."

"No, we can't. It's not that they wouldn't necessarily believe it," said Betancourt, "for Chrissake, they're guarding an alien space craft. For one, as you have so graciously pointed out, we are wanted for the murder of a four-star general."

"Right…that small matter," said Peter wryly.

"The other thing is that Area 51 has state-of-the-art security. I'm talking stuff no one even knows exists, even within our own military."

"So they'll think they can handle whatever Kafka throws at them," said Peter thoughtfully.

"Something like that."

"Sir, have you ever been to Area 51?"

"Once. And let me tell you, the security is amazing."

"I heard that the site is no longer used for anything."

"That's what the government would have you believe, but the Janets still take off from Las Vegas and land regularly on the Area 51 air strip."

"Janets, sir?"

"The white airplanes with the red stripes that bring Area 51 employees into the site."

"Whatever security they have won't be worth a damn," said Peter. "Kafka can use his new trick with the portable RGT to turn guards into zombies as he waltz's right into the base."

"Exactly. So our best bet is to stop him when he makes his attempt."

"How are we going to do that? There's only two of us?"

"Yeah, but you're more powerful than one soldier," said Betancourt.

"But I'm not as strong as Carl," reminded Peter. "In a straight out fight he would win. He saw to it that all of his little clones are watered down versions of himself."

"What about your little friend inside your head?"

"He pretty much confirmed that Carl is stronger, and he'd never help me. In fact, to get out of his limbo he'd probably tell me how to get killed, so he'd be released from his purgatory."

"Nevertheless, keep your ears...uh, mind open. He may accidentally tip you off to something crucial."

"Or he may lead me to believe that he let something accidentally slip to get me killed, but I get your drift, sir."

"I think our primary objective is not to kill your brother," said Betancourt. "We just have to get to the ship first and destroy it before he can use it. Then we deal with him."

"What about Elicia and her sister? We can't drag them into this. They're civilians."

"Actually, I think the mighty Tronika can come in handy given our situation," said Betancourt.

"I don't follow, sir."

"We have to consider the very distinct possibility that we are going to fail."

Peter looked down thoughtfully. "Yeah, that's crossed my mind on more than one occasion."

"We need Elicia to fire up her blog and get the word out. She needs to tell everyone to drop off the grid."

"That would be suicide!" said Peter. "They'd track her, find her."

"Peter, I know that your first instinct is to protect her, but we are at war. This is all bigger than any one person. We're talking about the fate of the whole human race."

Peter stood up and turned away from Betancourt. "I don't like it. We saved her life so that now we can use her."

"You don't have to like it, son."

Peter turned on Betancourt. "I'm not your fucking son. I bet you had this planned out from the beginning. I bet it's why you changed your mind about going back to save Brittany. You figured if we saved her sister, she'd be willing to play her part."

"What's your point, Major?"

"My point is that you, Major Lewis, General Ramses…we're all just pawns for you, to be manipulated, all in the name of the greater good. Elicia is a person, with a life and a family."

"You don't get it," snapped Betancourt. "If this all plays out to its grisly conclusion, there will be no people. There will be no families. There will be no life.

"And, for the record, I am no Lewis or Ramses. I don't enjoy making the tough decisions, Major, but it is my duty, and you have to do your duty to stop the extinction of the human race."

"Elicia is not just a spectator in all of this. She actually has the platform to do something about it. Maybe she won't be so averse to all of this like you think. Why do you think she started her blog and podcast to begin with?"

"The NSA will track her down and come for her," said Peter bitterly.

"Whether or not she takes that risk is up to her," said Betancourt. "So I suggest that you deal with whatever feelings you have for this girl and do your duty. Your country…shit, the WORLD needs you. So get your head straight."

Peter stormed out of the room, passing a startled Brittany who batted her eyelashes at him. "Is everything okay, Peter?"

"No, it's not," snapped Peter.

"Need some company?"

"I just want to be alone right now," replied Peter icily, not even looking at Brittany, who was doing her best to accentuate her best features. She frowned as he descended the stairs. She heard the back door slam downstairs.

Betancourt came out of the bedroom and into the hallway where Brittany stood disappointed.

"Colonel, is he going to be okay?"

"He'll be fine. I need to talk to your little sister."

"We heard you guys yelling through the wall. I have to say that I don't approve. Don't you think she's been through enough?"

"Brittany, this country is in great danger. The world is in great danger. You don't know the half of it."

"Elicia told me about the monsters at the army base. It's so surreal."

"Brittany, it's beyond surreal. At this point it's about to get real, and I believe your sister can help."

Elicia appeared in the doorway wiping tears from her eyes. "It's okay Brittany."

Brittany turned to her sister. "Elicia, you don't need to…"

"I said it's okay. The Colonel and I have to talk."

"They can do this without you, Elicia."

"Brittany, please. Let us talk."

Brittany shot Betancourt a sullen, icy look and went downstairs.

"She's just trying to be a good big sister," said Betancourt.

"She was never a good big sister," said Elicia. "She was always focused on herself. She never took the time to understand me. If she did, she'd know why you and I had to talk."

"Elicia, we have to take into account the possibility that we won't be able to stop Kafka."

"You want me to fire up the old podcast again to tell people to stay off the grid."

"Yes."

"You have to realize that I won't reach everybody, and out of those I do reach, not all—if any—will listen. But I've been thinking about that, and I think I have a way."

"Really?" Betancourt sounded impressed. Or maybe he was just desperate for ideas. "How?"

"We'll have to fight fire with fire, and I think I know just how to do it."

"And how's that exactly?"

"Well, you said that Kafka is going to use a master RGT console to send his digital signal through cell phones, computers, and televisions…"

"That's right."

"Well, what if I told you that I've been scanning operating systems and firmware for mobile phone companies for side money."

"I don't follow."

"I check the systems for what are called open ports, vulnerabilities that a virus can exploit. Then I patch up the vulnerabilities."

"So you're saying that you can patch up whatever 'port' Kafka is using?"

"Not yet. There are too many of them. He's obviously using a pretty sophisticated ephemeral port to launch his digital virus, but I can crash the system, taking all devices out of the loop, while I figure out how to patch the weakness."

"How would you crash the system?"

Elicia smiled. "With a nasty little virus of my own."

"But there are lots of different mobile companies. Do you have experience with all of them?"

"No, but I don't have to. Thanks to the Open Mobile Alliance, all of the operating systems and firmware are standardized. What I can do for one, I can likely do for others."

"Are there any current weaknesses we can exploit?"

"There are a few, but I have ephemeral ports of my own that I have access to for my work. I have my hands on a nasty virus that uses a polyalphabetic cipher that I can unleash to burn the operating systems."

"That sounds like Tronika's handiwork."

Elicia shrugged. "You have to understand the disease to create a cure."

"I wish the army followed that logic when fooling with THV," said Betancourt ruefully.

"I can also tank the firmware, which is the ultimate burn. We're talking hardware damage that's not easily repaired."

Betancourt raised his eyebrows and rubbed his temple with his right index finger and thumb. "I'm not even going to pretend that I know what the hell you're talking about. What about your employers? Won't they be pissed that you are using their weaknesses to trash their systems."

"I think a little business interruption is nothing when it comes to national security," she said wryly.

"Try the safety of the world, but computers and televisions aren't cell phones. How will your plan work for them?"

"While they are not cell phones or mini-coms, these days, televisions and computer tablets and such are all mobile devices. Televisions are no longer one-way; they have touch screens and two-way communication ability."

Betancourt put his hands on his hips and couldn't help but smile.

Elicia smiled back. "You're impressed. I can tell."

"How did you learn all of this stuff?"

"Well, let's just say I haven't been busy all these years cultivating a social life, so I've had lots of spare time."

"What about the NSA? They'll track your activities."

"As Tronika, I've created a whole bot network that I can reactivate and use to hide my activities, or at least slow them down."

"Bot network?"

"I've garnered access to other computers using rootkits I designed." She saw the confused look on the Colonel's face. "A rootkit is a virus that grants me privileges to other computers remotely as if I was the main user, but the beauty of a rootkit is that it disguises its own presence so that the main user—or administrator—can't detect its presence. The compromised computer is called a 'zombie' computer, which can be used to launch attacks while making it look like it's the unsuspecting user who is doing it."

"Zombie computers," said Betancourt. "How ironic."

"Then I can start hacking into the Area 51 system and do what's called a core dump analysis to try and find out how Kafka is hacking into the system…what. Why are you looking at me like that?"

"I just realized that Peter was right to rescue you and your sister."

Elicia frowned. "Yeah, but I think I liked his reasoning better."

"Hey, that's not what I meant," said Betancourt defensively. "What you are about to do is very brave."

"Yeah, yeah. I know. I'm a real American hero."

"Elicia, there's a good chance that Peter will fail in trying to stop Kafka. Kafka is very powerful, more powerful than Peter, but if he can buy you the time you need, you might just save the country. What do you need?"

"I need a computer with access to the internet."

"That will be very risky."

"I'll activate one of my bots and then access my code for my port scanners, rootkits, and the virus that I have dropped in a virtual safety deposit box."

"Clever girl. Just in case your equipment is stolen, your work isn't."

"Right."

"I think Marcy's father has a computer or laptop around here somewhere. If they detect you, it will lead them to your bot?"

"Yup. Then I'll close the port before they complete the handshake."

"Handshake? Jesus, you hackers love your lingo."

"They will use data packets to sniff out my open port to the bot computer. Once they detect it, the packets will draw out my port and they will connect, in effect finding me out."

Betancourt, resigned, put his hands up. "I'll take your word for it. I'm too old for this shit. Go find Peter. I need to discuss our strategy for breaching Area 51. It won't be easy."

"No, I imagine not. Why do you want me to go find him?"

"He feels terrible about attacking you. He's a good kid. Give him a chance to apologize."

"That's not important, right?" said Elicia, blushing.

"It is to him," said the Colonel.

Peter was walking around in the fenced-in backyard, kicking stones as he walked. He heard the back door creak open and shut, and he looked up. His heart nearly jumped into his throat when he saw Elicia.

He froze in his tracks as she approached him.

"Hi. How are you feeling?" he asked self-consciously.

She looked down for a moment, and when she looked up, she bit her lip. "I'm fine. No permanent damage."

"Listen, I'm sorry about what happened."

"No need to apologize. I realize you didn't know that you were attacking me. The Colonel told me everything about the voice in your head."

"Oh. Good, I guess." He felt her heart flutter.

"Can you hear it now?"

"No. It doesn't always speak to me, but I get the feeling that it's always listening. You must think I'm some kind of freak."

Her vitals lit up like a Christmas tree. "Peter, you saved my life, and you saved my sister's life."

"And now Betancourt wants to cash in on the favor," said Peter bitterly.

"I know," she said. "We already spoke, and it's okay. Really."

"You know the NSA will track you down. They'll take you."

"I know, but it has to be done, right?"

"I don't think so," said Peter defiantly.

"Oh, come off it, Peter. Why do you think I started the blog and the podcasts in the first place?"

"Elicia, you don't have to be a hero."

"So you're the only one fit to play that role?"

"That's not what I'm saying."

"Peter, you've only recently become a freak. I've been a freak my whole life."

"C'mon, what are you talking about?" he replied awkwardly. He didn't know why she was getting angry, and he wasn't sure what he was supposed to say.

"Oh, really? Come on, you saw my sister. She's a freaking model. She's always been my parents' favorite, she's always been popular. She's never had to apply any real effort to get boyfriends. She's gets through life by batting her eyelashes, and then people can't throw gifts at her fast enough.

"But this isn't about her. It's about me. The ugly duckling, who had the misfortune of having to develop a personality and intelligence because I couldn't manipulate people with my looks."

"I don't think you're ugly," said Peter matter-of-factly. His sincerity stopped her dead in her tracks, and she began to blush. Her heart fluttered again, and his did in kind. "My little brother, Carl—now the mighty Kafka—used to feel that way. He was always the brains in the family. He saw it as a curse, but he had options. More options than I did."

"And look at which option he chose," said Elicia. "I am choosing a different option. Yeah, I'm a misfit, I always have been, but that doesn't mean I have to be so bitter about it that I turn dark. Because of what I can do as Tronika, I have a responsibility to do the right thing.

"That's what makes you different from your brother. You may not have his brains, but you took on responsibility. Responsibility to protect our country. "

"Believe me," replied Peter, "responsibility isn't all it's cracked up to be. I've seen many horrors. I've seen many good people—friends, my family—die."

"And that is what makes you a hero, Peter—the fact that you choose to shoulder the burden knowing exactly the cost of doing so."

Peter paused, weighing her words. "You really are smart."

Elicia blushed again and smiled. "And I believe you said I was pretty, too."

Peter flirted back. "No, I just said you weren't ugly."

"What about my sister? She's got eyes for you. You're exactly her type."

Peter smirked. "Not anymore. Now I'm a responsible freak like you."

"Really, now."

"Elicia, are you really sure you want to do this?"

"Trust me. Only I know how to go about it."

"How?"

"I'm going to out hack your brother. There's no time to explain. The Colonel actually sent me out to get you. He wanted to discuss the defenses at Area 51 and an attack strategy."

"Duty calls."

"So do you really think your brother can infiltrate Area 51?"

"Hey, my brother infiltrated Guantanamo Bay. I don't put anything past him."

Chapter 14

Beeville Carnival
11:29 HRS

Petrela roamed the grounds of the carnival in daylight. Because it opened at 11 am, the crowds were sparse, which meant less cover. Less cover made Petrela nervous.

He went over what happened—or at least what he thought may have happened—in his head. Bejko and Vllasi never left Kafka's hideout. There was an explosion. All of this meant that the meeting went wrong. Kojic was right, or at least it seemed. Even about the "drones" milling around out back.

He was at the center of the carnival and he sent out a ping from his mini-com. Minutes passed, and then almost a half hour without any return ping. Petrela looked around nervously. Maybe the site had been compromised.

Suddenly, his mini-com emitted a tone indicating that he had been pinged back. He walked the grounds until the ping became louder, and he stopped right in front of the tent for the freak show.

A cartoonish looking carny with oily black slicked down hair, a waxed mustache, and drab clothing beckoned him. "Step right up, young man, and we'll make a true believer out of you."

It was the code.

Relieved to be found, Petrela didn't hesitate. He stepped into the tent and sat on one of the long, backless wooden benches.

The carny produced a plastic tie from his pocket. "Where are the others?"

"Something went wrong. They didn't make it."

The carny bound his hands behind his back, and two other men entered the tent with a black sack. Petrela nodded. He knew the drill.

However, all four men were surprised when the curtains behind the stage opened and a tall, dark, lanky figure with four blinking eyes and a toothy grin stepped out onto the stage.

"What the hell is this?" one of the men asked the carny.

"I don't know," shrugged the carny, as confused as everyone else.

"Welcome all to the Beeville freak show, where we make true believers out of everyone!" said the four-eyed monster.

"Kafka?" gasped Petrela, who now wished his wrists weren't bound behind his back.

"The one and only, in the flesh! And do we have a treat for you tonight!"

The carny and other two men pulled handguns and trained them on Kafka.

"Ladies and gentlemen, boys and girls, we have a very special act for you tonight. No doubt, you have met my friend, Luka Kojic. Snappy dresser, wonderful singing voice, but not much in the loyalty department I'm sad to say."

"Where are Bejko and Vllasi?" asked the carny.

"Bejko is fine. Never better. As for Vllasi...well, he's around..." Kafka gestured widely around the tent. "But today, I want to introduce to you someone very special, a personal creation of mine, you all know her as Marina, Kojic's lovely wife..." Kafka stabbed the air with his long index finger, "...but at the Beeville freak show, she is known as no other than the Zombie Girl!"

Marina staggered out onto the stage and began to awkwardly pirouette, ending in a horrific curtsey. The men gazed upon the stage in horror.

"What is the meaning of this?" demanded the carny.

"This is a warning," said Kafka with great menace. "It was this easy to track you down. Tell your cell to mind their business. If not, I shall add them to my morbid little menagerie of monsters. Savvy?"

"This is not our way," said the carny. "The jihad you wage is not according to the Law."

Kafka shrugged sardonically. "Well, you know what they say about rules. They're made to be broken. Really, I don't know why you guys are so outraged. It's not like you're a bunch of boy scouts."

"You are not OIL. You are a monster."

Kafka smirked, revealing his right fang. "You say tomato, I say tomato. I can call you a bunch of deranged mass murderers and you can call me four eyes, but why resort to sophomoric name calling?" He hopped down from the stage, looming over his frightened prey. "I don't want to fight you guys. We share the same enemy. Those who hurt you have also hurt me...Can't we all just get along?"

"You're...going to let us go?" The carny swallowed hard and nervously licked his dry lips, afraid of the answer.

"Of course I am," said Kafka with mock surprise, "but I am keeping Bejko as a souvenir, for my trouble and all. You tell Bushaj and Murati—I believe those are your cell's leaders—to back off or I'll be dropping by to collect some more souvenirs…" He pointed to Marina. "Like Kojic's wife here."

The carny pulled Petrela off the bench and the four men slowly backed out of the tent.

"Be sure to tell Kojic that his wife is better at jumping around on a stage than a trained poodle," Kafka called after them.

They exited the tent and Kafka was left alone with Marina, who was still twirling around on the stage, nearly toppling herself over.

"You know you can stop that now." Marina stopped dead and stared at him with that vacant expression that the undead wear perennially.

Kafka called her over, and she hung on him like the head cheerleader on a quarterback. "I have plans for you, my pretty. What do you say to a little makeover?"

***

12:47 HRS
Marcy's Father's Residence

"So there's closed airspace above Area 51 monitored by radar," said Betancourt. "Groom Lake abuts one side, which is why it has the codename Groom Lake in some communiques."

"I've heard it referred to as Dreamland."

"That's in reference to all of the classified research projects that supposedly go on there."

"Supposedly," said Peter, shooting Betancourt a 'you've got to be kidding' look.

"There are armed guards around the perimeter in roving white jeeps. Once you've passed the point of no return, they shoot to kill. You'll see plenty of signage to that effect, but there's something else."

"Of course there is."

"The military has been running statistics on the amount of deaths in combat since the new, fractal camouflage was instituted. There's been a marked increase. So, in response a private consulting group has been experimenting with a material that naturally bends light."

"Great. Invisible guards."

"That's right. This new camo is one of the Dreamland projects. Now, just imagine if Kafka converts all of those guards with his portable RGT."

"Invisible zombies. Jesus Christ, this just keeps getting better."

Suddenly they heard the crackle of a bullhorn outside. Peter and Betancourt looked at each other.

This is the U.S. Army. We have the house surrounded. Exit the facility unarmed with your hands in the air. Failure to comply will result in the use of deadly force.

"What the…"

"How?" asked Peter.

"Where's Brittany?" asked Betancourt.

Peter ran into the living room and pulled back the curtain to the bay window. "MP's, and lots of them!"

Elicia ran into the house from the back yard. "Colonel…"

"I know. Where's your sister?"

They heard footfalls down the steps. It was Brittany. "There's a bunch of army guys outside…"

"Brittany, what were you just doing?" asked Elicia, now in the living room with Peter and Colonel Betancourt.

"There's nothing to do around here. I was just watching a little TV in the bedroom."

"You mean it was watching you," said Betancourt.

"Great," said Peter, "just great."

"She didn't know," snapped Elicia. "We never really explained it to her."

"Know what?" asked Brittany.

There was the breaking of glass and two canisters of tear gas began to spew on the living room rug.

"Everyone to the back of the house!" shouted Betancourt. They all ran into the kitchen with their hands trying to cover their face.

"Why didn't I sense them?" muttered Peter, cursing himself under his breath.

"You were a little preoccupied," said Betancourt. "No time for blame."

A tear gas canister crashed into the screen door and dropped, sending the tear gas into the kitchen with the breeze.

"Close the sliding door," shouted Betancourt.

The front door crashed in as several MP's wearing gas masks in column formation breached the house and stormed into the kitchen. Peter saw MP's breaching the back fence and crossing the back yard. Everything was happening so fast.

"They followed the breadcrumbs," Peter said to Elicia.

"Hands up! Back away! Hands up!" shouted the MP's.

Everyone backed against the kitchen counter by the sink and put their hands up. The soldiers grabbed them and dragged them out into the back yard. Peter, Betancourt, Elicia, and Brittany were all choking, gagging, and frantically wiping their eyes.

Peter and Betancourt heard a familiar voice.

"Really, I didn't think it would be this easy. I'm disappointed, Colonel Betancourt." It was Assistant Director Wolff. "You, Birdsall, and the infamous hacker, Tronika, all in one place. It must be Christmas."

Peter thought he heard an excited clicking coming from the man. "Screw you, Wolff."

"No thanks," replied Wolff icily. "Cuff them and load them up into the ASV."

"Jesus, an ASV for little ol' us?" quipped Betancourt.

"For the murderers of a four-star general and a cyber-terrorist," corrected Wolff, "I'm taking no chances."

"I'm no cyber terrorist," protested Elicia.

"Tell it to the judge," said Wolff. "I really don't give a shit. This is going to look great on TV. Three baddies in one sweep. A tribute to interdepartmental cooperation."

The MP Lieutenant rolled his eyes behind Wolff's back.

"Let my sister go. She had nothing to do with this," demanded Elicia.

"Aiding and abetting three fugitives. I'd say she has plenty to do with this."

"You bastard," hissed Peter.

"Okay, let's go," said the MP Lieutenant.

Peter, Betancourt, Elicia, and Brittany were all led out front, where several Humvees were parked on the front lawn and street, and placed into the ASV before all of the prying eyes of the neighborhood. And wouldn't you know it, as if by design, the press was there and documenting it all like sharks at a feeding frenzy. Wolff probably chummed the water ahead of time.

The four prisoners sat side-by-side inside the ASV on the floor.

"What are we going to do now?" asked Elicia in a hushed tone.

"I don't know," said Betancourt. "I didn't see this coming. I just don't know."

Brittany began to sob. "I didn't know. I didn't know."

"It doesn't matter now," said Betancourt. "This is what Kafka wanted all along. To keep us out of the way."

"Looks like he succeeded," said Peter reaching out with his senses. "Wolff is the only infected one. The MP's are all human."

"They're innocents following orders," said Betancourt. "They have no idea what is going on."

"A lot of atrocities were committed by those just following orders," said Elicia thoughtfully.

***

New OIL Safehouse
12:30 HRS

"I told you," said Kojic, "your men would not return. Kafka is not one of us."

"So it is true," said Bushaj looking away. "It has all happened as you said."

"So now you see that we are with you?" asked Ehsan.

"How could your cell have allowed this monster to take over?" asked Murati. It was an accusation more than a question.

"We told you," said Kojic, "He was accepted by Simon Belmont. They worked very closely together. Kafka was his lieutenant."

"Belmont didn't see the monster in Kafka until it was too late. Are you accusing him of being stupid?" asked Adnon. It was also an accusation more than a question.

Bushaj put his hand on Murati's arm to silence him. "Simon Belmont was a great man. A real visionary. No one is accusing him of anything. This Kafka must be really clever."

"He found your men at the carnival rather easily," said Kojic pointedly.

"Yes," said Bushaj contemplatively, "yes, he did."

"So what do we do?" asked Ehsan.

"We know where Kafka is. We strike back," said Murati pounding his fist on the table in emphasis.

"He will have cleared out by now," said Kojic. "He will attempt to infiltrate Area 51. It is his obvious move. We should intercept him there."

"There is no way he's getting into Area 51," said Murati dismissively. "We get him where he lives."

"You are not listening," said Kojic. "This man led a successful assault on Guantanamo Bay. He is always one-step ahead of everyone. Our obvious move would be to attack him at his hideout. He'll be prepared for that."

"He thinks he frightened us away," said Bushaj. "He will not think we will come get him."

"He may already be heading to Area 51," said Ehsan. "All he would need to do is use this portable RGT device and he could walk right through the front gate."

"We have not seen this portable RGT device that you speak of," said Murati. "How do we know it exists?"

"How do we know it exists?" Kojic stood up in outrage. "Haven't I been right about everything so far? Why would you now doubt me on this?"

"I say we hit his hideout," said Murati to Bushaj, ignoring Kojic's outburst.

Bushaj sighed deeply. "Kojic, we know you are our brother and we will take you in to our cell, but I think Murati is right. We hit him where he lives. He wanted a war, he'll get a war."

"We came to your cell because ours was compromised and we needed help to fight Kafka," said Adnon.

"We will help you," said Bushaj. "We are taking the fight to Kafka."

"You will have your revenge in good time," said Kojic, "but right now, we need to stop Kafka from carrying out his plan. He means to infect us all, even true believers. He is the ultimate enemy."

Petrela came running into the room. "It's all over the news. The army captured Kafka's army brother, another officer—the ones who murdered that general—and some cyber-terrorist girl."

"Where?" asked Kojic.

"Mathis. They're going to be transporting them back to Fort Bliss."

"Bushaj," said Kojic, "my two friends and I request a fast vehicle and weapons." Ehsan and Adnon looked at him questioningly.

"Why? To what purpose?" asked Bushaj.

"You are attacking Kafka's hideout. I want to get his brother."

"His brother? Why?" asked Murati.

"For leverage. He's kept his brother alive for some reason. If we have him, then we have leverage over Kafka."

"What makes you think Kafka will care if we have his brother?" asked Murati.

"He's right," said Bushaj officiously. "We cannot waste resources on a fool errand. We need you with us."

"Bushaj, please," implored Kojic. "We came to you and told you the truth about everything. We tried to warn you about Kafka. All I ask in return is that you grant me this. Please, Bushaj."

Bushaj waved a hand at Kojic. "Take it. You'll only be in our way anyway. Petrela, give them some weapons and the key to the 2021 Mustang."

"Yes," said Petrela, and he left the room.

"Good luck with your wild duck chase," said Bushaj. "Murati, round up the men."

Murati nodded and both men left the room leaving Kojic with Ehsan and Adnon.

"What are you thinking?" asked Adnon. "Why are we going after Kafka's brother? He probably doesn't care about him."

"You are probably wrong about that, Adnon, but that is not why we are going after his brother."

"Well, then why are we doing it?" asked Ehsan.

"I overheard Kafka talking to the NSA man," said Kojic. "He instructed him to hunt his brother and keep him occupied."

"Yeah, so?" said Adnon.

"If he wants his brother out of the way, then his brother must be trying to stop him," said Ehsan.

"Right," said Kojic. "We came to this cell for help, but help has left us. Kafka's brother is like us. He's infected. He's worth at least twenty of these idiots here."

"What makes you think he'll help us?" asked Adnon.

"We'll be rescuing him for one," said Kojic. "We all want to stop Kafka from carrying out his plan."

"The enemy of my enemy is my friend," said Ehsan.

"Exactly."

"What about the officer and the girl?" asked Ehsan.

"Maybe we kill them," said Adnon.

"A computer hacker might prove useful," said Ehsan.

"How?" asked Adnon.

"I don't know."

"Ehsan is right," said Kojic. "We need every soldier we can get on our side. Besides, if we kill the officer and the girl, then Kafka's brother may not want to help us."

"What makes you think that the three of us can pull this off?" asked Ehsan.

It was time. No more secrets.

"Have you been feeling the changes? Since the dream?" asked Kojic.

Both Ehsan and Adnon nodded.

"I don't know about you, but I feel...different. Stronger, faster."

"It's the infection," said Ehsan. "I feel it too."

"Me, too," said Adnon.

"It's a good seven hour drive," said Ehsan consulting his mini-com's navigation app. "They'll be sticking to the main highway, Interstate 37. We can take a short cut and catch them if we leave now."

"We can do this," said Kojic. He thought about what Petrela said. He thought about Kafka's remark about Marina. His blood boiled just thinking about it, and he had revenge on his mind.

"We have to do this."

***

15:57 HRS
Interstate 37

"I'm sorry you got dragged into this," said Peter to Elicia.

She regarded him with a weary look. The nonstop chases since she left Fort Bliss had taken their toll on her. Her sister sat with her face buried in her hands. She might have been sleeping.

"I dragged myself into this. I never was super serious about the whole hacker thing. I had a lot of free time on my hands, and I was pissed off at the system."

"Did anyone ever get hurt from one of your hacks?"

"No. Never," she answered quickly. "I never stole money or data or crashed anyone's system. I infiltrated systems and left my calling card, just to see if I could do it, but I never did any of that Black Hat stuff."

"Black Hat?"

"Illegal, criminal stuff. Stealing, damaging. I wanted out. I tried to stop, especially when the FBI was getting close on campus, but it was too late."

"Yeah, too late," said Peter pensively.

"Not that it matters much now," said Betancourt. "If Kafka succeeds, we won't live to see a trial. This is just to get us out of the way."

"Do you have a boyfriend?" asked Peter. That particular question out of left field took Elicia off guard. "You know, somebody to warn? Some other hacker?"

Elicia blushed and sighed deeply. "No boyfriend, I'm afraid. Hackers don't make a habit of communicating with each other offline. Safety precautions."

"Right."

"Never really met anyone that interesting anyway. Just a bunch of frat boys at school."

"I think I'm pretty interesting," quipped Peter, smirking.

"I make a habit of not dating half-aliens," said Elicia wryly. "It's kind of a deal-breaker for me."

Brittany looked up rolling her eyes, her eye makeup smeared all over her face. "Oh, will you can it, Elicia?"

Elicia looked stunned. "What?"

"You finally meet a good guy whose life just might be more fucked up than yours, and you push him away?"

"I was only kidding, Brit. Jesus. We're all going to die soon in a zombie apocalypse anyway."

"I didn't take any offense," assured Peter.

"No," said Brittany adamantly. "She always does this and I'm tired of watching it. Elicia, you always accused me of not trying to understand you, but I get you just fine. You don't understand yourself."

"I have no idea what you're talking about," said Elicia defensively.

"Of course you don't. You are so damned insecure that you look for any excuse to push guys away so you don't have to stick your neck out there. Yeah, we're going to die, so why not go out going against your nature and be adventurous?"

"Come on, Brit. What are we going to have our first date at the jail in the military base?"

"Major," said Betancourt.

"Yes, sir."

"Do you see how they're discussing you right in front of you, as if you aren't here?"

"Yes, sir."

"That's what my ex-wife used to do."

"Which one, sir?"

"Both of them. You should see when they imitate you. They use this weird voice, like you're John Travolta."

"Who, sir?"

"It's never too late, Elicia," continued Brittany. "For once, I'd just like to see you connect with someone. I want you to be happy."

"Kinda hard to be happy when we're in a military police vehicle on our way to prison to await a death sentence brought on by an alien invasion."

"Your sister has a point there," said Peter to Brittany.

"*You* stay out of this," snapped Brittany.

"I don't need you to defend me," snapped Elicia.

"Just don't get involved," said Betancourt. "Trust me, it's safer that way."

Adnon had the pedal to the metal, engine roaring, and was tearing down I37. "There they are."

They saw an ASV surrounded by what looked like six Humvees. Three in a vee formation in front and three in reverse vee formation in the back.

"What do we do?" asked Ehsan from the back seat. "Pull up close to the rear vehicle," said Kojic. "Real close. And be careful."

Adnon shot him a nervous look, but he pushed forward towards the rear vehicle. Kojic slung an Uzi over his shoulder and lowered his passenger side window.

"What are you doing?" asked Ehsan.

"After I go, you follow me," instructed Kojic.

"Follow you where?"

Kojic did not answer him. He undid his seatbelt, and he pulled himself up and out of the window in a single deft move. The wind was blowing through his hair as Adnon gained on the rear vehicle.

Kojic pulled himself up, clutching the top rim of the car window and resting his feeton the bottom rim, and he swung himself onto the car hood still clutching the top rim of the passenger side window with his left hand.

He heard Ehsan swear out loud, but he ignored the remark and turned around on the hood to face the upcoming back end of the Humvee. He waved for Adnon to pull closer.

Kojic saw inside the Humvee that he had been noticed, and the soldiers were talking to each other frantically. They were raising their weapons as a voice came over a bullhorn.

You, behind us. Back off or we'll use deadly force.

But it was too late. Kojic had leapt from the hood of the Mustang to the back of the Humvee and was pulling himself onto the roof.

The Humvee began to swerve as Kojic steadied himself on top. They swerved a little too close to the left flank of the reverse vee.

Perfect.

Kojic jumped from the rear Humvee as bullets tore through the roof and landed onto the back of the left flank vehicle. He pulled himself up to the roof as he heard Ehsan shoot out the back tires of the rear vehicle.

As he tried to steady himself atop the flanking vehicle, it began to swerve away from the ASV, but it slammed into the Mustang. Adnon was trying his best to keep it in place as Ehsan joined Kojic on the roof of the vehicle, leaping like a panther from one tree branch to another.

Kojic pointed to the ASV and leapt onto it as Adnon careened the Humvee into the rear left panel of the ASV. Ehsan followed as the Humvee popped up onto the right side of the Mustang, crushing it, and using the Mustang as a ramp flipped over on its side.

The Humvee rolled over and over behind them on the road and Kojic knew—no felt—that Adnon was all right. He felt a quickening of pulses inside the ASV and he grabbed on as the gun turret swiveled around, taking Ehsan off guard.

Ehsan slid off the side of the turret but grabbed firmly onto the barrel. Unable to get a clear shot, the turret continued to swivel around so that Ehsan was hanging in front of the driver.

A voice inside Kojic's head—that of the doppelgänger now within him—told him to pull out his mini-com. He held it up to his eye and a code uploaded onto the device. He then initiated the code and the digi-lock to the hatch disengaged.

Kojic felt a quickening from somewhere in front, and he looked up in time to see Assistant Director Wolff leaping onto the ASV, morphing in midair into a four-eyed beast, and landing with a thud.

His gripped Kojic's hand holding the mini-com and crushed it inside Kojic's grip with his own. "What are *you* doing here?" he growled.

However, before Kojic could answer, Ehsan hoisted himself back up onto the top of the ASV and the gun turret swiveled around, knocking both Wolff and Kojic off balance. The top hatch opened as a soldier emerged with a handgun.

Gunfire erupted from the front two flanking Humvees and the rear right flanking Humvee as soldiers hung out of the windows. The bullets hit Wolff, Kojic, and Ehsan like a barrage of bee stings, causing them to stagger around the turret like drunkards. The soldier in the hatch took aim at Kojic but was knocked off balance from inside and fell back into the ASV.

Suddenly, all six tires of the ASV screeched to a halt, sending Wolff and Ehsan flying forward, but Kojic grabbed Ehsan by the wrist. The three Humvees in front skidded sideways to stop about one hundred feet in front of them, as did the two rear Humvees about as many feet behind them.

Kojic swung open the hatch, and he and Ehsan dropped inside. They each grabbed a soldier as Peter yelled, "Don't hurt them!"

They shot Peter a quick glance, bearing their fangs, and slammed the soldier's heads into the inside wall of the ASV, knocking them unconscious.

The driver tried to draw on them, but Ehsan crushed his gun hand and slammed his head into the top of the ASV. Gunfire erupted outside as they lit Wolff up like a Christmas tree.

"Major, don't," Betancourt warned.

"They're not here to kill us," said Peter with a certainty that even he couldn't understand.

"That's right," said Kojic. "How did you know?"

"They're firing on the beast," said Ehsan. "We need to get out of here." They heard footsteps on the roof.

"Close the hatch," ordered Peter.

Kojic nodded and re-engaged the digi-lock. There was pounding on metal from above and voices shouting to open the hatch.

"Free me," said Peter.

Kojic nodded and cut the ties that bound Peter's wrists. Peter stood up and took the knife from Kojic, freeing Betancourt.

Outside the soldiers fired at Wolff in beast form, but he only snarled and howled, refusing to go down. Suddenly, the ASV's loudspeaker blared.

Step away from the animal, form a wide perimeter, 30-foot spread.

Recognizing military commands the soldiers outside backed away. The gun turret wheeled around and took aim at Wolff, who struggled to his feet, his chest heaving.

There was a loud bang, and a projectile took Wolff's head clear of his shoulders. Blood erupted from the open neck as his body fell limp to the pavement.

There were cheers and then someone asked where the other two assailants were. There was another boom as one of the now empty Humvees blasted off the ground, rolling over and over down the highway.

The path cleared, the ASV began to pull away, the soldiers on top hanging on tight. The top hatch opened and Betancourt popped up pointing an assault rifle at the hangers on.

"Sorry, fellas. This party's by invitation only. No crashers." They looked at him, incredulous, but he gestured with the barrel of his rifle to jump off. They looked at each other, one soldier shrugged, and they all jumped off the top of the moving ASV.

Betancourt climbed on top for a better look and saw them rolling on the pavement. He got back inside and sealed the hatch. The turret swiveled around and fired at the other two Humvees in front as the MP's took cover on the side of the road.

The ASV picked up speed and tore down the highway.

"We have to get off," said Betancourt. "They'll be sending air support and we're sitting ducks on here."

"I have an idea," said Peter.

He pulled off at Kerrville, and it wasn't long before he found a wooded area away from any traffic and residences. He pulled under a thick group of trees and turned off the ASV. Elicia was rubbing her wrists, tender from the tight plastic ties, and Brittany was crouching behind her little sister nervously eyeing their new guests.

"This should shield us from air support," said Peter. The radio went wild as search parties combed the area for them.

"Why did you rescue us?" asked Betancourt.

Kojic ignored him and addressed Peter. "You are Kafka's brother, yes?"

Peter looked at Betancourt uncertainly and then nodded his head. "Yes, I am."

"You are like us?"

"If you mean a piece of shit terrorist, then no. I am not."

"I mean you are infected," said Kojic.

"Yes, but I think you already know that. You are too, and your friend here."

Ehsan shot him a sharp glance.

"That is correct," said Kojic. "Before you were captured, what were you doing?"

"We are not at liberty to say," said Betancourt.

Kojic shook his head in frustration, as if he wasn't being understood. "Were you trying to stop Kafka?"

"Yes. We were," replied Peter.

"Don't tell them anything," said Betancourt. "They're with him."

"If they were with my brother, they would've killed us already," said Peter. "They sure as shit wouldn't have tried to rescue us. Kafka put us in this situation, remember?"

"That is correct," said Kojic. "We are not with Kafka. Not anymore. We need your help."

"And what makes you think we'll want to help you?" snapped Betancourt.

"Because we know that Kafka plans to infect the entire country," interjected Ehsan.

"So isn't that a part of your jihad?" Elicia asked. "Isn't that what you want?"

"No," said Kojic shaking his head. "It is not."

"That's because he plans on infecting all of OIL, too," said Peter. "What, no ultimate sacrifice for the jihad?"

"Kafka is waging an entirely different jihad than we are," said Ehsan. "His is against all of the planet."

"Yours might as well be, too," said Elicia. "You're against everyone who isn't you."

"You misunderstand," said Kojic. "We will fight, and we are prepared to kill for our Cause, but we prefer assimilation."

Peter chortled at Kojic's explanation. "Isn't that what Kafka wants? Full conversion. A zero-sum war. Our losses are his gain. Victory through attrition in our ranks and conversion to his."

"We don't want to turn everyone into zombies," said Kojic.

"No, you just expect blind disobedience to your Law," said Elicia.

Ehsan appealed to Elicia. "Someone like you should understand. You are called a terrorist for fighting for what you believe in."

"I am not a terrorist," she corrected, "and someone like me—a woman—would be treated like a second class citizen or an animal under your Law. So you're barking up the wrong tree."

"Without splitting hairs, here," said Peter, "it sounds like you want to help us stop Kafka. My question is: why us?"

"We tried to appeal to our OIL brothers," said Kojic. "We explained everything, and they saw it for themselves, but they are misguided and don't fully understand our enemy."

"So you're saying that they're not going to help you."

"They think they're helping," said Ehsan. "They're attacking Kafka at his lair as we speak."

"They're walking into a trap," said Peter.

"Exactly. You know your brother. His is very cunning. The only chance we have is to get to the master RGT apparatus first and destroy it."

Peter and Betancourt exchanged knowing looks.

"So it appears we aren't the only ones who came to this conclusion," said Betancourt. "The question is, do we align ourselves with terrorists?"

"Hey," said Elicia as she examined the instrumentation onboard the ASV, "this vehicle is loaded with some pretty sophisticated equipment, and it's a rolling internet hotspot."

"An *armored* rolling internet hotspot," Betancourt corrected smiling. "Will this equipment be what you need?"

Elicia's eyes were wide with excitement. She looked like a kid in a candy store. "It's exactly what I need, and because it's a vehicle, we can stay mobile. It'll make us harder to track."

"So what's it going to be?" asked Peter.

Betancourt pondered the possibilities for a moment. "Okay, we'll play ball. We ride to Nevada and intercept Kafka. Brittany will stay behind and drive around the desert in circles while Tronika here does her thing."

"No," said Peter. "You stay behind with them. They'll need protection in case they catch some heat."

"Major, I don't think that you should be alone with…"

Peter knew where he was going. "It's all right. We three are the best equipped for dealing with Kafka. No offense, sir, but you'll only be a liability. With the three of us and our enhanced abilities, I really think we stand a chance."

However, Peter could read Betancourt's mind. Thanks to the serum, Peter didn't have the same level of ability as the other two. They were somewhere between Peter and Kafka in power. If they decided to turn on him…

"I'll just need you to delay him," said Elicia. "He won't see me coming. Once I unleash my virus into the mobile operating system and firmware, his whole viral distribution mechanism will be toast."

"Fighting fire with fire," said Betancourt.

"Virus with virus," corrected Elicia.

"What's the fastest way to get to Nevada?" asked Peter.

"By train would be quickest," said Betancourt. "Your men's attack on Kafka's lair should buy us some time. Plus we're a little closer than he is."

"It'll buy us time if he's still there," said Ehsan. "He might already be on the move."

"All right," said Peter. "Let's get moving," he said to Kojic and Ehsan."

"What about Adnon?" Ehsan asked Kojic.

Kojic smiled weakly. "If I know cowardly little Adnon, he's already on his way to Mexico."

Ehsan frowned and nodded his agreement.

Betancourt looked at Peter. "I'll have my connections wire some funds to your phone so you can purchase a train ticket. It'll get you into Nevada, but it won't get you close. You'll have to improvise once you're in state."

"I don't think Amtrak runs that way. We'll have to hotwire a car," said Peter.

"You won't have to," said Elicia. "I'll send you ignition codes depending on the make and model of the car."

"Won't that be dangerous with Kafka running around transmitting his virus?"

"He'll be heading to Nevada like you and out of range to get me," said Elicia. "I should be fine."

Peter looked at Betancourt. "Find some deserted area to drive around in circles. With Wolff out of the picture, maybe the NSA won't be on your back now. Keep the girls safe. I have to take Elicia out if we survive this."

Elicia looked up, startled, her pulse quickening. Then she smiled. "Be careful, Peter."

"I'm with two terrorists headed to Area 51 to try to kill my half-alien brother and prevent a zombie apocalypse. What could possibly go wrong?"

He smirked and then climbed out of the ASV with his new partners.

Chapter 15

Outside Kafka's Lair
16:01HRS

Bushaj pinged his rooftop snipers on either side of the building, as he demanded radio silence. He, Murati, and their assault team crept along the side of the building. While Murati worked on breaching the side entrance, Bushaj walked all the way back to the fenced in back area.

It was empty. Completely empty. No shadowy figures lumbering about. He began to question his men's account, attributing their hyperbole to the mystique that surrounded this Kafka.

He rejoined the team just as Murati breached the side door. Murati gave the thumbs up.

"Camaj, come in," said Bushaj into his mini-com.

"Camaj, here."

"Did you scan the building?"

"I only pick up one life form with a strange signature."

"That's him," said Murati.

"Standby," said Bushaj into his mini-com.

"Standing by," replied Camaj, who waved to them from the rooftop opposite them.

"Marco, did you do your scan?"

"Yes. I'm only picking up one strange signature."

Murati nodded.

"Good, stand by," said Bushaj.

"Standing by."

"All right. He's in there all alone. He's one man. Let's make him pay for what he did to our brothers."

Everyone nodded silently. They all raised their automatic assault rifles and filed into the old factory building. Bushaj whispered a prayer to Allah and brought up the rear.

They crossed a dark stairwell, passing a small security camera mounted overhead, and filed into a long, dark corridor. They followed the corridors, working their way deeper into the interior of the building towards the factory floor at its center.

Murati peeked through the window in the door to the factory floor, checking for movement. "It's deserted."

Bushaj jerked his head to the side and put up a finger to shush Murati. He heard the echo of footsteps.

Lots of footsteps coming in their direction.

He pointed his index finger in the air and made a circular motion, and the team began to spread out, going away from the factory floor.

Murati went down a hall to the left with two others and listened intently for the source of the shuffling footsteps. They rounded a corner and heard the shuffling getting louder. Murati put up his hand and made a fist, signaling for the other two men to stop.

They waited, Murati down on one knee, rifles aimed at whatever was going to be coming. He nearly slipped and pulled the trigger when he heard one of the others screaming in terror from some other corridor. There was gunfire.

About a dozen bumbling silhouettes spilled into the end of the hallway hissing and growling, swiping their hands in the air as if trying to grasp them from afar.

"What the hell..." muttered Murati.

As if they heard him, the figures picked up pace and were growling as they lurched towards them. As they got close, their ghoulish features were revealed under the staccato lighting of the overhead fluorescent lights.

"Fire!" Murati commanded, and the hallway erupted into gunfire, the muzzle flashes creating a strobe effect. The bullets sank into the lumbering bodies, but it only slowed them down.

Horrified, Murati signaled for them to retreat. They ran backward, tripping over each other, as they unloaded on the tide of undead coming down the corridor.

They rounded the corner from whence they came and backtracked to the area outside the factory floor. That was where they found the others firing wildly down the other corridors.

"It was a trap!" shouted Bushaj, panicked.

No shit, thought Murati, who continued to fire at his band of zombie pursuers. He regretted ever doubting Kojic, and he regretted even more that Kojic's sorry ass wasn't there to share his fate.

"Onto the factory floor!" shouted Bushaj, and the group retreated inside. "Lock the doors!"

Murati ran forward and tried to trigger the digi-lock. To his surprise it worked. There was a tone and the lock engaged.

"Circle the floor, lock all the doors!" commanded Bushaj. The group fanned out and secured all of the doors. When they finished, they all stood back from their respective doors and waited.

The zombies pounded on the doors, but it didn't pose much of a threat. They were safe...for the moment.

"Everyone, spread out and find a staircase leading to the offices upstairs!" shouted Bushaj.

"This wasn't much of a trap," said Murati looking around the floor.

"That's what worries me," said Bushaj. His mini-com chimed. He picked it up. "Come in, Camaj."

"That strange signature is leaving the building."

Bushaj shot a confused look at Murati.

"What?" he shouted into his mini-com.

"Bushaj, Kafka has left the building."

"Coward," hissed Murati. "He keeps us in here while he slips away."

There was a chime over the PA system and a mechanized woman's voice came on.

Twenty...nineteen...eighteen...

"What is that?" asked Murati looking up at the ceiling.

"It's a countdown," said Bushaj. After a heartbeat, his eyes widened in terrible realization. "He corralled us into this place. Activating the locks to the doors triggered the countdown."

Fifteen...fourteen...thirteen...

Bushaj grabbed his mini-com. "Camaj, come in!"

Eleven..ten...

The zombies pounded on the doors.

"This is Camaj."

"Camaj, you need to get us out of here! We're trapped."

Seven...six...five...

"I'm coming in."

Murati put a hand on Bushaj's shoulder. "It's already too late, my brother."

Three...two...

Bushaj and Murati clasped hands in a soul shake, like they were going to arm wrestle, the handshake of brothers-in-arms.

One...

Bushaj and Murati closed their eyes, bracing themselves for the blast...

...but none came.

Bushaj opened one eye and looked around. Then he opened both. Murati opened his eyes. "Thank Allah."

The PA system crackled on.

Now you didn't think I was actually going to blow up my headquarters, did you?

"He's toying with us," said Bushaj out loud, looking around the factory floor.

"What now?" asked Murati, annoyed by the farce at their expense.

Oh, no. I have something more…interesting planned for you all. I left you a couple of playmates while I dispense with your snipers.

"That is impossible," said Murati. "Our scans only picked up one life form."

It was nice knowing you all, brief as it may have been, but I have more pressing matters to attend to. Ta ta.

Murati looked at Bushaj, who only shrugged.

"We have to warn Camaj and…"

Before Bushaj could finish his sentence, they heard the ground shake, as if from a heavy footstep. There were the sounds of gears turning and hydraulics' working.

"What the hell was that?" asked Murati, wide-eyed.

"I don't know," said Bushaj, gripping his assault rifle. "Be ready!" he shouted to his men.

There was another heavy footstep, followed by two more coming from another part of the factory floor. It sounded like heavy metal on concrete. There was the whining of motors and gears echoing off the walls of the defunct factory floor.

"Holy shit!" someone shouted.

There was a hiss and the churning of motors, and one of the men screamed as blood spattered in the air off to the left behind a conveyor belt.

"Bushaj, what is going on?"

Bushaj pointed to his right. "You take the right. Flank it. I'll come in head on."

Murati nodded and slipped down the right side of the factory floor.

There were screams of terror, gunfire, and some more heavy thumping. Bushaj saw blood spray and body parts tossed up in the air like a salad just ahead of him, behind some heavy machinery.

He quickened his pace and vaulted a small conveyor belt as he trained his rifle ahead of him.

There were more screams to his far left and the whirring of motors and gears. More gunfire erupted, but it didn't last long.

Bushaj wiped the sweat from his brow with his sleeve, his hand trembling over his forehead. He looked to the right for Murati, and he caught a glimpse of him creeping along the far wall.

Murati stopped dead in his tracks, raising his rifle up high. Whatever he was aiming at was obscured from Bushaj's view by some equipment, but it must have towered over him.

"Murati!" he called out, but Murati never took his eyes off what he was looking at.

There were more mechanical sounds and two heavy footsteps. Murati yelled out and opened fire in frantic bursts. There were quick swipes of metal, flashes of quicksilver, and Murati crumpled to the floor in pieces.

Bushaj cursed under his breath as he began to back away, but he had the odd feeling that he was being watched. He turned to his left and saw a hulking mech standing there, heaving like a large predator, separated from him only by a conveyor belt.

It was a bramble of wires and pistons, shards of metal and sharp blades. Atop its neck, if that was what you would call it, sat a makeshift head housing a large monitor.

On the large monitor was a face, one that Bushaj did not recognize. It was a horrible face, and it glared down at him, curling its lip in feral hatred.

Bushaj raised his rifle and opened fire as it roared at him, flashing blades and spinning buzz saws from everywhere on its body.

It rushed him, slicing through the conveyor belt array as if it was made of butter, and Bushaj turned and ran. He heard stomping coming from behind him as the mech picked up speed in pursuit.

Bushaj meandered through the floor machinery, doing his best to lose the mechanical monstrosity chasing him, but whatever it couldn't circumvent it merely smashed through like it was crushing empty beer cans.

Bushaj just had to make it to one of the doors.

Camaj had just exited the front door of the building next door and was closing the distance to the factory. He pulled open the side door and slipped inside, pushing into a corridor and making haste towards the factory floor.

He turned a corner and ran into the area just outside the factory floor when he saw dozens of zombies pressed up against the door, looking in through the window.

His boots squeaked on the floor as he skidded to a stop before crashing into them. The sound caused a few of them to turn around, and Camaj nearly gasped when he saw their decayed faces, eyes frenzied with hunger for flesh.

They began to reach for him, snarling and hissing. Camaj turned around, feeling grasping fingers on his back, and began to run back in the direction that he came, the shuffling of his pursuers echoing in the corridor behind him.

As he passed a door, it opened, and he felt his head pulled back by his hair. There was a quick flash of pain, and he felt his throat open up like someone pulled a zipper.

He was released and he dropped to the floor, clutching his throat as he bled out crimson all over the dust-covered ground.

Kafka stood over him like a nightmare, licking the blood off his large hunting knife. Camaj stared up in horror, unable to respond except for some gurgling and blowing bubbles of blood out of the open wound in his throat.

The zombies closed in on him as he lay there on the dirty floor, his life slipping slowly away from him but not fast enough. The first of the zombie onslaught got down on their knees and began to bite into his flesh while he was still alive.

Bushaj made it to one of the doors, running into it with his body. He looked out the window and saw a horde of zombies looking right back at him.

He looked back over his shoulder and saw two mechs, one with the female face on its monitor and one with an older man's face, gaining on him, twirling blades and sporting sharp metallic fins.

If it was a choice between facing these things or the zombies outside, Bushaj was going to take his chances with the zombies. He reached into his pocket and pulled out his mini-com to disengage the lock on the door, but it wouldn't disengage.

"Shit."

The two hulking mechs bounded towards him. He turned and raised his rifle, taking aim at the monitors that appeared to serve as heads. He fired, but they raised their arms and deflected the bullets with their metallic fins.

The one with the older man's face on the monitor stepped forward first, twisted, and swiveled its limbs, dicing Bushaj's rifle and his arms with its numerous sharp edges.

Bushaj looked down at his stumps in horror, his face covered in blood, his mouth open wide in terror, but no sound escaping.

The horrid face of the older man on the monitor looked down at his prey and hissed as the mech with the female face joined them.

There was a nonverbal, guttural understanding that passed between them, and the mech with the man's face stepped aside. The one with the female's face leaned in so that her monitor was level with Bushaj's face.

Her screen began to flicker to a staccato rhythm, and Bushaj had a brief moment of recognition before he went slack, staring blankly into the monitor. When the mech backed away from him, Bushaj was nothing more than an armless zombie.

The two mechs parted and allowed him to stumble between them. Marina Kojic looked on through her monitor like a mother animal watching its young take its first steps, grunting her approval. Barry Birdsall looked on through his monitor and let out a tinny, digital gwarp of a laugh.

Marco saw a door open through his sniper scope, and Bushaj stumbled out into the daylight, tripping over his own feet and falling down in the dust, spurting blood everywhere from the two stumps he now had for arms.

Marco gasped at the sight and frantically scanned the area. There was no movement anywhere. He waited a bit, watching Bushaj flounder around, armless in the dirt, until he decided he could stand there and watch no longer.

He shouldered his rifle and left the rooftop. A moment later, he swung the door open to his building and trained his rifle, sweeping the area. Satisfied that there was no movement, he cautiously stepped outside and began to walk over to his fallen comrade.

As he got closer, he noticed that Bushaj was making grunting and growling sounds as he rolled around in the dirt, kicking up a cloud of dust around him.

"Bushaj."

No answer.

"Bushaj, what happened?"

Bushaj stopped rolling around and lay still, making strange rasping sounds, like a wild animal.

Marco inched over to Bushaj, training his rifle on the opposite building, and he reached down to grab his fallen comrade in the dust.

Bushaj craned his neck up and bit Marco on his hand. Marco cursed out loud and jerked his hand away, now training his gun on Bushaj. The dust began to settle and Marco began to see that his comrade was no longer himself.

Bushaj began to push forward in the dirt with his legs, snapping his jaws at Marco. Marco put his friend's head in the crosshairs and pulled the trigger.

As the echoes of the shot bounced off the side of the building, Bushaj lay face down in the dirt with his brains blown out of his head.

Marco backed away, looking at the nasty bite on his hand, and let himself back into his building. He stationed himself by the window and trained his rifle on the building opposite, his mind racing, thinking of what to do next.

He decided to exit the abandoned building out the other side and make his way back to his car. His bite was stinging him terribly, and he felt like he was burning up.

He threw his rifle into the back seat and slid into the driver's seat. He started the car, praising Allah for sparing his life, when he saw a tall, dark figure standing in the middle of the road holding a machine gun.

He put the car in gear and began to make a hasty three-point turn. The figure just looked on as Marco put the car in gear and sped away in the opposite direction.

Marco got away with his life, barely. He would go back to the safe house…or even try to make contact with another cell. They would…take him in. He would…lay low…for a while. He…he would…h…

Kafka watched as the car swerved and careened into a parked car. He casually walked up to the car, his machine gun pointed down at the ground, and the sniper in the car was clawing at the glass and growling at him. He glared at Kafka with dead white eyes. Kafka smiled back at him.

"Welcome to the family."

***

Needles, California
The Next Day
09:03 HRS

They had been taking turns driving for hours in their little hatchback, and they needed to stop for gas. Kojic wanted an SUV, but Peter insisted on a small car for fuel economy. Time was of the essence, and a smaller car meant fewer stops.

Kojic and Ehsan had been mostly silent on their trek across Interstate 40, which was fine by Peter. Any conversation was awkward and brief, and truthfully, the whole arrangement made Peter uncomfortable, but he knew it was a necessary evil.

He had made it clear hours ago in one of their brief exchanges that this alliance was temporary, and in no way made them friends.

"I don't like this one bit, but I think we all agree it's necessary. We can't kill my brother as individuals," said Peter, *"but together…"*

"Yes, don't worry. You don't have to invite me to dinner or let me fuck your sister," said Ehsan.

"I don't have a sister," said Peter, *"but if I did, I'd punch you in the mouth."*

Kojic shot Ehsan a dirty look in his vanity mirror and Ehsan, taking the hint, sat back in the backseat and looked out the window.

"Let's save our anger for Kafka," advised Kojic. "We cannot turn on each other."

"I just want you to know that this doesn't make us friends," pressed Peter. "I don't want any misunderstandings. When this is all over, you are still terrorists."

"You are assuming that we will survive to play out the aftermath," said Kojic coolly. He wasn't going to let Peter goad him into an argument. "You've made your point. We'll cross that bridge when we get to it."

Peter wasn't sure what was going to happen if they actually beat Carl. Would they immediately turn on each other? And what about their battle with Carl? Will these two just help each other while Carl makes minced meat out of Peter?

There were so many uncomfortable possibilities and the fragile alliance created enough tension to choke a grizzly bear. Peter hoped that they would remember their main objective and save the hostilities for the after party.

He pulled into a gas station off the highway that had a small diner and gift shop called the Covered Wagon. Quaint. Peter pulled up to the pump and put the car in park, turning off the ignition with his mini-com. It was able to access the car's computer, thanks to Tronika.

"I'll run in and get us some snacks and drinks," said Peter. "Why doesn't one of you make yourself useful and pump the gas?"

Kojic looked back at Ehsan, who huffed in protest, but when Peter got out of the car, Ehsan pushed the driver seat forward and got out to pump the gas. Peter waved his mini-com over the pump sensor to provide payment, and then he walked into the diner.

It was an old cliché, the tawdry roadside diner in the middle of nowhere. There were outdated jukeboxes at every booth with the numbers worn off the buttons. One had an out of order sign printed in all caps on a yellowed scrap of paper taped to the glass front, obscuring what Peter was sure was a very outdated catalogue.

He saddled up to the counter and took a seat right next to the payment kiosk on a rickety stool attached to the floor. It squeaked as he sat down, metal grating on metal.

"May I help you?" asked a waitress without bothering to muster up any modicum of enthusiasm.

"Three coffees and egg and cheese sandwiches please...on rolls."

The waitress entered it into her palm organizer, turned, and left without saying anything else. Peter looked around the diner. The clientele looked almost as dingy as the diner itself did.

There were groups of what looked to be couples at the booths holding hands and laughing, some tourists and some locals, as well as truckers and cab drivers at the counter. They all looked road-weary and grateful to replenish themselves in this simple oasis.

There was a young boy sitting next to his mother and across from his father in the booth closest to the front entrance. He had to have been around five years old, in Peter's estimation. He was drawing on the paper place mat with a broken green crayon taken from a worn plastic souvenir cup. The cup was filled with pieces of crayons, provided by the manager no doubt.

Peter allowed himself a smile, a small luxury in difficult times, and turned his head to the left, peering into the gift shop. It was filled with all kinds of bric-a-brac and California state paraphernalia.

He found it odd that all of these patrons sat here in this establishment living their lives, blissfully unaware of the secret war that was being waged in the shadows beyond their awareness.

However, when Peter saw the little boy coloring quietly as his mom and dad talked about their trip, their jobs, whatever, he realized that this was exactly what he was fighting for. He was amused by the fact that he was throwing himself, once again, into the breach to fight secretly for those who would know nothing of their danger or what he was doing for them.

Just like Tijuana and Xcaret.

Peter felt his mini-com vibrate on his hip and was absent-mindedly about to grab it from its holster, when all of the cell phones in the diner appeared to go off. Peter had an ominous feeling.

The 50-inch flat screen television above the counter began to flicker, the lines and static playing out that dreaded, familiar rhythm.

As Peter looked up, he saw that almost everyone in the diner had been transformed into the undead...everyone except the waitresses and the kid. They didn't have cell phones or mini-coms, and they weren't looking at the television. There were a few patrons who focused on their meals and didn't look at their phones or the television.

There was the grating sound of plates shattering on the floor, and one of the waitresses let out a scream. The little boy was tugging on his mother's arm trying to get her attention.

His mother eerily turned her head slowly to the left, eyes wide with animalistic hunger. Peter was already off his stool as the waitress who took his order came out with the sandwiches in a brown paper bag.

He heard her gasp behind him, and he heard the paper bag hit the floor behind the counter…but he was focusing on the little boy.

All throughout the small roadside diner, there were screams as the dead attacked the living in a wild feeding frenzy. The little boy's mother awkwardly grabbed his small head in her hands. He gazed into his mother's eyes in horror as she leaned in to take a bite…

…but Peter was there first. He punched the husband in the forehead as he attempted to stand up, sending him falling backward into the booth and rolling off the seat and under the table.

Peter dove across the table, sending the cups of coffee and the boy's juice crashing into the base of the old jukebox and toppling the sugar. He grabbed the woman by her long, brown hair and pulled her head away from her son just as her jaws began to close.

The little boy screamed as he made to dive under the table to get away from his mom.

"No!" shouted Peter. The boy's father would be waiting for him under there. "Up here! Hurry!"

The boy's mother flailed about wildly, struggling in Peter's grip as the terrified boy climbed up on the tabletop next to Peter. Peter slammed the mother's head into the table twice, the second time forcing her to bite down onto the worn edge. He brought his hand down in a karate chop on her neck, effectively severing her spine. She rolled off the table and fell underneath, joining her husband who was banging the bottom of the table in his attempts to stand up.

Peter grabbed the boy in his arms and rolled onto his back as a clerk from the empty gift shop named "Martha" (it was printed on her nametag with a cheap label maker) reached out for him, her jaws snapping loudly and slicing her own tongue.

Peter gave her a swift kick in the face with his boot, sending her crashing into the stool he sat on mere moments ago. She fell to the ground on all fours and was trying to get up as Peter got to his feet with the screaming boy in his arms.

Two new zombies entered through the front entrance, so Peter stepped on Martha's back and rolled over the counter as the two entering zombies advanced on him.

He landed on the hard tiled floor behind the counter and hit his head. He cursed under his breath, clutching the boy tight, wondering where the hell his two terrorist friends were.

Kojic sat in the car fiddling with the radio as Ehsan pumped the gas. Ehsan squeezed the trigger of the pump and looked at the road, his back to the diner. Kojic had found a soft music station and lazily cranked the volume up louder, unwittingly concealing the screams and chaos in the diner behind them.

Ehsan let go of the trigger before the tank filled. His eyes were fixated on the road behind them. There was a large tractor-trailer barreling down the road in their direction, but it was veering off to the left, towards the gas station…

…and it didn't look like it was slowing down.

Kojic looked up and saw Ehsan staring at the road. "What is it?"

Ehsan's eyes widened. "Brother, out of the car."

Kojic regarded him quizzically. "What's wrong?"

"Now, Kojic!"

The little boy screamed when he saw two zombies on the other end behind the counter tearing off shreds of flesh from a poor waitress with their teeth. The scream got their attention, and one of the zombies—a middle-aged man in a now bloodstained tee shirt, tattered blue jeans, and trucker hat—started crawling towards them.

"Great. Just great," muttered Peter, as he shoved the boy under him. He reached up on the counter to the left by the cakes and grabbed a large serrated knife. The trucker was closing in and reaching out for the little morsel under Peter.

Peter shoved the knife into the zombie's left eye socket and twisted, but it kept reaching for the boy, pushing the knife deeper into its own skull as it pushed forward.

Peter looked up and saw Martha leaning over the counter with one of the two new zombies who entered the diner. Their fingertips scratched at the top of his head. The other zombie was rounding the payment kiosk and shuffling behind the counter. The whole scene was going from bad to worse.

Kojic stepped out of the car and pointed at a zombie woman chewing on her husband or boyfriend's arm in a car parked in front of the diner. The man was crying out for help, reaching for the car door handle, but she pushed him forward with her weight, pressing his face against the window. The poor man clawed at the glass with a bloody hand as she sunk her teeth into his neck.

"Holy, shit," gasped Kojic. There was an impending sound of rolling thunder approaching his back, but before he could turn around Ehsan was on the other side of the car and pulled him away.

At last, the trucker had driven the knife far enough into his own brain that he suddenly stopped moving. Peter slid the knife out of the trucker's head and stood up. The boy's father, on his feet and approaching the counter with several other zombies, and the one at the end by the payment kiosk were all closing in.

Shit. This was it. Peter had his knife, but it wouldn't be enough. There were just too many of them. Even with his strength and speed. Already infected, he would likely survive the onslaught of bites—if they didn't tear him apart—but the little boy wouldn't.

There was a rumbling outside and a flash of metal that caught Peter's eye. He looked out the glass window to see Kojic and Ehsan dash out of the way of an oncoming tractor-trailer.

Peter shoved the boy's head down behind the counter as he, too, took cover. There was a crash outside as the truck barreled through the pumps and the old Mustang came crashing through the front of the diner.

The whole diner shook and broken glass flew everywhere, raining down on Peter's head as he covered the boy's head and face with his arms. The approaching zombie behind the counter was thrown into the cake display and was hung up on shards of glass. It reached out for Peter but was unable to pull itself off of the display.

The zombie munching on the waitress at the other end of the counter stood up to look at what happened. Peter stood, grabbed the boy, and threw him over the counter where they were at the middle. He then hopped up on the countertop and swiveled to the other side as the curious zombie muncher reached out for him.

The diner was a mess of broken booths, stools, and glass. Peter snatched up the boy, who was taking in the scene in amazement, and proceeded to climb out of the large hole in the front of the diner.

As he found his footing outside, he stalked over to Kojic and Ehsan. The roof of the diner caved in behind him, pushing several zombies attempting to follow Peter back inside.

"Where the hell were you guys?"

"We were pumping the gas," snapped Ehsan.

"You didn't see what was going on in there?"

"I had the radio on loud," said Kojic sheepishly. "We did not hear."

"I'm beginning to reconsider your usefulness on our mission," said Peter menacingly.

Kojic was staring at the little boy in Peter's arms. "What are we going to do?"

"We have to go," said Ehsan. "Kafka did this. He knows we are coming. He's trying to stop us."

"No," said Peter, "he's trying to slow us down. He must be close by in order to do this."

"We have to go now if we are going to catch up with him," said Kojic.

Peter put the little boy down. "Ehsan, take him across the street." Ehsan looked to Kojic, who nodded his approval. "Kojic, find us a car, one of the one's parked in front."

"But they have the dead inside."

"You're infected now," barked Peter. "Deal with them and bring me a car."

"What are you going to do?" It was more of an actual question than an accusation.

"We can't just leave here. The authorities don't know what they are dealing with. They'll be overrun and we'll have zombies roaming the countryside. I have to torch the place. Nothing remains."

Kojic nodded and ran around the tractor-trailer to the cars parked out front to the right of the crash. The smell of gasoline was in the air as it spurted up like a geyser from the broken pump.

Peter rounded the truck and opened the front door. A dazed zombie driver reached out for him, but Peter let him fall to the ground. He then began to stomp on its head repeatedly until the driver's skull crunched underneath his boot and it ceased to move.

Peter climbed up into the cab and looked around. He heard Kojic wrestling with a zombie on the other side of the truck. Then there was silence. An engine turned over and Peter heard a car pull around the truck and stop behind him. He saw a sawed off shotgun behind the driver seat, but nothing he could use.

He backed out of the cab and lowered himself to the ground. Kojic got out of a rather plain, mid-sized sedan.

"Kojic, where are the weapons?"

"In the Mustang."

"Go get them. Be careful but hurry."

Kojic nodded and climbed up onto the Mustang that was halfway into the diner. The passenger side door was pushed in from the impact, so Kojic reached in through the hole where the window used to be. He reached in and grabbed the assault rifles from the backseat as a zombie reached out and grabbed his right forearm.

It was a woman, half her face missing, her left eyeball entirely exposed in its socket. The effect was almost as unnerving as the moans coming from inside the diner. Kojic saw them milling around, looking for a way out so they could have a hot lunch.

He pulled himself out of the car, taking the woman with him. He dragged her out of the battered Mustang and down to the dirt. He dropped two of the rifles but held onto one, pointing the barrel at the woman's head as he held her down with his boot.

Peter was searching the body of the truck driver he dispatched and found what he was looking for...a lighter. He was startled by the report of Kojic's rifle. He stood up as Kojic ran over to him.

"Give me one of those," said Peter, gesturing to one of the assault rifles. Kojic did as he was told and handed him one. "Take the car and pick up Ehsan and the kid."

Kojic looked concerned. "We can't take the child with us."

"We sure as shit can't leave him here. We'll drop him off with someone down the road."

Kojic looked uncertain, but he nodded and got in the car. As he pulled away, Peter stepped into the gift shop. A clerk lunged at him from behind the store's payment kiosk, but Peter blew his brains out on the back wall.

The zombies in the diner caught sight of him and made their way to the doorway to the gift shop, but Peter closed the door. He pulled down a shelf filled with jams and syrups in front of it. It would hold them, but not for long.

As fists pounded on the other side of the door and sticky sweet jam and syrup pooled on the floor like blood, Peter searched the store. There were cookbooks, post cards, belt buckles, wide-rimmed hats, even scorpions behind glass. Peter found Tex-Mex style ceramic jars and grabbed one. He also took a dishtowel and ran back outside.

He walked over to the broken gas pump, but the gasoline was no longer spurting up. So much for making a Molotov cocktail. Peter tied the dishtowel around the ceramic jar and rolled it around in the gasoline. Then he stood up and crossed the street.

There were sirens in the distance. They didn't have much time. Kojic was in the backseat with the little boy and Ehsan was behind the wheel. The engine was running.

"What are you going to do?" asked the little boy.

Peter smiled. "You know the Fourth of July?"

The boy sniffled and nodded earnestly.

"We're going to start the festivities a little early."

Peter took the lighter and lit the rag tied around the jar. He walked halfway back across the street. The first responders were closing in—two police cars and a fire truck. Ever the quarterback, he chucked the jar into the center of the spilled gasoline. It quickly caught fire as the flaming jar rolled around.

Peter walked back across the street to the car without looking back and hopped in. Zombies were starting to crawl out of the hole in the front of the diner and the entrance to the gift shop.

"Let's get out of here."

Ehsan put the new borrowed car in gear and tore off down the road, as there was a massive explosion behind them. The little boy turned to look out the rear window in time to see a bright orange fireball rise into the air and leave thick black smoke in its wake.

Several of the escaping zombies were ablaze and, after staggering around for a moment, dropped to their knees and succumbed to the flames. The police car and fire truck stopped in front of the site across the street, forming a perimeter and frantically calling for backup.

They all drove down the road in silence for a bit, digesting what had just happened. Peter wondered if Kafka had stayed behind to watch the fruits of his dirty work.

I told you you'd lose, Peter.

Was it the voice of Kafka or Peter's own demon?

You cannot ignore me. I am inside you, but soon I'll be outside. And when I am, I'll be coming for you as my first order of business.

Peter turned around. "Hey, kid. What's your name?"

"Bobby," said the boy meekly.

And then I'm coming for young Bobby, here.

"How old are you, Bobby?"

"Four-and-a-half."

"Bobby, do you know what just happened back there?"

"There were monsters."

He doesn't realize he's still with monsters.

Ehsan watched the boy in the rearview mirror.

"Bobby, you are absolutely right. Those were monsters. I know it looked like your parents were trying to kill you..." Bobby started sniffling again, his mouth contorted as he attempted to hold back his tears. He let out a *Baaah* as young children do when they try to suppress a cry but fail. Tears streamed down his red cheeks. "...but those weren't your parents anymore. Those were monsters."

"Mommy tried to bite me," cried Bobby.

"That was no longer your mommy, Bobby. I can't really explain it to you, but that thing, that monster, was no longer your mommy."

But Bobby continued to cry. Kojic shrank into the corner of the backseat, sitting there awkwardly.

Snap his neck like a toothpick. That will silence him.

"Bobby, you know how an ugly caterpillar turns into a beautiful butterfly?"

Bobby nodded as he sobbed.

"Well, your beautiful mommy transformed into something ugly, but it wasn't her."

"It wasn't?" sniffled Bobby between wails.

"No, it wasn't," reassured Peter. "Just like a butterfly isn't the same thing as a caterpillar. Right? They're two different bugs."

Bobby nodded, wiping his eyes with his forearms the way little kids do. It was a clumsy explanation, but it calmed the kid down for the moment.

"Bobby, do you have any aunts or uncles?"

Because we're going to kill them, too.

He nodded. "Aunt Darma and Uncle Harry."

"Great. Do you know where they live?"

The kid shook his head, and Peter cursed himself for his stupidity. The kid was four years old. Of course he didn't know where they lived.

"I don't suppose you know your Aunt Darma's phone number?" The kid shook his head. "Great," he said with sarcasm that was lost on young Bobby, who wondered why that would be great.

"We can't just drop him off at a police station," said Kojic. He didn't want to say why in front of Bobby, but Peter caught his drift. There'd be questions, and they didn't have the time. And they were wanted for terrorism and murder.

"We'll drop him off at a hospital," said Peter.

"This is costing us more time," said Ehsan impatiently.

Time, time. Time for what? Your futile little suicide mission? Why be in such a rush to die?

Peter knew Ehsan was right, but what could he do? What would they have him do? He didn't want to entertain their notions.

"So he rides with us until we get to Groom Lake. Then we hand him off to some kind of government employee."

He interpreted their silence as agreement.

"Hey, Bobby, you're going on a road trip."

"We were going to California," whimpered Bobby.

"Vacation?"

"Yes, sir."

Peter didn't know what to say. The boy's parents were just turned into flesh-eating zombies. There wasn't going to be a vacation. Peter plucked him from the jaws of death only to bring him to ground zero of the impending zombie apocalypse.

"Let's listen to the radio for a while." Peter turned it on and tuned in to the news. There were reports of riots all throughout Nevada, bouts of cannibalism on the Las Vegas strip, a shootout in front of the Bellagio fountains. The press was labeling it as "mass hysteria" or "riots."

However, Peter knew what this was. Kafka was creating distractions. Nevada would pour all of its resources into putting out these fires, so to speak, and Kafka would waltz right into Area 51 with his new toy.

There'd be no defense, and chances were that he already had a head start on them. But how was Kafka able to be in California and Nevada at once? It didn't make any sense.

Peter prayed that Elicia would come through. He had faith in her, she was sharp and an accomplished hacker, but a little prayer never hurt.

***

Yesterday

Elicia was getting dizzy from driving around in circles. "Hey, Colonel, don't you know any other shapes?"

"Which shape would you like? I thought you're supposed to be doing your hacking thing."

"I am. I opened up my ephemeral port and have activated my fourth bot. I figure four should do it."

"Hey, you're the expert. I'm just your goddamned chuffer. I really wish you'd get on with it."

Elicia's fingers were like lightning on the keyboard inside the ASV. "Patience, Colonel. Genius takes time."

She was thankful that they decided to drop Brittany off before continuing. It was her idea, actually, but the Colonel didn't protest. Less dead weight.

Elicia remembered the exchange between them when Elicia said goodbye to her sister.

"Trust me, Brit, you'll be safer this way. Just tell the police that you were taken hostage. They'll realize you had nothing to do with all of this."

"Elicia, you don't have to do this."

"I don't expect you to understand, but I do. If not, there won't be anything left."

"But why you? Why can't the Colonel do it?"

"Because he doesn't know how."

Brittany stood outside the ASV awkwardly, tears welling up in her eyes. "I don't know what to say."

Elicia hugged her big sister.

"I know I haven't always been there for you..."

Elicia shook her head. "Don't, Brit. I wasn't exactly the most normal little sister."

"You're a lot braver than me," said Brittany, wiping her eyes, smearing the faded makeup even more. She looked like a raccoon.

Elicia smirked. "You know, you look like one of the zombies. You'd better clean up before the police accidentally shoot you."

Brittany laughed, slurping up the snot dripping from her nose most unattractively. "You be careful."

Elicia nodded. "I always am."

They held hands for a brief moment. Betancourt cleared his throat rather loudly, and Elicia took the hint. "Goodbye, Brit."

"Don't say it like that. I'll see you later."

Elicia smiled. "I'll see you later." She knew it was a lie, but her big sister needed that lie right now. She got back onto the ASV, and Betancourt pulled away.

Elicia retrieved her virus code and custom made rootkit from her online safe deposit box. She activated the rootkit and entered the mobile firmware update system.

A small dialogue box with a red exclamation point appeared on the top left of the screen. "Shit."

"What?" asked Betancourt. "Is everything okay?"

"They found my first bot."

"That was fast. Should I be worried?"

Elicia began to upload the virus code as she launched the rootkit to cover her tracks. "Not yet. They only found the first..."

Another dialogue box with a red exclamation point.

"Double shit."

"What now?"

"They discovered bot number two."

"So quickly?"

"That's fast," said Elicia, impressed. "That's real fast."

"Is it supposed to be that fast, or are they really good?"

"*They* are really good." The virus code uploaded. "I've uploaded the virus. We're in business." Her fingers moved quickly across the keyboard as she began to download the virus into the mobile firmware update system. Two percent...five percent...

Another dialogue box popped up. This time it had a message. *I know what you're doing, and it won't work.*

"He just found bot number three."

…eight percent…eleven percent…

"He?" asked Betancourt, looking quizzically over his right shoulder while trying to steer the ASV in the desert.

"It's Kafka. He left me a message. He knows what I'm up to, or so he says."

…thirteen percent…fifteen percent…

"How do you know it's him?"

"I don't think the government would send me a message saying they know what I'm up to."

…eighteen percent…twenty-two percent…

"You're probably right."

…twenty-six percent…twenty-nine percent…

"Shit, he's found us."

"What do you think he'll do? We're out here in the middle of nowhere. He's probably miles away," said Betancourt, trying to reassure himself.

…thirty-three percent…thirty-five percent…

"How much longer kid?"

"We are a third of the way through the download."

…thirty-seven percent…forty percent…

"How much longer?"

"I don't know. Soon."

"How soon?" pressed Betancourt.

…forty-three percent…forty-six percent…

"Asking me repeatedly won't speed it up any," Elicia snapped.

…forty-nine percent…fifty-one percent…

"We just passed fifty percent," she announced as they both heard a screeching sound in the distance carried to them on the desert wind.

…fifty-four percent…

Elicia looked up at the closed hatch of the ASV. "What the hell was that?"

…fifty-seven percent…

"That's an aerial drone," answered Betancourt.

…sixty percent…

"That can't be for us," said Elicia.

"We're out here in the middle of nowhere. Who else can it be for? Kafka sent it in."

…sixty-four percent…sixty-seven percent…

Betancourt looked at the sky out of his front window as something soared overhead. "Elicia, take the wheel."

She nodded and got up from her seat, making her way up front. Betancourt slipped out of the driver seat and guided her into it.

"Keep it steady. If you see it approach, start to zigzag," he instructed her.

"What are you going to do?"

"I'm going to try to shoot it out of the sky."

...seventy-two percent...seventy-five percent...

Betancourt made his way to the gun turret controls.

...seventy-seven percent...seventy-nine percent...

"I think I see it," shouted Elicia, terrified. "It's coming real fast."

Betancourt scanned the sky until he saw it. "Hold her steady!"

...eighty-four percent...eighty-seven percent...

"I thought you told me to zigzag!"

"Hold her steady, dammit!"

He got a lock on the zooming bird and got tone as it began to open fire on the ASV. Elicia braced herself as bolts of light flew at the ASV, bullets pelting the armor...

...ninety-one percent...ninety four percent...

A few of the bullets took out the front tires, pulling the ASV to the right until the front axle grinded to a halt, and some others penetrated the armor, lighting up the inside cabin.

...ninety-six percent...ninety-six percent...

Betancourt got a shot off as he fell to the floor clutching the rather large hole in his upper right thigh, but the aerial drone exploded above them.

...ninety-six percent...ninety-six percent...

Elicia slid out of the driver's seat and crawled over to where Betancourt lay bleeding all over the floor. They heard a helicopter approaching.

Elicia pulled off her belt and wrapped it around Betancourt's thigh above the wound. He pulled it tight and slipped the prong in the hole, grunting in pain.

He looked at her gravely. "You know that's him."

Elicia nodded. "Can't be. How would he get here so fast?"

"What about the virus? Did we do it?"

She crawled over to the computer on her hands and knees and hoisted herself up to look at the monitor.

...ninety-six percent...ninety-six percent...

She started punching away at the keyboard. "Shit." She slammed both hands down on it.

"What?" asked Betancourt, already knowing they failed.

"The drone knocked out our communications, our wireless capability. It's frozen at ninety-six percent. The connection was severed."

The helicopter was getting closer. It sounded like it was right next to the ASV.

"Help me up," said Betancourt. "I'll blast him with our canon."

Elicia looked over at the controls. "The equipment's Swiss cheese."

Betancourt nodded and pulled his handgun.

"What are you going to do with that?"

"I can do us both. So we don't have to become monsters."

"He'll take us alive," insisted Elicia, wide-eyed at Betancourt's intention.

"What makes you say that?" Betancourt was looking pale.

"He stopped the virus download. If he just wanted us out of the way, he'd be high-tailing it to Area 51, but he's come to take us hostage."

"To use us as leverage against Peter," said Betancourt, finishing her line of thought. "I can't allow that."

Betancourt aimed the handgun at Elicia. "I'm sorry, Dear. You remind me of my daughter, but I can't let him take you."

Elicia shuddered at the sight of the gun being pointed at her and the conviction in his words. She closed her eyes, forcing tears out of them, and prepared herself to accept her fate.

She knew the Colonel was right, but she still wanted to live. She became desperate, squirming as she sat on her heels, choking back sobs. She heard the Colonel let out a stifled cry as he pulled back the hammer on his gun.

She could've sworn she heard his hand trembling. His conviction eroding, his ambivalence made the moment all the more unbearable for her, an unwanted eternity that she wished would end with the bang of a gunshot.

There was a tone from above, the hatch opened, and Betancourt hesitated for a moment, looking up out of reflex as sunlight was cast down upon him in a column, like the tractor beam of an alien spaceship.

Elicia opened her eyes and saw his tears reflecting the light, like shimmering diamonds in his eyes, and a bullet from above tore through his skull, putting out his lights permanently.

Kafka slipped into the cabin and blinked at her with all four eyes. "So you're the one causing me all of this trouble."

He looked over and saw the virus download on the computer monitor stuck on ninety-six percent. He shot out the monitor and then the computer, causing Elicia to jump.

"You're very talented. I could use someone like you."

"If you're here, then who was on the other end..."

Before she could finish her thought, he was upon her, taking her into a forceful embrace as his fangs extended on queue. He sunk his teeth into her neck and infected her with his gift, his curse.

Elicia fought at first, but after a moment, she became slack. She was exhausted. She was exhausted from running. She was exhausted from being chased all over God's green earth by government, aliens, and monsters. She was tired of fighting.

No more fighting.

As her head sagged loosely on her shoulders, she caught a glimpse of the poor Colonel lying still on the floor of the cabin, tears streaming down his face mixed with his own blood.

The fight was now Peter's.

Chapter 16

Area 51
Groom Lake, Nevada
The Next Day

Peter, Kojic, and Ehsan were sitting in their little car just outside the perimeter of Area 51. Peter was relieved to have been minus Bobby; they dropped him off at a pediatrician's office in some small town along the way. They would see to it that he was taken care of properly.

No more distractions. It was back to business.

The three men sat there awkwardly, unsure of their next move. It was Ehsan who broke the tense silence.

"What do we do now?" His question was directed solely to Kojic, which irritated Peter.

"How do we know if he's in there?" asked Kojic.

"There are supposed to be a roving patrol of white jeeps," said Peter, looking up at a rather severe warning sign promising draconian consequences for passing it. "If we go much further, they would normally intercept us."

"So you are saying we have to risk getting caught by the authorities to see if Kafka is inside?" asked Ehsan, his tone indicating that he thought the idea was ridiculous.

He doesn't trust you, Peter. He's afraid of you, and that makes him dangerous.

"It's not so crazy," assured Peter. "If we are detained, all we have to do is wait. When Kafka comes, we'll know it."

"And if he doesn't come, we'll be detained and at the mercy of the U.S. Government," Kojic warned.

"He'll come," said Peter, reaching out as far as he could into the compound, feeling for his brother. Nothing. "He'll come."

"I don't know about this," said Ehsan. "What if they shoot us?"

The terrorist doesn't understand your plan. He's weak and stupid.

Peter sighed. "First of all, brain-o, bullets cannot kill us. Only dismemberment can, and *my* people aren't accustomed to doing such things."

"You'd be surprised the kind of things *your* people are accustomed to," snapped Ehsan.

Kill him. Do it now before he kills you.

"All right, that is enough," admonished Kojic. "Our fight is with Kafka, not each other. Right?"

Neither Peter nor Ehsan acknowledged his sentiment, but neither refuted it. There was reluctant agreement through silence.

"What if the American let himself get captured and we wait?" suggested Ehsan, once again like Peter wasn't in the car with them.

They're plotting against you, even now.

"Oh no," said Peter, "I'm not letting you two out of my sight."

"You said so yourself," said Kojic, "he will come. So what is there to worry about?"

"I'm a fugitive like you two, wanted for the murder of a four-star general."

"But he will come, as you say, so there is nothing to fear."

"Then why don't you come with me, if you are so certain," insisted Peter.

Do yourself a favor, Peter. Kill them both. You don't need them. They'll only slow you down.

The voice inside his head was distracting and this argument was going around in circles. Peter was regretting his tenuous alliance with these terrorists.

"If for some reason he does not come, we will come for you," said Kojic, eliciting a dubious look from Ehsan. Kojic's vitals were steady, meaning he was well intentioned...or a good liar. Ehsan's fluttered.

"Your partner doesn't share your sentiment, Kojic."

"Ehsan will do as he's told."

"What assurance do I have of that?"

"None. You'll have to trust me."

"That, my friend, is a risky proposition."

"Think about it. It's not good tactics for all of us to be in the same place."

"So why don't you get caught, and I'll remain behind with your buddy, Ehsan, here," said Peter.

Ehsan sucked his teeth at the suggestion.

"If it would make you more comfortable, then yes," said Kojic to both Peter's and Ehsan's surprise.

"Luka, no," protested Ehsan.

Kojic looked Peter in his eyes. "The both of you will see that I am rescued. Yes?"

Peter looked back into his eyes. "Yes."

Kojic got out of the car. Peter rolled down the window. "No weapons. They won't shoot if you are unarmed."

"What if he is already here and they are zombies. I'll need to be armed."

Peter reached out with his senses. "I'm not picking up any sign of zombies or Kafka."

"You can sense that?"

"I can, too," said Ehsan.

Kojic nodded in awe of his two comrades' ability, one he had not yet mastered. He handed his gun inside the car to Peter.

"Good luck," said Peter.

Kojic nodded. He put his hand on Ehsan's shoulder, and Ehsan nodded. It was then that Peter realized that these two terrorists had prior military training. This was how soldiers said goodbye. No words, no tears. Just an understanding.

Kojic began to walk down the dirt road past all of the signs intended to frighten emboldened tourists away, as Ehsan backed the car down the road in the opposite direction.

Kojic walked on for what must have been fifteen minutes or so, hopeful that the guard had already been turned. He didn't want to be detained by American soldiers. He preferred to deal with zombies. He tried to reach out with his senses, but he wasn't very good at it.

He was startled when he heard the roar of the engine of a white jeep, just as the American described. He stopped in the middle of the road and put his hands up in the air.

The jeep closed in on him and stopped. Two soldiers in full camo jumped out, rifles trained on him.

"Keep your hands in the air," one of them commanded. Kojic complied.

The other soldier shouldered his rifle and approached Kojic, turning him around and pulling his hands down, placing his hands behind his back.

"What are you doing here? Couldn't you read the signs?" asked the soldier, as he bound Kojic's wrists together with a plastic tie.

Kojic responded in Serbian.

"He's a foreigner," said the soldier with the rifle trained on Kojic.

"What's he doing out here?" asked the other, thinking out loud. He turned Kojic around so they were face-to-face. "Are you here alone?"

Kojic again responded in Serbian.

"What language is that?"

"I don't know. We better take him in. I get the feeling he's illegal."

Kojic smiled to himself. Illegal. They had no idea. He was one of the world's most talented cyber terrorists, and he had committed many crimes ranging from espionage to sabotage.

The soldier who bound him talked into his military-issue mini-com multi-tasker, "Attention base, we have a wanderer in custody and are bringing him in."

"Roger that," crackled a voice on the other end.

Kojic went quietly as they put him on the back of the white jeep and drove back into the compound.

"I don't like this one bit," said Ehsan bitterly in the car, watching a Janet plane approaching the compound. "He was taken."

"Yes," agreed Peter, "I can feel the guard, too." He slapped Ehsan on the shoulder. "Look at the bright side, partner," he said in a thick Texan accent, "the rodeo hasn't started without us."

There was a great explosion, and the approaching Janet burst into a bright orange ball of flames. Ehsan and Peter saw a small flying object dart across the sky away from the falling pieces of the plane.

"That's an aerial drone," said Ehsan.

"He's here," said Peter.

Kojic was bouncing around the back of the jeep as it receded further into the compound. He focused on the two soldiers' vitals as he took in the barren grounds around him.

They looked completely deserted, but Kojic felt that someone was there, hidden. More guards, well camouflaged.

Suddenly, there was an explosion in the sky, and he felt the soldiers' heart rates flutter as they commented on the plane that exploded in midair.

Then something changed.

The soldier's vitals ended and were replaced with...something else. As Kojic craned his neck to get a glimpse of his captors, the jeep veered sharply to the left at top speed, throwing Kojic on his side. The soldier in the passenger seat reached out for him, eyes white and glassy, snapping his jaws.

Kojic rolled off of the back of the careening jeep before the soldier grabbed him, and tumbled in the dirt until he came to a stop.

He looked around him and saw that the jeep kept on its random trajectory away from him. He rolled over into a sitting position in the dirt as the hot sun beat down on his face and neck.

He struggled with his bindings behind his back, but his hands were well secured. All he could do was sit and wait for Ehsan and the American to find him. Surely, they sensed that Kafka was here. He reached out with his mind in an attempt to reach them...

...when he found something else.

Kojic heard footsteps all around him. He frantically scanned the area with his eyes, but saw no one. His senses picked up something...peculiar, like what he felt when the two soldiers in the jeep were turned.

The footsteps and the odd sensations were growing closer. He squinted in the sunlight as he saw distortions, patches of bent light, closing in around him. He heard wheezing and snarling as they drew closer.

There was another explosion in the distance as the aerial drone soared overhead.

Kojic didn't know what was happening, but something in his reptilian brain screamed for him to get the hell out of there.

He struggled to his feet and began to run away when he bumped into something solid and was knocked off his feet. He felt fingers finding purchase on his legs as he saw nothing but a bending of the horizon in front of him.

He rolled out of the ghostly grip and into more probing fingers as he felt putrid breath on his face and neck. He squirmed as something bit him on the shoulder, sending a shockwave of pain through his body like a bolt of lightning.

He squirmed on the ground like an exposed earthworm writhing desperately to find refuge. More fingers clamped down on various parts of his body as disembodied teeth and jaws became exposed, sinking into various parts of his anatomy.

Kojic let out a scream, as he lay there powerless to defend himself when a shot rang out. Blood sprayed directly above him and painted the invisible assailants around him, and Kojic saw his attackers.

He kicked one in the face and then rolled to the side. He kicked another, and then another, as they scrambled to grab him and have a bite.

There were more gunshots, each successive one growing closer, and heads exploded above him. He wriggled free of the throng that was descending upon him, rolled away, and struggled to his knees and then his feet. He saw Ehsan and the American shooting at the invisible guard all around him.

He ran towards them, his bites stinging, and away from the wheezing and growling and disembodied snapping jaws.

He crossed the distance between the zombies and his saviors and practically collided with Ehsan. "What took you so long?"

"We hit traffic," quipped Peter, taking down the invisible guard using his senses.

"Turn around," said Ehsan, shouldering his rifle. Kojic turned and he felt his plastic ties being cut. When he turned back around, the firing had stopped.

"What happened?" asked Kojic. "Are they gone?"

Peter nodded. "We got 'em."

"What were they?" asked Ehsan.

"Soldiers clad in a new, experimental camouflage. It's a material that bends light around it. I'd say it worked pretty darn well."

Kojic gave Peter a sardonic look. "You think?"

"Kafka's here," said Peter. "We have to get to the compound quickly. An aerial drone took out our ride, so we go on foot."

"That second explosion was you," said Kojic, remembering the second explosion and what he saw in the sky.

Ehsan nodded.

"Thank you for helping me."

"Well, let's not break out the champagne just yet," said Peter. "There'll be more of them, and if we're lucky enough to make it to the compound, we have Kafka to contend with." He looked at Kojic, who was bleeding through his clothes on his legs and shoulder. "Can you make it?"

Kojic nodded. "I can make it. Let's get moving. Give me a gun."

Ehsan unslung an extra rifle off his shoulder and handed it to Kojic. Peter took a rifle off one of the dead camouflaged soldiers as a spare. Kojic and Ehsan followed suit. The rifles were covered in the light-bending material as well, but they were covered in blood spatter, making them somewhat visible.

Peter sized up his ragtag team. They weren't his first choice, but they were all he had at the moment and each possessed the power of several men. It was do or die time.

He smiled. "Oh, hell yeah."

***

They made it across the open grounds with very little incident, quickly dispatching any zombie guards roaming around. Peter experimented with a few of them, reaching out, trying to control them like Carl did, but to no avail.

He thought he got one to look at him for a moment, but it could've just been a coincidence. Who knew what those damned things were really seeing anyway with those milky, lifeless eyes?

Peter figured it was the serum that prevented him from being able to connect with them. He wondered if Kojic and Ehsan sensed the serum pumping through his veins, making him weaker than them.

He hoped not.

Peter cleared his head and prepared for the endgame. His main objective was to stop Carl from turning the whole damned planet into zombies. If he succeeded in stopping his brother…and that was a big if…and these two terrorists killed him, so be it.

At least the world would be safe.

"Look," said Ehsan, pointing at a medium-sized building.

It was a rectangular building with a rounded roof, just like most of the others. It had two large bay doors in front, which were closed at the moment, nothing unremarkable for a building on a base with an airfield. It was a very nondescript building…

Except for the mass of zombified Groom Lake employees, patrolling the perimeter like a moat of drunk people staggering around.

Peter sighed. "He's in there all right."

"That must be where the master RGT console is," said Kojic gravely. "I only hope we aren't too late."

"I don't think so. Those guards who took you into custody were just turned, so he had to have just arrived," Peter reasoned.

"So what's the plan?" asked Kojic.

Peter hesitated for a moment. The time for playing his cards close to his vest had passed. "I have this trick I can do. It'll make them think I'm flanking them on both sides. Hopefully, I can lead them away in either direction."

"How? That's impossible," demanded Ehsan.

Peter smiled sardonically. "Does any of this seem possible to you?" Kojic shot Ehsan a reproachful look. "Trust me," continued Peter, "I can do this."

He wanted to say that he used it on OIL operatives, like the man with the van outside of Frisky's, but he didn't want to instigate problems with his new, tenuous alliance.

There'd be plenty of time for that later.

"Okay, so you lead them away from the building," said Kojic. "Then what?"

"We reach in with our senses and get a sense of what is going on in there, how many Kafka has with him. That will determine our plan of entry."

Kojic nodded his agreement. Ehsan was staring at the zombies milling around the front of the building. He was sulking like a recalcitrant teenager, avoiding eye contact with Peter.

Peter walked towards the building, a full frontal approach, strolling casually as Kojic looked on in fascination. Even Ehsan was curious.

"What is he doing? He's crazy."

"Watch," said Kojic expectantly.

And watch they did. They watched Peter close the distance between him and the building. They watched the zombies outside look to the left and the right as if they saw something. None of them appeared to see the American.

The zombies began to part like the Red Sea, each side following someone or something that wasn't there. Peter walked right down the Middle like Moses himself, unseen and unmolested.

When both groups had wandered off, Peter gestured for Kojic and Ehsan to come. They looked back and forth, hesitant, and then they began to walk over.

Nice trick, but they'll be back. It was Peter's doppelgänger. Great. His little voice inside his mind always had the best timing.

'You're trying to distract me. I'm not listening to you,' thought Peter.

You have no choice, Peter. I don't come with a mute button.

'You must be getting nervous. We're close to getting Kafka and here you are, on queue.'

Nervous about what? Kafka is going to rend you limb from limb and I will be free.

Peter reached inside the building with his senses. He detected Carl. He was alone…no, wait. There was someone else. The other's signature was a little different from a regular person. On a continuum it was somewhere between Kafka and a regular human, but much closer to a regular human.

It was someone recently infected.

I wouldn't go in there if I was you, but since I'm not you I hope you do go in there.

'Oh, I plan on it, only I think you'll be disappointed with the end result.'

Kojic and Ehsan slowed as they approached Peter, looking tentative.

"What? What's wrong?" asked Peter.

Kojic blinked as he saw Peter's doppelgänger standing next to him, whispering in his ear. He looked at Ehsan, who apparently saw it too.

"What is this?" asked Kojic, gesturing to Peter's left.

"What the hell are you talking about?" Peter snapped, irritated by the voice in his head.

"Nothing," said Kojic, exchanging another glance with Ehsan. Peter felt their vitals flutter.

"How did you get the zombies to go away?" asked Ehsan. He sounded afraid. Peter felt it.

"Never mind that now. Kafka is inside with a recently infected human, but the other is weak."

"How do we know you aren't secretly with him and you're not leading us into a trap?" asked Ehsan.

"There's no time for this," Peter insisted. "The zombies will be back."

"It's a fair question," insisted Kojic.

Peter narrowed his eyes. "Why? What did you see?"

Kojic looked at Ehsan, weighing whether or not he should tell the American what he saw. "We saw your double standing next to you, whispering in your ear."

Peter felt a chill creep down his spine, as if someone had walked over his grave. "You *saw* it?"

Kojic and Ehsan both nodded.

"What was it whispering to you?" asked Ehsan suspiciously.

"I've been hearing it from time to time in my head. It's getting nervous because we're close. It wants us to fail."

"What about you?"

"What *about* me?"

"Do you want us to fail?"

"Of course not."

"How come we don't hear voices?" asked Ehsan, smelling blood in the water.

Because you don't have the serum in your veins, asshole. "Is this really the time for this?" asked Peter, growing antsy. Was this all going to fall apart right now when they've come so far?

Kojic put his hand on Ehsan's shoulder. "I heard my double."

Ehsan regarded him incredulously. "When?"

"When we rescued him," he said, pointing to Peter. "I told me what to do, like an idea in my mind."

"Really, Luka?"

"Yes."

"Great, now that we established that we're all hearing voices, can we get back to our mission?" demanded Peter.

Kojic nodded for both he and Ehsan, who was still flummoxed.

Peter pointed in the distance to the undead Groom Lake employees, who were beginning to circle back around. "Let's go around the side. I'm sure there's a side door where we can slip in."

"What's the plan? We can't just go in there," argued Ehsan.

"Kafka already knows we're here," said Peter.

"How?"

"We sensed him, didn't we?"

"Yes."

"So what makes you think he didn't sense us?"

"He's right," said Kojic. "There's nothing left to do but go inside."

Inside, in the center of the room surrounded by all kinds of control panels, monitors, and computer equipment, was a small vessel about the size of an automobile. It was a shiny metal craft in the shape of an elongated skull. It emitted an eerie, low-pitched hum.

Kafka was standing over it wearing his portable RGT headset. Elicia was on the floor next to him. She looked pale and weak.

"Gentlemen, I thought you'd never come," said Kafka without looking at them.

Peter, Kojic, and Ehsan all looked at each other.

"Who are you kidding? You knew we were here."

Kafka turned around and regarded his brother with four dark eyes. "Oh, there's no slipping anything past you, Pete. I see you have an entourage. I have to warn you, they're not very reliable."

"Maybe they didn't like their boss," said Peter.

"Peter, I'm sorry," said Elicia, her eyes wide with terror. "He got to me before..." her voice trailed off.

"It's not your fault, Elicia," said Peter. "He bit you?"

She nodded.

"Aww, such a sweet reunion," said Kafka, pretending to dab his eyes.

"Why did you do it?" asked Peter.

"Pete, she's my gift to you. I want you to have companionship when the world turns. I don't want you to be alone. Not like you wanted me to be alone."

"Carl, Yvette was trying to kill me. I had to defend myself. Elicia wasn't trying to kill you."

"She was trying to stop my transmissions. A firmware virus, very clever."

"He used the portable RGT to read my memories," blurted Elicia. "He knew you were coming with help."

"It doesn't matter," said Peter. "There's three of us and one of him. So that's your mother ship? A little small, isn't it?"

Kafka sighed in mock exasperation. "Didn't you listen to that voice inside your head? It only needs to transmit the activation code for the virus. Sleek, efficient, elegant, environmentally friendly, great on gas. Oversized vehicles are so New Millennium. This is the future."

Kafka grinned, flashing his fangs. "Kojic, Ehsan, siding with an American soldier to save the world. That's got to burn your ass, even just a little."

"What burns my ass," snapped Kojic, "is what you did to Marina. Now you are going to pay."

"What about you, Ehsan?" asked Kafka. "These two have a dog in this fight. I've done nothing to you. In fact, by infecting you, I've spared you the fate of becoming a mindless zombie. You were to be one of my hand-picked lieutenants. Yet here you are, fighting on the losing side."

Kafka felt Ehsan's vitals flutter. He smiled at the confirmation that he struck a nerve. Ehsan was ambivalent. Somewhere, deep down and now rising to the surface was the poison of doubt.

"Your jihad is not mine," replied Ehsan. "You betray the Order and its Cause."

"Really?" mocked Kafka. "You don't sound certain yourself. Pete, a chain is only as strong as its weakest link, and I think I've found yours."

Kojic shot Ehsan a reprimanding look.

"Where's Adnon?" asked Kafka, pouring salt on the wound, exploiting the lapse in conviction of this small team. "Let me guess, he cut and run the first chance he got. Quite the group you have here, Pete. Do you think they have what it takes to stop me?"

"You underestimate their hatred for you," said Peter. "That might be the only motivation they need."

"So it's three against one, is that it?" asked Kafka, obviously unafraid. His cavalier attitude made Peter nervous. He reached out once more with his senses, scanning the building and the outside. All he detected were the zombies staggering around outside the structure.

"It would appear so," said Peter.

Kafka clapped his clawed hands together. "Well, this has been such a wonderful reunion. Why stop here?" He began to click in excitement like an oversized cicada. "Peter Birdsall, Luka Kojic, this-is-your-life." He sounded like a game show host from the 1970's. "We have two mystery guests here who would be dying to meet you if they weren't already dead."

"Oh, hell," said Peter.

"Mystery guest number one, please step out."

There were the sounds of gears turning and motors whirring as a hulking mech stepped out from behind a large control panel. The ground shook as it stomped over, taking its place next to Kafka. It was a mess of rods, pistons, and wires with a monitor for a head.

Kojic gasped when he saw the face on the monitor. "Marina."

She swiveled her limbs, brandishing blades, buzz saws, and all kinds of sharp appendages.

"Jesus," said Peter in awestruck terror.

"Yes," continued Kafka, gesturing grandly over the mech with a sweeping hand, "we all know her as Marina Kojic, wife of Luka Kojic. She was turned into a zombie when, in a tragic accident, Luka tried to kill her. Once an unfaithful wife, now she is an obedient mechanized soldier, a deadly weapon in the transition to the new world order, a marvel of science and metaphysics!"

Peter and Ehsan trained their assault rifles on Marina. Kojic only stood there gawking at her, a long tear streaming down his left cheek.

"But that's not all," Kafka announced. "Would mystery guest number two step out?"

Another hulking mech stepped out from behind a stack of crates on the other side of the room. It stomped over, taking its place on the other side of Kafka.

Peter's mouth dropped open when he saw the face on the monitor it had for a head.

"That's right, folks," continued Kafka, "I'd like to introduce you to Barry Birdsall, father of yours truly and Peter Birdsall, disgraced ex-Major of the U.S. Army. Abandoned by his country that he served so diligently, Peter turned to the only family he felt he had left. Barry took him in, gave him a place to stay and a job. How did the prodigal son repay him? He allowed him to become a mindless zombie when he had the chance to save him. So, once again, I took it upon myself to intervene. Now Barry, too, is a walking marvel of bio-digital technology, an evolved being in his own right."

"You're a monster," said Peter to Kafka.

"No, you and Kojic are the monsters. You made them what they are today, and boy do they have a bone to pick with you guys."

"Dad," Peter called out, but the digital face in the monitor, the plastic countenance of his father, gazed back at him with empty eyes. "Carl, Dad always defended you, even with all of the horrible things you've done. Now he's nothing more to you than a remote controlled toy?"

"I told you to infect him, Pete. Right there in the hardware store. The ball was in your court, but you dropped the ball. Didn't you?"

"Don't turn this on me, Carl. This was all you. You're the monster. Dad was the only family we had left, and you turned him into some kind of…abomination."

"Pete, you're the one doing the mental gymnastics. You couldn't protect your squad in Tijuana or Xcaret, you couldn't protect those poor people in Italy, you couldn't protect me, and you let Dad down."

"What about *you*, Carl? You let Mom down."

"Nice try, Pete."

"You had to look at that enlistment center in the mall..."

"It's not going to work, Pete."

"You had to have that argument with her..."

Kafka squirmed a little. "Stop it."

"Just enough time. You bought that suicide bomber just enough time..."

"Shut up, Pete."

"Just enough time to line Mom up..."

"I said that's enough." All four eyes were blinking quickly. Kafka took a few steps backward.

"Shit, you even backed your car out of the way so he'd have a clear shot at her..."

"THAT'S ENOUGH!"

Kafka took off his RGT headset, dropped it at his feet, and lunged at Peter. Both mechs rushed forward and Kojic and Ehsan opened fire on them. Peter grappled with his brother, but he was quickly overpowered.

Kafka forced him to the ground, holding his wrists in his long hands, his claws digging into Peter's wrists. As Peter struggled, Kafka kicked him in the face repeatedly and then flung him across the room.

Kojic ducked as the Barry mech swiped all kinds of sharp instruments at him. The Marina mech was chasing Ehsan around the room.

Peter got up as Kafka descended on him. Peter tried to block his punches, but Kafka was too fast. His fists moved in a blur, striking Peter in his midsection and face. Kafka delivered a swift sidekick, knocking Peter on his back.

Ehsan hid behind a control panel and fired at Marina, hitting her monitor. The picture of her face flickered as he heard Kojic scream from across the room, "Don't you touch her! Don't you ever touch her!"

It only took a hot second. Ehsan turned to look at Kojic as Marina advanced upon him. She hopped the control panel, landing with a heavy thud behind Ehsan

The mech reversed its features in a whine of motorized parts and grabbed Ehsan in a bear hug. Kojic, dodging the blades of Barry's mech, had a second to look Ehsan in the eye one last time as Marina swirled her mechanics, dicing Ehsan into little pieces.

"I told you, Pete," said Kafka, "I'm stronger than you. Betancourt screwed you when he gave you that serum."

"He saved me," insisted Peter. "I'm still human, not a monster like you."

This time Peter threw some punches, but Kafka blocked them relatively easily. He punched Peter in the throat and then in the jaw, dislocating it. He delivered a body blow that sent the wind right out of him, feeling Peter's ribs crunching under his fist.

Peter dropped to the floor, clutching his midsection, coughing up blood, moaning through a mouth horribly distorted by the unnatural angle of his mandible.

"Peter, no!" cried Elicia, powerless to do anything.

Kojic was cornered by Marina as the Barry mech approached, covered in gore. "My Marina," he pleaded. She stooped down until her monitor was at his level. He stroked her monitor delicately with his hand. The digital face recoiled, hissing at him.

Kafka grabbed Peter by the roof of his mouth, his long, greasy fingers reaching inside, gagging him. He dragged Peter over to where Elicia was sobbing on the ground.

"Here, watch your boyfriend. I have work to do," he commanded.

Across the room, Marina reached out and took Kojic into her arms. He went willingly, closing his eyes as he was pressed against her metal parts. It was his Marina. She wouldn't harm him now. He would give himself to Kafka's Cause.

If it was the only way he could be with her, then so be it. Even if it meant the extinction of the human race. At least he would be with his Marina. She was better than she was before. She was powerful.

He opened his eyes and saw that her monitor was looking down at him. She was looking into his eyes. For a moment, he saw...recognition. She recognized him. She saw her husband.

Her face disappeared from the screen and memories popped on the monitor...her memories of him. How they first met in Serbia on her father's farm. How her father told her they would be married. Their wedding day. Their tender wedding night.

Kojic saw himself through Marina's eyes, in first person view, and he wept in her strong, mechanical arms. He saw himself above her, making love to her in their marriage bed. He saw her hand rise up and stroke his face tenderly.

He saw her watching him work tirelessly in the kitchen from her view in the living room, tinkering away with his electronics. He became distant, not just physically but emotionally. Marina's view became more of a spectator's than a participant's.

Then he saw himself guiding her to sit on the toilet as he placed the portable RGT headset on her head. He saw himself change right before her eyes. His expression changed from inquisitive to incredulous, and then to rage.

He saw himself grab her and throw her into the bathtub. Water filled the monitor as he saw a distorted view of his own hands hold her down. The monitor shuddered with her death rattle, and he shuddered in her robotic arms.

Then the screen went black.

"Marina, I'm so sorry. My sweet Marina."

Her face reappeared on the screen so suddenly it startled him. Her milky eyes were narrowed in anger as she hissed at him, snapping her digital jaws through the monitor.

Kojic felt the twisting of mechanisms against his chest. In a fraction of a second, he felt searing pain slash throughout his body. Marina looked him in the eye with her cold, dead eyes and she released him from her cold embrace.

Kojic looked down at his body as blood oozed from everywhere, and his last sensation on this earth was that of his body falling to pieces. He was dead before they all hit the floor.

Kafka pressed a button and a hatch opened on the small, skull-shaped casket of a spacecraft. He lowered himself inside, and the mechanism immediately responded to his presence. Little electronic wires and fibers reached out like cybernetic vines, embracing him, enveloping him.

The headrest in the seat opened up, metal teeth separating, as Kafka's head disappeared, the teeth closing back over it. He became mummified in what looked like liquid mercury.

Elicia cradled Peter in her arms, his head in her lap. He tried to speak to her, but his jaw was too swollen to allow intelligible speech. His tongue flapped around his mouth like a fish out of water suffocating in the toxic air.

"Sssh. It's okay. We did our best. We did our best."

The two mechs lumbered over and stood on either side of the small sarcophagus-shaped craft. Elicia moved herself and Peter out of the way, making room for the Barry mech.

Zombie mechs. Now Elicia thought she'd seen it all. This was her future. To be surrounded by all things undead, a vile melding of man and machine…

…a melding of man and machine.

She looked down at Kafka's discarded portable RGT headset. She reached out and grabbed it. She looked nervously up at the two massive mechs, but they were preoccupied with watching their master.

She placed the headset on Peter's head and started turning knobs on the portable tower. Peter asked what she was doing, but it came out virtually unintelligible.

The humming of the craft dropped a few octaves, rattling the fillings in Elicia's teeth.

"Peter, listen to me carefully. You have the serum inside you, like an antivirus."

Peter nodded his head.

"I want you to reach out to Carl, use your memories. This technology seems to run on memories. Think of your childhood, your most precious memories. Lure him to you. Then infect him with the antivirus."

"Ha," he said, which he meant to come out as *How?*

Elicia was grasping at straws here. She really didn't know if it was going to work. "You'll know. You'll feel it, just like Carl does."

Peter nodded his head in her lap, and he closed his eyes. He tried to focus through the pain. His body was going into shock, which helped him.

As he felt himself disassociate from his own body, he began to think of him and Carl as kids. He thought about playing tag in their back yard. He thought about birthday parties, family vacations...

What are you doing? Stop that. It's no use.

Peter wasn't sure if this was the voice of his doppelgänger or Carl, but as he slipped into shock the voice became more distant. As it became more distant, it became more desperate.

Listen, you little asshole. It's not going to work. You're too late. The invasion is here. Do you hear me?

Peter thought of watching his little brother as an infant in his mother's arms. He remembered her words. 'Peter, this is your little brother. He's all yours. You have to look after him.'

The voice in his head was gone. He started to feel something else.

He thought of his mother, her smiling face, putting Carl's birthday cake in front of him as they all sang happy birthday. He struggled with blowing out the candles. Peter remembered standing behind him and blowing them out over Carl' head and Carl's squeals of delight in thinking he actually blew out the candles.

Peter felt it. He felt Carl. Carl was being drawn to Peter's memories like a magnet. He resisted the memories, but Peter felt the tendrils of

Carl's mind involuntarily reaching out for them, like moths drawn to a flame.

Peter thought of his family sitting around the Christmas tree, his mother watching in delight as he and Carl opened the presents, his father getting a fire going in the hearth. He felt the warmth of the fire, the warmth of his parents' love enveloping him like a warm terrycloth robe on a cold winter's night.

The tendrils of Carl's mind were touching the tips of Peter's memories. Peter reached out...

There was a handshake. Peter's memories latched onto Carl's mind and flooded it, and with it the serum in digital representation. Peter felt himself pouring into Carl, the two becoming one.

When Peter opened his eyes, he saw Elicia looking down at him; her tears were falling on his face. He tasted their salt as he raised his head off of her lap. He saw that Kafka had been released by the craft, the wires and liquid metal receding in rejection.

Kafka looked confused. "What happened?" He looked down at Peter wearing the RGT headset. "What did you do?"

Peter didn't know what made him do it, but he sent out a mental command to the Barry mech. It reached out and embraced the craft, crushing it in its grip. Metal grinded on metal. When it let go, the hatch was fused to the craft.

Kafka was banging on the inside. He was shouting at the mechs. "Let me out! Goddammit, let me out!"

They stood there, looming over the small craft that was to become Kafka's coffin. Peter sent out another mental command, and the Barry mech reached out and began to rip wires and circuit boards out of the Marina mech. Marina stood there stoically as her lights went out.

The Barry mech threw the mechanical carcass to the ground and began to stomp it to pieces under its heavy metal feet. After a moment it stopped. It stood there, awaiting Peter's next command.

Carl punched the inside of the hatch with all of his might, recoiling at the pain it caused him. Peter and Elicia looked on in amazement.

"You did it," she said. "He's weak. You interrupted his virus, isolating the code."

She helped Peter to his feet. He looked at her and tried to speak. It came out garbled, but somehow she knew what he was saying.

"We'll have to go outside and see. If we're in the middle of a zombie apocalypse, then I guess we were too late."

Peter looked up at the mech that was his father. He remembered what the voice inside his head said. The bio-digital code that was their soul never died. It just went dormant. If he removed his father's hard drive, his CPU containing the code of his existence, he'd never really be dead.

However, he looked up at his father's image in the cracked monitor, into the glazed eyes. This abomination was not his father. Barry Birdsall was dead. He had to let him go.

Peter clenched his teeth and choked back a sob as he sent out a thought, and the Barry mech again embraced the small craft.

"Pete, what are you doing?" Kafka cried out.

Barry's face in the monitor was face-to-face with Kafka's in the pod. There was the digital ticking of a countdown coming from the mech.

Peter limped over to the pod and put his hand on the hatch. He put another on the mech. He was saying goodbye to his family.

"Dammit, I was always on your side, Carl."

All four eyes blinked in unison, tears welling up and streaming out of them. He put his hand on the inside of the hatch opposite Peter's. "I know, Pete. I'm so sorry."

"I know you are, Carl."

"You're not responsible for what I did. I chose this."

Peter looked into his brother's eyes, his own tears now streaming down his face, and reached out with his senses. He knew he was now talking to Carl, not Kafka. The serum was holding Kafka back, if only for a moment, so that Carl could say goodbye.

Elicia put her hand gently on Peter's shoulder. "We have to go."

He nodded.

As they walked away from the building, the zombie employees just stood there in a daze, awaiting their next commands that never came. They were even devoid of their hunger for flesh.

Peter looked at Elicia. "Conul Befanct?"

She shook her head. "The Colonel's dead."

As Peter limped, supported by Elicia, it occurred to him that the only official person who was aware of their innocence and their role in saving the human race—the only person in the position to exonerate them—was dead.

They were still fugitives.

When they were a considerable distance away, there was a large explosion, a flash of light, and a shockwave that nearly shoved Peter and Elicia off their feet. The spacecraft, Carl, and his father were all gone in an instant, as were Kafka and the Automaton.

Good, bad, or indifferent, all that was left was whatever world lay outside Groom Lake.

Chapter 17

Tucupita, Venuzuela
One Month Later

A pretty young woman entered the bar. Dressed in beige shorts and a black tube top clinging to her for dear life in the humidity, she strolled passed the tables with a tablet computer under her arm and saddled up to the bar.

Although she was attractive, and a gringa no less, she curiously didn't draw any looks from the half dead patrons in the sleepy bar. She put her tablet flat on the bar, pressed a button, and waited.

The bartender said something; the computer identified it as Warao and translated it as, "Are you lost?"

She shook her head and ordered. Her tablet translated her speech into Warao.

"One beer, please."

The bartender smirked at her manners and poured her a beer that smelt like rat piss in a dirty glass with a hairline crack running down the side. She pressed a button on her tablet, paying the bill, and she grabbed the pint.

She raised the glass to her parched lips and gulped the warm rat piss down heartily until she emptied the glass. She let out a loud belch and wiped beer head from her lips with her tongue.

Once again, no one looked up.

"Another beer, please," she called out to the bartender.

The bartender snickered, but he obliged the gringa girl. He took her dirty glass and poured her another pint of warm rat piss. He slammed the glass down in front of her.

"Thirsty?"

"I've been looking for someone all day, and I was told to come here."

The bartender regarded her disdainfully. "You're a long way from home, young lady. Maybe you should go home and forget about this man."

"Funny," said the young girl, taking a long swig of the beer, "I never said it was a man I was looking for."

The bartender glared at her. She had his full attention now.

He smiled, shrugging it off. "Well, I figured a pretty young girl like you would be looking for a man. You'll find plenty in here."

A few of the patrons looked up from their drinks momentarily. The place was as quiet as a tomb.

"Yeah, well the man I'm looking for is not from around here, if you catch my drift." This garnered a few more looks. "He's a Muslim."

The bartender laughed, but he wasn't smiling. It was a mechanical laugh that wasn't meant to fool anyone. "There are no Muslims here. Try looking in the next town over."

The girl reached out and grabbed the bartender's wrist in a surprisingly tight grip before he could walk away. She noticed that the patrons' eyes were now glowing in the shadows of the bar like cats' eyes.

"Well, the thing is, I'm looking for him here, and I'm not leaving until I find him. So maybe you can make things easy on yourself if you just tell me where he is. His name is Adnon."

The bartender leaned over the bar and looked right into her eyes. "If you don't let go of my hand, your loved ones will be looking for *you.*"

The patrons were on their feet and reaching out for the girl, jaws open wide for a hot meal. A man burst into the bar and began shooting them in the heads, popping them like balloons.

Tables turned over, glasses shattered on the tiled floor, and bodies went flying every which way. The bartender tried to free himself from the girl's unnatural grip, but she held him fast.

"I'm not through with you," she said. She hopped up onto the bar and slid over on her butt to the other side. The bartender reached under the bar for a gun, but she was too fast.

She grabbed the sawed off shotgun and jammed it under his nose, pushing forward until his back was to the bottles against the dirty mirror. They clinked together under his weight.

The man finished dispatching the ghouls on the other side of the bar. Then he trained his gun on the bartender.

"See, Adnon had to leave one human behind to manage any people poking around asking questions. So I think that if I pull this trigger, your brains will splatter all over your liquor bottles and you'll be as dead as Julius Caesar."

"Shit," said the man, her partner, "anything you do here will be an improvement." He looked at his watch and took out a small plastic bottle. He popped the cap and tilted the bottle, placing two pills on his tongue. He chewed them as he stared at the bartender.

"I tried to be nice," hissed the girl in the bartender's face. "Now that time has passed. Where's Adnon?"

"He's in a hut down by the river, in the swamp. You'll need a canoe to get there. No one will rent you one."

"Who said anything about renting?" asked the girl. She let him go and slid across to the other side of the bar in one deft move.

"You've been relieved of your post," said the man, her partner. "If I were you I'd get the fuck out of Dodge."

***

Adnon was sitting on a crudely constructed wooden pier outside his hut off the Caño Manamo River, looking out over the swampland and watching the sun rise, when he felt it.

He turned around slowly.

"Hello. Adnon, is it?"

Adnon's eyes went wide. "How did you find me?"

"I followed the trail of breadcrumbs."

"You sound like...is he dead?"

"Yes."

"I didn't have anything to do with anything that happened in America," Adnon pleaded.

"I wouldn't say *that*."

"I didn't support Kafka. I ran away. I don't know why you're bothering me."

"Yes, I guess that's what you do best. You run away."

"I severed all connections with OIL. I have nothing to do with them now."

"But you did once, and now you're infected."

"I'm not hurting anyone. I keep to myself now."

"What about those ghouls in town? They were once human."

"I had to protect myself. I'm not going to turn anyone else, I swear it."

"There are crimes that you've committed that have gone unanswered. And you're infected."

"So are you! So what?"

"So, you know that means I can't allow you to live, a terrorist infected with alien DNA."

"You're a hypocrite. By that logic, you shouldn't be allowed to live either."

"Don't you talk to me about logic. There is no logic in what you do. Me...I've served my country. I've done my duty."

Adnon shook his head vehemently. "No, you are a criminal, just like me. Your government turned its back on you."

"That changes nothing about your fate," said Peter. "Not one bit." He pulled out a machete and brandished it in front of the coward.

"Why do you want to kill me? I've done nothing to you. If anything, I helped rescue you from your own military."

"Kojic told me you were driving the car."

"Tell me one thing: what ever became of Kojic?"

"He was reunited with his wife."

"He's dead?"

"Yes."

"And Ehsan?"

"Dead, too."

"See, it was wise that I fled."

"Wise indeed," said Peter sarcastically. "Do you realize that if Kafka had succeeded, you would've been surrounded by an entire world of flesh-eating zombies? Oh, that's right. You're infected. So either way, whether Kafka succeeded or not, you'd be okay."

"I didn't want him to succeed. That was why I ran off with Kojic and Ehsan. That was why I helped them rescue you."

"Then why did you run?"

"I was afraid."

"Not a true believer, 'ey?"

Adnon looked down in shame.

Peter shook his head. "You're such a coward that you figured if your friends didn't succeed, you'd still be able to get back in Kafka's good graces. Being a lieutenant in his army is better than being zombie meat."

"I am very sorry that Kojic is dead."

"Not Ehsan?"

"He was an asshole."

Peter smiled wryly. "Now there's something we can agree on."

"Do you still hear the voice?"

"I chew anti-psychotics to drown it out."

"Does it work?"

"Mostly."

"So what now? You are going to try to kill me?"

"Who said anything about trying...but, yes. I'm afraid so, partner."

Adnon nodded. "Then you will be joining your brother in hell."

Peter's expression soured, his last shred of good humor lost. He suddenly made a move for Adnon, but Adnon vanished. Gone. Poof.

Shit.

Everyone who was infected had their own bizarre talent, and no two were the same. Apparently, this was Adnon's.

Peter heard a shuffling from inside the hut. He kicked the thatched door in and Adnon came at him with his own machete, fangs bared. Sparks flew as the blades collided over and over again. Both men moved with such speed that their arms were a blur amongst the sparks.

Adnon, having no serum to limit him, was a little faster. He nicked Peter on his arms a few times, drawing blood. Peter kicked him away. He raised his machete to slash at him but poof...Adnon was gone again.

Dozens of holographic ads flashed around the hut simultaneously, making the inside of the hut look like a disco. The diversion did its trick and bought Adnon the time he needed.

Peter heard a splash outside and the engine of a motorized canoe. By the time he was outside, Adnon was barreling down the river.

Elicia was on the riverbank running alongside the canoe in the river and keeping up. She leapt into the air and sailed over the water, unsheathing her machete, until she landed on the canoe.

Adnon sensed her presence and anticipated her move. He turned and met her blade with his as they slashed away at each other, the metal blades sparking in the dawn. Elicia, unhindered by the serum, was faster than Peter, and she blocked every strike and countered with lightning speed.

Adnon knew it was an even match, so he disappeared, nearly sending Elicia over the side of the canoe with the shift in weight.

He reappeared on the bank of the river and turned to run when a machete swung out and lopped off his head. Peter slashed away at the rest of his body, dismembering him in the mangroves.

Elicia swung the canoe back around and ran aground on the bank where Peter was. He shoved the canoe back into the river and quickly jumped in. She started the motor and they headed back in the direction from which they came.

"So that's it now," Elicia said.

Peter nodded. "Yeah, he's the last one."

"Besides us, you mean."

"Yeah, besides us."

"He somehow figured out how to create ghouls. They were watered down versions of your brother's zombies though."

"Yeah, well, the only living copies of the virus now reside in us."

Elicia looked out at the sun rising over the horizon. "So what do we do now?"

"I don't know, but we have generations to figure it out. I was thinking of Italy."

"Italy?"

"Yeah, you ever been?"

She shook her head.

"When I was there last, I saw this beautiful sprawling countryside in Tuscany. I could get lost there for a decade or so. Care to join me?"

"Seeing as how I can't go back home, I don't see why not." But she was okay with that. For the first time in her life, she was free to roam the great big world. There was nothing for her in Texas.

"How are we going to live?"

"I suppose we could do odd jobs here and there. I hear the locals have a real problem with the local bosses. Maybe we can help out, make our own way."

"What, like mercenaries?" she asked.

"We make a good team, Elicia—an ex-soldier with preternatural abilities and a world renowned computer hacker who also happens to have extra-terrestrial blood running through her veins. They won't stand a chance."

"Really."

"Yeah, we can kick some serious ass, help some people…"

Elicia laughed. "Like a couple of superheroes fighting injustice wherever they're needed."

Peter shook his head. "No, just a couple of responsible misfit freaks trying to make their way in the world."

Back at the bar, the mortal bartender was cleaning up the remains of the slaughtered ghouls on his tile floor with a mop. This was the first time that floor had been cleaned…

…well, since the last slaughter. But the last time the ghouls won.

The door opened, casting a pillar of bright sun into the bar, and two men walked in. After the door closed and his eyes adjusted, the bartender saw that the two men were Asian. Great, more outsiders.

"We're closed. Come back tonight."

One of the men flipped open a mini-tablet and pressed a button. When he spoke, the mini-tablet translated his speech.

"We are looking for two individuals, a man in his twenties and a teenage girl. We were told to come here."

"They were here," said the bartender putting down his mop. "They tore up my bar real good."

The two Asian men looked around at the body parts strewn all over the floor. "Then perhaps you can tell us where they went."

"Sure. They went upriver looking for someone. What's this all about?"

"These two individuals owe us a great deal of money that we paid for a certain service that wasn't delivered."

The bartender chortled. "Good. I hope you find them."

Mr.Joeng opened the door, spilling light back into the bar. Before stepping out, Mr. Kao said, "Don't worry. We will."

***

São Paulo, Brazil

A young woman sat in a waiting room of Prognosticorp on the nineteenth floor overlooking the city down below. The Prognosticorp Tower was awash in a sea of skyscrapers tightly packed together, the spread of the city looking like it lacked any coherent layout. But that was São Paulo.

"They are ready for you now," said the secretary who walked over from her desk. "Would you like to bring your espresso inside?"

"No, thank you." She made to pick up the small cup and saucer, but the secretary gestured for her not to.

"I'll take care of that. They're waiting."

The young woman stood up and walked past the desk and into a boardroom with another spectacular view, not unlike that in the waiting room. There were four men seated around the table. They all stood when she walked in.

"Please, have a seat," said a man in a ten thousand dollar pin stripe suit. She had never met him before. He must have been important.

She took her seat at the head of the conference table opposite them. She recognized two of the men. One was the project manager, Mr. Antunes, who she originally contacted. The other was the programmer, Mr. Valmor.

"My name is Mr. Silva," said the man in the ten thousand dollar suit. "I am the Vice President of Research and Development."

"Pleased to meet you," she said.

Mr. Silva continued, never introducing the fourth man who just sat their quietly. He must've been someone really important. "Our team has had a chance to review the code you've provided us with…"

"I have to say," interjected Mr. Antunes, "We've never seen anything like it. It's very comprehensive. The language is the most extensive we've ever seen. It's like a genome."

"Where did you say you obtained the code?" asked Mr. Silva.

"I didn't."

"Why have you given this to us?" asked Mr. Silva.

"Because I don't have the resources to develop this further on my own."

"May I be frank?"

"Yes."

"I really don't see how you've developed it at all. In fact, this smacks of stolen technology."

"Mr. Silva, I assure you that this technology is not stolen. It was developed to a point by my team, but we ran out of funding. We are another casualty of this Rollercoaster Recession."

"What was the name of your group? We aren't aware of any new AI developers."

"Our group was part of a larger company that didn't specialize in Artificial Intelligence, which is why the project was mismanaged. They were forced to make cuts, so R&D took a beating."

"You still haven't said who the company was," pushed Mr. Silva.

"They'd prefer I didn't. They had me sign a gag order."

"So you expect me to believe that this mystery company, who made you sign a gag order, just let you waltz out the front door with this marvel in Artificial Intelligence technology?"

"They didn't know what to do with it and they didn't appreciate the progress we'd made. I purchased it with whatever funds I could scrape together."

"So you have investors?"

"That is none of your concern."

"On the contrary," insisted Mr. Silva, "it is entirely my concern. I'd like to know who I'm getting into bed with, particularly when the project seems too good to be true."

The young woman smiled humorlessly. "Mr. Silva, I've come to you with the most advanced AI system ever developed, far ahead of anything out there currently. I am offering you a healthy cut for waltzing in at the end, and you are hesitant? If the terms of my offer are unacceptable to you, I can certainly take this to your competitors."

"Wait just a minute," said Mr. Silva, squirming in his seat. "Let's not react in haste. My superiors are merely concerned about being beholden to a group of mystery investors."

"Don't worry about them. Their payment comes out of my end."

"We will have that in writing, of course."

"Of course, Mr. Silva."

"This code," said Mr. Antunes, "will take us decades, maybe even a couple of generations to understand. With all due respect, ma'am, this is not as near to completion as you would have us believe."

"The programming is self-adapting," said the young woman. "It aids in its own development as you progress."

"That's why I said it was like a genome," said Mr. Antunes. "It's like it is life itself, in digital form. Self-adapting, autonomous. This is what AI is supposed to be like in theory, but no one has ever come this close before."

"This will be a long-term investment," agreed Mr. Silva. "Which makes me wonder what you stand to gain out of this? You're not asking for anything up front. If this ever came to fruition, your children would stand to gain from it. Maybe even your grandchildren."

"Who gains from it on my end is not your concern. That is my affair. The question is: Is Prognosticorp too short-sighted to invest its resources in the next revolution in technology?"

Mr. Silva chortled at the question. "We are called 'Prognosticorp' for a reason. We have many projects in development that won't see the light of day for decades."

"So we have an agreement?"

"Ms. Yvette, our attorneys will have a contract drafted and sent to you by the end of the day."

Yvette stood up. "Thank you. I look forward to it."

She turned and left the conference room.

As she entered the elevator, she was overcome with a melancholic excitement. She did as her beloved Kafka asked. She stayed away despite the fact that she yearned for him, his touch, every minute of every day.

She understood, however, the importance of her keeping her distance. She understood that one day, if he failed, she would receive a massive download of his digital genome, a redundant copy of himself.

When that day came, she wept until there was no more hydration left in her body and was exhausted from racking her body with sobbing. She allowed herself a brief time to grieve, but her beloved wasn't really dead...

... just dormant.

She had a job to do, and it would take time...generations. But thanks to his gift that he gave her when they made love on the floor of the sacristy in Italy, she had nothing but time. Her spirit was strong, which was why she came back more as a vampire than a mindless zombie or ghoul after her impalement in Italy.

She would bide her time until her beloved would return in the form of a new gift to mankind, a gift that would become their ultimate undoing. After all, you can't eradicate evil...

...you can only suppress it.

The End

www.ingramcontent.com/pod-product-compliance
Lightning Source LLC
Chambersburg PA
CBHW070739180626
46818CB00007B/2920